Little Bird

A Novel

BARBARA VINIAR

Sibylline
DIGITAL FIRST

Sibylline Press

Copyright © 2025 by Barbara Viniar
All Rights Reserved.

Published in the United States by Sibylline Press,
an imprint of All Things Book LLC, California.

Sibylline Press is dedicated to publishing the
brilliant work of women authors ages 50 and older.
www.sibyllinepress.com

Sibylline Digital First Edition
eBook ISBN: 9798897409969
Print ISBN: 9798897409976
Library of Congress Control Number: 2025938479

Cover Design: Alicia Feltman
Book Production: Aaron Laughlin

For my grandmother

PART I: THE JOURNEY, 1910

CHAPTER 1

The three men sat around the scarred wooden table, finalizing the terms of Feige's betrothal. Papa, his cousin Charles, and the Rabbi were arranging her marriage to Charles's son, Caleb, in America. They lingered over glasses of schnapps while Feige and her mother listened anxiously from the kitchen.

"Business is better than ever," said Charles. He enjoyed bragging about his success since leaving Russia twenty-five years ago and had even changed his name from Chaim Finkelstein to Charles Fine. "Our customers prefer an American name," he said. Feige looked at her mother. Was she also wondering what other changes there were? Surely Papa didn't approve, but his silence made it clear he didn't want anything to stand in the way of their arrangement.

"Thanks to the changes Caleb made at the factory, we're growing every year. It won't be long before he'll be running Fine and Sons. And he's good-looking, too."

"A nice picture," Feige heard her Papa say. She couldn't wait to see it for herself. Was her husband-to-be as handsome as his father claimed?

"Your boys are doing well," Charles added. "I made Daniel a salesman—he can charm anyone into buying. Noah, I keep on the floor—the men look up to him there. You should be pleased."

"I can't wait for the family to be reunited," said Asher. "It seems longer than four years since the boys left and violence against the Jews is getting worse. The pogrom in Bialystok was too close for us not to worry. Seventy of us died there, Charles, and even more were beaten. Some of them were children. And what they did to the women ... What if we're next? Feige is sixteen. I must keep my family safe."

"This is what life has always been like for us," said the Rabbi. "Tsars come and go, and we suffer. Let's sign the contract and say goodnight. God willing, Feige and Caleb will be married by the end of the year. You have agreed that the Fines will pay for Feige and Asher's passage to America this summer. Asher will work for Charles until he saves enough to come back for the rest of the family. Sign here, gentlemen."

"Caleb is lucky to be marrying a girl who's been raised to be a traditional wife," said Charles. "Modern ideas are fine for the factory, but not for the home. It's time for him to settle down."

"I was the lucky one when my parents chose Bluma. Feige will be a fine wife and mother, just like her," said Feige's Papa. She heard the clink of glasses. "*L'chaim*!" the men proclaimed. "To life!" Did they even think about her, the girl whose future they had just decided?

"Bluma, Feigele, come join us," her Papa called as soon as the Rabbi left.

Feige's mother wept as she grasped her daughter's hands. "A *kallah*. My daughter, a bride. It's what I've always wished for."

"Even though I'll be so far away? You're still happy?"

"You'll be with family, Feigele. And we'll be together soon enough. Come, let Papa give you his blessing."

Feige could see her father blinking back tears as he embraced his wife and daughter. Placing his hands on Feige's head he recited the ancient blessing he gave his children every Friday night. "May the Lord bless you and keep you ..."

Mama began to clear the table.

"No, Feigele," she said when Feige began to help. "Go to bed. Papa and I will be catching up with Charles for quite a while."

Feige leaned over to kiss her Papa and cousin goodnight. "Goodnight, Feigele," said Charles. "Your Cousin Miriam will be so happy you're coming to join our family."

And Caleb? Would he be happy? She stole a glance at the picture on the table before her mother kissed her on the forehead and sent her out of the room.

Feige undressed slowly and got into bed. But with so many unanswered questions on her mind, sleep eluded her. What else would be decided that night? What would she tell her friends in the morning? That she was going to America with Papa, leaving Mama and her brother and sister behind to marry a stranger? Family, but still a stranger. Not one of their brothers or someone she had seen at *shul* or at the market. She had expected to be happy when her betrothal was arranged. Wasn't marriage what they all waited for? She hadn't realized she might be frightened.

★ ★ ★

"Go, Feigele, go. I can tell your mind is somewhere else. You can finish your chores later."

"Thank you, Mama!" Feige threw her arms around her mother. She didn't even stop to take off her apron before dashing out to find her friends at the market. She ran through the crowds, narrowly avoiding crashing into shoppers and the carts loaded with foods and housewares. Depending on which way the breeze was blowing, the street was filled with the aroma of freshly baked breads and pies or the pungent smell of horse droppings that would be cleaned at the end of the day. Farmers and peddlers yelled out to the townspeople in Yiddish and

Russian, vying for business. "My prices are the cheapest! Stop here for the best quality!" Solomon the dairyman reached out to grab her arm, but she shook him off. "No time now," she called back over her shoulder.

"Gittel! Raisel!" she shouted as soon as she saw her friends at the fruit stall where they had agreed to meet.

The girls ran toward her, holding hands. Both petite, with light brown hair and brown eyes, they were often mistaken for sisters. Today they each wore two long braids that bounced behind them as they ran. Like Feige, they wore plain cotton dresses covered with long white aprons.

"Feige, we've been waiting forever. Tell us everything. Is he handsome? Is he rich? When are you getting married?"

"One question at a time! Yes, he's handsome. Well, maybe his ears are a little big." She giggled. "In his picture he wears a suit and bow tie. He's twenty-seven, and an important business-man, not a boy." She couldn't help boasting a little.

"Never mind how he looks. Is he rich?" asked Raisel. "You'll be living like a princess in America, and I'll be stuck in Kamenetz forever with who knows who they'll choose for me to marry."

"*Sha*, Raisel. Who cares about you today? Let Feige talk," said Gittel.

"They own a big metal factory. My Papa's cousin said they have a hundred workers and it's well known in America. My brothers already work there and now so will Papa. So I guess they're rich, at least compared to here. They have a house in a place called Brooklyn. We have to cross a bridge to get there.

"I knew it," sighed Raisel.

Gittel silenced her with an angry look. "When will you leave, Feige?"

"I'm leaving—" Feige's smile disappeared, and she began to cry.

"What's wrong, Feige? Tell us. This is what we've been dreaming about since we were little girls. Your parents found you a handsome, rich man. Why are you crying?"

Feige struggled to regain her composure. "I'm leaving at the end of May, in less than two months. Papa and his cousin will set the wedding date after we're there. But Mama won't be there, and neither will you. We were supposed to dance at each other's weddings. Now I won't have any friends to dance at mine."

She began to cry again, and the girls took her in their arms.

"We'll miss you too and we want you to be happy. Please, aren't you even a little excited?"

"I'm scared. It's so far away. It will take us weeks to get to America, and you know my Papa, he'll hardly speak the whole way there. And what do I really know about the man they've chosen for me? What good is handsome and rich if he's mean?"

Gittel and Raisel were silent.

"You see, you know I'm right."

"It's true, Feige. But even if the husbands they choose for us are from nearby, how do we know what they're like? What do I know about my betrothed, Abe, the butcher's new apprentice?" Gittel took her friend's hand. "Look at your Mama. She met your Papa on their wedding day and she's happy."

"And who wouldn't love you?" said Raisel. "You're the prettiest girl in Kamenetz."

"And the sweetest," added Gittel. "And—"

"And a good cook!" Raisel concluded firmly. "So that settles it." She crossed her arms in front of her chest and stamped her foot.

"No one could be mean to you," said Gittel. "So dry your eyes and let's go get a sweet from Moishe. That will cheer you up. And then we'll talk about wedding dresses."

Feige dried her eyes and blew her nose. The girls set off arm in arm, as they had so many times before. They never noticed the small group of Cossacks in their red uniforms, eyeing the crowd from a distance.

★ ★ ★

The weeks passed quickly. Tonight would be Feige's last *Shabbos* at home, the last with Mama, Freyda, and Levi until Papa had saved enough to bring them to America.

She and her mother had worked quietly together all day, cleaning the house, polishing the candlesticks and the *Kiddush* cup for the wine, and preparing the meal. Feige watched as her younger sister braided three strands of dough for the *challah*. They weren't quite even, but she was improving.

"You're learning quickly, Freyda," said Feige. "Soon your challah will be as good as mine."

Freyda beamed at her sister's praise. "But I wish you weren't going, Feige. Will you buy a dress in America for your wedding? Will it have lace? I wish I could be with you to see how pretty you'll look."

Feige smiled. Her sister reminded her of what she had been like at her age, dreaming of being a bride. *She'll be in America when it's time for her to marry. I wonder if things will be different for her.*

"Enough, Freyda." She put the challahs on a baking sheet and covered them with a towel to rise. "I'll send you a picture from my wedding so you can see my dress. Maybe I'll even save it for you to wear when you get married."

"Oh, yes, even though I could never be as beautiful in it as you'll be."

"Don't be silly, you're just a little girl and you're getting prettier every day. Feige put her hands on her sister's shoulders and looked her in the eyes. "You must behave while I'm gone and help Mama. Promise me you'll be good."

"I promise," said Freyda, putting her arms around the sister she idolized.

By midafternoon, the aroma of freshly baked bread, roast chicken, and soup with onions and dill drifted throughout the house. They set the table with the good dishes and a tablecloth Feige's *bubbe* had embroidered. Her grandmother had taught her the stitches when she was a little girl. As she got older, she taught herself to combine them into elaborate patterns. She was taking one of the cloths she had designed with her to America.

When everything was ready, they went into their rooms to put on their Shabbos clothes. Feige changed Levi and helped Freyda with the buttons on the back of her dress, noticing that it was getting short on her. She heard Papa arrive just as she finished putting on her own dress.

As soon as they were gathered at the table, Mama lit the candles. She brought her hands to her face three times and covered her eyes to recite the prayer. *"Baruch, Atah Adonai..."* Feige had watched this ritual ever since she could remember, but tonight her thoughts were melancholy. This was the last time she'd watch Mama light the candles. Soon she would be lighting them in her own home.

Then it was Papa's turn. First, he recited the *Eshet Chayil* from the Bible in praise of his wife:

A woman of valor, who can find?
For her worth is far above rubies.
Her husband's heart trusts in her and he shall lack no
fortune...

Feige had never really thought about these words before. *Look how he looks at her. This isn't just a prayer he says every week. It's the way he says, "I love you."* She wondered if Caleb had learned this prayer from his papa. Would he honor her on Shabbos? Would he love her the way Papa loved her Mama?

Next, Asher gathered the children to him. Feige held a squirming Levi in her arms as Papa put his hands over their heads to recite the blessing, asking God to grant them peace. When they were seated, he blessed the sweet red wine and the challah, tearing off a piece for each of them. Now they were ready to eat. Feige and her mother rose to get the soup, followed by the rest of the weekly dinner that ushered in the Sabbath, chicken, *lokshen kugel,* and vegetables.

"Every week your mother outdoes herself, Feigele," said Papa. "How lucky you are to have such a wonderful teacher. Are you ready to cook for your husband? I'm sure my cousin Miriam will help you in America."

"Yes Papa, I'm ready. Mama has taught me well."

Before she knew it, Papa was saying the prayers after the meal, and it was time to go to bed. Feige took her time getting undressed. She knew that the next time they were all together she'd be a married woman, maybe even a mother. The family would come to her home for Shabbos dinner. Daniel and Noah would come with families of their own and Caleb would say the blessings. But that time was far away; she needed to make her memories of home last. The smell of the herbs Mama added to the soup, the Shabbos candles flickering as they burnt down, Papa's deep voice as he blessed them. She'd never forget them. Freyda trying to be serious and failing—how that child loved to laugh. And Levi always underfoot and getting into everything. And most of all, Mama. Always working, but never too tired to smile. Her hands were rough from housework, but her touch was gentle. *No one is more beautiful than my Mama.*

Mama carried Levi into the children's bedroom to put him to sleep. She tucked Freyda in and bent to kiss Feige. Feige reached up to give her a hug, holding on tightly until her mother gently removed her arms. "*Gey schluffen, mamaleh.* You need your rest to finish preparing for your journey."

"Good night, children. God bless you," she said as she closed the door.

"Feige," whispered Freyda. "I don't want you to go. It will be so lonely without you."

"Come here, little one." Feige held up her covers so Freyda could climb into bed with her. "I'll miss you too. You'll be so grown up when you come to America. By then you'll have a little niece or nephew to play with. Won't you like that?"

"Yes," she said, drifting off to sleep in Feige's arms.

Feige was still thinking about leaving. It wasn't just home she would miss. Tomorrow was her last Shabbos morning at shul with her friends and their mothers in the balcony. Who would she sit with in America? She put Freyda back in her own bed and gradually drifted off.

★ ★ ★

As Feige waited for her mother to help her pack, her mood was somber. I've slept in this bed for the last time, she thought, fingering the coverlet she'd had since she was old enough to sleep in a bed. This was the room where she looked over at her little sister's red curls peeking out from under the covers and at Levi, sucking noisily on his thumb as he slept. *I'll never—*

"Stand up straight, Feigele." Mama interrupted Feige's thoughts as she came into the room, wiping her hands on her apron. "Your height is a gift from God."

Feige sighed at the familiar reminder. How could she explain that the fear of what was in store for her was weighing her down? She rolled her shoulders back.

Bluma was an unusually tall woman with ample breasts and full hips. Her waistline had slowly disappeared as she bore her five children. There were wrinkles around her hazel eyes and strands of gray ran through her dark brown hair. No one feature of hers stood out, but her smile was always welcoming. Her kindness led everyone to believe she was a beautiful woman.

Like her mother, Feige was tall, but she had an hour-glass figure that was the envy of all her friends. Her skin was smooth and fair, her upturned nose narrow, and her lips generous. Her thick brows arched over eyes so dark they were almost black. A small mole on her left cheek only emphasized the symmetry of her other features. Her thick, chestnut brown curls reached halfway down her back. For the most part, Feige was unaware of her beauty; her hair was her one vanity.

"Come, show me your things and we'll start packing. Miriam and Caleb will be impressed with all the things you've made."

"Do you really think so? I won't be ashamed? They must have so many fine things in America."

"Of course not," her mother said as she picked up an apron Feige was bringing to give her cousin as a gift. "These flowers are beautiful. And the cross stitching on your sheets and pillowcases is just right, not too feminine for your husband. It's no wonder Feige Dorfman's embroidery is sought after by so many Kamenetz brides. Now, where are your underthings?"

Feige began to hand her mother five matching sets, each delicately embroidered in pastel colors and so light they would barely take up any room in her valise. "These are my favorites," she said, stroking the silky-smooth fabric. "Look how the pink ribbons running through the lace on the chemise match the roses on the petticoat. And this is the nightgown for my wedding night."

"Feigele, sit down a moment. There are some things I need to tell you."

Feige sat. Was this going to be the talk she had been waiting for? The talk that mothers had with their daughters about married life?

"Do you remember what I told you when you started to bleed?"

How could she forget? The first time she bled, Mama slapped her face. Then, before she could recover from the shock, Mama took her in her arms to tell her she had become a woman. Now she could have babies.

"Yes, Mama."

"Men's bodies also change. You've seen Levi's little *petseleh*. When a boy gets older it gets bigger, and when he's married, he puts it inside his wife, in the place where she bleeds, so she can have a baby."

Feige tried to imagine how that would happen, but stayed quiet as her mother went on.

"It will hurt the first time, mamaleh, but it gets better, I promise, and it's a husband's duty to please his wife."

Feige was bewildered. Why would it hurt? And how much? But her mother had finished talking and held out her hands for the next thing to pack. Together they carefully folded the nightgowns, shawls, tablecloths, and handkerchiefs Feige had been embroidering for years. As the last item was packed, Feige's lower lip began to quiver. She tried to be brave, but as the valise snapped shut, she collapsed into her mother's arms, sobbing.

"Mama, it's such a long journey and I've never been away from you. What if something happens to Papa? What will I do?"

"Now, Feigele—"

"What if I never see you again?" she wailed.

Her mother drew her close. "Hush now, you'll be fine."

"Why can't we wait, and all go together in a year or two? I'm sure there won't be pogroms here. Kamenetz is too small for the Cossacks to bother with us."

"No, Feige. The Cossacks may seem harmless now, but their numbers are growing, even here. It's too dangerous to stay, especially for a beautiful young woman. You must leave now, and we'll come as soon as we can. The Fines have been good to your brothers, and they'll be good to you. You'll have a nice home, more than you could ever have here."

"But I don't care about those things, and I don't know the Fines." She cried even harder. "How can I stand under the *chuppah* without you? Who will take me to the *mikveh*? Who will help me with my dress and veil? How can I get married without you, Mama?"

"I wish I could be at your wedding. I've been dreaming about it since you were born. But Papa's cousin is a good woman. She was like the big sister he never had when they were growing up. She'll take care of you."

"What about Caleb? What if he turns out to be short and fat, or smells bad? What if he's not gentle on our wedding night? What if he's mean to me? How will I be a good wife then?" She paused. "How will I remember to do everything you've taught me, Mama?"

"Feigele, please calm—"

"And when my first baby is born, who will be there for me? Who will hold my hand when the pains come?"

"Feigele, my sweet little bird, please stop crying." She cupped Feige's chin and looked at her.

Feige drew back to look at her mother. How could she be so selfish? Her poor Mama was going to be alone with the children. She would have to take care of the house, and them, and mind the shop until Papa's cousin Hershel came to help.

"Oh, Mama, please forgive me, thinking only of myself when I should be worried about you. Who will help take care of Freyda and Levi? How will you manage without me?"

Mother and daughter clung to each other.

"I'll be fine." Feige stood up straight, ashamed of the fuss she had been making. She was going to be a married woman, but she was acting like a spoiled child. "I'm ready to say goodbye now, Mama." She wiped her tears and smiled. "I'll be brave," she promised.

She had no way of knowing what those words were going to mean to her.

CHAPTER 2

It was time. Shmuel, the wagon driver, had finished tying down their valises and bundles in the back of the wagon. His large belly hung over his pants, which were held up by a cracked leather belt tied where a buckle would have been and tucked into well-worn boots that were caked with dirt. His blue eyes were set deep in a face browned and wrinkled from the sun. A shapeless cap that perhaps had once been blue covered his stringy hair. As he took a handkerchief out of his pocket to wipe the sweat off his forehead, Feige noticed it was gray and dingy. Without a wife, who did his laundry?

She had dressed practically for the long journey in a plain, light brown cotton shirtwaist and skirt, with a wide-brimmed straw hat to keep out the sun. She would be in these clothes for weeks.

"Up you go, Feigele." Papa climbed up onto the bench next to Schmuel and helped her up after him. As usual, he had paid no attention to what he wore, donning the same old weekday knee-length black coat, pants, and hat he wore in his dry goods shop. His high leather boots were worn down at the heels. "My customers are here to examine the merchandise," he said when Feige and her mother urged him to buy new clothes. "Not me."

At least Mama made sure his clothes were always clean and in good repair and his old boots were polished. Papa was slender and average height, slightly shorter than his wife and daughter. He had the pale complexion of a man who spent most of his time indoors working and studying. His brown eyes were usually serious, although he was able to charm and flatter his customers. Unlike his sandy brown hair, his neatly trimmed beard was almost completely red.

Shmuel clucked at the horse to start moving. Feige looked back at Mama, Freyda and Levi waving goodbye. As the horse began its slow trot, she waved and shouted. "Goodbye, Mama!" She could see Levi tugging on her mother's skirt, eager to run off on his chubby little legs to play. "Be good, children. I'll write to you from America." She kept her eyes on them until they were nothing but far away dots and said a silent goodbye to the town she had grown up in, the only home she had ever known.

She longed for someone to comfort her, but Papa had taken out the prayer book that was always in his pocket and was reciting the prayers under his breath. She knew she couldn't interrupt him and that in any case he wouldn't hold her or reassure her as Mama would have. He would handle their money and documents, speak to the officials and the people selling food along the way, and shield her from dealing with strange men. But she could never confide in him. He had arranged her marriage for the good of the family. Even if he thought she was unhappy, it wasn't something he would discuss. The wagon bounced with every bump in the dirt road. Each time her body hit the hard wooden seat; Feige felt the jolt all the way to the top of her head. She held on tight to avoid falling off the side, trying to concentrate on the new sights around her. The late May weather was comfortable, and she took a moment to enjoy the breeze.

At mid-day, Shmuel stopped the wagon to allow the horse to rest and drink water. Feige and Papa had some of the bread and cheese Mama had wrapped for them, but their rest was brief. They still had a long way to go before arriving at Brest.

"Tell me again, Papa," she pleaded as they got back into the wagon. "Tell me again about our trip to America."

"Feigele," he responded patiently. "Tonight, we'll stay with my cousins in Brest. Tomorrow morning, we'll take the train west to Warsaw and then into Germany. We'll stop overnight a few times before we get to Antwerp, where we'll board the ship to New York. We're taking the same journey as your brothers, but on a newer ship."

Feige had never been outside Kamenetz, where she knew almost everyone, and they knew her. She had seen a picture of the tall buildings in New York in a book once but couldn't imagine what it would be like to live there. A new husband, a big city – it was too much to think about.

Hours later, after one particularly jarring bump, she was surprised to realize she had been asleep, and it had gotten dark. They had reached the outskirts of Brest. Papa's cousin, Eli, a short, thin man with a long dark beard, was waiting at the crossroads as he and Papa had arranged by letter.

"Asher!" He greeted Papa loudly with a bear hug, helping with their things. "And you must be Feige, the kallah, on your way to be married in America. *Mazel Tov*!" He led them quickly to the house, where Gussie, his wife, warmed up some vegetable soup. She was as round as her husband was thin and as fair as he was dark. Her light brown hair was tied back in a kerchief. She smiled with her whole face, instantly making Feige feel at home.

The children were already asleep when Feige crawled into bed next to the youngest. Papa, Eli and Gussie talked softly in the next room, but their words carried.

"You're smart to be leaving now and to bring your family to America. We're going to leave too," said Gussie, "To live near family in Warsaw. Things are too unsettled here. One of these days the Bolsheviks will succeed in overthrowing the Tsar, but meanwhile the Cossacks are out of control. And another revolution may be good for the workers, but it won't help the Jews."

"I'm glad you're leaving. And maybe you'll consider America one day? The Fines are your family too."

"We remember Chaim and Miriam from before they left. How fortunate that they've done so well and have a son for Feige to marry."

"Yes. I only worry that they've abandoned our ways. Chaim is now Charles. He says an American name is better for business. He wants a traditional wife for his son, but I don't think Caleb was brought up to obey our laws, not like my Feigele. I hope that doesn't make it too hard for her."

Feige shivered in spite of the warm night air and pulled the quilt over her. What had Papa done? Caleb wouldn't want her. He would think she was too old-fashioned. Wasn't there any other way to keep the family safe? *I know you did it because you love us, but did I have to be the price?*

It seemed as though she had just closed her eyes when she was being shaken awake. "Feigele, Feigele, it's time to get up." Gussie urged her to dress quickly and eat the bowl of hot porridge on the table for her. They had only a few minutes before leaving for the train station.

★ ★ ★

Feige shrank back against the walls of the station, overwhelmed by the monstrous black locomotive belching smoke, the first train she had ever seen. The narrow platform was as crowded as market day at home. When the piercing whistle announced the train was boarding, Papa led her toward the back of the train where the third-class passengers boarded.

They found two spots on the plain wooden benches which were as uncomfortable as the wagon had been. There were only a few windows to let in fresh air. The noise of the engine and the vibrations of the metal wheels shook Feige's whole body; she didn't know how she would stand it for days on end. But everywhere she looked she saw people just like her and Papa. She imagined their bundles held clothes and featherbeds like the ones she and Papa had with them, the few precious things they were able to carry. Were they also fleeing pogroms, or just looking for a better life?

"Papa," she asked. "Do you think these people are also going to America?"

"Well, some of them are probably going to Warsaw or the other big cities, but yes, I expect many of them are."

Husbands and wives gathered their children to them. Single men sat alone, and she was shocked to see there were a few women, and even young girls like her, traveling by themselves. How would they manage? Papa might not show his affection the way she wished he would, but he would keep her safe. She had promised Mama she'd be brave, but she could never do this alone.

Feige caught the eye of a little girl whose curly hair reminded her of Freyda. She was sitting with her parents and five other children. She was thin and pale and wore a simple pinafore over a faded blue dress, which Feige imagined had been handed down from one of her older sisters but was clean and well mended. When Feige smiled at her she smiled back and grabbed her mother's hand to point at Feige. Her mother had dark brown eyes and blond braids wrapped around her head. Her dress was also old and faded, hanging loosely on her thin frame. A life of hard work was visible in the lines on her face, but she offered Feige a warm smile. *If I can help her with the children, maybe I won't feel so lonely. It's time to stop feeling sorry for myself and make the best of this journey.*

A few days later they were due to reach the German border. They had stopped several times in small towns and cities before and after Warsaw, with just enough time to get some food and water from the pump outside the station. The Warsaw train station was huge, noisy, and busy with people who all seemed to be rushing somewhere.

"Is this what New York will be like?" Feige asked her father. "I don't think I'll like being in a place with so many strangers."

"Feigele, stop worrying," her father chided her. "You'll get used to it like everyone else."

The train was hot and uncomfortable. At each stop, more and more people crowded on with their belongings. Those who couldn't find seats took spots on the floor. Feige rarely left her father's side except to play with the children and pass the time with their mother, Yetta.

"We won't be staying in New York," Yetta shared. "We're going to a city called Baltimore. My sister has arranged for me to work as a seamstress like she does, and my husband will have a job in the brewery with my brother-in-law. The children will go to school with their cousins." She smiled when she looked at her children. "They will become Americans," she said. "All we want is a better life for them."

Feige told her about her forthcoming marriage. Yetta heard the doubt in her voice and reassured her. "How lucky you are," she said. "I'm sure you'll be happy in your new life. And I can see from how you play with the children you'll be a wonderful mother."

Feige had been amusing the children with stories and songs. When she entertained them, they forgot about being tired and hungry and she forgot to be scared about her future. Now they clamored for another story.

"What, another one?" she laughed.

"Oh, yes! One with a princess! One with a monster! One with –"

"All right, all right. Settle down and let me think."

"*Amol iz given*, once upon a time," she began. "*A katz un a moyz*, a cat and a mouse –"

Halfway through the story, the train stopped without warning, wheels screeching, throwing Feige and the children into each other. The passengers were stunned into silence when German soldiers with guns at their sides boarded at the end of the crowded car, pushing their way through the crowd.

"Passports, passports, have your passports out," they bellowed.

Feige quickly went back to sit with her father and held on to his arm. She had put the dangers of the journey out of her mind, but now she clung to him as the soldiers stopped in front of each family. No one was permitted to stay on the train without the right documents, even if they were just passing through Germany on their way to another country. Thanks to Cousin Charles, Papa knew about the papers. He had gone to the regional capital and been away for almost two weeks. One night Feige overheard him whispering to her mother about the bribes he had to pay.

A tall, blond soldier in a blue uniform, a stiff cap and high shiny black boots stopped in front of them. "Papers," he demanded, looking at her father. Feige held her breath as her father handed him their papers. After examining them closely, the soldier appeared satisfied and handed them back, moving on to the next passenger without saying a word.

Yetta and her family were missing some papers and were ordered off the train.

"Please sirs, where will we go?" Yetta pleaded with the soldiers. "We have sold all our belongings to go to America. We have no money to return to our village, no money for food." She fell to her knees. The children clung to her, weeping, but the soldiers were unmoved and marched them off to the platform.

"Papa, we have to help them." Without thinking, Feige began to get up from her seat.

"*Sha shtil,* Feigele." Feige's father held her back.

"But Papa." She struggled to get free. "We can't let them do this."

"There is nothing we can do, Feigele. I'm sorry too, but it's too dangerous. We can't help them."

"Please, Papa, they're my friends. Do something."

"Sha. Don't draw attention to us or they may decide to throw us off too. What are papers to these thugs?"

Feige buried her head in her father's coat, muffling her sobs. *My little friend, my shy little friend. And Yetta, whose company I've enjoyed. How is it possible that we won't make the rest of the journey together?*

"I'll never know what happens to them," she wept. But she knew her father was right. It was too much of a risk and nothing they did would have helped. She turned her head away so she wouldn't have to watch her new friends being led away. She knew she would never see them again.

Before she had time to absorb her loss, the soldiers were back. "Off the train, off now, it's time for the showers. We can't let you bring any of your filthy diseases into our homeland. Take your things with you. Hurry up or you'll miss getting back on the train."

Feige and her father looked at each other without speaking. Showers? As much as Feige yearned to get clean, she knew this wasn't right.

The women and men were separated and herded into two shacks. Feige and the other women were pushed into a large, dirty room and told to get undressed. A woman in a gray dress with brass buttons handed them each some greasy soap and a threadbare towel. They looked around for curtains or places to hide their nakedness, but there were none. They did the best they could to keep their eyes averted and to turn away from each other. Feige had never seen a grown woman naked before, not even her mother.

When the attendant turned on the showers along the wall, the cold water hit Feige's skin like icy rain, and she began to shake. "How could they?" she fumed under her breath. "We were healthy until now, but this could make us sick. Why are they treating us like this?"

As she hastily dried herself and put her clothes back on, she saw the attendants spraying the women's belongings. *My beautiful things, please don't let them be ruined.* But she didn't dare complain out loud.

Her hair, which she had not unpinned, was wet and heavy on her neck. It was going to take a long time to dry. But that was the least of her worries.

"Hurry, get back on the train," shouted the soldiers, prodding stragglers with their rifle butts. As quickly as they had been taken off, they were rushed back onto the train. She had barely settled onto a bench next to her father before the doors closed and the train started to move.

"Are you all right, Feigele?" Her Papa's hair was also wet. He was hunched over, staring at the floor even as he spoke to her.

No words came. How could she tell her father she had been naked? She wanted to forget. Forget the pain of losing her friends, forget the humiliation. She made no effort to stop her tears but stayed silent.

The train rumbled on through the night and day, the rhythm of the wheels lulling Feige to sleep, her head falling against her father's shoulder. Finally, the conductor announced that they were approaching Berlin. Feige and her father got off at the station. They would take a different train the next day that would take them out of Germany and on to Antwerp and their ship.

As they left the platform, Feige's father took a folded piece of paper out of his pocket. It told him how to find a hostel run by the German Jews where they could get a clean place to eat and sleep. After walking a short distance away from the station along the banks of the river, he pointed to a small wooden building that looked newer than the others they had passed. "I see it, Feigele, I see it. There's the sign, *Zentralbureaus fur Judische Auswanderungsangelegenheiten*, Central Jewish Committee for Jewish Travelers." He held up the paper and matched its writing to the sign, haltingly reading the German, which was somewhat like the Yiddish they spoke at home.

"Come, Feigele. The Jews who live in Berlin will give us shelter here."

"Why will they do that for us, Papa? No one else has shown us any kindness."

"Jews take care of each other, Feigele. Doesn't the Torah command us to welcome the stranger?"

Feige walked heavily, barely able to put one foot in front of the other. She dragged her valise along the ground, stopping often to rest. So much had happened, she hardly cared where they were going. She didn't think it could get any worse and doubted it would get any better.

She was wrong. The woman who greeted them at the door smiled warmly and spoke to them in perfect Yiddish. She was wearing a spotless white apron over her black dress.

"Welcome. I'm Frau Bergman," she introduced herself as she led them to a clean room with rows of freshly made-up cots. "You will sleep here, but first you'll eat. And please don't worry, our food is strictly kosher. You can wash your hands there, at the sink."

Feige and her father took seats at a long wooden table, nodding to a family seated at the other end. A man and his wife and two children who looked about Freyda's age were already eating, talking softly among themselves. Had they endured the same treatment as Feige and her Papa? She couldn't tell by looking at them and wondered if she and Papa looked different after their terrible experiences on the train. She felt different inside.

"Please, enjoy," said Frau Bergman. Almost immediately, a younger woman brought them steaming bowls of soup.

"Mmm. Doesn't it remind you of home?" said Feige between spoonfuls. They devoured the stew that followed and finished with tea and slices of lemon cake.

"We are so grateful," Papa said to Frau Bergman as they prepared to leave the next morning. "It's been a difficult journey. How is it for the Jews here in Germany?"

"We have a good life here," she answered. "Our musicians and poets are revered. We're not like you— poor, uneducated Jews from Russia and Poland. We're happy to help our fellow Jews, as long as you're moving on. We don't want you to ruin it for us."

Feige gasped. She could see her father stiffen. He thought they were performing a *mitzvah*, but it was self-protection, not charity in their hearts.

"Papa, why—" she started to ask as soon as they left.

"Let's not talk about it, Feigele."

She wished she could ease his disappointment. In the world he believed in, Jews wouldn't hold themselves above other Jews. Saddened, they walked toward the station to board the train to Antwerp where their ship awaited them. Forewarned of the terrible conditions awaiting them, she dreaded the ocean crossing.

CHAPTER 3

The trip from Berlin to Antwerp was uneventful. Feige tried to rest, but her fears about the next part of their journey kept her on edge until they reached the pier.

"I hear music, Papa, where's it coming from?" she asked as they inched forward in yet another long line to board the ship. The S.S. Lapland was one of the Red Star Line's newest steamships, with four tall wooden masts and two shiny black and white funnels. Smoke was beginning to rise from one of them.

Feige looked up in awe at the enormous ship in front of her. It was so much bigger up close than she had imagined from the picture on the tickets. To get from one end to the other would be like walking the whole length of the market street at home. And it appeared as though as many people as who lived in Kamenetz were getting on. How did it stay on top of the water?

"I expect the music is to welcome the rich passengers, Feigele. Can you see them boarding over there?" He pointed to a separate gangplank. "They will have their own sleeping rooms, a dining room for fancy meals, salons where they can sit and talk or play cards, and a ballroom for dancing."

Feige craned her neck to get a glimpse of the first-class passengers. She wondered what was waiting for her and the other passengers in third class.

"Do you ever wish we were rich, Papa?"

"Who is rich, Feigele? The sages teach us 'A rich man is one who is happy with his lot.' I have a family I love and I'm taking my daughter to be a bride in America. Don't you think I'm rich?"

Feige nodded. *He still has his faith. Even after what Frau Bergman said. He's a good man, my Papa.*

"I may not dance on the ship, Feigele, but I'll dance at your wedding. Just remember, when the ship docks, we'll be in America. Keep thinking about your new life, no matter how uncomfortable it is on board."

Daniel and Noah had written about how terrible it was. The meager, tasteless food, the airless and dirty sleeping quarters and above all, the terrible smells. She hoped things would be better on the ship she and Papa were boarding. "I'll remember, Papa." She would try not to disappoint him.

They finally reached the end of the line where inspectors in bright red uniforms were waiting. First a doctor briefly examined their eyes, ears, throat, and scalp. Feige flinched as he poked through her hair. Then, after taking their tickets, another man questioned them.

"Name?" he began. "Age? Religion? Where were you born? Occupation? Have you ever been in prison? How much money do you have with you? Who will you stay with in America?" Thanks to the Fines, they had sufficient funds and a place to stay. Papa had a job waiting for him in New York. They were allowed to move on.

"Leave your luggage here to be disinfected. We'll give you a tag. There is no room below except on your bed, so don't try to take anything big with you."

Feige's father put his valises on the large pile the crew member pointed to, keeping only a small bundle with the *tallis* and phylacteries he needed for his daily prayers clutched to his chest. He was allowed to pass. Feige hated to leave her things but did as she was told. She carried one small bundle with her hairbrush, a few items of clothing, and a warm shawl.

"Women and children this way, men that way. You'll see each other later."

I will be brave, I will be brave, Feige repeated to herself as she and Papa were separated.

The women were led down a steep, narrow, metal staircase into a large room with about a dozen beds on either side, one on top of another. They were each handed a metal cup, a bowl, a fork, and a spoon.

"Keep these with you," said the crew member handing out the utensils. "You'll need them to eat, and you only get one. Here's your life preserver, which is also your pillow. Don't lose it!"

Feige went to the next available bottom bed, where she found a thin, straw mattress and a gray blanket that was too thin to keep anyone warm. It gave off a faint chemical smell, which she hoped meant it had been cleaned. She put her bundle on the bed and looked around. At the end of the room, she could see through a doorway into another room, filled with long tables and benches. Some of the women and children were already seated there, waiting, although no one seemed to know what came next.

"The women's toilet and washing room is down that way. The men's quarters are on the other side of this wall. The deck for you is up those stairs," announced the crew member. "Food will be brought down here, but you can take it up on deck. You can go up any time unless the crew tells you to stay below. Do not, I repeat, do not go anywhere beside your assigned deck without permission."

Feige wondered if permission was ever granted. Were they passengers or prisoners? *I don't care what Papa says, in this world it's better to be rich.*

"What's your name?" asked the woman who had claimed the next two beds. "Are you alone? I'm Hannah and these are my younger sons, Ephraim and Joshua. My husband and my older boy are with the men."

The woman who greeted Feige appeared to be about her mother's age. Her face was beginning to show wrinkles, especially around her eyes. Her light brown hair hung in a single braid down her back. She wore a faded green floral dress that Feige imagined was once quite pretty and had brought out the green of her eyes. The simple woven shawl around her waist would come in handy to fold into a pillow or spread over the children. The boys, who appeared to be about six and seven years old, were fair like their mother, but dark-eyed. They wore identical blue short pants and white shirts and matching blue caps which they politely took off when Hannah introduced them.

"Where are you from? Are you going to live in New York?" Hannah asked.

"My name is Feige. My father and I are traveling together from Russia. Please forgive me while I go to look for him." Feige turned toward the stairs to the deck. Hannah seemed nice, but Feige couldn't bring herself to talk to her. She didn't want to be rude, but what was the point in making new friends? Friends got taken away. Just thinking of Yetta and the children brought tears to her eyes.

"Don't be upset. We'll be here if you need help." Hannah tried to comfort her, mistaking the reason for her distress.

As nice as she seemed, Feige didn't want to tell this stranger why she was crying and was determined to rebuff any offer of friendship. "Thank you," she said as she rushed off.

The deck was crowded with people standing by the rails or sitting on the floor. It didn't seem like there was any more room, but men, women and children continued to arrive, calling out for their loved ones. Feige tried to work her way across, scanning the crowds for her father. When she didn't see him, she squeezed in along the rail in a central spot, keeping her eye on the stairs rather than the harbor, barely noticing who was next to her.

"Who are you looking for?" asked the young man on her right, smiling and doffing his cap. "Perhaps I can help you."

"No thank you. I'm sure my father will be here in a minute." Feige gave him a curt nod.

She wasn't about to have a conversation with a man she didn't know, but she couldn't help noticing how tall and handsome he was. He appeared to be slightly older than she was, with red hair that reminded her of her oldest brother, Daniel, and sparkling green eyes. Tiny freckles were sprinkled across his nose and cheeks. He wore long blue pants held up by brown leather suspenders and a blue checked shirt. His boots were worn but well taken care of like her Papa's.

Feige looked around anxiously. *Please hurry, Papa, I'm all alone with him.*

"My name is Samuel. I'm waiting for my mother, Hannah, and my younger brothers," he said, ignoring her lack of response. "They were not happy to be with the women, I can tell you that."

"Oh, I met them," Feige blurted without thinking. "They're on the beds next to mine."

"Well then, you're already a friend of the family. And you are?"

"My name is Feige."

She could at least be polite to Hannah's son. And were they really alone while they were surrounded by hundreds of passengers? Nevertheless, she hoped Hannah or Papa would come soon.

"And where is a pretty girl like you going?"

"I'm going to be married in New York," she said, thinking that would put a stop to the conversation. Surely he didn't speak to girls he didn't know like this at home. But were the rules the same now? They were on their way to America, to a new life. Maybe there were new rules.

"Lucky man," said Samuel.

Feige had no idea what to say next. She was relieved to see her father coming toward them. "Papa," she called out. "Over here."

Before she could say a word, Samuel extended his hand to her father. "Pleased to meet you, sir. I'm Samuel Greenstein. My mother, Hannah, and your daughter met below deck."

Feige's father was taken aback. He shook the young man's hand but looked at Feige with a question in his eyes. "Asher Dorfman. I'm glad Feige already has a woman friend on the ship." She could tell her Papa disapproved. But he hadn't been there. She had done nothing wrong.

"There they are! Mama, Ephraim, Joshua," called Samuel.

When Hannah finally pushed through the crowd with her boys, she was pleased to see Feige, who introduced her father. "I'm so happy you've met Samuel," said Hannah. "He'll be such a help to all of us while we're on the ship."

"Where's your father, Samuel?"

"Just getting settled, Mama. You know he likes to know everyone and everything in a new place. He'll be up soon."

"And you're just like him!" Hannah kissed her son. His face turned almost as red as his hair, but he embraced her in return.

Just then the whistle sounded, shocking them all into silence. Passengers lined up three deep at the rail to watch as the crew removed the heavy ropes that kept them tethered to the dock. The dark water began to swirl around the ship and more smoke rose from the smokestacks. Orders were being shouted in Dutch, a language most of the passengers didn't understand, but the crew obeyed quickly, performing a well-rehearsed dance.

There were people on the dock waving handkerchiefs and shouting farewell. Feige could hear people on the deck above them responding, but the third-class passengers were far away from home. They had said their goodbyes a long time ago and they had no one to wave to now.

"*Zei gezunt, alt lebn*! Goodbye, old life," shouted Samuel as the ship slowly made its way out into the harbor. "We're on our way to *Die Goldene Medina*!"

"The golden land," echoed Feige, silently praying that it would be golden for her.

Most of the crowd stayed where they were, watching until land faded from sight.

Feige finally turned away. There was no turning back now. She knew what she had left behind, but not what lay ahead. Fear and hope warred inside her. She wished she could be as enthusiastic as Samuel.

The crowd dispersed, some families sitting together in groups, some separating and going below to acquaint themselves with their quarters. Feige and her father and Samuel and his family stayed on deck. His father had found them just as the ship began to move. As dusk fell, the crowd started to buzz. They were bringing the food down below. Feige, Hannah, and her boys said their goodbyes and started toward the women's quarters.

"Come back up later, Feige," said Samuel. "It will be cooler up here. I'll wait for you at this spot."

"Me too, me too," cried Ephraim and Joshua.

"Hush boys. It's almost your bedtime." Hannah held onto them firmly. "You'll see Samuel tomorrow."

"I'm very tired, Samuel," said Feige. "Perhaps tomorrow for me too. I'll see you in the morning."

She wanted to talk to him again, but she had no experience talking to a man her family didn't know. What would they talk about? She turned toward her father, who had been praying silently. "Goodnight Papa, sleep well."

"Feigele, stay a minute," he said, taking her aside. "You're a good girl, Feigele. What were you doing with this boy? Remember, you're on your way to be married."

"Papa, how can you doubt me? I know what's right."

"Of course, child, but please be careful."

"Yes, Papa," said Feige, keeping any disobedient thoughts to herself. *What does it mean, be careful? Don't talk to him? I want to talk to him. After we get to America, I'll marry Caleb and never see Samuel again. But for now...*

When they got below, they could see lines forming. Three men behind huge barrels were ladling food into the bowls the women and children held out. Those who had their food took seats at the tables. When Feige got to the front she could see potatoes in one barrel, vegetables she couldn't identify in another and some kind of meat floating in a brown sauce in the third. She moved her bowl away to avoid the meat, which she couldn't be sure was kosher, and took a seat near Hannah and the boys. The food had no flavor, but she would have been glad for a little more of it.

When she looked around for a place to clean her bowl, she realized that the only water was in the same room where they were expected to wash themselves, not far from the toilets. She was horrified, but once again had no choice. After washing as best she could, Feige lay down on her bed. Samuel was probably right. It would be cooler on the deck than in this space with no windows. The rumbling of the ship's engines was so loud she was sure it would keep her awake all night, but the day's events caught up with her and she was soon sound asleep.

"Wake up, Feige, wake up." Someone was shaking her.

"I'm coming, I'm coming, Mama." In her sleep, she thought Mama was waking her to start her chores.

Someone shook her again. "Feige, it's me, Hannah. Wake up, or you'll miss breakfast."

"Thank you," murmured Feige, coming awake and remembering her hunger from the night before. She rushed to get washed and offered her bowl to the man behind the barrel for her helping of lumpy porridge. Her first mouthful was cold and tasted burnt, but she made herself finish it. It was better than nothing.

Breakfast, lunch, dinner. Barrels of porridge, barrels of herring, barrels of potatoes. Sometimes hot, sometimes cold. The meals marked the hours as the days passed. On her first night, Feige discovered small scratch marks on one of the iron poles connecting her bed to the one above her. She began to do the same, wondering about the woman who had gone before her. Where did she come from? Was she alone? Was she as frightened as Feige?

The first three days she marked off, the seas were calm. Only a few people got sick, but the smells started to grow stronger. The floors were swept by the crew every morning before the ship's Captain made his rounds but not washed. The women did the best they could to keep the room and themselves clean, but it was a hopeless struggle.

Feige spent most of her time on deck with Samuel. At first Papa sat at a distance with his book, keeping a watchful eye, but he was one of the first to get seasick and had to stay below. Samuel and his father assured Feige that they would watch out for him. Now she was glad she had made friends. For the first time in her life, Feige didn't have either of her parents watching over her. She and Samuel walked around the small deck allotted to them, talking about their hometowns and the friends they had left behind. Samuel's family, he told her, was from a town near Lodz, Poland.

"It was close enough for me to go to the gymnasium there," he said. "To study science. And when we get to America, I'll learn English and go to college to be a doctor."

"Won't you have to work to help the family?" Feige asked.

"Yes, I'll get have to get a job while I study, but I know I can do it."

"I'm sure you can, Samuel."

"And what about you, Feige?"

She didn't answer right away. What was it like to have a dream like his? She had never thought of being anything but a wife and mother, like her Mama and her Mama's mama before her. She was on her way to America to make a home for the stranger she was pledged to marry and raise the children they'd have. All she wanted was to be happy.

"I loved growing up in Kamenetz. I went to school as a girl, but mostly I learned from my Mama and my bubbe. My bubbe taught me how to embroider when I was a little girl and when I got older my Papa sold the things I made in his shop. I embroidered things for a bride's trousseau or new home."

"When we get to America, I'll buy something from you for my Mama."

Feige nodded, but she knew they would be going their separate ways. She would never see Samuel again after they arrived in New York.

"And what about your family?"

Feige told him about her Mama and her brothers and sister. "My oldest brother, Daniel, has red hair like yours. He always made time to tell me stories and teach me games. My other brother, Noah, was the scholar, always with his nose in a book. He would have loved to go to a gymnasium like you. They've both been in America for four years, working in my cousin's factory. I can't wait to see them again."

"And the little ones still at home?"

"Freyda is ten, growing up quickly. Levi is three. He's full of mischief, but easy to love."

"And your Mama? You don't look like your Papa, so your beauty must come from her."

Feige blushed. "I'll never be as beautiful as her. She's patient and kind and generous. Her smile can make you forget all your troubles. I miss her so much." She told him how hard it had been to say goodbye to Gittel and Raisel. She said very little about the marriage that had been arranged for her.

Each time they were together Feige found it easier to talk to Samuel. They sat together on the deck, trying to keep out of the wind and ocean spray. Feige's long hair often came loose in the wind, and she struggled in vain to keep it pinned. Once, Samuel reached to fix a curl, but Feige stopped him with a look. Touching was too much to allow.

"Good morning, Feige, did you dream of your prince last night?"

"Don't be silly, Samuel. I dreamt about the village fool, and as I recall, he looked just like you."

"Oh, Feige, how you wound me," Samuel clutched his heart.

Feige surprised herself by being able to joke with him. She began to look forward to their time together and was disappointed if rainy weather kept them apart. After a few more days the wind grew stronger, and the ship started to roll with the huge waves. Most of the passengers were seasick. The lucky ones who were able to get themselves up to the deck vomited over the rails. Those who stayed below lay in their beds, moaning. They vomited on the already soiled floor and the stench grew.

Feige and Samuel were together every day as the weather got worse. They were among the hearty few, along with Samuel's father and brothers, who stayed healthy. Even on the windiest days, Feige was strong enough to navigate the steps and walk on deck. It was the only way she had to get away from the smell below. She did what she could to help Hannah, who was not so fortunate, bringing the boys up on deck as often as she could.

"Have you ever seen the ocean before, Feige?" asked Samuel. "It's as big as the sky. I could watch it forever."

Feige looked out at the ocean. She had expected the water to be blue, but today it was a cold, dark gray.

"Doesn't it frighten you?"

"Don't worry, I'll protect you from the sea monsters."

"Can't you ever be serious?"

"Well, maybe sometimes it scares me a little."

"Only a little, I'm sure. You're brave, not like me."

"How can you say that, Feige? Here you are, far away from your home, your Mama, and your friends. You couldn't have come this far if you weren't brave."

"I'll try to remember that when I'm alone and scared."

"You're not alone now. You've got me—and my family," he added hastily.

"Thank you," she said. But she didn't feel brave. If she were truly brave, wouldn't she tell Papa she didn't want to marry Caleb? But wasn't it also brave to do what was right for her family, even if it wasn't what she would have chosen?

The next day they sat quietly, huddled as far from the railing as they could to stay out of the wind. Feige had her woolen shawl wrapped tightly around her. She was quiet, still thinking about bravery, still feeling it would always elude her.

"Oh look," she said when a wind gust blew Samuel's jacket open. "It's because you're losing a button. Let me go below for a needle and thread and I'll fix it for you." She began to stand.

"No, stay," said Samuel. He ripped the button off, grabbed her hand and dropped it onto her palm. She tried to pull her hand away, but he held tight and wrapped her fingers around it. "Keep it," he said. "As a good luck charm—and to remember me by." He released her hand.

Feige nodded wordlessly and put the button in her pocket. She couldn't find the words to tell him how much it meant to her and was relieved when Samuel's brothers came running over, demanding his attention.

After another three days the weather finally improved. Passengers who had been sick gradually came up on deck. "Oh, Papa," Feige cried when she saw how gaunt he was. She tried to ignore how much he smelled; he would be ashamed. Besides, they were all dirty and smelly. Nevertheless, she took Samuel aside and asked him if he and his father could take him below and help him wash, comb his beard, and change his clothes.

"I'm fine, I don't need your help," her father said when Samuel offered. He turned to go below himself, but when his knees buckled Samuel took his elbow firmly.

"I was just about to go below myself," he said.

"He's a nice young man," Feige's father told her when they returned to the deck. That was high praise from Papa, even if it didn't change anything. She took his arm and led him on a short walk around the deck.

She had marked off eight days on the bedpost. Could it get any worse? Only her time with Samuel made it bearable. Finally, after five more seemingly endless days, the crew told them it wouldn't be long before they got to New York. When they did, every passenger, walking on their own or helped by others, came up for their first glimpse of America. A hush came over them as they gazed up at the magnificent Statue of Liberty, her shiny torch held high above the harbor. Feige stood next to her father, Samuel and his family beside them. She knew the statue couldn't promise her liberty. Whatever was in store for her, it wasn't freedom.

"There's one of the men I've been praying with. I'll go say goodbye to him while you say goodbye to Samuel, Feigele. I'll just be a minute."

"Thank you, Papa." He gave her a chance to say goodbye.

"If only—" Samuel said quietly. He reached for her hand, and she let him take it. It would be the last time before they said goodbye forever.

"Sha, Samuel. I'll miss you too, but it's almost time to go on to our new lives. Be happy, Samuel, and please, wish me the same."

"I hope he deserves you," said Samuel, squeezing her hand tightly.

Feige held on for a moment before letting go and turning away. She didn't want him to see the tears in her eyes. She reached into her pocket to hold the button he had given her. *If only… I'll always wonder what would have happened if we had met at another time. I'll never forget you.*

She caught Hannah's eye, feeling as though the older woman could see into her heart, before going to join her father. As they glided past the Statue of Liberty, the crowd erupted in cheers. America, their new home.

PART II: AMERICA, 1910-1911

CHAPTER 4

The deck hummed with excitement as the ship neared the shore, but their hopes were dashed when the crew informed them only the first-class passengers were allowed to disembark.

"I should have known," Feige grumbled. "Once again, the rich people get special treatment."

"Sha, Feigele," said Papa, putting his arm through hers. "Our turn will come."

The third-class passengers were put onto a ferry and taken to the island where they would have to pass inspection to stay in America. Any hint of illness or infirmity and they could be sent away; everything they had been through would be for nothing.

When the ferry docked, Feige and her father joined the lines walking toward a castle that took up almost the entire island. The hall they entered was grander than anything she could have imagined. Sunlight streamed through the rounded windows and a red, white, and blue flag that stretched the width of the room hung from the ceiling. She gazed in awe at the arched ceilings high above her.

Hundreds of new arrivals, many speaking languages Feige had never heard, climbed the stairs in long lines. Men in uniform watched them, occasionally pulling someone off the line. She knew they were looking for reasons to turn them away. Please God, she prayed silently. Let us make it through this final trial. And please take care of Samuel and his family.

The doctor checked her hair and eyes and touched her face and neck and hands. She felt violated, but stayed silent, terrified that he would write a letter on her clothes as he had done on some of the others. That would mean he had found something that could send her home.

Next, they waited to be questioned by officials sitting behind large wooden tables covered with piles of papers. When it was their turn, an interpreter translated the questions into Yiddish. They were the same questions they had been asked before they were allowed to board the ship, to make sure they wouldn't be a burden on the American government. The Germans hadn't wanted them and now it appeared neither did the Americans. Did anyone care about the persecution and violence that had driven them from their homes?

Finally, the official stamped their papers with a loud bang and handed each of them a card granting them permission to live in America.

"Papa," cried Feige. "It's official. We're in America now." She held out her card and threw herself into his arms.

Another interpreter helped Papa exchange their money for American dollars and they picked up their belongings from a storage room piled high with valises and bundles. Feige was relieved to be reunited with her things.

At the foot of the stairs, they saw men, women, and children hugging and kissing each other. Many were weeping. They joined the crowd of families, anxiously scanning the faces of each new person who came from outside. *At last, I'll meet Caleb and begin my new life.*

Papa saw them first. "Charles, Noah, Daniel," he yelled. "Over here!"

"Asher, Feigele, thank God you're here safe," Charles welcomed them in a booming voice and reached out to his cousin. He was tall and stout, his hair and neatly trimmed beard more gray than brown. In his striped suit, starched white wing collar, bright burgundy tie and fine, polished shoes, he looked like what Feige presumed a wealthy factory owner should look like.

Her brothers had changed so much in the four years since she had last seen them, she barely recognized them.

"Feige," shouted Daniel, lifting her in the air. "Where is the baby sister I left in Kamenetz? Who is this beautiful young woman?"

"Put me down, Daniel," she laughed. "Let me look at you."

Tall and slender, his hair was dark red, like Papa's beard, falling in soft curls over his forehead. But his eyes were hazel like Mama's. Feige had missed him. He had never scolded her for following him around, and when he wasn't getting into trouble for running outside instead of studying, he would play with her. He was never too busy or too tired for her endless questions.

"My turn," said Noah, hugging her. Although closer in age to Feige, he had never been a playmate. He was always too busy reading and got annoyed if she interrupted. His straight, light brown hair framed a round baby face, but he too was tall and thin. Neither of her brothers had a beard. They wore caps, but no *yarmulkes*.

"You have become Americans," said Feige.

"No yarmulkes," said Papa after holding his sons close. "What else have you given up, my boys?"

"This is America, Papa. Things are different here," said Daniel.

"Perhaps too different," said his father.

They had only just arrived, but Feige could already see how different this world was from the one she and Papa had left behind. Would he be able to accept it? And where was Caleb? She had been sure he would be there to welcome her.

"What, no Caleb?" Papa asked as though he had read Feige's mind.

"He's much too busy at work," scoffed Charles. "I expect you'll see him tonight. Come, let's get to the ferry quickly. Miriam is home making dinner, and it will take us a while to get there. Boys, take the baggage. Feigele, stay close." He turned and started walking.

Cousin Charles was clearly used to taking charge. Feige was grateful he was there to lead the way, but she couldn't stop thinking about Caleb. Important businessman or not, didn't he want to see the bride his father had chosen for him? There was no time to worry about it as she hurried to keep up with the men.

As the ferry churned across the river, Feige had another chance to see the city. She gazed in astonishment as they approached the tallest buildings she had ever seen, silhouetted against the dusky sky. The reflection of the sun setting behind the ferry turned their windows bright gold.

Charles laughed as he watched her looking up. "Those are called skyscrapers," he announced. "See that one? That's the Singer Building, forty-one stories high! The company that makes sewing machines built it."

"Do people live in those buildings?" asked Feige. "There are so many stairs to climb."

"Not in the tallest ones," answered Charles. "Those are offices for banks and businesses. And you don't have to walk because there are elevators, little rooms pulled by electric cables, to take you as high as you want to go." Feige couldn't imagine venturing into an elevator or looking out a window at the top of a skyscraper.

When they emerged from the terminal on the other side of the river, the street was crowded with newly arrived passengers, stevedores, horse drawn carts and wagons and a few delivery trucks with large, lettered names painted on their sides. Feige had never seen an automobile before. Men were shouting. Boat whistles blew and horns blared. She held onto Papa, afraid they would be trampled, but Charles steered them quickly through the crowds.

"This way," said Charles. "We'll take the trolley to the bridge that will take us to Brooklyn. Then we'll take another train to the house."

At the bridge they climbed the stairs to the train which began rumbling slowly along the tracks high above the river. The river was barely visible through the high metal railings, but still Feige was frightened. Daniel held her hand and assured her it was safe. On the other side they climbed down and boarded another train. Feige watched out the window. The three and four-story buildings were so close to the tracks she could almost see into people's windows. As the train climbed, she clung to Daniel and Noah on either side of her.

"Don't be afraid, Feigele," said Charles. "The tracks are under us. You're perfectly safe."

"It's called the El, for elevated. We take it every day to work," said Noah.

"You'll get used to it," added Daniel. "And wait until you take the new subway train that goes under the ground."

Feige doubted she would ever get used to trains that floated in the air or went under the ground. She tried to stay calm as she watched the electric lights come on as if by magic in the streets below. "How beautiful," she murmured.

At last Charles announced, "Get ready. We get off at the next stop. When we came to America, Brooklyn was a city by itself, but now it's part of New York. It's much quieter here than in Manhattan, a good place to raise children."

Feige hoped she wasn't blushing, sure he was hinting at the children she and Caleb would have.

It was a short walk along a wide tree-lined avenue to the Fine's two-story brick house. Light poured from the open windows. There were small flower gardens on either side of the front steps surrounded by a low, black iron fence. Yellow and white daisies and mounds of pink, purple and red flowers Feige didn't recognize were in bloom, giving off a sweet scent.

How grand the house is. They must be very rich.

Charles, Daniel and Noah ignored the *mezuzah* as they walked through the front door. The small wooden cylinder affixed to the doorpost contained a scroll inscribed with their most sacred prayer. Papa appeared ready to say something to his sons but stopped himself. He and Feige paused to touch the mezuzah with their fingertips and raised their fingers to their lips.

As Charles ushered them into the house, Feige detected the familiar smells of chicken and soup. And there in the hallway was Cousin Miriam, a short, trim woman in a rose-colored dress and flowered apron.

"I thought you'd never get here," she cried. "Welcome to your new home." She wept as she embraced Feige's Papa. "It's been so long, Asher."

"I've missed you, Miriam. Thank you for taking care of my boys." He too had tears in his eyes. "You're looking well."

"You mean not too bad for an old woman?" Then she took Feige in her arms. "Feigele, my soon to be daughter, how wonderful to finally meet you – and you're even more beautiful than your picture."

"But come everyone, let's eat. I'm sure Asher and Feige are exhausted, but they haven't had a decent meal in weeks. Let's have a bite before they're off to bed."

★ ★ ★

Feige awoke with a start. She had been aware of footsteps and murmured voices earlier in the morning but had barely stirred. It felt too good to rest her head on the soft pillow and feel the cool, smooth, linens on her skin. The light quilt was just right for the June morning. "Just a few more minutes," she thought. Snuggling deeper, she had fallen back into a deep sleep.

It was her first good sleep since leaving home. After the train's wooden benches with only Papa's shoulder as a pillow, the thin dirty pallet on the ship, and the groans of seasick passengers throughout the night, being alone in a clean bed was a luxury. She could stretch her arms out wide without fear of touching anyone else, or worse, something crawling nearby. She was savoring the moment when suddenly she remembered where she was. They had arrived in America. They were in her cousin's home. One of the voices she had heard could have been Caleb.

She wished she could remember what the voices sounded like. Did Caleb have a deep, manly voice? Would that tell her anything about him? Was he stern or kind? Handsome or plain? What would he think of her?

Fully awake now, she glanced around the pale-yellow room. There was a dressing table with a mirror and a matching chintz-covered bench in between two tall windows. The floral chintz curtains that matched the bench were still drawn to keep out the sun. The tables on either side of the bed each had a glass lamp on a lace doily. The polished wood floors were partly covered by a wine-colored carpet.

There were no personal items on the dressing table or the nightstands. It clearly belonged to a woman, but Feige had no idea who. She saw her valise near the door, which she must have opened for her nightclothes, but she was reluctant to take out anything more until Cousin Miriam told her whose room it was.

With these questions on her mind, and becoming rather desperate to use the toilet, Feige wondered what to do. She vaguely remembered that there was a toilet inside the house, in a big white room. The toilet had a chain to pull to remove the waste.

Water for hand-washing came out of taps over the sink. She thought it wasn't far from this room. But could she simply go find it on her own? Could she leave the room in her nightgown and robe?

Before she could gather the courage to peek out, she heard a soft knock at the door. "Are you awake, Feigele?" It was Miriam. "It's almost noon."

Feige was shocked. She threw open the door without stopping to put on her robe. "I am so sorry, Cousin Miriam, this has never happened before."

"Nonsense, dear, you were exhausted from your journey and needed your rest. The men all left for work hours ago and I have been getting ready for Shabbos. There was no reason to wake you."

"I have never slept this late before, but the bed was so wonderful. Whose room is this?"

"It's yours. It was Max and Rachel's room before the baby was almost due and they moved to a place of their own. We made it over for you until the wedding. Do you like it?"

"I love it!" Feige hugged her cousin.

"I'm so glad. I've never had a daughter, and I was hoping it would suit you. Now I'm sure you'll want to unpack and bathe. Then I'll show you around the house and introduce you to Bridget, who comes in every day to help me with the cleaning. You can watch as I finish preparing dinner."

"Come, put on your robe." She held out her hand to Feige. "Do you remember where the bathroom is?"

Miriam led Feige down the hall and opened the door to the room Feige had used briefly the night before. The floor was tiled with large white porcelain squares. Smaller white tiles went halfway up the wall; blue striped wallpaper covered the rest. A large window with frosted glass let in ample light, even without the fixture hanging in the center of the room. The toilet, sink, and bathtub were shiny white. Everything was sparkling clean.

"Remember, just pull the chain over the toilet when you're done. And there is soap, a washcloth and towels next to the tub. I've also left you some lavender oil to put in the water. It will smell delicious and make your skin feel wonderful. I use it every time I bathe and if you like it, I'll get more just for you. Or if you'd prefer a different scent, just let me know. And don't be shy, Feigele. This is your home now."

Miriam lifted Feige's heavy braid. "Can you manage your hair on your own?"

"Yes, thank you. But how will I heat the water?"

"Oh, how silly of me. I forgot that you wouldn't have a tub like this at home. Hot and cold water come out here. Just turn these knobs—this one for hot and this one for cold, until you get it just the way you like it. This plug will keep the water in the tub, just pull it when you're done. The sink has a plug too."

Miriam walked over to the sink to point out even more new things. "Here's a new toothbrush and some dental powder. We didn't have brushes or powder when I left Russia." She showed Feige how to mix the powder and chattered on as Feige tried to absorb all the new information.

"In the mornings when everyone needs to use the toilet, we don't take very much time in here, but no one is home now, Feigele, so you can take as much time as you need. You don't even need to lock the door. I promise no one will disturb you. And just leave everything when you're done. Bridget will clean it all up. And I'll ask her to unpack and hang your clothes while you're bathing. She'll make sure you have something fresh for Shabbos."

Feige could hardly take it all in. No need to go outside to the toilet? No need to heat the water? Surely everyone in America didn't live like this. She'd try hard not to disappoint Cousin Miriam by making a mistake.

After using the toilet Feige couldn't resist pulling the chain again to watch the water swirl and disappear like magic. She put the plug in the tub and carefully let in the water, testing it with her fingers until it was as hot as she thought she could stand it and adding the oil. It smelled as wonderful as her cousin had promised. She slowly eased her body into the water until she was fully submerged from the neck down.

She began washing, feeling lighter as the dirt of the journey came off. She scrubbed her scalp until it tingled, trying to rid herself of the memory of the doctor touching her.

I'll be married soon. Will Caleb see me naked? Will my body please him? Other than what Mama told her about making a baby, Feige had no idea what to expect from married life. Her best friend Gittel's cousin had brought a novel with her when she came from Warsaw. Feige was too afraid to read it, but Gittel said when the man and woman in the story kissed the woman felt it "deep inside her." Neither of them understood exactly what that meant.

Feige ran the soapy cloth over her body. Her nipples hardened and she felt a shiver between her legs. Was this it, this feeling deep inside her? It made her want to feel more of it, to touch herself. She started to slide her hand down toward the sensation but jerked it away. Surely it was a sin. But was that what Caleb would do to her when they were married? She willed herself to stop thinking about it and rinsed off quickly.

A hot bath that smelled like a garden, a room with a door that locked, all the time she wanted, and someone to clean up after her. She must be dreaming. Any minute Mama will be yelling for her to hurry up because she needed to get warm water for the children's baths.

Feige felt guilty when she thought of Mama. Here she was, relaxing in a bath like the Empress of Russia, while Mama was still at home. It was Mama who deserved this hot bath, Mama who should be treated like a queen.

As she dried herself with the thick white towels, her thoughts turned to meeting Caleb for the first time that night. He had not arrived in time for dinner the night before and she had gone to sleep immediately after they ate. She prayed they would like each other. Her future happiness was in his hands. She began to plan what she would wear and how she would do her hair to make a good first impression.

* * *

Caleb's chair was empty. Feige tried to avoid looking at it. Why hadn't he come home yet? They hadn't met, so it couldn't be anything she had said or done. And she had worn her best dress with lace trim and fastened her long curls with a comb decorated with colored stones just to impress him! She looked around the table at her new extended family, determined not to let anyone see how upset she was. Cousin Charles was seated at the head of the table. He didn't appear at all concerned that his son was late for Shabbos dinner.

"Where is Caleb, cousin?" her father asked. "Surely he won't miss Shabbos?"

"The business comes first, Asher. He's working on a big order for one of our most important customers. He'll get here soon enough. Come, let's eat." He said a hurried prayer over the wine and challah and began to carve the chicken Miriam placed before him.

"No Eshet Chayil, Charles? You don't honor Miriam on Shabbos?"

Miriam answered before her husband had the chance. "Asher, please. We don't observe all the old ways here. I don't need a prayer to know Charles is proud of the home I keep." She went to get the soup. "You sit," she told Feige when she started to get up. "Tonight, you're a guest."

"So, Asher, you'll start working right away," Charles told Feige's Papa after they had finished the meal. "You're family, and a job is waiting. But the work will be hard."

Asher bristled. "Of course," he replied sharply. "I'm no stranger to hard work. I built the shop I took over from Bluma's father into a good business, just like you did with yours."

Feige was proud of her Papa. He wore his traditional plain black coat and trousers, but she thought he was even more handsome than Charles in his striped suit and gold pocket watch and chain stretched across his middle. Yet she worried about him here in America. Would he learn English quickly? He was used to being in charge. Would he allow himself to follow orders from his cousin? She hoped they wouldn't argue at their first Shabbos dinner together.

"You're a lucky man to have a job waiting for you," Charles continued, unperturbed by his cousin's response. "I had no one to help me when I arrived in America twenty-five years ago. Everything you see here is because I worked hard for it." He waved his hand at the luxurious furnishings surrounding them.

Feige looked around the room. The starched linen tablecloth was set with fine china, cutlery, and etched crystal glasses. The Shabbos candles in their tall silver candlesticks sat on a carved oak sideboard. Drapes that matched the green velvet chairs hung in soft folds to the floor. She wondered if she and Caleb would have nice things when they had their own place to live, but how would she know how to shop for them?

Before further words could be exchanged between her cousin and her papa, the aroma of the freshly baked chocolate cake Miriam was bringing out of the kitchen filled the room.

"Ah, my favorite," said Charles, patting his stomach contentedly. "If Miriam doesn't stop feeding me, I'll have to have my new suit let out."

"Caleb loves it too, Feigele." He looked down the table at Feige. "You'll have to learn to make it for him."

Feige glanced at Caleb's empty place.

"I know you're disappointed he isn't here," said Charles. "You know, Feigele, your intended is already an important man here in New York. He was the one who got us the patent from the government that helped make our factory the biggest in the city. Now he's a big shot."

Feige had no idea what a patent was. She hated to reveal her ignorance, but it would be worse to say the wrong thing in front of Caleb. "What is a patent?' she asked her cousin timidly.

Charles enjoyed showing off. "A patent means that no other factory can use the method we invented to roll thin tin sheets without paying us. You must expect some late nights, but you should be proud of your future husband. One day he'll take over Fine and Sons."

Feige glanced at Max, Caleb's younger brother. He was fair, of medium height and build. She noticed that his pale blond hair was already thinning. He also worked at the factory, but it seemed Charles had little regard for him. How awful to be slighted in front of the family. Surely her cousin didn't treat him like that in front of their workers.

Max's wife, Rachel, sat next to him. Her face betrayed nothing, but Feige could see the clenched fists she was hiding in her lap. Feige had hoped she and Rachel would be friends, but her future sister-in-law had barely said a word all night. Did she resent Feige for marrying the favored son? She was so pale and withdrawn Feige felt sorry for her. Maybe she was just tired from taking care of her three-month old son, who Bridget was minding in the parlor.

"Another round of schnapps," Charles announced, "A toast to our expanding family."

"Asher, as the guest of honor, you'll lead us in prayers after dinner."

"My boys," Asher looked lovingly at his sons. "Will you say them with me? Do my American sons even remember the prayers?"

"Of course, Papa," replied Daniel. "We're happy you're here and we'll pray that Mama, Freyda and Levi can join us soon. We've missed you all."

"And we missed you," said Feige. Looking at them, she was sure it wouldn't be long before they too were married. And she was confident they would help their Papa adjust to America. They knew as well as she did that he needed to earn enough to return home quickly for Mama and the children. Along with the traditional Shabbos prayers, Asher thanked God that he and Feige had arrived safely and that he and Miriam were reunited.

"I've been so worried about you," said Miriam when he finished. "Ever since you wrote to us about the pogroms. According to the paper, things are getting even worse, and I won't be happy until Bluma and the children are also here with us. And we are delighted that Feige is joining our family," she added.

When the prayers ended, Max and Rachel took the baby, his little head barely peeking out from his swaddling, and said their goodbyes. Charles and Asher continued to drink their schnapps and talk about business while Noah and Daniel listened intently, interrupting occasionally with questions about the factory.

While the men were occupied with their conversation, Miriam turned to Feige. "You look lovely tonight, child. Caleb is going to regret not coming home sooner."

Feige could feel her cheeks turning red as Miriam continued.

"I know you'll miss your Mama, dear, but I'll take care of you as if you were my own daughter. I'll help you prepare for your wedding and shop with you for your new home. And I'll teach you to make Caleb's favorite foods."

"Thank you. Mama taught me to bake and cook, but I'll count on you to teach me what foods Caleb likes and how they make them in America."

Feige had been drawn to her father's cousin from the minute she had come to the door to welcome them. She was warm and affectionate, just like Mama. Now, as they sat quietly together, Feige had a chance to admire her cousin's simple blue silk dress and the small gold brooch at her throat. She had never seen anything so delicate. Miriam wore a plain gold wedding band on her left hand, but the purple and green gems in the two rings on her right hand sparkled when they caught the light. Her auburn hair, threaded with silver, was neatly pinned up. She wore her beautiful things as though she had always had them, although Feige knew that she had been a poor country girl in a town not far from Kamenetz before Charles married her and brought her to America.

"And I'll be with you when the first baby comes," said Miriam. "You'll have nothing to fear. Charles and I are waiting for you and Rachel to fill our house with grandchildren," she added with a smile.

Feige felt her face grow even warmer and her eyes filled. Thanks to Miriam, she was starting to feel a little less worried. She vowed to herself that she would be a good daughter-in-law.

"I promise—" Before she could finish, there was a commotion at the front door.

"I'm home!" yelled Caleb.

Feige gasped. Now that the moment she had been waiting for had arrived, she would give anything to delay it. It had been hours since she had dressed so carefully and done her hair. She barely had time to compose herself before Caleb burst into the room.

She thought he had a pleasant face, with brown eyes and generous brows beneath a high forehead. His wavy light brown hair came to a prominent widow's peak. Feige tried to remember if that revealed something about him. What was it that the old women of Kamenetz said about a widow's peak? Always self-conscious about her height, she was relieved to see that he was tall. Like his father, he was dressed in a light-colored suit, but he sported a bright blue bowtie that gave him a more youthful appearance.

Caleb's eyes were on Feige as he bid *Gut Shabbos* to his father and cousins.

"Cousin Asher, it's so good to see you at last. We were all waiting anxiously for you and Feige." He bent to kiss his mother. "Gut Shabbos, Mama."

Miriam chided him gently as she rose to get him the dinner she had saved. "So late, Caleb. It was very wicked of you to keep Feige waiting."

She turned to Feige before she left the dining room. "This is my son, Caleb. I'm sure he's about to apologize to you."

"Caleb," she said, "This is your bride, Feige. Now come sit near us, dear, so the two of you can get to know each other."

Caleb moved the empty chair to sit opposite Feige and gave her an appraising look. "I'm sorry, Feige, and happy to meet you at last," he said with a disarming smile.

"It's good to finally meet you too, Caleb," said Feige shyly. "Your father explained the delay. He's very proud of you." She struggled to think of what to say next.

"How was your journey?" asked Caleb. "I was so young when we came to America, I barely remember the train or the ship. Was it a smooth sailing? You were so lucky to be on the Lapland. I read all about her when she launched last year. She's one of the fastest steamships crossing the Atlantic."

"Yes, thank you," stammered Feige. Some day she hoped she could confide in Caleb. She yearned to tell someone about the friends she had made and lost along the way. But tonight was for polite conversation as they looked each other over. She knew her face was turning red, but Caleb didn't appear nervous at all. She couldn't believe this self-assured American was her future husband.

"And I see Mama has served my favorite chocolate cake," said Caleb, echoing his father. "You'll have to teach Feige how to make it, Mama, or I'll be coming home for dessert every night."

"Oh no," said Feige. "I'll learn to make it for you."

"Don't worry, I was only teasing. I promise I'll stay home to eat any dessert you make for me. Just ask Mama how much I love sweets."

He grinned as he began to concentrate on the generous slice his mother had given him.

Miriam cleared her throat loudly. "Caleb," she said.

Caleb glanced up from his plate, saw his mother's expression, and put his fork down to look at Feige. "You must be tired. It's my fault for making you wait. How can I make it up to her, Mama?"

"Why not—"

"I know, I'll take you to the park for a picnic. We'll go on a Sunday when I can leave the factory early. You'll love it. It's pretty and cool there all summer long."

Feige looked at Miriam in a panic. Was this how it was done in America? Did he mean they would go alone?

"And who will go with you?" asked Feige's Papa, making no effort to hide his disapproval.

Miriam sensed Feige's discomfort and moved to reassure Asher that his daughter's reputation would be safe. "What a wonderful idea!" she said. "Young couples go to the park on their own all the time here, Asher. They'll probably meet some of Caleb's friends strolling in the new garden."

American custom or not, Feige asked her father's permission. "May I go with Caleb, Papa?"

"Yes, Feigele," he said, although clearly still displeased. "If Miriam says it is proper in America."

"Then it's settled," said Caleb. "I'll let you know as soon as I've made a plan."

Feige rose to go to her room. She had survived their first meeting. "Good night, everyone." She went to kiss her Papa and brothers.

"Good night Feigele, we will walk together to shul tomorrow?"

"Of course, Papa."

"And you, my sons?"

"We'll join you tomorrow, Papa, because it's our first chance to be together. But we don't go every Shabbos." said Daniel.

"No yarmulkes, this I understand, but not to pray?" He raised his voice. "Are you still Jews?"

"Yes, Papa, but not in the old way. Let's talk about this another time," Noah answered him.

Feige turned to leave. She wished there was something she could do to make it better for Papa. It was going to be hard for him to accept how much Daniel and Noah had changed, and he was going to be so lonely without Mama.

"Good night, Feige," said Caleb, as he turned to his father. "So, Papa, let me tell you what happened with the order ..."

That was it? "Happy to meet you" and back to business? Feige thought she'd be relieved when the evening ended, but it had done nothing to alleviate her fears. Who was this stranger who cared more about business than his bride?

★ ★ ★

28 June 1910

Dearest Mama,

We have arrived safely, thank God!

The journey was hard, but now that we're here there's so much to do, I'm sure I will soon forget what we suffered.

Wait until you see Daniel and Noah. I almost didn't recognize them! They have both grown into such handsome young men. Papa is worried about how much they've changed in America, but I'm sure they're still the good sons you brought them up to be.

The buildings in New York reach to the sky! I feel like a small child again here, a child who knows nothing about the world. There are so many wonderful things here we didn't even know existed in Kamenetz and I can't wait for you and the children to see them with me.

Cousin Miriam is wonderful, just like you told me she would be. She made up the prettiest room for me to sleep in until the wedding. I never dreamed of having a room all to myself!

Two girls help her take care of this big house, but Miriam is a baleboosteh just like you.

About Caleb, I don't know what to say yet. He didn't come to meet us the day we arrived. Cousin Charles said he was too busy at work. Then he was very late for Shabbos dinner, again working. It seems that for Caleb, business comes before everything. I will have to get used to this when I am his wife.

A big hug and kisses for Freyda and Levi - I'll write again soon.

Your loving daughter,

Feige

A few days later, Feige was sitting at the kitchen table writing a letter to Mama when Miriam came in to invite her to go with her to visit Rachel and the baby.

"I'd love to," said Feige. "I was just writing to Mama."

"Please send her my love. I'll write my own letter soon."

When they arrived at Rachel and Max's apartment later that day, Rachel opened the door with the baby in her arms. She looked far more relaxed than she had at dinner and the light pink blouse she wore gave her face more color. Her pale, almost white-blond hair, which made her dark brown eyes stand out, was tied back with a narrow ribbon.

Miriam immediately held out her arms for her grandson and beamed when he let her take him. She brought him into the living room to sit on a comfortable-looking gold sofa and reached into her purse for the new rattle she had brought.

"Look, *Doovidel*, look what your bubbe brought you."

She shook the rattle and was rewarded with a smile.

"Feige, will you come help me get the tea and cookies ready?" asked Rachel. "They won't even notice we're gone," she added with a grin.

Feige followed Rachel down a hallway adorned with family pictures. The apartment was small, but she could see Rachel had taken care to make it look inviting. The kitchen was painted white. Sunlight streamed through a large window, casting a glow on the table covered with a cheerful red oilcloth.

"What pretty dishes," said Feige, admiring the flowered teacups and saucers and the matching sugar bowl and pitcher.

"Thank you," said Rachel. "They were a gift from Miriam for every day. She picked them out, but they're just what I would have chosen."

To Feige, they looked elegant enough for Shabbos.

"Come sit while I put the kettle on," said Rachel as she filled a shiny copper kettle with water. "I hope you don't mind store bought cookies. Since David was born, I haven't been doing much baking during the week. Only for Shabbos."

"Of course not. Please don't fuss on my account. I'm just happy to spend time with you. How long have you and Max lived here?"

"Just a few months. We stayed with Miriam and Charles for a while after we were married. My parents' apartment is small, and my three younger brothers are still at home. But with the baby coming we wanted a place of our own. And I wanted to be closer to my mother. Every girl wants her—" Rachel stopped herself. "Oh, I'm sorry, Feige. You are without your mother. I should have realized—"

"Don't apologize. You're right. I miss my Mama, but Miriam has already made me feel at home. It's hard for Mama too, waiting at home." Feige unconsciously began to nibble on a cookie. "Tell me about you and Max. Did the *shadchen* arrange your marriage?"

"No, we didn't need a matchmaker. Our families have known each other since we were children. We lived in the same neighborhood when we arrived in America, and we were practically raised together. I have no memories of life without Max."

Rachel poured the hot water into the teapot and filled the pitcher with milk she took out of the icebox. She filled their cups and brought a plate with lemon slices over to the table.

"Even though Max's father became rich and mine doesn't do nearly as well as a butcher, the families stayed close. I think our parents always planned for us to marry and since we had been together all our lives it seemed natural to us too. We were married two years ago, when I was seventeen and Max was twenty."

"How wonderful." Feige fixed her tea and took another cookie. "I wish I knew Caleb better. He's going to take me on a walk in the park soon. Such a thing never would have been allowed at home, but Miriam says it's acceptable here."

"You can trust Miriam. And you couldn't ask for a better *shviger.* She's such a wonderful mother-in-law; my friends are all jealous of me."

"I can already tell that about her."

"Max and I didn't spend time alone like you and Caleb will, because my parents are still more attached to the old ways than Miriam and Charles. We did have a big wedding, but not too extravagant. The Fines wanted it to be fancier, but my papa insisted that it only be what he could afford. I'm sure it will be different for you because of Caleb's role in the business. They'll want all their important friends there. And I'm sure they'll set a date quickly. They want Caleb to settle down."

"Can I tell you something, Rachel?"

"Of course, Feige. We're going to be sisters."

"The truth is, I'm scared. I've never really thought about being anything but a wife and mother, but I don't know how I'll make Caleb happy. Things are so different here."

"Don't be scared, Feige. What Caleb wants most of all is to be American. I think he might have had ideas about choosing his own bride, but Charles would never allow that. He would never risk letting the heir to the business make a bad choice on his own—maybe even, God forbid, a *shiksa*. Can you imagine, a girl who isn't Jewish?"

"But what if Caleb holds that against me? If he wanted someone else and they are making him marry me—"

"No, no, it wasn't like that. There was no one in particular. Just a fast crowd that Charles didn't like. But you're so beautiful and sweet, just like his mother, who he adores. You're sure to win him over."

"Do you think so?"

"Yes, I do and—"

"Rachel," said Feige, turning red and lowering her voice. "I'm frightened of the first night."

"Of course, you poor thing, I was too. And it did hurt the first time. But that goes away, Feige, I promise. We learned together, Max and I." Now it was Rachel's turn to blush. "I've never said this to anyone else, but I look forward to it."

"Thank you, I—"

They were interrupted by a wail from the other room, followed by Miriam carrying the baby into the kitchen. "He's getting fussy. Is it time for a nap or is he ready to be fed?"

As soon as the baby saw his mother, he reached for her.

"He's all yours, Rachel. Crying babies go back to their mamas."

"I think he's hungry." Rachel took him in her arms, unbuttoned her blouse and began to nurse. "Please help yourself to the tea. Feige and I have been talking so long I hope it hasn't gotten cold."

Miriam had her tea and the three of them chatted comfortably, mostly about bringing up children, until it was time to leave.

"Thank you, Rachel," said Feige. "For everything," she whispered in her ear.

CHAPTER 5

A few weeks later, Feige sat at the Fine's kitchen table trying to write a letter to Gittel and Raisel. Since her first morning in America, when she had been so exhausted from traveling and the emotional reunion with her brothers she had slept half the day, Feige made sure to rise early and come down to the kitchen as soon as the men left for work. She wanted to be ready to help her cousin in any way she could, and she had come to love this quiet time.

She never got tired of looking around the gleaming kitchen, still in awe of the modern appliances she had never seen before, like the brand-new white enamel gas oven Miriam had shown her how to light. But this morning she was struggling to describe these new things in a letter to her friends. How could she tell them about the bathroom and the kitchen, filled with conveniences no one in Kamenetz had? Would they think she was putting on airs? As she was thinking of the best way to write about them, Clara, the girl who helped Miriam in the kitchen, walked in.

Clara was Bridget's younger sister. The two girls, now teenagers, had come from Ireland as little children and had been working for the Fines for several years. They both had dark, almost black hair and bright blue eyes. They worked hard but always had a smile for the family. Feige had learned just enough English from them to say hello and ask for simple things.

"Good morning, miss. The water is ready for your tea if you'd like."

"Yes, thank you." Feige accepted the steaming cup. Clara took a pitcher of cold milk from a large oak icebox with shiny chrome handles. Every day the ice man called out from the street to tell his customers to get ready for his delivery. He lifted the large blocks of ice with giant tongs and carried them inside on his back.

Feige chewed on her pencil, at a loss for words. Finally, she began.

18 July, 1910

Dear Gittel and Raisel,

I am overwhelmed by all the new things I must learn about in America. My family lives in a big house with many things I don't know how to use yet. Today Papa's cousin is going to teach me to bake Caleb's favorite cake. Thank goodness she is here to guide me. You would like her. She's warm and caring, just like Mama.

Caleb is so busy with the factory I rarely see him. But this afternoon we are going for a walk in the park - alone! Can you believe that? I was shocked when he suggested it, but Cousin Miriam says it is permitted here. Papa wasn't happy, but he agreed. I am very nervous about meeting Caleb's American friends. I miss you both so much – please write to me soon.

Your friend in America,

Feige

Feige sighed and folded the letter. It was the best she could do. She got up to get more hot water, admiring the gleaming copper countertop that ran the length of the kitchen on the wall opposite the stove. Pots and pans of all sizes were stacked on the shelves above. Those for dairy were on one side and those for meat were on the other. Even though the Fines had abandoned many of the customs from the old country, they maintained a kosher home. Foods, pots and pans, dishes, and utensils were strictly separated, and some foods, like pork and shellfish, were never allowed in the house.

A table and six chairs were in the center of the kitchen. This was where the family ate breakfast and where she was now enjoying the sunlight coming in through the windows. If the women were alone, they ate lunch in the kitchen. Otherwise, meals were served in the dining room. A tea kettle always sat on top of the stove, ready to boil water for a cup of tea. But Caleb, she had learned, only drank tea at night. In the mornings he preferred coffee. His mother brewed a pot for him every morning and served it with the thick cream that was delivered along with milk before the sun came up. Feige sometimes heard the horse drawn wagon and the bottles clinking in their wire baskets.

That past Sunday, when Caleb was going to the factory later than usual and they were both eating breakfast with Miriam, Feige watched Caleb add two heaping spoons of sugar to his coffee. Then he topped his bowl of cold milk and Kellogg's Toasted Corn Flakes with more sugar. He certainly did love sweets!

The corn flakes and other ready-made foods were stored in a large pantry. There was even a can of "instant" coffee. It was so easy to make, a man could do it himself. But Feige would make sure to prepare Caleb's coffee every morning just like his mother did. Today, she was baking his favorite chocolate cake as a surprise for the picnic they were taking to the park that afternoon. Although she had been learning from her own Mama since childhood and already knew her way around a kitchen, she was eager to please Caleb by making his favorite foods. Didn't the old proverb say the way to man's heart was through his stomach?

"Good morning, Feigele." Miriam smiled as she joined Feige at the table. "You're up bright and early as usual." Miriam had gotten into the habit of going back to her room in the morning after serving breakfast to the men in the family. "I must confess, dear," Miriam shared as she started her tea, "Now that everyone is grown, I enjoy a few minutes to myself in the morning, as I see you do. After I had Caleb, I never thought this time would come! He rarely slept through the night and when he started to walk, he was into everything. I couldn't turn my back for a minute. And his questions, always with the why? why? why?"

"Just like Levi," laughed Feige. "Mama and I are always chasing him."

"But look at Caleb now," said Miriam proudly. "I think it's his curiosity that makes him such a wonderful businessman. He finds ways to do things differently and better than everyone else." Miriam glanced at the clock. "Look at me, chattering away when we should be baking."

"Oh no, I love hearing your stories about Caleb. It's nice to hear how he became the man he is today."

"Well, just the same, let's get started. We want to finish before he gets home." She walked toward the pantry but stopped and turned back toward Feige.

"I almost forgot." She reached into one of the cupboards to get a package wrapped in brown paper and tied with a string. "This is for you."

Feige unwrapped the package, carefully setting aside the paper and string to use again. *"Lehr-bukh vi azoy tsu kuchen und bakhen,"* she read. "By Hinde Amchanitski."

"It's a recipe book by a lady who runs a restaurant," explained Miriam. "Some of the foods we eat here in America may be new to you. And I have another one for your Mama when she comes."

"Thank you, I'm sure I'll use it often." Feige glanced through the book. "What is a macaroni?" she asked.

"It's *lokshen*," said Miriam. "Italian noodles. When we first came to America, Italians and Jews lived in the same buildings. We could smell each other's cooking, and we learned to use each other's ingredients. Like macaroni in chicken soup."

"And is the chocolate cake recipe from this book?"

"Oh no, it was my mother's and her mother's before her." Miriam handed Feige a well-worn piece of paper with a hand-written recipe.

"And someday I'll give it to my daughter," said Feige.

"Then what are we waiting for?"

Miriam began showing Feige where each ingredient was kept and which bowls and pans to use. She watched as Feige lit the oven so it would be warm enough when the cake was ready for baking. Feige measured carefully, sifted, cracked the eggs with a practiced hand, stirred the batter with a big wooden spoon, and poured it into a round, fluted cake pan. She put it into the hot oven and checked the time on the large wooden wall clock.

"Thirty-five minutes until it needs to be checked," said Miriam, "Let's have another cup of tea while we wait, and I'll tell you about the time Caleb swallowed a marble."

After forty minutes the cake was done. Feige took it out of the oven and set it on the counter until it was cool enough to invert onto a plate. It was perfect.

"Excellent," said Miriam. "I should have known you'd know exactly what to do. Bluma would be proud."

Feige put slices of cake into the large wicker basket Miriam had put out on the counter. When they were ready to leave, she would add the cold brisket sandwiches, potato salad, and pickles they had stored in the icebox the night before. Feige was nervous about the picnic and especially about meeting Caleb's friends, but at least now she was confident he would like dessert.

* * *

Feige was ready early that afternoon, even after spending longer than usual fussing with her clothes. Her choices were limited by what she had been able to bring with her when she came from Kamenetz, but she finally chose her light brown traveling skirt and a square necked white blouse with a row of buttons down the front. Her belt was trimmed with a deep red braiding she had embroidered herself. Her somewhat battered straw hat was perched at an angle atop her curls.

She waited anxiously at the front door. Caleb was so often late coming home from the factory, sometimes missing dinner altogether, she was afraid he'd be late for their outing. Sunday, when all the American businesses were closed, was a regular workday for Fine and Sons, making up for closing on Shabbos. It had taken him several weeks to find a day when he thought he could leave early enough for the picnic he had promised her. What if he didn't make it at all? She paced by the door.

As if worrying about when Caleb would come home wasn't enough, she was even more concerned about meeting his friends. They were sure to examine her critically. Would she make a good first impression? Would Caleb be proud to show her off? Finally, she saw him hurrying down the street.

"I'll just be a minute," he said, rushing up the stairs toward his room.

When he came back, he had changed from the clothes he had worn at the factory into tan pants with brown suspenders, a white shirt, and a light blue bow tie. He too wore a straw hat. Feige thought they looked well together.

It was a pleasant walk along Eastern Parkway, a boulevard with substantial homes like the Fine's on either side. The weather was mild for late July. Feige hesitated when Caleb offered her his arm, but she was in America now. He swung the picnic basket in his other arm, chatting easily about how the neighborhood had grown since the subway had opened. The parkway ended at their destination, he said, Prospect Park and the Botanic Garden.

"Wait until you see it. The Garden has only just opened but it's already a popular spot for a stroll. My friends and I go often."

Feige looked at him, wondering how he felt about taking her there. Was she intruding on things he enjoyed doing with his friends? She spotted a domed building with an imposing staircase leading up to its columned entrance. Even Brooklyn, it seemed, was filled with architectural wonders. "What is that?" she asked.

"A museum. The Brooklyn Institute of Arts and Sciences."

"A museum?"

"Where they have paintings and statues. And old machines like the ones they used in the factory when Papa started it."

"I would like to see such a place."

"And it has stuffed wild animals like lions and bears." He made his fingers into claws and reached them toward her, growling playfully.

"Well, maybe not those."

Caleb laughed. She had never seen this charming, easygoing side of him. Soon they were at the plaza at the entrance to the park. Feige craned her neck to gaze up at the statues on top of the arch that towered above them.

"Those statues are in honor of the soldiers and sailors who fought for the Union in America's Civil War," Caleb explained.

"There was a war in America?"

"Yes, almost fifty years ago—the North fought the South."

"But why?" Feige knew nothing about that war. She had so much to learn about her new country. *I must be careful not to reveal my ignorance in front of Caleb's friends.*

"Well, mostly about slavery, but we can talk about that another time—let's hurry into the park. I want to make sure we have time to meet my friends after we eat."

Feige saw lots of couples in the park, some with baskets like theirs, some just walking arm in arm. Some were dressed simply, others in costumes clearly meant to be shown off. Many of the women carried dainty pastel-colored parasols to block the sun. She was sure Caleb's friends would be among those elegantly dressed. She dreaded being judged by them.

As they walked deeper into the park, she tried to focus on the beautiful cool green forest. The trees formed a canopy over winding paths lined with flowering bushes and wooden benches. Many of these were occupied by couples holding hands as they talked to each other. Courting was certainly different in America.

Off to the side, couples were picnicking on cloths they had spread out on the grass and soon Caleb suggested they do the same. He found a shady spot far enough away from the others for privacy, spread the cloth that was in the basket, and helped Feige to sit. Together, they unpacked their lunch and began eating.

Conversation started slowly as they ate. "Tell me about Kamenetz and your family," prompted Caleb as they were finishing dessert. "Mmm, I love my mother's chocolate cake."

"I baked that for you with your mother's recipe." Feige was delighted the surprise had worked.

"Then you're a fast learner, this is delicious. Don't tell her I said so, but it's as good as hers."

Buoyed by her success, Feige began to relax a little. She told Caleb about Mama, Freyda and Levi. "You'll love my Mama," she said. "She's beautiful and kind, just like yours. And a good cook, too! I was sorry to leave her without help—the children are a handful."

"We'll have lots of children, Feige, sons to carry on the business."

"I've always wanted children, Caleb." Feige blushed but answered readily. She was even able to overcome her modesty to add, "And perhaps a daughter I can teach to make a home? Tell me more about your business, Caleb. Did you go to school before you started working with your father?"

Caleb told Feige about the Manual Training High School he attended because his father thought it would help prepare him to take over the factory. He described how Fine and Sons had grown and outpaced the many other metal factories in New York. He spoke with pride but didn't mention his own part as his father had at their first Shabbos dinner. Feige was glad he didn't brag about himself. It made him seem more like an ordinary person—someone she could talk to—rather than the intimidating "big shot" Charles had described. She was still nervous about his friends, but at least the two of them were getting along well.

"And speaking of school, Feige, you'll start learning English right away. The special night schools for immigrants will start again in September and you'll enroll. Most of my friends and business associates grew up here, like me. They understand Yiddish because their parents speak it at home, but everywhere else it's English."

"But I—"

"You're in America now. My wife must speak English."

Feige's heart sank at the prospect of school. She had gone to the girls' *cheder* in Kamenetz to learn her *Aleph Bet* and could read enough Yiddish to follow the *Tsene Rene* in shul with other women on Shabbos mornings or read the newspaper, but she had never wanted or needed more. Always shy, she dreaded being called on in front of the class. How would she overcome her fears in an American school?

"Of course, Caleb." He was going to be her husband, and he had decided.

"And now it's time for your first lesson. We need to give you a new name. Names from the Bible, like mine, are acceptable. Yiddish names like yours are only for "greenies" right off the boat. I hope you like the name I've picked out for you, Fannie. It's the name of a famous singer in New York. Although I must say you're much prettier."

Feige was so taken aback she barely heard the compliment. Give up her name? "Oh Caleb, must I? My whole life I've been Feige. To Mama and Papa and the people who love me I'm *Feigele*, their little bird."

Caleb would not relent. "We will probably meet my friends soon. What kind of impression will you make with a Yiddish name?"

Feige could feel tears coming. This wasn't like going to school or learning a new alphabet. Her name was who she was. How could she sign "Fannie" to her letters to Mama or Gittel and Raisel? It was a stranger's name. "Even your parents call me Feigele. It makes me feel like I belong," she said, wiping her eyes with her handkerchief.

Seeing her dismay, Caleb softened. "Maybe I'll call you Feigele at home after we're married. But from now on, everywhere else you're Fannie."

Maybe it wouldn't be as bad as she thought. She imagined them home, alone. She even dared to think of herself in his arms as he murmured, *my Feigele.*

He brought her back from her daydream. "Let's take a walk, Fannie, before it gets too late."

Feige tried not to flinch at the new name and hoped she would get used to it quickly to please him. She did her best to smile as he put the cloth back in the basket and helped her to her feet.

"This way." Caleb led her along one of the paths near where they had been sitting. "Let's see if my friends are here this afternoon."

They walked slowly, gravel crunching under their feet, enjoying the cool breeze. "These may not look like much now," said Caleb, pointing to the young trees and newly planted flowers. "But just imagine how lush they'll be when our children and grandchildren come here to walk."

Feige could picture herself walking there with her children, but it was harder to think of herself with another name. Fannie, she kept repeating to herself. *I'm Fannie now.* She had expected many things to change in America – she had already seen how different her brothers had become. But this, a name Caleb had chosen without consulting her, this was a terrible surprise.

They continued on in silence until Caleb spied his friends approaching from the other direction. "Simon, Mary!" he called out to them. "Come meet Fannie."

When the couple joined them, Caleb introduced them. "Simon and Mary, I'd like you to meet Fannie, my intended. She has only just arrived in New York and hasn't learned English yet. Fannie, these are my friends, Simon and Mary. They were married just last month."

"We're so glad to meet you," said Mary. "Everyone has been waiting to meet the lucky girl Caleb is going to marry. He's quite the catch, you know. Now I can tell everyone I've met the beautiful bride his father chose for him. Quite a few hearts will be broken."

Ever since her visit with Rachel, Feige had wondered about other girls Caleb might have married. Was there someone else he would have preferred? Someone who was already an American? At home it was the parents who chose, but maybe that wasn't always true here. Would he ever really love the bride his father had picked for him?

"Thank you. I'm happy to meet you, and Mazel Tov on your marriage," she said.

Mary was quite short, but carried herself with a confidence that made her seem taller than she was. Her light blond hair was elaborately curled around her oval face, setting off her dark brown eyes. She had the same coloring as Rachel, but Feige couldn't imagine two more different women. She even detected a hint of rouge on Mary's cheeks and her lips were definitely painted. Was this respectable in America?

Feige could see Mary looking at her clothes with barely disguised disdain. Even for a walk in the park, Mary wore a pale-yellow organza dress with a bright ribbon belt. Her wide brimmed hat was generously trimmed with so many flowers Feige wouldn't have been surprised to see birds nesting in it. Her soft leather boots were nearly white with delicate curved heels. Feige's serviceable brown boots looked clumsy by comparison.

"Welcome to America," said Mary. "I hope we'll be great friends. And as soon as you're settled, I hope you'll let me introduce you to the wonderful stores we have here. I would be happy to be your guide to the latest styles. After all, we can't let Caleb outshine his bride."

Feige felt the sting underneath her offer. "That is most generous," she said, swallowing her pride. After all, Mary was right. She couldn't embarrass Caleb by appearing in the wrong clothes. She would consult Miriam of course, but Mary might be just the person to help her. She would talk to Papa that night about what they could afford and still save enough for Mama and the children's passage.

Simon was a handsome man. Except for his bushy blond mustache, he looked so much like Mary he could be her brother. He greeted Feige with a mock bow and kissed her hand. "Caleb is a lucky man to have such a beautiful bride." Feige smiled at him gratefully as the two couples began to walk toward the exit.

Caleb and his friends tried to include Feige in their conversation, but she was content to just listen. They soon parted ways, with promises to see each other again soon. Feige and Caleb took a trolley back to the Fine's house where she went to help Miriam with dinner, and he went to read the newspaper until the other men returned from the factory.

"How was your day?" asked Miriam as she put the pot roast and vegetables on a platter. "Did Caleb like the cake?"

"The surprise worked! He thought it was yours."

"I knew it would." She handed Feige a stack of plates to put on the table.

"The garden was as lovely as Caleb said it would be. And so many people walking and picnicking. How wonderful to have a place like that for ordinary people to enjoy—and without paying even."

"Were any of Caleb's friends there?"

"Yes, we met Mary and Simon. She's so pretty and her clothes were beautiful. She offered to help me shop for new clothes. What do you think?"

"What a wonderful idea. You couldn't ask for a better person. Let's arrange it soon. Now I think everyone is home, so let's bring the dinner in."

Feige wanted to tell Miriam about the other surprise, about the new name Caleb had chosen for her, but she couldn't do it without revealing how much it disturbed her. And it wouldn't be right to complain to his mother. Maybe she already knew and approved. Maybe she too was concerned about Feige fitting in.

The men talked about the news over dinner. For the first time, a Negro boxer had defeated the white champion. After his victory on the American Independence Day, riots broke out. Negroes all over the country were killed and injured, just like the Jews were during the pogroms at home. At home they hated the Jews. In America they hated the Negroes. Why was that? It saddened her to think about all the innocent people who suffered from other people's hate. Wasn't that why Papa had brought her here, to escape the outbreaks of senseless violence?

When the men had finished eating, the women rose to clear the dishes and bring out tea and cake.

"Is this more of the cake you made?" Caleb asked when Feige brought out dessert. "Fannie made a cake just like Mama's for our picnic," he told the others. "It was delicious."

"Fannie? Who is this Fannie?" asked her father.

"That's Feige's new name," Caleb answered. "So she'll be more American."

"She needs a new name to be American? Feige is the name her mother and I gave her when she was born, after my grandmother, her great-grandmother, may her memory be for a blessing. The Shabbos after she was born, I was called to the Torah and announced her name to the congregation."

Asher looked toward Feige, waiting for her to say something. She was silent, but Caleb responded quickly. "I mean no disrespect, Asher, but that name is from the old country and Fannie is in America now. When she's my wife she'll be with people who've lived here a long time and speak only English.

They would know as soon as they heard her name that she had just come off the boat."

"And what's so terrible about that? Everyone in America came off some boat and needed time to learn new ways. It is a *shanda*, what you're doing," he said, his voice raised in anger. "A shame."

"Papa, please," Feige tried to placate him. "Let's not argue at the dinner table."

Without answering her, he rose so abruptly he nearly knocked over his chair and turned to leave the room. "I'm no longer hungry. Please forgive me everyone."

"Wait, Papa." She stood up to go after him. Caleb reached out to stop her, but she shook him off.

"Papa, let's talk for a minute." She took his arm and led him into the parlor.

"You'll go along with this, this terrible idea?" he said.

"Sit, Papa, sit. Don't you see, I'm going to be Caleb's wife. I don't like it either, my new name, but I must abide by his decision if I'm going to be the wife you and Mama taught me to be. Isn't that why Cousin Charles wanted this match, because he knew I'd be a traditional wife? Please understand and don't be angry, Papa. I'll always be your Feigele."

"No, not my Feigele anymore. Now you're Caleb's Fannie." His voice cracked. Then he lowered his gaze and was still. It seemed like forever to Feige before he spoke again.

"You're right," he said when he finally looked up at her. "This is how it should be. I knew he was brought up differently here in America and I should have expected something like this."

He stood and was quiet another moment. "I will apologize to the family."

"I'll go back in with you."

"Come here, child, and give your poor Papa a kiss."

The next morning Feige stayed in her room to write to her mother. She knew Miriam would never read over her shoulder, but she wanted to be alone.

19 July, 1910

Dear Mama,

I wish you were here. Caleb and I took a walk in the park yesterday, which betrothed couples do here. Miriam assured us it was proper in America.

But that isn't why I'm writing. On our walk, Caleb told me that he was giving me a new American name, Fannie. I don't want to be Fannie, Mama. I want to keep the name you and Papa gave me, but what choice do I have if I'm to be a good wife?

When Papa found out he got angry and had words with Caleb. I have never seen him like that.

I tried to make him understand that doing as my future husband asked was the right thing, and what you would have expected. Isn't that true, Mama? But he was so sad. If only you had been here to comfort him.

We miss you and need you so much.

I will send more news in my next letter. Papa is working hard - it won't be long before we're together again. Please give Freyda and Levi a hug for me.

Your loving daughter,

Fannie

Feige read what she had written. She couldn't send this. Her Mama would only worry and be upset that there was nothing she could do. She tore the letter into pieces and started again.

Dear Mama,

Caleb has given me an American name, Fannie. Papa and I were both sad at first, but I promised him I will always be your Feigele ...

★ ★ ★

Fannie sat in the parlor reading the *Forverts*, the Yiddish newspaper Charles brought home every night. The small brass clock on the mantel had just chimed eleven. She had settled in one of the two wine-colored armchairs flanking the fireplace, facing an overstuffed cream-colored sofa. A crystal chandelier sparkled in the sunlight and the wood floors were covered with a Persian carpet. The room was elegant, but comfortable, which was surely Miriam's doing. When she and Caleb had a place of their own, she would try to emulate her cousin's good taste.

A dark wood piano with elaborate carvings on the front panels stood on the wall between the windows, but Fannie had never heard anyone play. She herself was not at all musical and wasn't even tempted to touch the keys, but one day she hoped her children would play. She imagined a little girl in a pink dress with a big bow in her hair sitting on the bench practicing. She was so young her feet didn't reach the pedals, but she smiled as her pudgy fingers pounded the keys.

The top of the piano held an electric lamp and family photographs. Miriam and Charles were young and handsome in their wedding portrait but held themselves stiffly and barely smiled. Rachel and Max were as comfortable looking in theirs as Rachel had described them. She wondered how she and Caleb were going to look the day they married. In another picture, Miriam sat with an infant Max on her lap, while Caleb, in a sailor suit, stood beside them. Fannie looked closely but she couldn't see the man Caleb had become, except perhaps for his ears.

The windows were opened wide to let in the summer breeze but other than an occasional trolley passing by there was little noise from outside to disturb Fannie's concentration while she read the letters in that day's *"Bintel Brief."* Ever since Miriam had shown her this advice-to-readers column, it was her favorite part of the paper. The letters were easy to understand and taught her a lot about how people lived in America. New immigrants like herself asked for advice about everything from marriage to working conditions. Fannie was shocked to learn how poorly workers were treated in America. One boss, she read, had taken two cents away from a thirteen-year-old boy's pay just because he came to work ten minutes late. The poor child only earned two and a half dollars a week, and Fannie, who always had a soft spot for children, was sure he had a good reason for being late. He could have been helping his mother with the other children. How could anyone be so cruel?

What would "Dear Editor" tell her if she wrote a letter, she wondered. Last week Papa and Cousin Charles had met with the Rabbi and set the date for her wedding. It was five months away, in late December. She'd be seventeen then, older than many girls when they married, but she wished she could wait a little longer. What harm would there be in waiting until June?

She looked at the picture of Caleb again. They didn't see each other often, but when they did, he was nice to her. On the other hand, he picked out a new name for her without asking. He expected her to be Fannie, the perfect American wife. She knew he'd be happier when she spoke more English. Couldn't they wait until she'd had more schooling?

The more she thought about it the more upset she became. She had no idea how Caleb felt. He hadn't looked unhappy when their fathers informed them, but he could have been hiding his feelings as she hid hers. And it really didn't matter how either of them felt. Their fathers had arranged their marriage and now they'd arranged the wedding. She was sure "Dear Editor" would tell her to respect her parents, but it didn't seem fair that even in America, where everyone was supposed to be free, neither she nor the workers had a say.

"Fannie, there's a telephone call for you." Clara's announcement startled her.

"For me? But I've never spoken on a telephone."

"Oh it's easy. Come, I'll show you."

Fannie took the earpiece Clara gave her and spoke into it.

"No," Clara explained with a good-natured laugh. "This way. You listen here and speak into this part."

Fannie started again. "Hello?"

"Hello, Fannie, It's Mary. I hope you've been well since we met in the park. I know there's so much to learn."

"Oh, hello, Mary. How nice of you to call."

"I'm calling to invite you to go shopping with me. I would love to take you to a new department store right here in Brooklyn. Everyone is talking about it. They have beautiful clothes and shoes and everything you could wish for."

Fannie had seen advertisements for department stores in the *Forverts,* but she wasn't entirely sure what that meant.

"They even have a restaurant for ladies inside the store. "My mother is visiting her family in Boston with my brother and sisters, but perhaps Caleb's mother would like to join us and we can have lunch there. Are you free next Tuesday?"

"I'll ask Miriam."

"Wonderful. Call me back as soon as you know. Applegate 6631."

Fannie hung up. Perhaps Mary was nicer than she had thought the day they met. And it would be nice to shop for something pretty. Miriam had introduced her to the stores for meat, fish, and fruits and vegetables. There was even a store just for pickles, and, her favorite, one with all kinds of candies. Fannie was confident she could handle grocery shopping by herself. Mama had taught her how to pick out the freshest ingredients and get the best price. But this was different.

She went to find her cousin in the kitchen, hoping she'd be able to go. With Miriam along, Fannie would be less likely to make a mistake that marked her as a "greenie."

"What a wonderful idea," said Miriam, who was just putting the finishing touches on a salad for dinner. "I'm sure she's talking about Abraham and Strauss, and I would love to go. It's such a beautiful store; I wish I had thought of it. Let's see, you'll need clothes for *Rosh Hashanah* and *Yom Kippur* in October. Everyone wears new clothes for the High Holy Days."

She went to get a piece of paper and pencil from the drawer and sat down to make a list. "Some pretty dresses for visiting friends like Mary and Simon," she wrote. "And we mustn't forget fancy clothes for the theater. Caleb loves the theater, and he'll want you to look your best." She put down the pencil. "Anything else?"

Fannie was struck dumb. What else could she possibly want? And how could Papa ever afford all the things on the list? But as she thought about it, there was one thing. "Boots," she said, remembering how shabby her boots looked compared to Mary's. "I need new boots."

"Of course." Miriam added them to the list. "And hats, before that straw hat you brought with you falls apart."

Fannie knew Miriam was right, but she would be sad to give up her poor little hat. It had traveled so far with her.

"The store even has its own bridal shop, Fannie, so we can start looking for your wedding dress. You're going to be such a beautiful bride."

This time Fannie stayed silent. She had always expected she and Mama would sew her wedding dress together, and now she would have to choose without her.

"And Fannie dear, the clothes will be my gift to you. I already think of you like the daughter I never had. Rachel shopped with her own mama before her wedding, so I have never had this chance before – and it will give me so much pleasure to see you with Caleb in pretty new things. Let your Papa concentrate on earning the fare for your Mama and the children." She reached out to take Fannie in her arms. "And we'll let it be our little secret."

"Thank you, Miriam, for this and everything." Fannie held on tight to her cousin, knowing she would cry if she let go.

"Before we go, I have some lady's magazines for you to look at. They're in English, but you'll be able to tell from the pictures what the latest fashions are. And I know Mary will be helpful. She's always dressed so beautifully. I feel young again myself just thinking about all the nice clothes we'll find. It will be an adventure."

CHAPTER 6

They were taking the subway directly to the store. It was the first station of its kind anywhere, and although Fannie had nothing to compare it to, Miriam and Mary were proud it was in Brooklyn. The three women were seated together on the smooth fabric seats as fans circulated overhead. Bulbs hanging from the ceiling provided light inside, but nothing was visible outside the car.

Fannie couldn't help being envious of Mary's light pink dress and delicate white boots. She looked as pretty as she had in the park. Miriam was wearing a simple light gray dress with a shiny black leather belt and matching shoes. Her clothes were more conservative, but equally smart.

"I don't think I'll ever get used to this," Fannie said as the train sped along. "Being underground and not knowing what's happening overhead."

Miriam reassured her. "Just remember it's new for all of us. The subway only opened a few years ago. Get ready for the doors to open, we're almost there."

As they stepped out of the train, Fannie immediately saw the shop windows. Every window was arranged with different merchandise. Some had women's dresses, men's suits and children's clothes. Another had a shiny new stove with pots and pans.

"Now I see," she said. "Different 'departments,' all in one store!"

As they walked through the doors, Fannie looked up and gasped. They had entered a huge courtyard with a marble fountain in the center. Five balconies with sculptured railings reached to a glass roof.

"The Tsar's palace can't be any grander than this," she whispered, awestruck.

Before she could ask how they would get to the upper floors, Miriam and Mary stopped in front of a large door. When it opened, a man in a black uniform with shiny buttons, wearing spotless white gloves, slid open a brass gate and announced, "Going up."

"Women's clothes, please," said Mary as they stepped into what appeared to be a small room paneled in polished wood.

"Yes, Ma'am. Third floor."

He pulled the gate shut and the outer door swished closed behind it. Unsure of what to expect, Fannie held on to her cousin as they began to move slowly upward. This was one of the elevators Cousin Charles had told her about!

The elevator stopped and the man opened the gate. "Going up."

A few more women got in, dressed so elegantly Fannie felt even more self-conscious about her plain clothes. As soon as they got off at the third floor, a young woman in a black skirt and white blouse with a pink flower pinned to her collar approached them. "May I help you?" she asked.

"Yes," replied Miriam. "We're looking for some dresses for my young cousin." She pointed at Fannie. "Some for now, and some she can wear in the fall. She will also need hats, gloves and shoes. And we'll need a Yiddish translator."

"Yes, Madam. Please follow me and we'll start with the dresses."

Fannie had never seen so many beautiful things, in every possible color and fabric. How would she choose?

"I think blue is your color," said Mary, holding up a dress for Fannie. "It looks great against your fair skin. Maybe a lighter shade, like this one." She offered Fannie another dress.

The saleswoman measured Fannie and began showing her dresses just like the ones she had seen in the magazines and that Mary appeared to favor.

"So many choices. You'll both have to help me," said Fannie.

"Let's leave it to Mary," said Miriam. "I'm too old to know the latest fashions."

"I'm happy to help. I don't need anything for myself—I did all my shopping for the season before I got married. You have such a beautiful figure, Fannie, you can wear anything."

"We'll make sure your new clothes show off your tiny waist," added the saleswoman.

With advice from Mary, Fannie finally decided on a few lightweight silk and organza dresses for the rest of the summer in pale blues, greens and yellows, colors that reminded her of the park on a sunny day. Mary convinced her to add ribbons and decorations. "These dresses don't have to be practical," she said.

"But we should add a few plain skirts and blouses," suggested Miriam.

"Not too plain," countered Mary.

Fannie barely said a word as the two women discussed what she needed. She felt like a doll they were dressing for a tea party. For the High Holy Days, when the weather would be cooler, they selected a royal blue poplin suit with a long cutaway jacket and a violet light wool dress with a wide velvet collar. She had expected to go home with a few dresses and perhaps some new boots, not a whole new wardrobe. She was overwhelmed.

She had never dreamed of becoming a person who spent the day shopping for new clothes with women like Mary. If her mother and her childhood friends saw her now, what would they think? Did these clothes make her Fannie? Was she leaving Feige behind for good? She suspected she was.

"And undergarments, Miss?" asked the saleswoman.

"Not today, thank you," Miriam answered. "My cousin is an expert needlewoman and has brought beautiful, hand-embroidered things with her."

Fannie smiled at her cousin, grateful to be complimented in front of Mary. The saleswoman sent for shoes and gloves to complete her new outfits.

"Look at these boots, Fannie," said Mary. "I love this pale gray color. You can wear them with everything."

"They're beautiful," agreed Fannie. Gloves and shoes were easier to choose than dresses.

"After our hat purchases," Miriam told the saleswoman, "we're going to have lunch. Can you please have whatever doesn't need to be altered ready for us to take when we're done?"

"My pleasure, Madam, and I hope you'll come again soon."

They took the elevator back down to the millinery department. Mary and Miriam were eager to see the selection of styles and to introduce Fannie to the fun of trying on hats. Fannie quickly got into the spirit, preening in front of the mirror with each new hat. She tried on a summer hat with a wide brim and flowers.

"What do you think, Mary?"

"I love it. You're learning fast. And try this one for the fall. It will go perfectly with the clothes for the holidays." She handed her a darker hat with an upright brim and a single, long feather. Fannie put it on. Already tall, the hat made her appear even taller.

"It's perfect," said Mary. "You'll make a grand entrance!"

Fannie stared at the elegant young woman in the mirror. *Can this really be me?* She turned to admire her reflection from every direction. There had never been a reason to show off in Kamenetz, now she was going to "make an entrance." She hoped Caleb would be proud of her for becoming a fashionable American woman.

"Now let's eat," said Mary as the saleswomen were putting their hats in pink and white round boxes. "Shopping always makes me hungry," she said as she steered them toward the restaurant.

Fannie sank gratefully into her seat. A trio of musicians played softly in the background. The table linens, upholstered chairs, wallpaper and carpets were pale pink, white and apple green. There were flowers on each table and tall potted plants around the room.

"You'd never know the city is just outside," said Fannie.

Fashionably dressed women in small groups sat at the tables, drinking tea and coffee in crystal glasses and delicate china cups. Fannie wanted to tell them she would soon look like them. She was going to fit in. Men in formal suits brought sandwiches and small iced cakes for dessert.

"Do you have enough energy to visit the bridal salon, Fannie?" asked Miriam. "You don't have to decide anything today, but you can get an idea of what you like."

"Oh, please do," echoed Mary. "I can't wait to see how you'll look."

Fannie hesitated. As much as she loved her cousin and appreciated Mary's advice, she wasn't sure she could face buying her wedding dress without her mother. But they were already in the store, and she didn't want to appear ungrateful. Since it had to be done, she supposed today was as good as any to get started.

"Yes of course," she said.

The bridal salon was deep in a secluded corner of the women's department. The saleswoman ushered them into a private room with off-white silk drapes and thick beige carpets. Three-way mirrors stood in front of spindly gilt chairs.

"Who is the bride and when is the wedding?" asked the saleswoman.

"She is," replied Miriam, gesturing toward Fannie. "And the wedding is in December."

"Satin is a nice fabric for winter, and you'll want something with long sleeves. Let me bring you some samples."

The first gowns the saleswoman showed them probably would have pleased her little sister, Freyda, but they were all too fussy for Fannie. She may have been lost when it came to everyday clothes, but when it came to her wedding dress, she knew her own mind. After all, she had been dreaming about it since she was a little girl. Finally, she saw a simple dress she liked enough to try on. The saleswoman took her into the dressing room and had Fannie hold up her arms to slide into an ivory satin gown with a high neck and sleeves that ended with rows of tiny pearl buttons at her wrists. The skirt flared slightly at the floor and swayed gently when she walked. Then she helped Fannie slip on a slightly lighter colored lace coat with short, capped sleeves and tied a wide satin sash around her waist.

"Oh, how beautiful," said Fannie as she twirled around in front of the mirror. "I never knew a dress could make me feel like this, like a princess in one of the stories I used to tell my little sister."

"Let's go show your mother and your friend. They're going to love it," said the saleswoman.

Fannie tried in vain to hold back her tears.

"Oh no, what's wrong?" asked the saleswoman, offering Fannie a clean white handkerchief. "Have I said something to offend you? Shall I fetch your mother?"

Fannie hid her face in the handkerchief until she could speak. "She's my cousin," she said, dabbing at her eyes. "My mother won't arrive in America until after my wedding. She'll never see me in my wedding dress."

Fannie caught her breath and composed herself. "But please, let's go show them. I don't want them to worry." The saleswoman opened the curtains and led Fannie out.

"You're as beautiful as I knew you would be," sighed Miriam. But then she noticed the dampness in Fannie's eyes and rose to embrace her.

"It's perfect," said Mary, clapping her hands. "Just perfect. This is the one."

"I agree," said the saleswoman. "It's traditional, but the latest fashion. You're the first person to try it on and I can't imagine anyone looking better in it."

"You don't have to decide today," said Miriam. She could see Fannie was struggling to contain herself. "You can think about it, and we'll come back another day."

"No, Miriam, I love it. This is the dress I want to be married in."

"An excellent choice. Let me find the right headpiece and veil," said the saleswoman. "And we'll write up the order so it will be ready for a fitting the month before your wedding. You can see to the shoes then."

"Thank you for including me in this special moment, Fannie." Mary hugged her when they were ready to leave the bridal salon. "I can't wait to see you walk down the aisle."

Mary wasn't Gittel or Raisel, but at least there'd be one friend at Fannie's wedding. As soon as they got home, she sat down to write to Mama about every exciting thing she had seen in the department store. For Freyda, she drew a picture of her new hat and her wedding dress. She hoped that as sad as it was to be apart, they'd be happy for her.

★ ★ ★

Here it is. Fannie stopped in front of an imposing brick building that took up almost the entire block. P.S. 155.

She had passed the school on her way to the stores a little further along the parkway. It had been silent and unused over the summer, but once Fall arrived, it had come to life with children during the day and adults, mostly immigrants like herself, at night.

She hesitated at the foot of the steps leading up from the sidewalk to the tall double doors where a steady stream of men and women were entering the building. It was beginning to get dark, and she knew that many of the students were coming straight from a long day at factories and shops. Learning English was so important they were giving up their dinners, and here she was, dreading it. Since her first day at the Fines, Bridget and Clara had been teaching her English words to use in the kitchen and around the house. Miriam had been teaching her words to use when she went out shopping. But she was sure she'd forget everything she knew as soon as she went inside.

I hope I don't make a fool of myself.

She continued to hang back and checked the small black leather purse she wore on a strap over her arm. Miriam had given it to her when she arrived in America. It held a brand-new box of sharpened pencils with rubber eraser tips and a paper with the Fine's address and telephone number. "In case of an emergency," Miriam had said when she wrote it out that evening.

She reached for Samuel's button at the bottom, where she kept it underneath her handkerchief and coin purse. She rarely took it out; just knowing it was there comforted her. Now she grasped it tightly. Samuel was wrong. She wasn't brave, and there was no one there to reassure her as he had. She wondered if he was also starting school and couldn't help scanning the steps to look for his red hair.

Fewer and fewer students remained outside. She put the button away and shut the clasp on her purse, finally climbing the steps to look for her classroom. When she got to Room 202, she was happy to see that most of the seats were already taken so she could sit in the back without drawing attention to herself. She squeezed herself into a child-sized desk, barely able to get her knees underneath.

At least I wore the right clothes, she thought, glancing around at the other students. They were all dressed plainly, some in overalls and aprons and whatever else they might have worn to work. She had on a black skirt and white blouse. Her hair was pinned loosely in a simple bun. She had decided to wear her old boots instead of the fancier new ones from her shopping trip with Mary and Miriam. Fitting in here meant dressing like Feige, not like Fannie.

She shifted in her seat to look around the classroom. Tall windows lined one side of the room, open to let in the fresh air. It was still warm in September, but the room was comfortable. Seeing the children's drawings hanging on the opposite wall, she imagined the children she and Caleb would have. Maybe one day her little girl's drawing would hang there. She wouldn't be frightened because she'd be an American. And her brother would be smart like his father.

The English alphabet was written on white lines across the blackboard in the front of the room. An American flag hung from a pole in the corner. There was a large clock on the back wall, with pictures of men in old-fashioned clothes underneath it. Rows of globes suspended from the ceiling gave off pale yellow light.

As she turned back toward the front of the room, the girl at the desk next to her smiled. She was a petite, honey-colored blonde with light brown eyes. Like Fannie, she wore a black skirt and white blouse, but the long braid hanging down her back was tied with a bright red bow. Fannie admired the bold touch of color, something she was unlikely to wear herself.

The girl started to say something, but just then the teacher arrived, closing the door and marching briskly to the front of the room. She was short and heavyset. Her maroon dress strained across her chest and hips. She wore eyeglasses on a long chain around her neck and a small watch with a plain brown leather band on her left wrist, but no other jewelry. Her hair, pulled up tightly into a bun on top of her head, was completely gray. Fannie guessed that she was about ten years older than her Mama. *Please let her be patient.*

"Good evening, students," she began in a loud but pleasant voice. "My name is Miss Berg. What is your name?" She pointed to herself first, and then to one of the students in the first row.

"My name is Miss Berg. What is your name?" she repeated, pointing again.

The student looked around uncertainly, but finally ventured, "My name is Anthony."

"Excellent," Miss Berg responded, proceeding to the next student.

Fannie was relieved—something she already knew! *My name is Fannie*, she began practicing silently to herself. When it was her turn, she answered confidently.

The girl in the seat next to her was Anna.

Next, Miss Berg pointed to a spot on the map.

"I am from New York," she said. "In the United States of America." Her hand swept across a large section of the map surrounded by blue on either side.

Then Miss Berg pointed to another part of the map. "This is Europe. Here is Germany, and Austria, and Poland and Russia, and Italy," she said, each time pointing to another color. Fannie nodded along with the other students, absorbing the enormity of America and the ocean most of them had recently crossed.

"What country are you from?"

This time she started at the back of the room.

"I am from Poland," replied Anna.

"I am from Russia," Fannie said when it was her turn. More English words she already knew!

"Very good," said Miss Berg when all the students had been called on. "Soon you'll all be Americans." Then she motioned for the class to stand up. She faced the flag and put her hand over her heart, making sure they copied her.

"Repeat after me."

The students looked at each other, unsure of what she wanted from them, but she began, slowly and clearly. "I pledge allegiance to my flag." She paused, gesturing toward the students.

"I pledge allegiance …"

The students repeated the first two words.

"to my flag …"

It went on like this, a few words at a time, until they had repeated all the words or come as close to it as they could with their heavy accents.

"Good," said Miss Berg. "You just said the Pledge of Allegiance. We will practice this every day until you know it." She gave them each a piece of paper printed with the alphabet, and they practiced saying the letters aloud. Then she showed them on the board how to write the first three letters. She walked around the room as they practiced, stopping frequently to help students who needed it.

"Well done," she said looking over Fannie's shoulder. Fannie glowed with pride. Maybe school wouldn't be so bad after all. Finally, it was time to leave.

"Good night, students," said Miss Berg.

"Good night," they echoed.

As they filed out, the students started talking in their native languages. Anna walked beside her, barely coming up to her shoulder. She said hello in Yiddish and grinned when Fannie answered her. "I'm Anna. I only just arrived in New York last month. My brother came here first and brought my Mama and Papa and me. He's studying to be an engineer. I'm working in my cousin's apartment sewing ladies' blouses. We live nearby, but we're moving to another place across the bridge soon. I'm fifteen." She barely paused to take a breath. How long have you been in America?" she rushed on as they walked down the stairs together. "Where do you live? How old are you?"

How she talks. I hope we can be friends.

"I've been here three months," she answered, trying to keep up with Anna's questions. "I came with my Papa. We live with his cousin and her husband. I'm going to marry their son, Caleb, in December. My papa will go home after the wedding to get my Mama and my brother and sister. I'm seventeen."

"What is your job?"

"I'm not working now. My cousin's family owns a factory. My Papa works there and so do my brothers, who came over a few years ago."

Most girls her age who had just come to America worked. She didn't want to set herself apart from her new friend. "At home, my Papa used to sell things I embroidered in his shop. I'd like to do that again."

As soon as she said it, Fannie realized it was true. She would like to be paid for her work again. Even if Caleb didn't need her money, she could help Papa save up for the tickets for Mama and the children.

"Feige."

Fannie looked up to see her brother Daniel standing in front of the school. "Daniel, what are you doing here? And here at school, you must remember to call me Fannie."

"I was out with my friends and had to pass this way to come home. So I thought I would stop and get my baby sister. Come, we'll walk together."

"Not a baby anymore, a soon-to-be married lady!" She scolded him playfully and kissed his cheek.

"Anna, come meet my disrespectful older brother, Daniel." She held out her hand to bring her new friend closer.

"Daniel, this is my new friend, Anna. We sat next to each other in class."

"Are you waiting for someone, Anna? Can we walk you home?" offered Daniel.

"No thank you, I'm fine, it's just a short walk and some of the other students are going that way. I'll see you again tomorrow night, Fannie. Isn't it wonderful? We're on our way to speaking English like Americans!"

"Goodnight, Anna. I'll look for you out here and we can walk in together."

Anna took off, practically skipping down the street.

Fannie took her brother's arm as they began walking in the opposite direction. "What were you and your friends doing out so late, Daniel?"

"We play a little cards once in a while. Now tell me about school."

When they arrived home, Daniel said goodnight and went up to the room he shared with Noah and their father. Fannie was too excited to think about sleeping and went into the kitchen to get herself a cookie. Caleb and his mother were there having tea.

"So we'll have to hire more workers ..." she heard him say as she walked in.

When he missed dinner, Caleb often told his mother about his day over whatever she had saved for him from the family's dinner and a cup of tea. They would sit in the kitchen and talk before he went into the parlor to smoke his evening cigar. Would he share like that with her when they were married?

She hesitated near the door, not wanting to disturb them, but Miriam immediately got up to bring another cup to the table.

"Would you like something, Fannie? Come, tell us all about school."

"I have a lady teacher, Miss Berg. And I made a friend, Anna, from Poland. We're going to meet on the steps before class tomorrow."

"Good for you!" Miriam offered her a cookie.

"And I had the most wonderful idea when I was talking to Anna. I'm going to sell my embroidery in America, just like I did in Kamenetz. I'll ask Mary and Rachel and—"

"Absolutely not!" Caleb banged his cup on the table so hard Fannie jumped. "How could you even think of such a thing?"

"But Caleb—"

"Do you want people to think my wife needs to work, that I can't support her? You'll do no such thing."

"I never thought—"

"Caleb, let's think about this for a minute." Miriam spoke softly. "Aren't you being a little hasty?"

"Whose side are you on, Mama?"

"I'm not on any side, Caleb. I want you both to be happy. And it's not as though she would be working in a factory or a shop. Tell us more, Fannie."

"I haven't made a plan, but I could show my things to Mary and Rachel, and they could show them to their friends. If someone wanted something, I would embroider it in the colors and design they wanted. And—"

"It's a terrible idea. I won't—" Caleb shouted.

"Caleb, let Fannie finish. Go on, dear."

"Well, now I'm thinking, I could make baby clothes or gifts for the house, like the apron I brought you, Miriam."

"Yes, that was quite beautiful. Caleb, don't you think people will think it's just something Fannie is doing to amuse herself? You can tell your friends how happy you are that she's found a way to pass the time until the children come. I'm sure none of them will think less of you."

"How can I be sure she won't embarrass me and—"

"I never meant to cause a problem, Caleb. Please don't be angry," Fannie pleaded. "And I thought the money would help Papa save faster to bring the family here."

She fumbled in her purse for her handkerchief as she started to cry, instinctively finding Samuel's button. How could she be brave in the face of Caleb's anger?

"Now look what you've done, Caleb," scolded Miriam.

Caleb threw up his hands.

"You win, Mama, you win. Please stop crying, Fannie. I'll let you try it."

Fannie nodded, unable to speak for a moment. "Thank you. I would never do anything to make you ashamed. You'll see."

"Of course not. You just didn't think."

"Good, children, I'm glad you worked it out. Now let's say goodnight." She kissed them both as they rose to go upstairs.

Fannie was upset. As soon as she got to her room, she began a letter to Gittel and Raisel.

19 September, 1910

Dear Gittel and Raisel,

I still have no letter from you. Please write to me!

Tonight I went to English school for the first time - and guess what - I liked it! I was a little afraid at first, but I was able to answer the teacher's questions and now I can even write some letters. I even met a girl from Poland, and I think we'll be friends. Not like us, but I'm lonely here. It will be nice to have someone who knows what it was like in the old country.

When I got home, I told Caleb and Miriam I wanted to sell my embroidery like I did at home. Caleb thought it was a terrible idea, because his friends might think we needed the money, but Miriam convinced him. What his friends think is very important to him.

Since the last time I wrote to you Miriam bought me new clothes and I picked out a wedding dress. We went to a "department store" to buy it. Think of market day all in one building – clothes, pots and pans, everything! My dress is satin and lace. If only you could see it.

What news about a husband for you, Raisel?

Your loving friend,

Fannie

P.S. Fannie is my American name. Caleb gave it to me the day we walked in the park. It is hard to get used to, but he insisted it would help me fit in. I suppose that's what I want too, but I would have liked to keep my name.

CHAPTER 7

Time passed quickly. Much to her surprise, Fannie enjoyed school. She did her homework faithfully and took pride in her progress. She could carry on a simple conversation in English and read the books Miss Berg loaned them to take home. They were children's books, but they helped her learn.

When she wasn't studying, she was embroidering. Thanks to Mary, Miriam and Rachel she had a steady clientele. She often worked late into the night, but she didn't mind. Each sale brought Mama, Freyda and Levi closer to America.

She had worn her new clothes to shul for the High Holy Days. She could tell Caleb enjoyed showing her off. He took her arm possessively and introduced her to everyone he knew. She was glad he approved and appreciated the compliments from his friends, although she didn't like being on display.

In late October, Fannie finally got her first letter from home.

7 September, 1910

My dearest Feigele,

How happy I was to get your letter and find out that you and Papa had arrived safely. I think perhaps there is much you didn't say about the trip, but it is all behind you now. You can spend your time learning to be an American and preparing for your marriage. I am so glad you have Cousin

Miriam to help you. I know she'll be as good to you as she was to me when I married into Papa's family.

Please give Daniel and Noah hugs from their Mama. You say they have changed, but I know my boys. They will always have good hearts.

Caleb sounds very modern. Be patient, Feigele. It will take time for you to get to know each other.

I have a surprise for you. By the time you get this, Gittel will be a married woman! She stood under the chuppah two weeks ago. I told her and Raisel all about your letter, but you should write to them yourself or they will think you have forgotten them now that you're in America.

As much as I miss you both, I am so glad you and Papa left. Every day there are more Cossacks moving into the town. Thank God there has been no violence, but they watch us all the time, never smiling or saying good day. We still don't know what the Tsar is planning for us.

Write often, Feigele. We all miss you. Freyda can't wait to hear about your wedding plans. She is growing up quickly and is a big help to me. Levi is as mischievous as ever.

With all my love,

Mama

Fannie sat down right away to write back. According to Mama, Gittel and Raisel hadn't gotten her first letter. That made her glad she had written again without waiting to hear from them. And to think, Gittel was already married. She would have to write to her to say Mazel Tov. She just wished it didn't take so long. If only there were telephones to call home!

It didn't seem long before the wedding arrangements were complete. Fannie and her father wanted a traditional wedding ceremony. It wasn't what Caleb wanted, but Miriam and Charles had agreed, so he had no choice. The celebration afterward, however, would be "American." Men and women would sit—and even dance together.

Miriam had handled everything about the food and music. Fannie had no idea how things were done in America and was happy to let her future mother-in-law take charge, even if it made her feel like a guest at her own wedding. She had only one person to invite—Anna, her friend from school.

Fannie's wedding dress was hanging behind the door to her room, covered in a white sheet. Only Miriam had seen it. When she picked it up at the store it made her feel as beautiful as when she tried it on the first time. The dress was one of the few things she was happy about as the day approached. She dreaded being surrounded by people she didn't know. Thinking about how Mama, Freyda and her friends were going to miss what was supposed to be the happiest day of her life made her sad and lonely. And more than anything, she was nervous about the first night she and Caleb would spend as man and wife. Nothing in their brief times together over the last six months gave her any sense of what was to come.

★ ★ ★

"Miriam," Fannie said shyly as they sat in the parlor one evening two weeks before the wedding. Miriam was reading and Fannie was working on a tablecloth one of Mary's friends had ordered. "I need to go to the mikveh."

She had waited anxiously for her cousin to suggest that she visit the ritual bath. It was the custom for women to purify themselves before their weddings, and then again each month twelve days after they started to bleed. Only then did they resume relations with their husbands. Miriam hadn't mentioned it, so now Fannie had to ask before it was too late.

"Oh, Fannie, I never even thought about it. I stopped going myself long ago and I think most of the young women in our set think it's old fashioned. I'm sure none of them use it. But I should have realized you would want to go, at least this once. The only people I can think of asking are Rachel and her mother. I'll call them right now."

Miriam returned quickly from making the call. "It's all set for next Thursday," she said. They went back to what they had been doing, each lost in their own thoughts.

A week later, in a Brooklyn neighborhood just north of the Fine's home, Miriam and Fannie knocked on the door of a small red brick building adjoining a shul. The attendant, a short, squat woman in a light brown dress let them into a small, dimly lit room.

"You're the kallah?" she asked Fannie.

"You can wait here," she told Miriam, pointing to a straight-backed chair near the door. "You, she said to Fannie. "Come with me."

She led Fannie into another small room with a shower, sink and toilet. There was a hook for clothing on a second, closed door. "Shower, wash your hair, brush your teeth and clip your nails. Everything you need is here on this shelf. When you're done, come through that door."

Fanny did as she was told, but memories of the showers on the train came rushing back to her. She had to struggle to keep them from ruining her day.

She stepped through the second door, wrapped in a towel. The attendant was waiting for her next to a small rectangular pool of water that Fannie knew was rainwater that came in through a small pipe.

"Let me check." The woman examined Fannie's hands, feet and back closely, making sure there were no stray hairs or dirt. "You're ready. Do you know the prayer?"

Fannie nodded.

"Go under once—make sure you're completely under—come up to say the prayer, go under two more times." She held out her hands for the towel. "I'll watch to make sure."

Naked, Fannie went down the seven steps into the pool of water. Seven, like the seven days of creation. She submerged herself under the attendant's watchful eye, her long hair floating out behind her. She let the water flow through every crevice of her body before rising to say the blessing.

"Kosher," said the women, letting Fannie know that her entire body and all her hair had been under the water. The rules for the mikveh, handed down over thousands of years, were very strict.

Fannie went under the water two more times, reciting the blessing each time, before coming out. "Mazel Tov," said the taciturn woman gruffly as she handed Fannie her towel. "I'll see you back outside."

Fannie hadn't known what it would feel like. She thought it would just be like an extra thorough bath. But she found herself moved. She felt renewed and pure, as though the waters had washed away her suffering and erased her bitter memories. Although still frightened, she felt ready to give herself to her husband.

As she dressed, Fannie couldn't help thinking about her wedding night. Would she have feelings like she had in the bath the morning after she arrived? What was she supposed to do, or did Caleb do everything? Were all brides this ignorant? She finished quickly and dried her hair as best she could, pinning it up under her warm woolen hat. She rejoined her cousin and handed the women who had overseen her bath an envelope with the expected donation before they went out again into the cold winter night.

★ ★ ★

The following morning, Fannie, Caleb, Miriam and Fannie's Papa arrived at the apartment Fannie and Caleb would be moving into after the wedding. Caleb had insisted that they move to a place of their own immediately after they were married. "We can afford it," he said. "We don't have to live together like greenies."

Fannie wasn't surprised when Caleb said he couldn't take time away from the factory to look for an apartment. She and Miriam went alone to look at some buildings that were going up a short trolley ride from the Fine's house. They easily found a two-bedroom apartment on the second floor of a six-story building, facing a pleasant courtyard newly planted with trees and shrubs. Caleb had looked at it one night after work and approved. He negotiated the rent with the landlord.

Now, as they stood at the front door, Fannie's father nailed a mezuzah to the right side of the door. He then repeated the process for the bedroom doors, reciting the blessing each time. It was customary to attach one to every doorpost.

"Thank you, Papa."

"Thank you, Asher," added Caleb. "Sorry to rush off, but I'll see you both later."

"Do you need to hurry too, Papa?"

"No, Feigele, let's talk a bit before I leave for work."

Miriam walked toward the door. "I'll just say goodbye to Caleb and come back in a few minutes," she said. Fannie was grateful to Miriam for giving her time alone with Papa.

"Come, Papa, sit on my new sofa. What do you think of the apartment?"

"It's very nice, Feigele. I pray you'll be happy here and be blessed with many children."

He took Fannie's hand and looked as though he were about to speak but hesitated.

"What is it Papa? Has something happened?"

"No, no, it's nothing bad. It's only that life is different for young people here in America, Feigele. Caleb may never touch the mezuzah I just blessed, and I'm afraid he cares little for our customs. I see it even in your brothers, how much they've forgotten. And I'm worried about them. I can see they're not happy at the factory."

"Oh Papa, I'm sure—"

"Especially Daniel, Feigele. He's gotten in with a bad crowd. I know America is different, but they have nothing but scorn for the old ways. They're a bunch of *gonifs* and I'm afraid they'll get him into trouble."

"Daniel could never be like them, Papa. You brought him up to know right from wrong and he would never bring shame on the family."

But then Fannie thought back to the night he had met her after school, out late playing cards with his friends. He had made light of it, but what if Papa was right? She couldn't bear to think of Daniel in danger. And how would he meet a nice girl?

"And Noah, our scholar, he says wants to go to the City College! I'm proud of him, but it's a hard life, working and studying. I'd like to see him settle down with a good wife, a girl like you, to take care of him. Who will want a poor student?"

"But isn't that why you wanted us to come to America, Papa? Noah wouldn't have been allowed to go to the university at home. He would have been conscripted into the Tsar's army and might never have come back. You know how they treat the Jews. I'm sure he can do whatever he sets his mind to, Papa."

"I'm sure you're right and I worry too much. But you'll see soon enough. When you're a parent, the worry never ends."

Fannie squeezed her father's hand. "I understand."

"It will be up to you to keep kosher, prepare for the holidays and light the Shabbos candles on Friday night, just like your mama taught you. And you must bring your children up to be good Jews. We came here so they will be born Americans, but they should know the history of their ancestors. They should know about our suffering."

"I'll make a proper Jewish home for them, Papa. I promise. And they'll have their bubbe and *zayde* close by. You'll take my sons to shul and Mama will teach my daughters recipes from the old country. We won't let them forget who they are."

"Good, that's all I wanted to say," he said, standing up. "Tomorrow, God willing, I will walk you down the aisle to stand under the chuppah with Caleb."

"If only Mama—"

"I know, Feigele, I know. We'll both be thinking of her and I'm sure she'll be thinking of you."

Fannie wiped away her tears.

"Don't cry, child," he said, wiping a tear from his own eye with his thumb. "This is what she wanted for you. Now give your Papa a kiss before I leave for work. Every day at the factory brings us closer to being together again."

Fannie walked her father to the door just as Miriam was coming up the stairs.

"Goodbye Miriam."

"Goodbye, Asher," she said, reaching out to embrace him. "Tomorrow we'll see our children married."

"Miriam, would you like to sit for a minute?" Fannie asked.

"Of course, dear. And I found some rugelach for us at the bakery down the street. But we mustn't use any of your new things before the wedding, so we'll just eat them straight from the bag." She held the bag out to Fannie. "Raspberry, your favorite."

The two women ate their pastries slowly, enjoying a moment of quiet away from the tumult of the wedding preparations. Fannie was the first to break the silence. "I'll never be able to thank you enough for everything you've done. Teaching me how to keep house in America, my new clothes, and helping me find and furnish this apartment. It's all because of you."

"I should be thanking you. I had no way of knowing when Charles arranged your marriage what a wonderful daughter you'd turn out to be. And soon you'll be a wonderful wife to my son. And I'm not just saying this because he's my son, Fannie, but deep down Caleb is a good man, even if he forgets to pay attention to the people he loves because he's so busy with the business."

She looked around the room and smiled at Fannie.

"Are you ready to go?"

"If you don't mind, I'd like to sit by myself a little. It still seems strange that tomorrow this will be our home. And I want to read the letter from Mama that just came."

"Of course, child. I understand. Take all the time you need." She embraced Fannie and turned to leave. "I'll miss you, Fannie. Now let me go before I start weeping."

Fannie shut the door behind her cousin and sat down on her new sofa to read her letter.

16 October, 1910

My darling Feigele,

I am writing this short letter now in the hope that it will reach you before your wedding. We just celebrated Yom Kippur. I prayed that you and Caleb will be sealed in the Book of Life for a good year.

Be happy, my child. Although I think of you always, I will be sending special thoughts and prayers on your wedding day. May God bless you and your new husband with a long and happy marriage and many healthy children.

I hope you and Papa and Daniel and Noah are well. Please thank Miriam for everything she has done for you while you and I are apart.

I will be waiting for a letter telling me all about the wedding.

With all my love,

Mama

Once again, Fannie found herself wiping away tears. She allowed herself a few minutes before getting up to walk through the apartment.

Caleb had given her a modest budget for furnishings, reminding her that they were just starting out and that she shouldn't expect lavish furnishings like his parents. Miriam had taken her in hand, however, and took her to places that helped her stretch her funds.

Now, as she walked around each room, Fannie was proud of the home she had created to start her married life. She ran her fingers along the smooth blue velvet of the new sofa and looked with satisfaction at the matching drapes. She had chosen a color she knew Caleb liked, although he'd hardly seemed to notice when he had taken a quick walk through the apartment the week before.

"Fine," he'd said, before rushing back to work. His father needed him to sign some papers. There was always something at the factory that demanded his attention. It meant long hours and lots of worrying, but Caleb would never allow himself to disappoint his father.

A low marble and wood table with a glass dish she planned to fill with candies was in front of the sofa. Two armchairs faced the table, one for her and a larger one for Caleb. The lamp standing between them would provide ample light for reading or embroidering. She hoped they would spend quiet evenings here, listening to music on the Victrola or talking about their days. And someday soon she would be sewing baby clothes.

She walked down a long hallway into a small dining area with an oval table and four chairs. Folding chairs were stored in the hall closet to accommodate the family when they came for dinner. Although the table was bare now, it would soon be laid with the tablecloths she had brought from Kamenetz.

This would be the place where she'd make all the recipes she learned from Mama and Miriam and from the American cookbook she had been studying carefully. This was where she'd serve Caleb his breakfast every morning and dinner when he got home from work. He'd smell the cooking as soon as he came up the stairs. She would read the *Forverts* over her tea and do her homework here.

On the other side of the table and chairs was a bright, clean kitchen with a large window. White cabinets filled with their new dishes and pots and pans went from the floor to the ceiling along the wall opposite the sink, icebox and stove.

As she walked back toward the door, she looked into the bedroom, trying not to think about the next night. The twin beds with their high walnut headboards were side-by-side, made up with the sheets and pillowcases she had embroidered. A glass tray and matching jewelry box, along with a hand mirror, comb, and hairbrush were arranged on her dressing table. Each piece was decorated with brass filigree and pieces of bright green glass that shone like emeralds.

She picked up the hairbrush. Would Caleb watch her brush her hair every night? Would he think it was beautiful? He'd only seen it pinned up.

The door to the second bedroom was closed. It would be empty until their first baby was born.

The bathroom was just big enough for a small sink, toilet and tub. Fannie straightened the new white towels that were already hanging on the porcelain racks. It wasn't nearly as luxurious as the Fine's, but still far more than she'd had at home. Tomorrow there would be two toothbrushes in the cup over the sink.

Just as she was about to leave, Fannie turned around and went back into the bedroom. She took Samuel's button out of her purse and dropped it into the jewelry box. It seemed only right to leave the talisman another man had given her behind. Now she was ready to go.

Please God, let me be happy here, she prayed as she reached up to touch the mezuzah before setting off for her last night at the Fine's.

★ ★ ★

Fannie was trembling.

"What's wrong, Feigele?" asked her Papa. "Everything is going perfectly. I may be a little prejudiced, but you're the most beautiful bride I've ever seen. Except for your Mama of course."

"I'll be all right, Papa. I'm just nervous about walking down the aisle and up the steps to the *bima* without stepping on the hem of my dress."

The lie came easily. She was frightened of so much more than tripping. But what else was there to say? She and Caleb, a man she hardly knew, were about to be married. Had Mama been this afraid? After all, Papa had been a stranger, and she too was only seventeen. If only Fannie had asked her before she left home.

It had been hours since they had arrived at the shul, just as the cold, clear December day was beginning to turn dark. The ceremony couldn't begin until Shabbos ended. Fannie had been led to a room with a throne-like chair, where she received congratulations from the women guests. It was her day to be treated like a queen. Miriam and Rachel had helped her dress.

"We know how you're feeling, Fannie," Miriam had assured her. "All brides are nervous before their weddings."

Rachel nodded in agreement. "I was petrified, and I had known Max most of my life."

Fannie knew Rachel meant well, but it only reminded her of how little she knew Caleb. Not even her perfect wedding gown and new silk shoes, or the huge bouquet of roses she would carry down the aisle comforted her.

Rachel had recently announced to the family that she was pregnant with their second child. It was barely visible in the high-waisted layered gown she wore, but Fannie noticed that her face was rounder and her complexion rosier. "You look especially pretty tonight, Rachel. Pregnancy agrees with you."

"I hope I'll be saying the same about you soon, but I don't know how you could look more beautiful than you do now."

Fannie was overwhelmed by the procession of well-wishers. How would she ever remember all these names?

She was relieved to see Mary, who had become a friend. Mary laughed when Fannie told her how pretty she looked. Always the first to wear the latest fashions, that night she had a rhinestone choker around her slender neck. "I'm just an old married lady now," she said. "But you, my dear, are as stunning as I knew you would be the day you tried on that gown. Caleb will be in awe. I'll see you in the sanctuary—don't forget to smile, Fannie."

Fannie's school friend, Anna, was among the last to arrive. Fannie had hesitated to invite her, not wanting her to be alone among strangers and worried that she wouldn't have the right clothes for a formal occasion. But she needn't have worried. Anna looked lovely in a simple dark red dress; her hair pinned up instead of in the long braid she wore at school. Except for her father and brothers, Fannie's life was centered around the people Caleb and the Fines knew. Even Mary had been Caleb's friend first. It felt good to have one friend she had made on her own.

"Oh Fannie, I'm so glad you invited me, and I could come celebrate with you. You look like a princess."

"Thank you, Anna. I can't wait for you to meet Caleb. I've told him so much about you. And you'll see Daniel again and meet my other brother, Noah, too. They promised to look out for you."

While the women fussed over Fannie, Caleb sat in another room at the groom's table, surrounded by male family and friends singing and toasting his good fortune.

"It's about time you settled down," said Charles.

"My sister will be a wonderful wife and mother, Caleb—be good to her." said Noah.

"Or else," added Daniel with a smile that didn't quite reach his eyes.

Two of Caleb's friends witnessed the signing of the *ketubah*, the marriage contract, and then, finally, it was time to begin. The men danced and sang with Caleb as he approached Fannie for the *bedeken* ceremony, when the groom saw his wife before she was veiled so he wouldn't be deceived like Jacob was in the Bible. As he bent over her to lower her veil, Fannie searched for some sign of Caleb's emotions. Was he nervous? Excited? Happy? He was smiling, but she couldn't guess how he was feeling.

Now he was waiting for her under a white silk canopy trimmed with gold fringe. His parents stood next to him. Miriam, regal in her dark blue satin dress and headband with matching feathers, was looking back toward her and smiling. It wasn't the same as having her own mother there, but she was grateful for her cousin's kindness.

Caleb too was smiling at her. He looked handsome in his black tuxedo with the cutaway jacket and brocade vest over a starched white shirt and white bowtie. Fannie thought his silk top hat made him look like one of the Broadway stars from the newspaper.

Fannie tightened her grip on her father's arm. Like Caleb, Charles and Max, he wore formal clothes and a top hat. She knew he disliked the dress clothes, but she was happy to see him looking so elegant. If only her Mama were here with them. She would have been dressed like the other women, but more beautiful than any of them.

The music started and they began to walk. She reminded herself to smile. When they reached the chuppah, Fannie's Papa kissed her and moved to stand next to her as she took her place to Caleb's right.

"You look beautiful," Caleb whispered.

How nice of him to say that. It will help me get through this.

After the Rabbi welcomed everyone, Miriam took her arm and helped her slowly circle Caleb seven times. She was creating a symbolic wall around them, announcing to the world that they were now a family. When she returned to her place, Caleb lifted her veil over her head and they each took a sip of wine from the cup the Rabbi had blessed. No sacred occasion was complete without the "fruit of the vine."

It was time for the ring. Caleb placed the plain gold band on Fannie's right index finger and recited the ancient vow. "Behold, by this ring you are consecrated to me as my wife according to the laws of Moses and Israel."

They were now officially married, but the ceremony was far from over. As the Rabbi read the ketubah, Fannie listened to the words that obligated Caleb to cherish, honor, and support her. He was required to provide food, clothes and necessities and to live with her as man and wife. Funds were to be set aside in case of his death or divorce. What she brought into the marriage remained hers. When the reading was complete, the Rabbi rolled up the scroll and handed it to Fannie. It was hers to keep, a contract designed to protect her.

Then the Rabbi began the seven blessings that celebrated the bride and groom's joy.

Seven steps into the mikveh, seven times around Caleb, seven blessings. My marriage is another of God's creations.

Fannie barely noticed what the Rabbi was chanting. Here she was, under the chuppah. It was every girl's dream—her own dream—but she felt more terror than joy. If she was a good wife and mother, like Mama and Miriam, would joy come?

Even in the midst of celebrations, it was customary for the Jewish people to pause and recall the tragedies that had befallen them. The Rabbi placed a glass wrapped in a napkin on the floor. In remembrance of the destruction of the temple in Jerusalem, Caleb raised his foot and stamped on the glass. As it shattered, the guests shouted "Mazel Tov!" They rose from their seats and began to clap as the newly married couple walked back down the aisle. They were on their way to the *yichud* room, where they would be secluded for eighteen minutes before joining their guests. They had gone places unchaperoned, but they had never been alone in a room before.

Caleb closed the door behind them. Fannie turned to him, unsure of what to do next. She closed her eyes as Caleb took her in his arms and gently pressed his lips to hers. She was surprised at how soft and smooth they were. He tightened his hold and the pressure of his lips grew stronger. *What do I do now?* She remained still until he pulled away.

"Until tonight, Fannie."

It suddenly occurred to Fannie that this might not be the first time for Caleb. He was an American, a man of the world. Did men like Caleb have experience before they were married? According to the ketubah, the bride was a maiden, but there were no rules for the groom. She was horrified to think he would be comparing her to someone else. It was better not to think about it at all.

Caleb held out a chair for her at the table laid with food, the first they would eat after fasting all day.

"I'll take care of you, Fannie. I'll honor my promises."

Was their marriage just another business arrangement? Did he care at all about loving her?

"Here, I have something for you," he said, handing her a small blue velvet box from the table.

Inside was a large round diamond ring. Caleb moved the plain gold band to Fannie's left hand and put the diamond on her right. She held out her hand to admire it. "It's beautiful, Caleb. Thank you."

She handed him her gift, also in a velvet box. Inside was a pair of onyx and gold cuff links she had picked out with advice from Miriam. "I hope you like them."

"They're perfect. Will you help me put them on so everyone can see them?" Together they removed the set he had been wearing and replaced them with the new ones. The moment their hands touched felt more intimate to Fannie than their kiss.

Only a few minutes later they were being called to join the others. At the door, Caleb kissed Fannie again and took her hand. They walked into the large, crowded social hall together, accompanied by lively klezmer music and cheers from their family and friends. The room hummed with anticipation. It was a sacred obligation to honor the bride and groom by eating, drinking and dancing at their wedding. Family and friends were ready to celebrate.

Caleb and Fannie joined their families at a long table in the front of the room. Even though she was expecting it, Fannie was still shocked to see men and women sitting together. Caleb, Charles, and Asher rose to say the blessings over the wine and the challah before the food started to come out on big silver platters. It smelled delicious, but Fannie barely had a chance to taste it before Caleb led her out onto the dance floor. Fannie had never danced with a man. In Kamenetz, women and men, including the bride and groom, danced separately. She had tried to demur when she found out it would be expected of her, but even Miriam, who usually supported her, maintained it was customary in America.

"I don't want my guests to be disappointed," she insisted.

"Don't worry," said Daniel when she went to him in a panic. "I'll teach you enough to get by." For several nights after dinner, he taught her some basic steps. "One, two, three, one, two, three." He led her around the room.

"Come," said Caleb as he reached for her. She stiffened as he held her in his arms.

"Relax," he said as he began to guide her around the room. She did her best but couldn't wait for the dance to be over. Fortunately, they had to stop frequently to accept their guests' well wishes.

Mary was one of the first to congratulate them. "What a beautiful ring," she said, picking up Fannie's hand. As soon as they noticed, the other women gathered around, eager to see what Caleb had given her. "What a lucky bride," they gushed. "Wear it in good health."

Noticing Anna at the edge of the crowd, Fannie called her to her side. "Next by you," she whispered before introducing her to the other women.

Daniel found a moment when the crowd around her thinned to hug her tightly. "You're all grown up now, baby sister, and beautiful. I hope he deserves you."

"And what about you, Daniel. When will I see you under the chuppah?"

"Come, let's dance," he said without answering.

Noah came over and took both her hands. "Be happy, Fannie."

"And when will I be dancing at your wedding, Noah? I got no answer from Daniel. Surely one of you will give me nieces and nephews."

Noah laughed. "Soon enough, Fannie. "Soon enough." He took her to join a circle of dancers.

Halfway through the evening, Caleb and Fannie were led to two chairs in the center of the dance floor and given a handkerchief to hold between them. Several of the men lifted the chairs as the crowd danced an exuberant Hora around them. Fannie held on to the edge of the chair with her other hand, shrieking when the chair dipped.

"Don't worry," laughed Caleb. "They haven't dropped a bride yet."

Fannie began to enjoy herself. She smiled as she held hands with the people she loved and even with the strangers who had come to wish her luck.

After the blessings after the meal, the Rabbi poured wine from two cups into a single cup, symbolically uniting the new husband a wife, and offered each of them a sip. All the rituals were over, but the crowd kept dancing until the band played its last song and it was time to say their goodbyes. The newlyweds stood together to see them off.

"We'll see you soon. I can't wait to see your apartment," said Mary. "And I'll expect plenty of good schnapps," added Simon as he and Mary walked out with their arms around each other.

"Will you be back at school soon?" Anna asked as she said goodbye.

"Yes, of course—I want my English to be perfect, don't I, Caleb?"

"She'll be there. It was a pleasure to meet you, Anna."

After what seemed to Fannie like hundreds of farewells, only their families remained.

Rachel and Max were the first to say goodbye. "It was a beautiful wedding. We hope you'll be as happy as we are. And we're waiting for cousins for baby David and his new brother or sister." The two couples exchanged hugs.

"We're looking forward to eating at your new apartment," teased Daniel and Noah. "We know Mama taught you well. You're a lucky man, Caleb."

"God bless you, child." Fannie's father said as he held her, tearing up. "Take good care of her young man," he said, reaching out to include Caleb in his embrace.

"Good luck to you both," Charles said gruffly. "I'm proud of you, son." He held them each briefly, letting go before tears could escape.

Miriam made no attempt to hold back her tears. "Thank you for making Fannie part of our family, Caleb. I love you both." She kissed them both, reluctant to let go.

They were finally alone. The room, so recently alive with music and laughter, was silent. They gathered their things, bundled up against the cold night, and left to spend their first night as husband and wife. Fannie wondered what Caleb was thinking as she took his arm. She was ready to make a home for him and raise their children. Did he have his own dreams for their future? She would soon find out.

PART III: MARRIAGE, 1911-1912

CHAPTER 8

"After you, Mrs. Fine."

Caleb held the door open for Fannie, who walked in and switched on the light. She took off her heavy coat, relieved to be out of the bitter cold, and began to hang it in the hall closet. "I'll do that," said Caleb. He locked the door and took Fannie in his arms.

"You can get undressed and washed first. Do you need help with your dress?"

"No thank you, I can manage."

Fannie went into the bedroom, chose her prettiest nightgown and robe and went into the bathroom to prepare herself. When she was done, she carefully hung up her wedding gown, unpinned and brushed her hair, and got into one of the beds. She was unsure whether to ask Caleb which bed he preferred, but she was anxious to get under the covers.

"I'm ready, Caleb." She lay still, her legs together and her arms stiff at her side. "Please let him be gentle," she prayed silently when she heard him come into the room. He came to her bed and pulled back the quilt.

"Let me look at my bride," he said, pulling her nightgown up to her neck. "You are even more beautiful than I imagined." He began to run his hands along her body.

Fannie shrank from his gaze. She had wondered if he would want to look at her and if her body would please him. It was what she thought she wanted, but now she was frightened by the hunger in his eyes.

"Try to relax, Fannie. It won't hurt as much if you relax. Your mama told you, didn't she? That it would hurt the first time? I'll try not to hurt you too much."

She could feel the bed sink under his weight as he straddled her on his knees and leaned over to kiss her, softly at first and then more forcefully. She didn't know if she was supposed to respond when he pushed his tongue in her mouth, but then he moved lower, kissing the base of her neck and then her nipples. It was like the feeling from the bath, as though an invisible cord pulled from her breasts, through her belly, to between her legs. *This is what I was hoping it would be like.*

Caleb kept his mouth on her breast, moving his hand down to between her legs, to the spot she hadn't dared touch herself. As he stroked her, her breath quickened and she couldn't help but move under him. But then suddenly he stopped and yanked her legs apart. As he raised his torso, she glanced down the length of his body. She had seen her brother Levi and other baby boys naked, and Mama had explained that they grew bigger, but the size of Caleb's erection terrified her. How would he fit inside her? She tensed, but Caleb held her legs open wide and pushed into her.

Fannie cried out.

"It's done. Everything will be all right now," said Caleb, thrusting slowly at first, then faster and deeper. He closed his eyes and moved as though Fannie weren't even there until with one final thrust he collapsed onto her, breathing heavily. He stayed like that for a few minutes, while Fannie wondered if she should say something.

"There," he said. He gave her a quick kiss and rolled over onto his own bed.

Fannie waited for him to speak, but soon she heard him snoring lightly. Her first time was over. She was a wife now. She reached over to turn off the light next to her and fell asleep at once. A few hours later she awoke to feel Caleb on top of her.

"I want you again, Fannie, I can't get enough of you."

This time there were no words of endearment, no kisses, no touches that aroused that new feeling inside her. She was tender from the first time, and it hurt. She waited for him to finish and go back to his bed, hoping this time he would let her sleep until morning.

Was this just because it was their first night together, or would he be waking her like this often? She had no way to know how a husband was supposed to behave. She sensed from the way he touched her at first that he knew how to please a woman, but he hadn't tried to please her. How could she make him understand what made her feel good?

The clock by the bed said seven AM when she awoke again, quickly glancing over to Caleb's bed to see if he was still asleep. He had usually left for work by this hour but had agreed to take the day off. Fannie eased herself out of bed quietly, took her robe and went into the bathroom to wash between her legs. Later, she would wash the sheet.

When she was finished cleaning herself, she began making Caleb's coffee and setting the table. She had no idea what they would do all day, but hoped their first day as man and wife would be special.

She walked into the living room to open the drapes and saw the ketubah on the sofa where she had dropped it the night before, next to her bouquet. Didn't the ketubah say a husband was obligated to please his wife? Now that the first night was over, would Caleb care about her desires as well as his own? Or was that too much to expect? Rachel said she liked it with Max.

And did pleasure matter as long as their lovemaking gave them children? Could there be a child from last night? She stared out the window without really seeing anything.

Lost in her thoughts, Fannie didn't hear Caleb come into the room. He put his arms around her from behind and pressed against her. She could feel that he wanted her again. He turned her around and began to unbutton her robe.

She held up her hand. "Caleb, please, I'm so sore from last night." The words escaped her before she had a chance to think. Would he be angry?

Caleb stopped and took a step back. "We'll wait until tonight. I hope you won't be frightened anymore, Fannie, and you'll learn to like it."

Would she? Would she get up the nerve to tell him how to help her enjoy it? Did respectable women say such things? She had no one to ask. It would be too embarrassing to go back to Rachel.

"Now, is that coffee I smell? What has my wife made me for our first breakfast together?"

★ ★ ★

A few days later, just after breakfast, Fannie was home alone, sitting at the kitchen table. The sun was just beginning to come through the window. On workdays, Caleb was always in a rush to leave in the morning, so he barely talked while he had his coffee and cereal, but Fannie rose early to make sure everything was on the table for him. She sat with him while he ate, waiting until after he was gone to have her own meal. Just as she was pouring herself a second cup of tea and getting ready to read the *Forverts*, the doorbell rang. She had no idea who it might be that early in the morning until she saw her father through the peephole. He wore a heavy overcoat, a muffler, a hat and gloves, but his nose was red from the cold. She let him in right away.

"Is something wrong?" She couldn't imagine what had brought him there before he had to go to work. He didn't want any special treatment from his cousin, who frequently reminded him of how lucky he was to have been given a job, so he made sure never to be late.

"No, no, I didn't mean to alarm you. But I wanted you to have this before Shabbos." He handed her a box wrapped in white tissue paper and tied with a blue ribbon.

"Come sit, Papa, and warm yourself with a *glezl tey*. I was just about to have one myself."

"Just for a minute, Feigele, I want to see you open the package. How are you? Caleb is good to you?"

"Yes, Papa, he is. We're getting to know each other."

She thought about how Caleb came to her every night. No matter how tired he seemed after a long day, he wanted her. "I can't believe you're mine," he would murmur. She tried to make him understand by how she moved her body what pleased her, too shy to say the words out loud. But as he had done the first night, he hurried to get inside her, satisfied himself, and went straight to sleep. She was sure it would get better. She just needed to overcome her embarrassment and tell him what she needed.

She ripped away the paper and lifted the cover off the box. "Oh Papa, they're beautiful." She took out two tall, intricately embossed silver candlesticks and set them on the table.

"These are a wedding gift from your Mama, Feigele. She wanted you to have them for your first Shabbos in your new home. One of them has an inscription on the bottom."

"Yes, this one," said Fannie after examining them both.

"Here, let me read it to you," said her father, taking the one Fannie pointed out and putting on his reading glasses. "May

God guide my daughter, Feige, from this day forward. Your loving mother, Bluma. December 10, 1910.ʺ

He put the glasses back in his pocket and handed the candlestick back to her. She ran her fingers over the Hebrew letters.

"But how?"

"Cousin Miriam took me to the shop where she buys silver as soon as we set the date. I had them inscribed with the words your Mama wrote down before we left home."

"Oh, Papa, if only she had been at the wedding. She would have been so happy. I wish she could have been there in a fine silk dress, letting all the other women honor her."

"I missed her too and I know she was thinking of you that day," he said. He took both her hands in his. "All she wants, all both of us want, is for you to be happy. We know it was hard for you to leave home and your friends. You have always had such a good heart, now you deserve to have someone take care of you. You're married to a man who will give you a good life. I can see from how my cousin lives that you won't lack for anything. It was a good match for you."

Fannie nodded.

"And you'll write to your mama and tell her about the wedding? You'll help her feel like she was there and give her a reason to *kvell*, to boast to her friends?"

"Of course I will, Papa. I have a letter already written; I'll just add a thank you."

"Good. I have to go now. You're Caleb's wife now, Feigele, but you'll always be my daughter."

Fannie gave her father his coat, tied his muffler around his neck and kissed him goodbye. After putting her beautiful new silver candlesticks on the sideboard in the dining area, she took the letter she had written from her drawer and sat down at the table.

12 December, 1910

Dear Mama,

It is hard to know where to begin telling you about the wedding. You should have seen all the fine clothes and jewels the women wore – even fur coats! But if you had been there, you would have been more beautiful than all of them.

Rachel and Miriam helped me dress and stayed with me in the bride's room. I was so afraid, Mama. They said all brides were nervous – but you never told me, were you?

I can't remember the names of all the ladies who came to wish me well before the ceremony. Miriam, Charles and Caleb have so many American friends and invited all the important people from their business. I was glad my friend from school, Anna, was there, but I was missing Gittel and Raisel.

You should have seen how handsome Papa looked. The men all wore formal clothes and top hats. They looked like movie stars. He told me I was a beautiful bride, but not as beautiful as you were. Even Caleb told me I was beautiful. You'll see our wedding portrait and judge for yourself.

Everyone was looking at me when I walked down the aisle. I just kept smiling and holding on to Papa's arm. If I had let go I'm sure I would have fallen over.

Caleb surprised me with a diamond ring! The women couldn't stop talking about it. I gave him cuff links that

Miriam helped me pick out. I was able to buy them with the money I've earned with my embroidery. He said he liked them.

There were bouquets of flowers and candles on every table in the hall. The food smelled delicious, and everyone said it was, but I hardly had time to eat. I didn't tell you it would happen before the wedding, but Caleb and I danced together! It's another thing they do differently here in America. I was lucky I had Daniel to teach me how.

I asked Noah and Daniel when they were getting married but they both avoided answering me. I hope by the time you get here they'll be ready to stand under the chuppah.

Please tell Freyda I have saved the dress and will put it on for her to see when you get here. Unless of course I'm expecting. Wouldn't that be wonderful?

Even though you weren't there, I could feel you with me, Mama. I hope you are all well and I can't wait for us all to be together.

You're loving daughter,

Fannie

P.S. I am writing my new address for you, Gittel and Raisel. Caleb and I are living in a small apartment not far from the Fines. It is not fancy compared to their house, but more than I ever dreamed of.

Mama – Papa came this morning with the beautiful

candlesticks. How can I ever thank you? The inscription brought tears of joy to my eyes. I will use them tomorrow for our first Shabbos dinner at home and every Shabbos after that. And every time I'll think of you.

★ ★ ★

After the excitement of the wedding, life settled into a routine. She discovered Caleb's tastes were simple. He had a healthy appetite, but he wasn't fussy about what he ate. She enjoyed being more creative with the dinners she made for their families. Daniel and Noah, who had moved into their own rooms in Manhattan, were frequent guests. She knew they wanted freedom from Papa's reproachful eye but thought they'd been foolish to give up a place as comfortable as the Fine's. And they obviously missed home cooking.

She visited often with Miriam and Rachel and the baby and had lunch occasionally with Mary.

Fannie did her homework faithfully every morning. She was eager to learn and was pleased with her progress. It became easier to join in conversations with Caleb and his friends. She paid particular attention to her pronunciation to avoid being identified as a "greenie." Caleb never said anything, but his friends complimented her.

At night, she concentrated on her embroidery. Mary's mother and friends bought her embroidery and told other friends about her. Her business was thriving; every dollar brought Mama and the children closer. If he wasn't in the kitchen going over business papers, Caleb sat in his chair reading the newspaper. He often played music on the Victrola, partial to lively songs like "Charles's Rag Time Band" and "Oh You Beautiful Doll," tapping his foot while he read. At first he insisted she dance with him, but she was so stiff and unsure of herself he gave up.

Occasionally, she would introduce herself to a neighbor she met on the stairs. As the weather got nicer, the young mothers gathered on the stoop with their baby buggies and let their toddlers play in the courtyard. She always stopped briefly to chat but felt excluded from their conversations about colicky babies and toilet training. Soon, she hoped, she would be one of them.

Finally, Spring came, and Passover, Fannie's favorite holiday. She loved the Passover Seder, the ritual dinner when the head of the family was commanded to tell the children the story of the exodus from slavery in Egypt. Special foods, like bitter herbs and matzoh, the unleavened bread the Jews ate as they hurriedly escaped, symbolized the journey. Only little David was there now, but one day soon her own children would be at the table.

As soon as they arrived at the Fines for the first Seder, Miriam handed Fannie a letter from Russia. "This came a few days ago," she said. "I hope you don't mind that I saved it for tonight."

"Of course not," said Fannie. She tore it open. "It's from my best friend, Gittel. It's the first letter I've gotten from her. I've been waiting and waiting." She started to read, and held the paper out to Miriam. "Look at the date. It took four months to get here!"

"It must have gotten lost somewhere. Why don't you go in the parlor to read it," said Miriam. "We're not ready to start."

15 November 1910

Dear Feige,

I finally got one of your letters—the one you wrote after your first night at school. Who knows if the other one will ever come.

By now I am sure you know a lot of English. Even if you didn't like school when we were girls, you were always very smart. You just need to believe in yourself.

I'm sorry you've been lonely but by the time you get this you'll be married, so you'll have a husband to keep you company.

I have news about Raisel. She has gone to Warsaw to be married! Her mother's family there helped to arrange it. He works in a factory. I can't remember what they make there, but they said he does well.

Now you're both gone, and I am without my two best friends. But I won't have time to be too sad because I've saved my news for last—I'm having a baby in May! My mama said it was bad luck to tell too soon, which is why it took me so long to write. I was sick all the time at first, but now I'm fine. Abe hopes it's a boy, but I don't care as long as it's healthy.

I can't wait to hear that you're having a baby. If only our children could play together like we did.

Write to me soon – I miss you,

Gittel

Gittel, a mother. Fannie was happy for her friend but couldn't help feeling a little jealous. She wasn't concerned after only three months, but Caleb was already starting to wonder how long it would be.

"Just believe in yourself," Gittel had written. Like Samuel, she saw something in Fannie that she hadn't seen herself. Perhaps it was time to start believing them.

Fannie loved watching the trees and flowers start to bloom. May and June were delightful, but July brought sweltering heat. There was little escape when temperatures rose just after the American Independence Day. Firemen let water out of the fire hydrants. People crowded into the parks, swarmed the beaches and jumped into the East River. Hundreds of people died. When workers started to pass out, Caleb and his father, like many others, closed their factory, although Caleb went into the office every day.

On one of those hot afternoons, Fannie's Papa came to her door unexpectedly. His face was red and shiny with sweat. He had even taken off his black coat; his shirt was sticking to him.

"Papa, come, sit by the electric fan. Caleb was lucky to get one of these. It only helps a little, but it's better than nothing."

"*Z'is heys*" He sank into the sofa wearily, mopping his face with his handkerchief. "It's hot."

"Let me get you a glass of cold water."

"Feigele, there's something I must tell you," he said as soon as she returned. "I've had a letter."

"Oh no, is it Mama? One of the children?"

"No, they're fine, but Mama sent some bad news. She wanted me to tell you myself." He reached out to take Fannie's hands.

"It's Gittel. She died giving birth."

Fannie was stunned into silence. How could that be? Bossy, fun-loving, Gittel, her friend since they were babies together. Dead?

"No, Papa," she wailed. "I've been waiting for news. I never thought ..." Fannie's body shook with her sobs. "And the baby?" she asked when she began to recover.

"A boy. A cousin has come to help the father take care of him."

"A son." Fannie moaned. "Why did God take her, Papa?"

"I can't answer that Feigele, no one can."

The two of them sat without speaking for a while.

"I need to be going back for dinner," said Asher. "Will you be all right until Caleb gets home?"

"Yes, Papa," Fannie told him. "Please take care of yourself in this dreadful heat."

That night she shared the news with Caleb. "So many women die giving birth. It's hard not to be scared."

"Don't be silly, you're young and strong. You'll be fine," said Caleb, dismissing her fears.

Didn't he realize that Gittel was young and strong? Did he even care that her best friend had died? He said nothing to comfort her. Gittel had written that Fannie wouldn't be lonely when she had a husband, but it hadn't turned out that way.

★ ★ ★

The heat wave broke, and life got back to normal, although Fannie's heart still ached for her friend. She had written to her Mama right away, asking her to tell Gittel's husband how sorry she was and to find out where she could write to Raisel. But in her heart, she knew both her friends were lost to her forever.

A few weeks later, Caleb walked into the kitchen waving an envelope. "Look what I have!"

Fannie looked up from the stove. "What? What's inside?"

"Tickets to the theater. Remember when you changed your name last year and I told you about the actress, Fannie Brice? We're going to see her in Ziegfeld's Follies."

"You mean when *you* changed my name," she said under her breath. Fannie had gotten used to her American name and liked the new, more confident person she was becoming in America. But she had not forgotten how surprised and hurt she had been when Caleb changed her name without consulting her.

"So, tell me more about the theater," she said when they sat down to dinner.

"Everyone is talking about this year's show with the Dolly Sisters and Bert Williams, a Negro singer. And just wait until you see the costumes. But Fannie Brice will be the best."

"I saw her picture in the *Forverts*. They said she was the star of the show. I couldn't believe it—a Jewish girl."

"Everyone loves her. The tickets weren't easy to get, I'll tell you. Simon and Mary are going too, and we'll all have dinner at Delmonico's after the show. Dress up Fannie, all the women do."

Not just the theater, but dinner in a fancy Manhattan restaurant. Fannie was still fearful of doing the wrong thing and embarrassing Caleb, but she was excited too.

Caleb helped himself to a large portion of the meat and vegetables, smothering them in gravy. "What did you do today, Fannie?"

Fannie was surprised he asked, he so rarely inquired about her day. Getting the theater tickets must have put him in a good mood.

"When I came back from the butcher our neighbor from across the hall was sitting on the stoop, so I stopped to talk to her a while."

"Which one is she? The one with the dark brown curly hair?"

"Yes, Sophie. She was a milliner until the baby was born."

Caleb looked up at Fannie as though he was about to say something but went on eating.

When they had finished, Fannie cleared the dishes and went to the icebox for the applesauce she had made that morning. She brought two small bowls of it to the table.

"Tea?" she asked Caleb when he had finished.

"No thanks, I think I'll just go have my cigar."

He went into the living room to smoke while Fannie washed and dried the dishes.

★ ★ ★

The following Saturday, Fannie and Mary walked arm in arm ahead of Caleb and Simon as they approached the theater. Fannie was wearing one of the dresses Mary had helped her pick out the day she bought her first new clothes in America. Although the evening was still warm, she carried a shawl of her own design with a border of vines and leaves in various shades of green. Mary's shawl, which Fannie had also embroidered, was covered in pink and yellow roses.

"Look, I'm wearing a Fannie Fine original," said Mary.

"Whenever you wear one of my shawls, I get more orders. Everyone who cares about fashion knows you're the one to follow. I can barely keep up."

"It's your one-of-a-kind designs and exquisite stiches. They sell themselves."

"Thank you. I'm proud of my work and glad to be giving Papa money for tickets to America for Mama and the children." If only Caleb was proud of her. He saw her sewing almost every evening, but he never asked to see what she was making, not even when she was working on baby clothes for Rachel's and Max's new baby.

"So, Fannie, are you ready to see the woman who inspired your name, the famous Fannie Brice?" Simon offered Fannie his arm as they stepped into the elevators that would take them to the rooftop theater.

"Yes, of course I'm curious to see the woman Caleb was thinking of when he gave me her name."

"I hope he told you that you're much prettier."

"He did, but I thought he was just trying to flatter me. After all, we had only just met."

"Oh no, it's true. You could be a Ziegfeld Girl."

"A Ziegfeld Girl?"

"You'll see. All the girls in Ziegfeld's shows are tall and beautiful, just like you."

"Thank you, Simon. I'm sure you're —"

"Let's find our seats and you'll see for yourself," said Caleb, putting a stop to Simon's gallantry.

Fannie took the time to look around. She was pleased to see that she was dressed as elegantly as any woman in the audience. I'm not a greenie anymore, she thought proudly. I belong here now.

The audience grew quiet as the lights dimmed and the curtain opened.

Fannie gasped. Perhaps she had congratulated herself on fitting in too soon. The stage was filled with girls in scanty costumes with tall, sequined headdresses made of ostrich feathers. She had never seen women reveal so much of their bodies in public. Should she be insulted that Simon thought she could be one of them? Did he think she would ever be so immodest?

"Caleb, you should have warned me."

"And ruin the surprise? I wanted to see the look on your face."

The crowd applauded as the girls turned and walked in unison, gliding across the stage. Fannie found herself clapping along with them. How beautiful and unashamed they were.

The Negro singer Caleb had told her about appeared in one of the skits and sang a solo. She wondered why he wore black face paint with exaggerated white lips, just like the white performers. Wasn't his own dark skin sufficient?

Fannie Brice was nothing like the Ziegfeld Girls. Their smiles never wavered; she made exaggerated funny faces. They seemed to float; she flounced around the stage. And she sang with an accent thicker than Fannie's.

"Second hand poy-ils," she sang as she twirled the long strand of pearls around her neck.

"I'm wearing second hand coy-ils," she continued as she tossed her curls.

"I never get a single thing that's new ..." she lamented, wiping a fake tear from her eye as the audience laughed and clapped along with the rhythm.

Fannie joined in. *I could do a lot worse than have her name. She's so brave.* Along with the other theatergoers she shouted "brava" as Brice moved to the center of the stage to finish her number:

"Everyone knows that I'm just Secondhand Rose"
"From Second Avenue."

The audience rose to its feet as she bobbed up and down in a childlike curtsy.

"Well?" Caleb asked.

"I'm glad to have her name," she told him.

"Let's go powder our noses before we go to supper," said Mary, pulling Fannie away from the men. When they got to the Ladies Lounge, dozens of women were crowded in front of the mirror. The brave ones like Mary applied powder and a touch of rouge to their cheeks and lips. Fannie watched them enviously. Mama would disapprove, but this was America.

"I'll be back in a minute," she said, excusing herself to use the toilet. Once she had locked the door, she saw that, as she had suspected, she was starting to bleed.

"What's wrong?" asked Mary when Fannie returned. "You look pale. Are you ill?"

"No, I'm fine," she said. "Only hungry and a little faint from the heat."

Fannie didn't want to tell Mary that she had found a spot of blood. Mary and Simon had been married just over a year, but not expecting didn't seem to bother Mary at all. In fact, Fannie sensed that Mary was rather pleased that her life of shopping, dining out and theater would continue without the interruption of bearing a child. At first, Fannie was also glad not to conceive. She wanted more time to adjust to her new life. But now that they had been married eight months, she felt ready. There were things she wished were better, like the way Caleb only used her body for his own pleasure and how he paid more attention to his business than to her, but she knew he'd be a good provider for their children. And perhaps a child would ease her loneliness.

She was disappointed that there wasn't going to be a baby and even more unhappy about having to tell him. For the last few months, she saw blame in his eyes every time she bled. She was sure he knew she was a few days late - he tracked her monthlies like it was one of his accounts—and he would be disappointed.

Sometimes she wondered if it was because she didn't go to the mikveh, but when she had broached the idea of waiting twelve days from the time she started to bleed to cleanse herself before they resumed relations, Caleb had sneered at her.

"You can't be serious," he said. "Take a bath here."

She knew she'd never convince him and certainly couldn't refuse him when he came to her bed. She didn't really believe she was being punished for not obeying the commandment, but it bothered her that she had been forced to abandon the tradition. She remembered Papa telling his cousins that Caleb hadn't been brought up to honor their ways. Now she saw what that meant for her.

"Let's go find our husbands," said Mary.

"Yes," said Fannie. "I'm sure they're hungry."

Fannie's cramps made her uncomfortable. Caleb noticed that she was only picking at her food.

"Are you unwell, Fannie?"

"No, a just a little tired."

"Then let's call it a night," said Caleb as he signaled for the bill.

The foursome made the trip back to Brooklyn together before going their separate ways.

The minute they were alone, Caleb began to question Fannie.

"You're bleeding again, aren't you? That's why you weren't well at dinner. What's wrong with you?"

"Let's not discuss this outside, Caleb. There's nothing wrong. Sometimes it just takes a little longer."

"How much longer?" he asked as soon as they were inside. "Max and Rachel have two children already. I thought you wanted children as much as I did."

Fannie hung up her coat. She started to protest but thought better of it. There was no use in reminding Caleb that Max and Rachel's first baby wasn't born until two years after they were married.

"Of course I do. Our time will come soon, I know it."

"Well, I hope so. That's why —"

"Why?"

"Never mind, let's go to bed." He walked toward the bedroom without another word.

CHAPTER NINE

One month later, Fannie scanned the crowd for her friend Anna as she approached P.S. 155 for her second year of night school. The year before, her first night had been filled with dread. But she had done well and, best of all, had made a friend of her own. Now she was eager to learn more, and, if she were honest with herself, relieved to be out of the house and away from Caleb. Every month she didn't get pregnant his silences grew longer. They still sat together in the living room most evenings, but she might as well have been alone.

Fannie had seen Anna twice during the summer. Once they had taken a walk in the Botanic Garden, and once Anna had come for dinner on a Saturday afternoon after shul. Anna had invited Fannie and Caleb to meet her parents and brother, but Caleb didn't see any reason to meet a working-class family he didn't intend to socialize with. She was appalled at his snobbery but made their excuses.

She and Anna had agreed to meet on the steps before class. She saw a few familiar faces as she looked around for her, but she knew many students left after just one year. They had enough English to get by and they couldn't spare the time, time they needed to earn more money for their families. Fortunately, both she and Anna were continuing their schooling.

Fannie wanted to learn more English to fit in with Caleb's American friends and business associates. She had made a great deal of progress in the last year but still felt like an outsider when their English was beyond her. Because she worked on her custom embroidery at home, she had ample time for school and homework, at least until she had children. Anna worked as a seamstress, but her brother, Jacob, helped support her and her parents. According to Anna, he was an educated man himself and was adamant she finish her schooling. After all, he told her, wouldn't she be her children's first teacher? Anna told Fannie he even supported giving women the vote.

Fannie was disappointed she hadn't been able to meet him. She was just beginning to read about women's suffrage in the *Forverts* and she didn't know what to think. After the vote, what else would women want? Surely not to run for office. Who would take care of their families? On the other hand, why shouldn't women have a say in making the laws that affected them and their children? They might even do a better job of it!

The men she and Caleb socialized with were opposed to allowing women to vote. She had heard them ridicule the idea, so she knew better than to bring the subject up when they were out with his friends. She was even afraid to discuss it with the women, who might report to their husbands that Fannie was a "suffragette." Caleb would be furious.

"Anna!" she cried, spotting her diminutive friend. "Over here."

"Fannie, how wonderful to see you again," Anna said as the two friends embraced. "Tell me all about your summer. And I have news of my own to share."

"You first. I have nothing new to report."

"Oh, I was hoping for—"

Anna looked down at Fannie's belly.

"No, not yet," said Fannie. "But tell me your news. Hurry, before class starts, and we'll talk more later."

"I'm going to be married!"

"What a wonderful surprise!" Fannie reached out to give her friend another hug. "Mazel Tov!"

"I met him at shul. He sits near my father and brother every week—I could see how handsome he was from the balcony. My brother introduced us after Shabbos services one afternoon. Between us, I think he was secretly planning the match all along. He knew we'd get along. My father met with his father, and it's all arranged for next spring. I'm so happy!"

"Then I'm happy too. Come, let's go in and after class you'll tell me all about him." Fannie took Anna's hand as they climbed the steps and searched for their new classroom.

Class went quickly. Their new teacher, Miss Anderson, was a petite young woman who looked like she had stepped out of a lady's fashion magazine. Her dark hair was pinned up like a Gibson girl and she wore a stylish skirt and matching jacket that showed off her curves. She was so young and pretty Fannie was sure she'd be married soon and then she'd have to stop teaching.

Class began with the Pledge of Allegiance, which all the students now understood and recited easily, even if their accents were still very thick. Miss Anderson explained that this year they would learn more about the history of America. She would tell them how to get library cards so they could get books of their own to read at home. Fannie had never been much of a reader, but maybe she would learn enough English to try one of the love stories like the one her friends read back in Russia. Here she wouldn't have to read it secretly. It wasn't as though Caleb would care or even notice what she was reading.

Fannie was no longer nervous about introducing herself to the class or reading aloud. When she mispronounced a word, Miss Anderson asked her to look at it again and waited patiently until she was able to correct it herself.

As soon as class ended the two girls rushed out to continue talking.

"You haven't told me his name, Anna. And what does he do?"

"His name is Nathan and he's in the fur business. He started as an assistant tailor—that's what he learned from his father back in Poland. But he was already promoted twice and now he works with the customers designing and sewing their coats. He plans to have his own shop in a few years. And I know he will because he's so smart. He even wants to go to the City College."

"Like my brother, Noah—that's wonderful."

"But that's not all. My family is moving to Manhattan. My brother found us a bigger apartment on One Hundred and Fifteenth Street. Some of my cousins will be arriving soon to live with us until they get settled, and it's closer to work."

"When do you move?"

Anna looked down before she spoke. "That's the only bad part—in two weeks. I won't be coming back to school here with you."

"So soon? But we'll visit like we did over the summer. Just be sure to send me your new address and a phone number where I can leave a message. And of course I'll expect an invitation to your wedding."

"I wouldn't dream of being married without you there. Oh Fannie, I'm so happy. But I'll miss you. And I can't wait to hear there's a baby on the way."

"I'll miss you too, Anna. School won't be the same without you. Please don't forget to call me right away."

"I promise."

Fannie and Anna held each other tightly. Finally, they kissed each other on both cheeks and turned in opposite directions to go home.

The tears Fannie hadn't wanted Anna to see began to flow freely. She was glad for her friend but already felt bereft. Until the moment Anna told her she was leaving, Fannie had not realized how much she had been counting on Anna's always cheerful personality to restore her spirits. It was hard to be happy in the face of Caleb's indifference.

She was so lonely. If only her Mama were there, but what would she tell Fannie except to make the best of it? She was jealous of Anna, marrying someone she knew and liked. Caleb was not the husband she would have chosen, and she didn't think he would have chosen her. He never said it outright, but he made it clear in so many small ways that he resented his father's choice of a bride from the old country. All she was good for was giving him a son, and she hadn't done that.

Fannie reached into her purse. She took out a handkerchief to dry her eyes and a nickel for the trolley. She wished Samuel's button was there. Tonight, she was going to insist that Caleb talk to her.

★ ★ ★

Caleb was going over some papers from the office at the kitchen table when Fannie got home.

"Can I get you some tea, Caleb?" Fannie asked as she turned the light on under the kettle. "A cookie?"

"No thanks, nothing for me." He barely looked up.

"Caleb, I need to ask you something." Fannie tried to make her voice firm.

"Yes?"

"I need new clothes for the holidays. Last week your mother reminded me that everyone wears their new fall clothes to shul."

"I'm not my mother, Fannie. What do you think, we're made of money? You'll have to make do. Why don't you just embroider something like you do for other women. And besides, new clothes will be a waste because you'll be expecting a child soon. Or at least you should be."

Fannie was shocked. They didn't have as much as his parents, but Caleb was a wealthy man. Was this a punishment for not having a baby? She tried to think of how to convince him. What would Mary say?

"Of course I can go without new clothes, Caleb," she began. "The men won't notice, but the women will talk. And they'll tell their husbands. I'm only afraid it will look like you can't afford to buy me clothes. But I'll do whatever you say."

"Very well, I don't want you to embarrass me. Buy something to wear to shul. But that's it. You can buy clothes when you're too big with a child to wear the old ones, but nothing else until then."

"Caleb. I'm as disappointed as you are that there's no baby yet. But many couples wait for their first baby. Even Max and Rachel had to wait. I think maybe you don't remember that Rachel wasn't expecting for more than a year."

"Well, that may have been fine for Max, but not me. I'm tired of waiting. What's wrong with you anyway?"

Fannie had finally reached her limit.

"Enough Caleb. It's not my fault. It just hasn't happened yet."

"I make love to you enough," he shouted. "It should have happened by now. I'm running out of patience."

"Love? It doesn't feel like love! You never ask me what I feel, what I want from you when we have relations. You never try to please me like a Jewish husband is supposed to please his wife."

Caleb glared at her. "What are you talking about? My father picked you because you were a nice girl. Did you trick us? Only a whore talks like that."

Fannie gasped. Caleb only sneered at her. He stood up, gathered his papers and left the kitchen. The door to their bedroom slammed.

Fannie folded her arms on the table, put her head down on them and wept.

How could he? What kind of man calls his wife that? *I finally stood up for myself, but now everything is worse. And now I know for certain he doesn't care.*

She stayed where she was, motionless, for quite a while. When she lifted her head, her tea had grown cold. She turned out the lights and went to wash up for the night. As soon as she got into bed, Caleb was on top of her. He finished quickly and rolled over into his own bed.

"That should make a baby," he growled.

Fannie let the tears roll down her face. Was this going to be the rest of her life?

That Saturday night Fannie tried to forget their argument as she made dinner. Mary and Simon were coming. She was trying a new recipe for chicken with fruit she had seen in the *Forverts*. It was really for the approaching holidays, when it was customary to eat something sweet for the new year, but she didn't see why they couldn't enjoy a little sweetness now. She certainly needed some. The apartment smelled delicious as she mixed the batter for what she still thought of as Miriam's chocolate cake, even though it had become one of her own specialties.

She put the cake in the oven and started to write a letter to her mother. There wasn't much she could say. What was the point in pouring her heart out when her mother was so far away, and when she thought Fannie was happily married and living a life of luxury in America? So she wrote about school, the new clothes she bought to wear to shul, and even the meal she was cooking. Mama loved to try new recipes.

Suddenly, she smelled something burning. How had she not noticed the time? She quickly got the cake out of oven but not before one whole side was blackened. She was sure Mary and

Simon would make light of it, but Caleb would be angry. Her cooking, the one thing she was sure of, had failed her. It would be one more thing that made her home unhappy.

CHAPTER 10

Fannie and her father were leaving shul on a crisp fall Saturday a few weeks after the High Holy Days. Fannie had worn her new clothes without any pleasure. When they prayed to be inscribed in the "Book of Life" for a good year, she prayed for a baby. Outwardly, nothing had changed between her and Caleb since their argument. He worked long hours; she shopped, cleaned, made his breakfast and dinner. Conversation between them at home was almost nonexistent, but when they were with family or friends, she did her best to keep up appearances. Only a baby, she thought, would make things better.

Fannie was surprised to see Noah at the bottom of the stairs, and even more surprised to see he wasn't alone. He was holding hands with a young woman.

"Gut Shabbos Papa, Feige," he said.

"Gut Shabbos, Noah," said Fannie.

"And who have you brought with you?" asked Papa, staring at the young woman.

"This is Eve, Papa. We're going to be married, and we've come to ask for your blessing."

Asher was still for a moment. "I'm sure I'm not hearing you correctly. Married? And this is the first I'm learning about it? You decided this without your Papa? Without a shadkhen? Young lady, please excuse us while I talk to my son."

Fannie stepped forward, ready to take the girl's arm and lead her away.

"No, Papa. Anything you have to say Eve should hear too. I would never have allowed some old man who cared nothing about my dreams to arrange a match for me. This is America. Eve and I are both students. We want the same things in life and we're in love. But you don't have to worry, Papa, she comes from a good Jewish family. They came from Germany many years ago. We'll be married under the chuppah, I promise you. And we'll wait for Mama to be here too."

"I shouldn't worry!" Papa sputtered. "My son who doesn't pray with me on Shabbos morning tells me he'll be married under the chuppah so I shouldn't worry. My son brings me this girl from a family I've never met and tells me he's getting married. Not asking, only telling. This is what a son does to his father in America?"

"Papa, please." Noah held out his hands, pleading.

"No. Let me be." He began to walk away.

"But Papa." Noah reached out to grab his father's arm.

"No 'but Papa' Noah. Is this why I'm working in a factory where my cousin bosses me around like a common laborer? Is this why I'm bringing my wife and children to America? So my daughter Freyda will meet a strange man and decide to marry him without asking her Papa's permission? So my youngest son, my Levi, will forget God like his brothers? So my wife Bluma's heart will be broken? No, better I should go home to Kamenetz and stay with them there. America is worse than the Cossacks for the Jews." He shook off Noah's hand and continued walking.

Noah and Eve remained where they were, silently regrasping each other's hands. Noah glared. Eve looked as though she were about to cry.

"Papa," said Fannie. "Don't go away angry. Let's find a place to sit and talk."

"Another time, Feigele. Another time." He strode away.

"Papa." Noah moved to follow him.

"No, Noah, let him go." Fannie held him back. "He needs time to calm down. This is just what he was afraid of when he saw how much you and Daniel had changed. I'll talk to him."

"Please make him understand."

"I'll try, Noah, but you must be patient. Now introduce me to this girl you plan to marry."

"Feige, this is Eve." He introduced the pretty, petite girl at his side. She had a heart shaped face, hazel eyes and golden blond hair in a long braid. Fannie noted that her clothes were well-made; they looked expensive. She wore small pearl earrings and a gold locket around her neck. Fannie wondered if she wore those clothes at school, or if she had dressed to impress Noah's father.

"It's good to meet you, Eve." Fannie reached out to take her hand. "Sometimes my brother forgets I am called Fannie here in America. I'm sorry you had to meet my Papa this way, he's a good man. It will take a little time, but I'm sure he'll give you his blessing." *Should I pretend when I'm not sure at all?*

"Thank you, Fannie." Eve smiled. "Noah has told me so much about you. I hope we'll be friends."

"I'm sure we will. Tell Noah to bring you for dinner soon and we'll get to know each other. Now, go enjoy the rest of this beautiful day and the colored leaves, you two. Let me go find Papa."

Fannie caught up with him at the Fine's home where the family was getting ready for Shabbos lunch. Caleb and Max, Rachel and the children had just arrived.

"Doovidel! You're getting so big." Fannie bent down to hold out her arms for her nephew who was just learning to walk. "And look how big Avigail's getting. May I?" She reached out for the baby who had been born at the end of June.

"Of course," said Rachel, handing her the infant and a cloth for Fannie to put over her shoulder. "Be careful. I just nursed her and she may spit up. I don't want your dress to get ruined."

I wouldn't care if all my dresses were ruined if I could have a baby like this. Fannie kissed the baby's forehead, but her pleasure was diminished by the expression on Caleb's face. She knew he was angry he didn't have a baby of his own yet.

Conversation over lunch was animated. Even though a few weeks had passed, they were still talking about the Rabbi's sermon on Rosh Hashanah. He had spoken in favor of more laws to protect workers from horrible conditions like those at the Triangle Shirtwaist Company. The fire there in March had killed over one hundred workers, mostly young women and girls. It was a shanda, he said, a shame that Jewish owners allowed such terrible conditions in their factory.

Caleb and his father were offended.

"He had no right to talk like that, as though we're all murderers," said Caleb. "What about all our hard work? We make our money honestly and don't treat our workers like the Shirtwaist Kings treated theirs. We don't need laws to tell us what to do."

Although she'd never say it, Fannie thought Caleb was wrong. She looked over at Papa, wondering what he thought, but he remained silent.

"Come sit with me in the yard, Papa," Fannie said as soon as lunch was over.

"I don't want to talk about Noah, Feigele."

"So, we'll just sit and enjoy the afternoon sun," said Fannie. "Soon it will be too cold to sit outside."

After a while, Fannie's father broke the silence. "He's a good boy, Noah. If he wants to marry this Eve, she's probably a nice girl. A student, I don't know, but maybe that's the right kind of wife for him. I don't think she'll be like you, Feigele, but I suppose he won't go hungry."

Fannie let him talk.

"But would it have hurt for him to come to me first? A shadkhen, maybe we could have done without. But permission? That's not our way. But married under the chuppah after your mother gets here, that's something. What do you think?"

"He loves you, Papa. And now he loves her too. If you make him choose, what then? Will I have to choose too? Shabbos dinner with my Mama and Papa, or my brother and his new family?"

"And what do I really know about this Eve's family?" Asher continued his litany of worries. "German Jews, Feigele, the ones who couldn't wait to get rid of us in Berlin and who look down on us here."

"Not all of them, Papa. Noah would never love a girl from a family like that."

"Maybe not. I don't want to lose him, and your Mama would never forgive me. But what's next? If he has a son will there be a *bris*? Will he obey the commandment for circumcision, or reject God's covenant with Abraham too? He's breaking my heart, Feigele. I need more time."

Noah, usually a regular at Shabbos dinners, stopped coming. Asher pretended not to notice. Miriam looked at Fannie for an explanation, but she said nothing. If Papa wanted to talk about it, he would tell Miriam himself. Caleb was contemptuous when she told him what was happening. "Your father's a fool. He's in America now. He'll drive away his sons and end up a bitter old man. Can't you make him see reason?"

Fannie had no response.

Several agonizing months went by. She knew her Papa was suffering but had no idea what to say or how to help. She wondered if he had written to Mama, sure that Mama would tell him to forgive Noah and make peace. Noah reached out to her often, but she had nothing to report.

Finally, Asher took Fannie aside. "Tell Noah to come talk to me after shul next Shabbos," he told her.

The following Saturday morning, Fannie was surprised to find Noah waiting for them before services, rather than after. She couldn't remember the last time he had come to pray. Father and son went into the sanctuary together as Fannie climbed the stairs to the balcony. When services ended, they met on the front steps and walked away from the crowd.

"Please forgive me, Papa," said Noah as soon as they were alone. "I should have come to you sooner."

"Yes, you should have."

"Please understand, Papa. I didn't set out to make you unhappy. I love Eve, and you will too if you'll give her a chance."

"I believe you, and I'm sure she's a wonderful girl, Noah, but this is not our way. What do we really know about her family? And what about your children? What kind of Jewish home will you make for them?"

"It's true our ways will be different, Papa, but my children will know they're Jewish. We won't let them forget who they are and after all, they'll have you and Mama to teach them."

"Here's what I propose, Noah. Let me meet with Eve's father. If we come to an agreement, then you'll have my blessing."

Noah looked toward Fannie, who nodded.

"Thank you, Papa. I'll arrange it," said Noah, weeping openly. The two men embraced and then opened their arms to include Fannie.

"Thank you, Papa," said Fannie. "Now, let's go have lunch before we all freeze."

12 November, 1911

Dear Mama,

For some time I've been afraid I wouldn't be able to write this letter. Just after the holidays, Noah told Papa he intended to marry a girl named Eve. Without asking Papa to arrange for a shadkhen or give his permission, he came to him for his blessing. Papa refused. He was so angry he wouldn't even talk to Noah.

Perhaps it's hard for you to understand, but things are so different here. Young people have more say about who they'll marry, which I think is a good thing. Not everyone who marries a stranger their parents choose is as lucky as you and Papa.

Noah has changed, but he still loves Papa and wanted his blessing. I don't know who was more heartbroken when he wouldn't grant it, Papa or Noah.

How I missed you then, Mama. I knew you'd know the right thing to say to make Papa feel better and to help them reconcile. I was afraid it wouldn't happen, and our family would be torn apart.

Papa finally relented on the condition that he and Eve's father would meet and come to a mutual agreement.

I don't know what they discussed, but Papa has blessed the marriage! Eve is beautiful and smart—I know you'll love her. And best of all, they're not going to be married until next year, when you'll be here. We'll all celebrate together!

From Daniel there is still nothing about getting married. Perhaps now that he's seen how happy Noah is, he'll think more about it.

> *I'm so happy for all of us, Mama.*
>
> *Your loving daughter,*
>
> *Fannie*

★ ★ ★

Fannie put the newspaper away. She had to get busy with dinner, but it was hard to tear herself away from the news about the Titanic. She read the descriptions of the survivors' terror when they realized the "unsinkable" ship was sinking fast and there weren't enough lifeboats to save them all. More than 1,000 people drowned. She wanted this dinner, the first time Eve was meeting the Fines, to be special, but she was having trouble concentrating.

Fannie had met Eve a few times and had heard the story of how she and Noah met at a café where they were both studying. He had asked her what she was reading, and she told him it was a book about the human skeleton. She was studying to be a nurse at the Bellevue Training School for Nurses, a dream of hers ever since she read about Florence Nightingale when she was a child.

Fannie couldn't help feeling bitter. Her one dream, to have a loving husband and children, had so far been denied to her. Caleb was cold and distant, and she had no one to confide in. *I don't know how much I'd tell Mama if she were here, but she'd still be a comfort to me.* She tasted the salty tears trickling down her cheek as she thought about how Mama always knew the right thing to say.

Stop dwelling on what you don't have, she told herself when she realized how late it was getting. Being bitter won't change anything. She picked up the lid to check on the chicken soup and took the *kneidlach* out of the icebox to add them to the pot to simmer. Her matzo balls were light and fluffy, just like her mother's. She checked on the brisket, which had been cooking slowly, surrounded by onions, potatoes, and carrots, and turned the oven down.

Once the table was set, she went to dress and wait for the family, hoping Caleb would be on time for once. Caleb didn't care about the traditions. He often came home well after she lit the Shabbos candles. Echet Chayil? It would never occur to him to praise his wife as a woman of valor, to acknowledge her hard work or the home she made for them. She had never felt so alone.

Papa was the first to arrive. "Gut Shabbos. How are you Feigele?"

"Good, Papa, you?" She put on a smile to hide the turmoil inside her and kissed his cheek.

"Not too bad."

The doorbell rang before they had a chance to talk, and Noah brought Eve into the apartment. Fannie had expected a girl studying to be a nurse to be plain and wearing glasses, her eyesight ruined from too much reading, but Eve was beautiful. Her eyes sparkled.

"Welcome." Fannie kissed them both.

"Thank you, Fannie." If Eve was nervous about her first dinner with the extended family, it didn't show. She handed Fannie a small white box from the bakery, tied with red and white twine.

"These are for you," said Eve. "You don't have to share them," she added with a smile.

Fannie smelled cinnamon and decided she'd save whatever was inside for breakfast the next day. "Come. Sit here in the living room while we wait for the others."

Noah and Eve sat together on the sofa and Asher took one of the armchairs while Fannie went to put the box away.

"Tell me more about nursing school. Is it very hard?" Asher asked.

"Yes, some of it. We're learning anatomy now, which is what I was studying when I met Noah. Have you heard about Florence Nightingale's methods for cleanliness in the hospital? My school—"

They were interrupted by the doorbell and Fannie went to greet Miriam and Charles. Rachel had called earlier to say that the baby had a cold, so they were staying home. Miriam admitted that she too had been feeling under the weather but was glad she could come.

While introductions were being made, Daniel, who already knew Eve well, arrived, and to Fannie's surprise, Caleb walked in just a few minutes later. She was relieved not to have to make excuses for him.

"Just in time. Come, everyone, let's sit down for dinner."

Fannie lit the Shabbos candles, covered her eyes and recited the prayer her mother had taught her.

Gut Shabbos, Mama, I think of you every time I use my beautiful candlesticks.

"Caleb, will you say the Kiddush and the *Motzi*?" It was not something he usually did, but in deference to his father-in-law Caleb recited the blessings, starting with the wine in the silver cup at his place. Then he took the freshly baked challah from under the silk cloth Fannie had embroidered and blessed God for "bringing forth bread from the earth." Everyone took a small piece.

The conversation over dinner naturally turned to the Titanic. They talked about the famous Jews who had died, men of vast wealth. John Jacob Astor, whose family had gotten rich from the fur trade, was descended from a Jewish family. Benjamin Guggenheim and Isidor Strauss, who owned the store where Fannie had gotten her wedding dress, had also drowned.

Fannie's heart raced as she imagined the other passengers left on board, hopeless and afraid. "I'm not surprised most of the people who died were third class passengers, people like me and Papa," she said. The family stared at her, surprised by her unusual outburst.

Daniel was quick to agree. "It never changes. The rich get richer, and the poor pay the price."

"And to think, soon Papa will be traveling to bring Mama and the children here—" Miriam put her arm on Fannie's to stop her. "You'll upset your papa," she said softly.

Fannie looked around the table, imagining her loved ones on the ship, or waiting for news. How long would it take for the news to reach people in small towns like Kamenetz? For people like Mama to find out that they'd never see their husbands, wives, sons and daughters, again? That their bodies were at the bottom of the ocean forever, their poor Jewish souls unable to rest because they'd never have a proper burial. What if it had been her and Papa?

Absorbed in her sadness, she almost missed Caleb telling everyone that the S.S. Lapland, the ship she and Papa had sailed on, was taking the surviving crew members home to England.

"Were you ever afraid the Lapland would sink, Fannie?" asked Eve.

Fannie thought back to her own journey. "Not really. I was too busy trying to survive the terrible food and smells and too worried about Papa to think about sinking. And Samuel—" Fannie caught herself. What could she say about him without revealing what he had meant to her?

"Who's Samuel?" asked Caleb.

She thought quickly. "He was the oldest son of the woman in the bed next to mine, Hannah. I met her and her two younger boys in the women's quarters the day we boarded. He and his father helped Papa when he was seasick." *I don't know why I said his name, but how can I think of the ship without thinking of him?*

"Is he in New York now?" Caleb pressed her.

"I don't know. Hannah said they were planning to settle here, but Papa and I said goodbye to them before we left the ship."

Caleb appeared satisfied and returned to discussing the Titanic. "I wonder what the investigation will uncover?"

"The company probably cut corners when she was built," said Daniel. "Anything to increase profits."

As the conversation swirled around her, Fannie's thoughts returned to Samuel. She imagined him with a little red-haired daughter. During the day he worked in a factory, but at night he went to college to become a doctor. Wouldn't it be strange if he and Eve met?

"Fannie, are you daydreaming again?"

Caleb's voice startled her out of her reverie. "Oh, I'm sorry, I can't stop thinking about all those poor people who drowned. I'll get dessert. I made chocolate marble cake."

When she came back to the table, Miriam was making her excuses. "I'm feeling worse than I expected. Please forgive me Eve. We'll talk another time, I'm sure." Caleb walked his parents to the door.

Eve and Noah got ready to leave after dessert. "We both have lots of studying to do tomorrow," said Noah. "Thanks for dinner, Feige, it was delicious, as always."

"Yes, Fannie outdid herself tonight," Caleb corrected Noah.

"Thank you both for having us." Eve and Fannie embraced warmly. "And my mother said to be sure to tell you that she would like to have the whole family over soon. She'll telephone you. Goodnight, Mr. Dorfman, Caleb, Daniel." She and Noah walked out arm in arm. Asher and Daniel left shortly afterward.

Caleb sat at the kitchen table while Fannie did the dishes.

"It's a terrible job, nurse," he said. "Think of all the diseases she might bring home."

"I never thought of it that way, only how important it is to help people who are sick or hurt. I would want someone like Eve to take care of me, wouldn't you?"

"A nurse is only a helper. It's the doctor who cures people."

It was just like Caleb to belittle a woman. "But the doctor can't do it alone. I like her and I'm sure she'd never take any risks that would harm my brother or their children."

Caleb shrugged. "Are you almost finished? I'm ready for bed."

"Just about." But Fannie couldn't stop thinking about the Titanic. "Do you think you know anyone who was lost on the ship, Caleb? Someone from business? How could such a thing have happened?"

"Machines aren't perfect, Fannie. Accidents happen. Are you done now?"

"Yes," said Fannie. "I'll go get washed."

That night, after Caleb rolled over into his own bed, Fannie couldn't fall asleep. She couldn't stop thinking about Samuel and what might have been. She had so many fine things she wouldn't have had with Samuel, but what good were they? She never cared about them before her marriage and would give them all up to be happy. Samuel would have wanted to please her. He would have loved her for who she was and waited for a baby without blaming her. *If only* ... She looked over at Caleb, already sleeping soundly. Maybe happiness was too much to expect.

CHAPTER 11

Fannie ran to the bathroom. Even her small breakfast of tea and cereal made her nauseous. This is what I prayed for, she reminded herself as she wiped her mouth and went back to the kitchen for a glass of ginger ale to take away the sour taste. She had not been able to hold down a meal for the last week.

Caleb had begun asking her if she was expecting as soon as she was a few days late. Now she was certain. "Yes," she told him after dinner that night. "This time, I'm sure. We're having a baby."

"I'm so glad," he said. "But when will you stop being sick?"

"I don't know, Caleb." She was so used to his criticism, she wasn't sure if he cared about her, found her being sick distasteful, or worried about the baby. He had been so cruel over the last few months it was hard to know.

"I can't wait to tell everyone," he said.

"Let's not share the news yet," she told him, "Let's wait until after the third month. We've waited so long, let's not tempt the *ayin hara* now."

"I can't believe you still pay attention to those silly *bubbe-meises*. Like you said, we've waited a long time. The evil eye is finally looking the other way."

"Please, Caleb, the beginning is the most dangerous time. Let's wait."

"Well, if you really think you can stand to wait that long before sharing such good news."

"Let's try."

That night, Caleb went straight into his own bed.

"We can't risk hurting the baby," he said, turning away and falling asleep quickly.

"Let's go to my parents for Shabbos dinner this week," he said the next morning at breakfast. "I don't want you to strain yourself making dinner for the whole family."

"I'm fine, Caleb. It's not too much trouble. Perhaps toward the end …"

"Are you sure?"

"Of course, I'll enjoy it."

But when Friday came, she was almost sorry she had agreed to make dinner. She was more tired than she had ever been in her life. Luckily, the preparations were second nature to her. Dinner was ready and the table was set with almost an hour to spare before the Sabbath began at sundown. She sat in her armchair and closed her eyes. I'll just rest for a few minutes, she thought.

The next thing she knew the doorbell was ringing. Papa, Miriam, and Charles had arrived. They all sat in the living room, catching up on the week. Fannie tried to stay alert but found herself yawning. She was relieved when Caleb arrived and they could start dinner. She ate sparingly, hoping no one would notice. But over dessert, as Papa shared a letter from Mama filled with funny stories about Levi, she couldn't stifle another huge yawn.

"Fannie," said Miriam, "I've never seen you like this."

"I'm just—"

"Oh my goodness. Are you—?"

"Yes, she is, we're having a baby at last," Caleb announced before Fannie could make any other excuses.

"How wonderful. How are you feeling, Fannie?" She reached across the table to take Fannie's hand.

"*B'sha'ah tovah*, my child," said Papa, getting up to embrace her. "In good time. I only wish Mama were here, but I'll write to her tonight to tell her she's going to be a bubbe. Soon all of Kamenetz will know."

"Well done, son," said Charles.

Before she could respond, Fannie covered her mouth and ran to the bathroom.

"You poor thing," said Miriam when she returned. She smoothed Fannie's hair back off her forehead where it had come undone. "I was the same way. But it passes."

"I'm so glad to hear that. I thought it was supposed to be morning sickness, not morning, noon and night sickness."

"Next week let's talk to Rachel about her midwife. She was wonderful and we should make sure she'll be available. And in a few months we'll shop for everything the baby needs. Of course we won't bring anything into the house until the baby's born. No use tempting the ayin hara."

"What, you too with the superstitions Mama?" Caleb laughed.

"Tragedies happen, Caleb, and you don't need a house full of baby things to torment you if they do," Miriam responded seriously. "Customs have a reason, even if they seem like superstitions to you. But don't worry, Fannie's a healthy young woman. Everything will be just fine."

Fannie couldn't help thinking of Gittel but quickly pushed the thought away. This was America and she'd have the best of care.

"Here's to Caleb and Fannie and their child." Charles raised his glass.

"To a healthy baby," added Papa. "He'll be crawling around when Mama gets here, and Freyda and Levi will think they have a new toy."

"And *naches* for all the grandparents," said Miriam. "Now you'll know the joy of being a zayde, Asher."

Fannie smiled as everyone drank. Her son—she had already started to think of the baby as a boy—would have grandparents who adored him.

★ ★ ★

"I know you wanted to wait to tell them, Fannie. But I'm just so proud I couldn't help myself," said Caleb when everyone had left.

"You were right, Caleb. It would have been hard to keep it secret. And I was relieved to hear your mother was as sick as I am. There will be other things she and Rachel can tell me, things only women who've had children will know. So really, it's fine."

"Sit down on the sofa and put your feet up. We need to get a footstool for your chair."

Fannie laughed and sat in her own chair. "Thank you, I'm fine for now. I've always dreamed of making things for the baby—for our baby—in this chair, and now I finally will."

1 May 1912

Dear Mama,

At last - God has finally heard my prayers. I'm going to have a baby! He will be born around the new year—and yes, somehow, I know it's a boy. That will please Caleb. He wants a boy to inherit the business.

I didn't want to tell anyone so soon, but Miriam guessed last night when I nearly fell asleep at the table. Were you sick at the beginning? If you were, I guess I was too young to notice, or at least too young to realize why. I'm sick all day long.

I can't help thinking about Gittel, Mama. But Miriam is going to call Rachel's midwife for me and I'm sure everything will go well, so please don't worry about me.

Of course, I wish you were here, but soon you will be, and I'll have a fat baby in my arms when I come to greet you. Maybe he'll already know how to say Bubbe!

Your loving daughter,

Feige

That Monday afternoon, the doorbell rang. When Fannie went to look through the peephole, a large Negro man was at the door with a footstool in his arms.

"Delivery for Mrs. Fine," he said. "From Mr. Fine."

Fannie let him in and had him place the footstool in front of her chair before he left. Dark blue with light blue and white flowers, it matched her chair perfectly, and when Fannie tried it out, was quite comfortable.

"Good," said Caleb when he arrived home and saw the footstool. "My mother helped me pick it out. Make sure to use it so the baby has a well-rested mama."

"Thank you, Caleb, it's lovely."

"I've spoken to my mother, Fannie. She said she can spare Clara one day a week to help you around the house and she'll look for someone to come more often toward the end. I don't want you carrying heavy packages up the stairs."

"Caleb, please. I may feel differently in a few months, but I can manage perfectly well for now." She thought of her own mother, who kept the house and cooked for four when she was carrying Levi. And what did Fannie have to do besides care for their small apartment and cook for two? Such luxury would be unimaginable to the women of Kamenetz.

The next two months passed uneventfully. Fannie's nausea passed. Her breasts were tender and swollen, but other than that her condition was hardly noticeable. When she looked at herself sideways in the mirror, she saw only a small bump which she knew wasn't visible to anyone else.

Life barely changed as she shopped, cooked, and sat and chatted with the neighbors, and yet everything was different. Now she felt like she belonged among the young mothers.

A few weeks later, Mary stopped by.

"I'm so happy to see you," said Fannie, putting out tea and home-made cookies.

"I'm so excited for you, Fannie, and you look wonderful."

"Look." Fannie drew her skirt tight across her belly to show Mary the tiny swelling.

"Better you than me," said Mary. "I'm just not ready. And Simon agrees. We like our life the way it is so we're going to wait. I got a pessary as soon as we got married. Of course our families are disappointed, so we just pretend it hasn't happened yet."

Fannie wasn't sure she understood what Mary was telling her, although, as she had guessed, Mary didn't want a baby yet.

"You look surprised, but that's probably because you've always wanted a baby. Have you heard about Margaret Sanger?"

"I've read about what she's doing for poor immigrant woman in the *Forverts*, but I thought it's against the law in America."

"Yes, it is, but it shouldn't be. Why should women be forced to have babies they don't want or can't afford? Why should the government decide when a man and wife start their families? Or how many children they have?"

"I never thought about it that way. I once heard Mama telling a neighbor about a woman who was desperate not to have her seventh baby, but she stopped talking when she knew I was listening. But what is a pessary?"

Mary blushed. "I've never talked about it before. And you promise not to tell anyone?"

"Please don't be embarrassed. I'm ignorant about so many things and I'd like to know."

"You put it inside yourself down there." She pointed between her legs. "That way you can't make a baby. I put mine in every time Simon and I—"

"You don't need to say more." Fannie stopped her. "Thank you for telling me. I didn't know about such things. And I'll keep your secret."

"Good, now let's talk about something else."

★ ★ ★

Chaya, the midwife, came to talk to her. "No need to eat for two," she said. "The baby will get plenty of nutrition if you eat normally. Walk every day and get plenty of fresh air." She took out a wooden instrument that looked like the earpiece of a telephone. "This is a Pinard horn," she said. "When you're further along I'll use it to hear the baby's heartbeat. Would you like to see how it works?"

She held the horn against her own chest and showed Fannie how to listen.

"I hear it." Fannie was in awe. "My baby will sound like that?"

"Yes," said Chaya. "It's a wonderful moment when you hear the heartbeat. And even though we know how babies are made; I still think of it as a miracle from God."

"So do I."

"Good. When your time is closer, I'll tell you what to expect during labor. Women will tell you lots of stories about their labor — don't listen to them. Every woman is different, and I'll help you with the pain. Besides, you'll be so happy when the baby is born, you'll forget all about your labor. If we didn't forget, who would want more children? Any questions before I go?"

Fannie shook her head and walked her to the door.

"Good, I'll see you next month. Oh, and relations with your husband are perfectly fine. Enjoy your last nights before there's a crying baby to interrupt."

"I'll tell him," said Fannie. She didn't want Chaya to know that Caleb hadn't come near her since learning about the baby. It wasn't that she missed it, he was too hurried and oblivious to her satisfaction for that, but hadn't he told her he had needs? Fannie knew there were men who went to other women to satisfy themselves. She had read letters about them from desperate wives in the "Bintel Brief." Could Caleb be one of them?

★ ★ ★

Although she and Caleb didn't talk much more than they had before, evenings felt different. He took an interest in the baby clothes she was sewing and glanced up frequently from whatever he was reading. It was as though he wanted to make certain that the baby was still there. One night, he even offered to help clear the table, something that never would have occurred to him before. She knew it was all for the baby's sake, but she liked this kinder Caleb. Her own happiness grew each time she finished a tiny article of baby clothing.

A few weeks later, as she cleared the breakfast dishes, Fannie felt the baby move. It was such a tiny flutter she couldn't be sure. She pressed her hands to her belly, but didn't feel it again until the afternoon. *My baby.* She sat down and wept. All the months of waiting, of Caleb scolding her, had taken their toll. Now she could rejoice. She was going to be a mother, and if Caleb wasn't the husband she had dreamed of, at least he had become more caring. Perhaps she had underestimated how important a baby was to him. Maybe it was only the disappointment that made him cruel.

She wondered what kind of father he would be. His own father was more devoted to making money than to people, even his own family. He rarely showed any tenderness. That's the side of Caleb she had seen most often. His mother, on the other hand, was quick to express her love. Fannie hoped he would take after Miriam.

"I thought you'd never get home," she said as soon as Caleb walked through the door that evening. Take off your coat and sit next to me." Caleb looked at her without understanding as she placed his hands where she had felt the baby move.

"What?" Impatient, he started to pull his hands away.

"Wait, be still."

And then he felt it too. "Is that—?"

"Yes, it's our baby, letting us know he's there."

"A son?"

"We won't know until he arrives, but somehow I feel sure."

"The next generation of Fine and Sons," he said. "Someday the company will belong to him."

Fannie's clothes started to get tight on her. Chaya told her to stop wearing her corset—it was bad for her heart and stomach—and she gladly complied. This time Caleb was happy for her to shop for new clothes.

"Being with child becomes you," he said. "I want everyone at shul to admire the woman having my child."

It was hard for Fannie to believe that she would actually fill out the clothes she bought. When Freyda was born she was only seven and when Levi was born her own body was changing so much she didn't pay much attention to what was happening to her mother.

Caleb noticed the baby kicking when she sat and sewed.

"Does it hurt?" he asked.

"No, it just feels strange. Imagine, soon this will be a baby who cries and eats and whose diaper needs to be changed."

"I'll leave the diapers to you," said Caleb, "But I can't wait to hold my son."

"Don't forget, Caleb, tomorrow your mother, Rachel and I are going to Macy's for baby furniture. Then we'll all meet for dinner at your parents' house."

The next morning before she left, a letter from her mother arrived.

1 June, 1912

My darling Feigele,

Your news made me so happy. By the time you get this I'm sure your sickness will have passed and you'll be showing. You'll probably be thinking you can't get any bigger, but you will!

I'll miss being there with you Feigele, holding your hand when the pains come, but I trust Miriam and Rachel and Eve to take care of you. I only pray you'll deliver safely and have a healthy baby. I can't wait to spoil my grandson—but I'll be equally happy to spoil my granddaughter.

And I am so glad your child will be born in America, where it is safe. Families are leaving Kamenetz all the time now. Some to Warsaw, a few to America. I know I will be sad when the time comes, but I will also be happy to leave the Cossacks behind. Until then, we'll keep going about our lives as usual.

Know that I am thinking of you.

With all my love,

Mama

Fannie put the letter away along with all the others she was saving and hurried to leave on time.

"It sems like so long ago when you took me to my first department store, Miriam," she said as she boarded the subway with Miriam and Rachel. "I was afraid of the subway and the elevator."

"I remember," said Miriam. "It was the day you picked out your wedding dress. And here you are about to be a mother."

The three women stopped to look at the store when they came up out of the subway. Even experienced New York shoppers were in awe of its size. Inside, they found their way to the baby department.

"Just look at these beautiful things," said Fannie, fingering the tiny white infant dresses.

"The dresses, blankets, and bibs you embroidered are even more beautiful." said Rachel. "You only need a pram and a cot. And diapers of course—and you should get those new rubber pants like the ones I have for Avigail."

"I wish they had been invented sooner," said Miriam. "It would have saved a lot of washing!"

Rachel and Miriam helped Fannie pick out a large gray wicker baby carriage.

"I can't wait to join the other mothers walking along the Parkway," said Fannie. "And Caleb will love walking alongside us on Saturday afternoons, showing off."

Next, she selected a white iron baby cot. "This is perfect for the nursery," she said. "I've already made white lace curtains."

After adding diapers and rubber pants, they had everything rung up and placed on hold for delivery after the baby was born and went up to the store restaurant.

"You can't imagine what a treat this is," said Rachel as they ate. "You'll see, Fannie, no matter how much you love your children, you'll look forward to a day out with grownups."

"And I'm glad you came," said Fannie. "I don't know what I would have done without the two of you to help me."

"We've only—" Miriam started to ask but was overcome with a fit of coughing.

"Here," said Rachel. "Drink some water." She held a glass out to Miriam.

"Are you unwell?" asked Fannie.

"No, I just swallowed wrong."

"I'm afraid I really must be going," said Rachel. "I don't want to take advantage of my mother."

"She's probably having a wonderful day with the children all to herself," said Miriam. "But we should go."

After dinner, Miriam told Fannie and Caleb to follow her upstairs. There, in the room that had been Fannie's, was a handmade wooden cradle.

"This was yours and Max's, Caleb. Rachel's parents gave her one from her family, so this one was still in the attic—just waiting for your children."

"It's beautiful, Mama. I hope we'll use it many times."

"And this is for you, Fannie." She held out a large white box.

"But you've given me so much already …"

"Please open it, dear, it will give me pleasure."

Fannie opened the box. Inside was a white silk bed jacket with blue ribbon ties. "It's lovely," she said, reaching to hug her mother-in-law. "Thank you so much."

"I know you make your own beautiful things, but I wanted you to have something from me for when the baby's born. You'll wear it when you're in bed, resting."

"My mother does love to spoil you, doesn't she," said Caleb when they got home.

"And I hope we'll spoil our child someday. It's a way to say I love you."

Fannie couldn't imagine being happier than she was now.

CHAPTER 12

Eve had stopped by for a visit on a day off from school. She and Fannie were sitting in the kitchen having tea and cookies.

"It's worth a trip just for your *mandelbrot*, Fannie," said Eve, helping herself to a second piece. "How are you feeling?"

"Fat," said Fannie, running her hands over her round belly to show Eve. "But seriously, I'm fine. Chaya said the baby's heartbeat is strong and I have about six weeks to go."

"Well, you look wonderful, and I've heard that means it's a girl."

"You too? Surely they don't teach you those bubbemeises in nursing school. Every woman I've met, even total strangers, has a prediction."

"Well, they're all right at least half the time," laughed Eve. "The most important thing is that you feel good, and the baby is growing on schedule. How is Caleb coping?"

"He's over the moon, Eve. Baby, baby, baby. I've never seen him this excited about anything that wasn't business."

"I'm so happy for you. And Noah is too—he can't wait to be an uncle."

"And how is he? I've barely seen him these last few months."

"He's so busy between working, classes and studying, but I'll make sure he comes by soon."

"And Daniel, do you see him often? I haven't seen him either."

Eve grew quiet. "No, Fannie. He has his own friends, and we hardly ever see him. I don't want to upset you, especially now, but Noah worries about him. Of course we'd never say anything to your Papa."

"Papa has been concerned about Daniel for a long time, even before my wedding. I promised him I would talk to Daniel, but he avoids anything serious when I try. He just tells me to stop worrying."

"He's a grown man, Fannie, making his own decisions. Even if we think he's wrong, there's nothing any of us can do."

"He's my brother, Eve." Fannie used her napkin to wipe the tears that were starting.

"Oh, you poor thing. I'm so sorry I upset you."

"It's not your fault. I know he's hiding something. After the baby comes, I'll make him talk to me."

"I'm still sorry I mentioned it, and I hate to leave you upset, but I need to go. Let me help you put these things away."

Fannie gasped and clutched her belly as she stood.

"What's wrong?"

"Oh, nothing, just a stronger than usual kick. This baby hardly gives me a moment's peace. He's going to be an Olympic star, just like Jim Thorpe last summer."

"Are you sure?"

"Of course. I should be used to it by now."

The two of them cleared the table and put the dishes in the sink.

"I'll finish later," said Fannie as she walked Eve to the door. "I'm so glad you came—it was nice for the two of us to have time alone."

"I promise I'll come again soon," said Eve. She put on her coat and hugged Fannie. "Take care of yourself."

Caleb arrived home a while later. As soon as dinner ended and the dishes were done, Fannie began to prepare for bed. "I'm especially tired tonight, Caleb, so I think I'll go to bed early."

"Sleep well."

Sometime in the middle of the night Fannie was awakened by a shooting pain in her belly and realized that the sheet under her was soaked.

"Caleb," she cried out. "Caleb, something's wrong. Call Chaya."

Caleb rushed out of the bedroom. When he came back, Fannie was moaning.

"My mother is on her way too. What can I do?"

"I don't know. This is what Chaya said labor would be like, but it's much too soon. I'm scared, Caleb."

"They'll be here soon. I'll wait for them at the door."

"Please, don't leave me."

Caleb sat helplessly on his own bed as she cried out with each new pain.

As soon as he heard the doorbell he bolted from the room and came back with his mother.

Miriam went right to Fannie and took her hand. "I'm here now, child. Everything will be all right."

Turning to her son, she said, "Caleb, bring some clean sheets and towels and go heat up the kettle."

Caleb, relieved to have something to do, left to do as he was told.

Chaya arrived a few minutes later to find Caleb pacing in the living room.

"The baby?" he asked.

"It's early, but I won't know until I've examined Fannie. Wait out here."

"Fannie, tell me what's happening. When did the pains start? Has your water broken? Miriam, I'm glad you're here."

"I don't know, I don't know," Fannie whimpered. "I may have felt something this afternoon, but I thought it was just the baby kicking. The bed was wet when I woke up and the pains are coming fast, not slowly like you said they would at the beginning."

"Slide down and let me look. I think this baby wants to come earlier than we expected. Miriam, can you help me get her to the end of the bed?"

Together, they helped Fannie slide her bottom to the edge of the bed and raise her knees. Chaya covered her with a clean sheet to examine her.

"You're in labor, Fannie. The head is down, and you're fully dilated—that means your body is ready for the baby to be born now. I know we haven't practiced yet, but do you remember what I told you about breathing? Miriam will hold your hand."

She glanced at Miriam; her worry clear to the older woman.

When the next contraction came Fannie screamed and Caleb threw open the door.

Chaya looked up at him. "It's normal for her to yell," she assured him. He retreated hastily.

The contractions grew stronger. Fannie panted and yelled and fell back, exhausted. "Am I going to die like Gittel?" she moaned.

"No, Fannie, I promise. On this next one, I want you to push. Good girl. Now rest up for the next one. It won't be long now. Are you ready? Push! That's it, that's it."

The baby slid out, tiny, quiet, and still. Chaya quickly cut the cord and massaged him vigorously. She breathed into his mouth and nostrils and rubbed him again. She kept trying—massaging, breathing, massaging. But she finally looked up at Miriam and shook her head.

"Miriam, please give me a blanket." She wrapped the baby and motioned for Miriam to take him. Tears were streaming down Miriam's face as she turned away from Fannie to shield her from the motionless bundle in her arms.

"Where's my baby? Why isn't he crying? I want my baby!" Fannie tried to sit up, looking around wildly.

"I'm so sorry, Fannie," said Chaya. "It was too soon."

"Noooo," Fannie wailed. "Give him to me. Let me hold my baby."

"Are you sure?"

"Please, I want to say goodbye to my baby."

Chaya took the baby back from Miriam and placed him gently in Fannie's outstretched arms. "Here he is Fannie."

Fannie slowly unwrapped her son and examined each tiny finger and toe. He was perfect. How could he not be kicking like he had inside her? She kissed his wrinkled forehead and handed him back to Chaya before collapsing into the pillows, wracked with sobs.

Miriam went out to Caleb. "I'm sorry son. The baby—" She broke down.

"What was it?"

"A boy." She reached out for him, but he turned away and, without another word, grabbed his coat and walked out the door.

"Caleb," Miriam called after him. "Come back, Fannie needs you."

But he was gone.

The following morning, when Fannie had been taken care of and the room cleaned, Chaya touched Fannie's shoulder gently. "Fannie, I have to go now. Miriam will take care of you."

Fannie opened her eyes briefly. "What did I do wrong, Chaya?"

"You mustn't think that, Fannie. Some babies just aren't ready for this world. It happens more often than you think, but women don't talk about it. All you need to think about now is getting strong again. I'll be back in a few days to make sure you're healing."

Miriam walked out with Chaya and returned with a bowl of soup. "You have to eat, Fannie," she said, holding out a spoon.

"Caleb?"

"He'll be back soon."

"He hates me for losing his son."

"Of course not, he just wants you to be able to rest."

Fannie took a sip of the soup. Miriam could make excuses, but Fannie knew better. Caleb would never forgive her. She turned her head away. "No more."

"Just a little," Miriam tried to coax her.

"Please, let me sleep."

Fannie dozed on and off in the darkened room, alone with her grief. She pretended not to hear the knock on the door, but Miriam walked in, followed by Asher.

He stood awkwardly by her bed. "My poor child."

"How could God do this to me, Papa?"

"It's not for us to understand, Feigele. It happened to your Mama twice after you were born. But then she had Freyda and Levi."

"I never knew."

"You were too young, but she suffered like you're suffering. The pain gets easier with time, I promise."

"You'll write to her? I can't, I just can't." Fannie sobbed.

Her father sat down and let her cry in his arms. "Rest, Feigele. I'll write to her. And listen to Miriam so you'll get well."

He kissed her forehead and let himself out quietly.

Fannie finally fell into a deep sleep. When she awoke, Caleb was in the room, taking some of his things out of his closet and drawers.

"You've come home."

"No, I'm just taking some things back to my parents' house."

"Please stay and talk to me, Caleb."

"What is there to talk about? You lost my son."

"Our son," said Fannie, weeping.

"I'll come back when you're better."

Rachel came a few days later. "I'm so sorry, but you'll have lots of healthy children, I'm sure of it," said Rachel, patting Fannie's arm.

"No one can be sure."

"You're young and strong, Fannie, your time will come."

Fannie listened politely but wasn't comforted. Young and strong hadn't saved her baby. "Thank you for coming, Rachel. I think I'd like to sleep now."

The next day, Eve came. "I'm so sorry, Fannie." She held out a large box of candy. "These are from Noah. He said chocolate is guaranteed to make you feel better."

Fannie took the box and put it aside. "I should have known something was wrong when you were here that day."

"You had no way to know. Come, let's get you out of bed. You should get up and walk a little each day."

She helped Fannie put on her robe and walk into the living room. "Miriam, why don't you go out for a while. You're looking tired and pale yourself. The fresh air will do you good. I'll sit with Fannie. Maybe she'll even share her chocolates."

Fannie laughed in spite of herself. "So that's why you brought them." She opened the box and took one of her favorite caramels before offering them to Eve.

"Go, Miriam, I'll be fine."

"I'll stay until Caleb gets home," Eve told Miriam as she was leaving.

Fannie began to cry silently as soon as the door was shut.

"What's wrong, Fannie?"

"He hasn't been home since that night."

"He's just trying to let you rest," she said, echoing Miriam's excuse, but Fannie could see the shock on her face. They both knew it wasn't true.

After Fannie had been able to get up and walk around on her own for several days, Miriam sat down to talk to her. "I'm going home tonight, Fannie. Caleb will be here with you at night, but until you're strong enough I'll come every day to prepare meals, or I'll send Clara."

She took Fannie in her arms. "It just takes time, Fannie."

Later that evening, Miriam sat on the sofa reading while Fannie rested in her chair with her feet up when Caleb arrived.

"My mother said you were better, but you still don't look well," he said when he saw her. He started to walk into the bedroom to put his things away, but turned around, still carrying his suitcase. "How did it happen? The one thing I wanted, and you couldn't give it to me."

"Please. It wasn't my fault."

Miriam stood up angrily.

"What's wrong with you, Caleb?"

"Taking her side as usual."

"I love you, son, but how could you be so cruel? You're not the only one in pain."

"Leave him be, Miriam. He's just disappointed." She had been expecting Caleb to react this way. There was no point in making him angrier.

Miriam embraced her daughter-in-law and walked past Caleb with a curt nod. "I expected better of you, Caleb."

Fannie watched Miriam leave, knowing the Caleb from before the baby was back and wondering how she was going to bear it.

CHAPTER 13

Fannie's recovery was slow. She had felt a new life inside her. Now she was hollowed out, empty. She asked Miriam to give away her maternity clothes.

"But I'm sure you'll be using them soon. Let me keep them for you."

"No, I'll never put them on again. I'll buy new clothes—if I ever need to."

At the beginning, each day brought a fresh reminder of her loss. The first time she went out, walking past her neighbors and their baby carriages brought tears to her eyes. But gradually they coaxed her into joining them. Without mentioning the baby, they let her know they understood her pain and steered the conversation to neutral topics.

When she started walking to the shops again, she was sure every shopkeeper was staring at her, wondering where her baby was. But Mr. Wang, the fruit store owner, a small Chinese man with a long handlebar mustache, simply urged her to taste an orange slice.

"The sweetest in all of Brooklyn, just for you," he said. Fannie took six of them to make juice for breakfast, dropping them into her mesh bag.

"The usual?" asked Sammy, the kosher butcher. He was a large man whose rolled up sleeves revealed thick, muscular forearms and who wore a blood-stained apron wrapped around his belly. "Just some chopped meat for us tonight," said Fannie, adding the package wrapped in brown butcher paper to her bag.

Helga, the woman behind the counter in the bakery, reached for the tray of rugelach as soon as she saw Fannie. "How did your husband like the cheese Danish from last week?" she asked as she tied the white box with the twine that hung from a spool.

"He loved them. I'll be back for more before the weekend."

She often spent afternoons with Rachel and the children. She was happy to sit on the floor and play with her niece and nephew. David, who was about to turn three, settled in her lap as she read to him from the book, *Mother Goose Rhymes*, that Miriam had given him for Hanukkah. She and Caleb had given him a bright red wooden caboose. For Avigail, they had chosen a "Teddy Bear," the stuffed toy animal invented by the owner of a candy store not far away in Brooklyn. For now, she'd make the most of being Aunt Fannie. But what if she never became Mama?

Fannie went back to night school after the new year, determined to keep improving her English. There wasn't another good friend like Anna there, but she exchanged pleasantries with the other students every evening as they walked up the steps. She liked her classes, especially when they learned about American history. Now when she went to Prospect Park, she could identify the Union heroes whose statues were on top of the arch.

She went to the neighborhood library regularly. The librarian, Mrs. Johnson, was a kindly woman who helped her pick out books she thought she'd enjoy. "This one just came in," she told Fannie one morning, handing her *The Secret Garden*, by Frances Hodgson Burnett. "It's meant to be a children's story, but I think you'll love it." Fannie had begun reading it immediately. Her progress was still slow, but the English dictionary Noah had given her helped. Novels were an escape from her grief.

Daily life returned to the way it had been before, and as she had feared, so did Caleb. Conversation at dinner was perfunctory and when they sat together in the living room, they barely spoke at all. Someone had taken away the unfinished baby clothes; she never asked where they were. When Mary asked if she would take orders again, she agreed. At least she could keep busy embroidering. When she wasn't sewing, she read the newspaper or one of her English books or just went to bed early. Caleb didn't seem to care what she did.

When Chaya had come to see her for the last time and told her she was perfectly healed and could start trying for another baby, Fannie didn't tell Caleb. Despite her yearning for a child, she would have been content if he never asked. But a few weeks later, instead of going to his own bed without a word, he stood at the foot of her bed.

"I want a son, Fannie. It must be all right to start relations again by now."

Fannie nodded mutely.

"Good, and this time you'll be more careful."

"It wasn't anything I did, Caleb. It happens to lots of women. Even my own mother lost two babies."

"I should have known. She must have passed her weakness on to you."

"You know that's not true. Why are you so hurtful?"

Without responding, he yanked down her blanket and began tugging at her nightgown.

"You'll tear it." cried Fannie.

Caleb ignored her and pushed inside her quickly. She didn't know what to hope for. If she didn't conceive, she knew he would be angry again, but it would be even worse if she lost another baby. She barely moved, waiting for it to be over.

The days were pleasant enough; she endured the evenings and the hasty relations Caleb demanded. She looked forward to

Shabbos dinners on Friday nights and to walking to shul with Papa on Saturday mornings. In shul, she allowed the familiar melodies to comfort her, but she no longer prayed. God had taken her baby and bound her to an unhappy marriage. What use was praying?

Before she knew it, spring had arrived. Fannie got busy preparing the house for Passover, trying not to let her loss ruin her favorite holiday. She scoured the house to remove every trace of *chometz*, replacing the forbidden foods with matzo and other special foods instead. Caleb brought the barrels of Passover dishes they would use only for those eight days up from the storage room in the basement. She cooked chicken soup with kneidlach, potato *kugel* and other holiday dishes. Keeping busy helped her let go of the winter's tragedy.

Just before the holiday began, she received a letter from Mama.

1 February 2013

My darling Feigele,

Papa wrote to me about the baby. Oh, how I wish I were there to hold you. Papa said he told you about my losses, so you know I understand what you're feeling. You're angry at G-d and thinking that somehow it's your fault—even though it isn't. You must believe that.

And most of all, the sadness, the terrible sadness I know you're feeling. That baby was real to you. He had a name and a place in your heart. But there was no funeral, no shiva. I don't know why, but women who lose their babies are just supposed to move on. It's cruel.

I hope by the time you get this the pain will be a little less. Not forgotten, but more bearable. I'm sure Caleb is helping you and thank G-d you have Miriam.

It won't be long before we're together, my child. Until then, please take care of yourself. Even if it seems hopeless, your time will come. You will be wonderful mama, and I will hold my grandchild in my arms.

With all my love,

Mama

Fannie folded the letter. It made her feel better—and worse. Caleb helping her? *Oh, Mama, if only you knew.*

Although it was traditional to wear new clothes for Passover, Fannie knew better than to ask Caleb for money. Although generous when she was pregnant, he had returned to his former stinginess, insisting he was not a wealthy man. She knew this wasn't true. From conversations with Rachel, she knew that Max, with a far less important job at Fine and Sons, made sure his entire family wore new spring clothes. No one would say anything to her if she wore last year's clothes, but she was ashamed. She embroidered a new belt and shawl to make one of her old dresses look new.

Caleb's penny-pinching made it all the more shocking when, the afternoon of the first Seder, he arrived home early and told her to come down to the street. There, he pointed to a shiny new automobile. It was midnight blue, trimmed in polished brass, with black leather seats and a black roof. Fannie couldn't help noticing how the car matched his own dark blue suit and bright yellow bow tie.

"Tonight, we're going to the Seder in style," he said.

"I don't understand," said Fannie. "This is yours?"

"All mine," said Caleb. "It's the latest Ford Model T."

"But so much money. I thought you said you didn't have a lot of money."

"Don't question me, Fannie. The man of the family makes the decisions about money."

"But for this? Something we don't need?"

"I wanted it, so that's all there is to it. After all, I have nothing else to make me happy."

Fannie saw no point in answering him.

"Get in, I'll drive you around the block."

Fannie shrank back. "It's safe?"

"Of course it's safe. I drove it here, didn't I?"

"I'll watch you go around the block first."

"Very well, but this is how we're going to my parents' house tonight."

Caleb began by pulling a wire in the front of the car. Then he got into the car, turned the key and, from what she could see, set a few levers. Then he got out again. He inserted a crank into the center of the front of the car and gave it a half-crank. Then he got back into the car again, turned some other dials, began pressing the foot pedals, and, slowly, it began to move! All this trouble, she thought. She had read about Mr. Henry Ford's invention and the cars he was making in a city called Detroit. Millions of Americans were buying them, but she couldn't believe this was truly "the way of the future." Why go to all the trouble when one could easily take a trolley or the subway?

Although she couldn't be sure it was the same car, she had seen an advertisement for a Model T in the English newspaper Caleb brought home, the *New York Evening Telegram*. The car cost eight hundred dollars. That was more than twice as much money as she would have needed for an entire new wardrobe. And not that he cared, but what did she have to make her happy?

Caleb soon reappeared and sounded the horn. Neighbors gathered to admire the car, which she knew would please him.

When it was time to leave, she braced herself for the car ride. She put extra hair pins in her hair and secured her hat with a long scarf over it. She wore her wool coat, knowing it would be much cooler when it was time to come home. It would also help keep the dirt from the street from soiling her dress. The ride was bumpy, and the mostly open sides did nothing to mute the traffic noise around them. At first, she was convinced they would crash at any moment, or worse, run over a pedestrian. Caleb had to use the horn constantly. As they rode, she gained confidence in his ability to avert disaster but couldn't stop herself from screaming when a bicycle swerved in front of them. Perhaps it would be more enjoyable outside the city, she thought, a nice way to enjoy the scenery.

When they arrived at the Fine's, the entire family was waiting in front of the house. Caleb had let them know about his new car earlier that afternoon. Daniel opened her door and helped her step down from the running board onto the sidewalk.

"How was it? he asked eagerly.

"I'm happy to be alive," she answered, still holding on to his arm.

"Surely not as bad as all that," he laughed.

"No, it wasn't really that bad. And I'm sure you'll love it." She gave him a quick hug.

"If you wait your turn," said Caleb, "I'll give everyone rides."

"You most certainly will not," said Miriam. "Dinner is on the table and it's time to begin the Seder." Reluctantly, they all began to go into the house.

"Next Shabbos after lunch," said Caleb. "Rides for everyone."

Fannie's Papa turned to look at him. "Riding on Shabbos?" he asked, frowning.

"You know we ride, Papa," said Noah quickly. "How else would we see you?"

"But not just for fun—"

"Sha, Asher, the holiday is starting. Let's get started." Miriam took him by the arm and led him into the dining room.

Fannie admired the table. The crystal, silver and china they used only for Passover was even more elegant than what they used for Shabbos. There was a *Haggadah*, the book that told the Passover story, at each place so everyone could follow along and join in the prayers and songs. She noticed a wine stain on the one at her place. They had probably been using it since before she was born.

When everyone had taken their seats and the wine was poured, Charles called upon Noah to start by reading the four questions. "You're the youngest," he said. "Until our David is old enough to read."

"Or his new baby brother," said Max, smiling. "There'll be a new baby next winter."

Fannie didn't dare look at Caleb as everyone congratulated Max and Rachel; she knew how much the news would upset him.

In response to the four questions, Charles explained the ritual foods on the Seder plate, like the roasted egg and greens, symbols of spring and rebirth. He read about the plagues God visited upon the Egyptians and how God "passed over" Jewish homes as he struck down Egyptian first-borns. The story never failed to inspire Fannie, although like everyone else she looked forward to its end so they could enjoy the feast.

Every year is different, thought Fannie as she looked at her family. Parents get older, children get married, babies are born. The world around us changes. Who would have thought we'd come to the Seder in an automobile? *I wonder what the next year will bring.*

PART IV: FAREWELLS,
1913-1914

CHAPTER 14

Two months later Fannie was at the docks with Miriam, Daniel, Noah, and Eve to say goodbye to Papa. The smell of salt water, the shouts of the stevedores, and the horns of the cars and trucks waiting for people and goods from the ships reminded her of her arrival three years ago. How little she knew then about how her life would unfold.

Along with crowds of others who had come to say goodbye, they yelled and waved to Papa, staying at the pier until the tugboat pulled the ship far out into the harbor, heading toward the Statue of Liberty. She remembered the solemnity of the moment the weary immigrants aboard the S. S. Lapland saw the majestic statue for the first time. How did Papa feel now, leaving her behind for his journey back to Russia for Mama and the children?

For a few minutes, none of them spoke. Except for Eve, who had been born in America, each of them had their own memories of the long, difficult journey. Fannie let her tears fall and saw her brothers wiping theirs away. Miriam wept noisily. Before he boarded, she and Papa clung to each other as though they would never see each other again. But after all, thought Fannie as she watched them, they knew the journey was dangerous. There was always a chance they'd lose each other again, this time forever.

Fannie had given her Papa a brief letter to Mama to take with him.

> *1 June 1913*
>
> *My Dearest Mama.*
>
> *Soon you will have to leave your friends in Kamenetz behind. I know how hard that is. But at the end of your journey, God willing, we'll all be together again.*
>
> *My English is now very good, and I'll be able to help you, Freyda and Levi get used to life in America. It is easier for children, but I know you'll do well.*
>
> *Tell Freyda I will take her to the biggest store in the world and tell Levi I will take him to see wild animals in the zoo!*
>
> *Noah, Eve, Daniel and I will be there when your ship arrives. Until then, be safe, Mama.*
>
> *Your loving daughter,*
>
> *Fannie*

If all went well, Papa would be gone only three months, traveling to Kamenetz, settling their affairs there, and returning with his wife and children. Finally, they would all be together in America. Fannie thought about the thirty dollars she had been able to give him. It had taken her a while, but her embroidery had grown in popularity. The fashionable young women from Mary's set didn't think twice about paying her a dollar to add her original designs to their shawls. She was proud she had been able to help.

"So, *knishes* at Schimmels before Fannie and Miriam go back to Brooklyn?" Daniel broke the silence.

Miriam demurred. "Thank you, Daniel, but I have an appointment uptown. I'll see you all soon."

"I'd love one" said Fannie. "I was so nervous about getting to the ship on time I didn't eat all morning. It's hard to believe Papa is actually gone and how much he will have to do in Kamenetz before they can all return. He's lucky cousin Heschel has done well at the shop and will be taking it over."

"The time will go quickly," said Daniel.

"The arrangements for the shop and the house won't take long, but who knows how long it will take Papa to get the papers to travel by train through Germany." Fannie had never spoken of Yetta and her family, the friends who had been forced to leave the train because they didn't have papers, but she began to share the story now, her voice hardening in anger.

"How awful," said Eve, putting her arm around Fannie. "And the ship, what was that like?"

"For Papa it was terrible. He was seasick. I hope it isn't as bad for him this time—he must be dreading it. But I wasn't sick at all, and a nice family helped the time pass. I think I told you about them." Fannie yearned to tell them about Samuel. She was certain that her brothers and Eve would understand, but she was afraid if she spoke about him she'd give away her feelings about her marriage. That, she thought, would have to remain her private sadness. No one had remarked on Caleb's absence. They had probably assumed that, as usual, he and his father were too busy at the factory and had said farewell earlier.

"Daniel and I were never sick either," said Noah. But the food and the smells were awful, and our ship was slower than yours. We sneaked up to the other decks until they chased us away."

"You must have been a bad influence, Daniel," said Eve, grinning at her soon-to-be brother-in-law. "I can't imagine Noah dreaming that mischief up on his own."

"You're absolutely right," said Noah, smiling. And speaking of dreaming things up, Papa won't be back until at least the end of the summer. That will give us plenty of time to plan a wedding for right after the holidays in October." He kissed Eve's cheek. She rolled her eyes, but smiled back at him and returned the kiss.

Fannie laughed at them. She was finally getting used to seeing them share their affection in public.

"We're here," said Daniel as they turned onto Houston Street. "What's your favorite, Fannie?"

"Kasha for me," said Fannie, practically drooling from the aroma.

"Put your money away," he said as Noah took some coins out of his pocket. She watched as Daniel peeled a dollar off a substantial roll of bills. Was he still playing cards? She reminded herself that she needed to talk to him.

"Mmm," she murmured as she wiped her chin with a napkin. "Perhaps another one—potato this time?"

"Gladly, Fannie. It's good to see your appetite is back. Anyone else for seconds?"

Noah quickly took him up on his offer.

When they finished, Daniel told Noah and Eve he would see Fannie home. They could stay in Manhattan and go about their day.

"Thank you," said Noah. "We both have studying to do."

Daniel offered Fannie his arm as they started walking to the train.

"Daniel, it's been so long since we've had a chance to talk. Eve said she and Noah hardly see you anymore. It's only natural for you to have your own friends, but I worry about you."

"No need to worry, Fannie, I'm fine. My friends just aren't the studious type like Noah and Eve. They'd have nothing to talk about, so I don't bother bringing them around."

"I couldn't help seeing how much money you had at Schimmels. It can't all be from your new job."

"Fannie, I occasionally play cards with my friends. I'm good at it, so I end up with a little extra spending money. There's nothing wrong with that."

"Isn't it dangerous?"

"I'm no fool, Fannie."

"I never said you were. But what about meeting a nice girl? Isn't it time, Daniel? Look how happy Noah and Eve are."

"And what about you and Caleb? Do you think I don't see how unhappy he makes you?"

Fannie hung her head, unsure of what to say. She should have known Daniel, the brother she had always been closest to, would guess the truth. She wondered if Eve and Noah also knew. *I guess I haven't hidden it as well as I thought.*

"But Daniel, I didn't choose my husband. It can be different for you."

"No thanks, Fannie, I'm not ready to settle down."

For the rest of their time together, they avoided anything personal. After exhausting the safe subject of the beautiful spring weather they were having, their talk turned to the suffragettes. Fannie had resolved her initial doubts and had been fully converted to the cause, even if there were few people other than Eve and her brothers she could talk to about it. Thanks to Mrs. Johnson at the library, she had read the novel *Suffragette Sally* and learned about the newspaper, *Votes for Women*. She had been thrilled when thousands of women marched in Washington D.C. the day before Wilson's inauguration, hoping he would help them get the vote. Daniel was skeptical of the president's support. It was the kind of conversation she wished she could have with Caleb. Even if they disagreed, it would be nice to talk about something important with her husband.

When they got to Fannie's subway stop, Daniel got ready to cross the platform and go back to Manhattan to work the rest of the day. Fannie prepared to leave the station. Daniel took her elbow to stop her.

"Fannie, you know you can always come to me. This is America. You don't have to suffer with a husband who mistreats you."

"Oh no, it's not like that. And you mustn't say anything to Mama and Papa when they come back!"

"I'll leave it up to you, Fannie," he said, hugging her tightly.

Fannie felt comforted in her big brother's arms. She stayed there a moment longer before she turned to climb the stairs to the exit. It was going to be a long wait for Mama and Papa.

CHAPTER 15

Shortly after Papa left for Russia, the Fines gathered for Shabbos dinner. Rachel was getting the children ready to leave when Miriam asked her to sit down with Max and stay another minute.

"I have some news for you," she said.

Charles got up from his place and stood behind her stiffly. He stared at the opposite wall without meeting his children's eyes. Miriam reached over her shoulder to grasp his hand.

Fannie looked around at the others; everyone looked as puzzled as she was.

"I've been ill for some time," Miriam said, almost in a whisper. "At first, we thought I was just catching a lot of colds or maybe I had become allergic to something. But I kept getting worse."

"Why didn't you tell us," Caleb interrupted. "We could have helped."

"I didn't want to worry you. She paused to take a breath and then rushed through what she had to say next. "A few weeks ago, I went to the doctor again. He sent me for another X-ray. It's cancer of the lungs, children." She dropped her gaze. "There's nothing they can do. I have only a few months."

"The best doctors, we saw them all," said Charles. "Not one of them had anything different to say." He held on to Miriam's hand, trying unsuccessfully to stifle his tears.

"There has to be something," said Caleb, raising his voice angrily. "This is 1913. Maybe a specialist in another city? Or we'll go to Europe. There must be something to try."

"Don't you think we've thought of that?" Charles shouted back at his son. His voice broke as he added, "There are no treatments anywhere."

Fannie tried to take Caleb's hand, but he pulled away.

"Are you in pain, Miriam?" she asked.

"Sometimes," said Miriam. "The doctor gave me laudanum for the pain. It helps me sleep."

"You can't leave us," said Rachel. Max put his arm around her, and she wept on his shoulder.

"I thought I'd have more time to watch David and Avigail and the new baby grow up and to see Caleb and Fannie's children born. And I was looking forward to welcoming Bluma and the children."

"Oh no, Papa—" cried Fannie.

"He knows. Living with us he saw how often I was sick and suspected it was serious. I told him before he left. He wanted to postpone his trip, but I wouldn't let him. Bluma and the children must come now, while it's still safe. There's too much trouble in Europe to put it off."

"And now he'll have to tell Mama," said Fannie. "It will be so hard for him."

"I'm so sorry children. How much time I have left is in God's hands. You must promise to be good to each other and to take care of your father." Miriam rose from her chair and held out her arms. One by one they went to embrace her. Rachel and Max carried the children over to her.

"Why are you crying, Bubbe? Did you hurt yourself?" asked David. "You should ask Zayde to kiss it and make it better."

Miriam managed to smile through her tears. "Why don't you kiss it for me. Right here," she said, pointing to her cheek. "That will make it all better."

"Me too, me too," cried Avigail, reaching out.

"Of course, my little angel, you can make it better here," she said, pointing to her other cheek.

The children hugged Charles too before they left.

Caleb, wiping furiously at his tears, held his mother close without speaking before turning to his father. "Don't worry, Papa." he said. "I'll take care of everything at the factory so you can be with Mama."

"That won't be ne—" Charles couldn't finish. He fell against Caleb and put his arms around him, sobbing. After some hesitation, Caleb put his arms around his father and held him.

Fannie watched the two men, so unused to showing emotion, struggle to help each other. As she thought back, she realized there had been signs. Miriam coughing, looking pale. She tried to remember how long ago they had started. Had she been too wrapped up in her own sorrow to pay attention? Was there anything she could have done?

"I love you, Miriam," said Fannie. "Whatever you need, please ask. We'll take care of you."

"I know you will, Fannie. I only hope I live to see you expecting again. You'll be such a good mama."

"From your mouth to God's ears. But now you need to rest." She tore herself away and waited for Caleb and Charles to release each other from their desperate embrace.

"Good night, Charles," she said. "Call us any time." She went to kiss him goodbye, but he surprised her by taking her in his arms.

"Thank you, Fannie. You're a good girl."

She and Caleb were both silent on the way back to their apartment. As soon as they were inside, he sat down heavily in his chair and held his head in his hands. "Oh Mama," he moaned.

Fannie sat in her own chair to wait for him to calm himself. She had never seen him like this. He was always so stoic and in control. She got up to stand beside him. "Let me help you," she said.

"Can you make her well?" he said without looking up. "Well, can you?" He raised his head to glare at her.

She shook her head mutely.

"Then there's nothing you can do."

Fannie tried again. She put her hand on his shoulder. "I'm your wife, Caleb. I can comfort you."

He shrugged her hand off. "Not now. Now I'd like to be alone."

"You don't have to suffer alone." She returned to her chair. "And what about me? I love her too."

"She's not your mother, she's mine."

Would he never cease to hurt her? "Please, let's get through this together."

Caleb stood up. "I can't talk to you right now. I'm going out."

Fannie also rose. "Wait," she cried. But the door had already slammed behind him.

★ ★ ★

Fannie waited for hours, but he didn't come back. When he wasn't home by morning, she dressed and went to shul. Even without Papa, it felt like the right place to be. God hadn't helped her, but perhaps he would be good to Miriam.

She hesitated when services ended but decided to go to the Fines as she usually did for Shabbos lunch. She would see how Miriam was feeling, and maybe Caleb would be there.

Bridget greeted her at the front door. "Oh Miss Fannie, I can't believe it. But Clara and I won't leave her side for one minute, I promise you."

"Thank you, Bridget. Where is she?"

"In the parlor, resting."

Fannie went straight in, Bridget following behind her. Miriam was lying on the sofa, leaning against some pillows. She smiled as soon as she saw Fannie.

"I was afraid you wouldn't come," she said.

"Can I get you anything Miss Miriam?" Bridget asked.

"Another cup of coffee would be lovely, and please ask Clara to fix Fannie some lunch and bring it here so we can sit and chat a while."

"Are you sure you're not too tired after last night?" asked Fannie.

"Of course not, I'm happy you're here. And then you can walk home with Caleb. He and Charles went out a little while ago."

Fannie was relieved to hear that Caleb had come, but uncertain what it would be like when he came back.

"Miriam—"

"Fannie dear, we can talk about anything but my health. I want to have a normal life with my children and grandchildren for as long as I can. Look, I saved you a new lady's magazine." She took the magazine off a side table and held it out for Fannie. "One day I expect there will be pictures of your embroidery in here. Your work is as pretty as anything these fancy stores advertise."

"Thank you. I never thought of it as anything more than a pastime, or a way to earn money to help the family, but who knows ... and even after we have children, it will be easy to do when they're asleep."

"What will be easy?" asked Charles as he and Caleb arrived in the middle of the conversation.

"Fannie's embroidery," she said. "Did you have a good walk? Fannie's going to have some lunch here with me. Would you like to join us here or eat in the kitchen?"

"We'll go into the kitchen," answered Caleb.

Fannie searched Caleb's face for a clue about his feelings. Was he trying to avoid her?

He nodded when she said, "I'll see you when it's time to go home."

It seemed like hardly any time before he was at the door. "I'm ready," he said. "And you shouldn't tire my mother."

"Don't be silly, Caleb," said Miriam. "I enjoyed the company. You'll come back soon, Fannie?"

"Of course, as often as you like," she said, bending down to give Miriam a hug. She could feel how thin she had become. *Why didn't I notice? Why didn't any of us notice?*

Caleb did the same and the two of them left.

"Shall we walk or take the trolley?" Caleb asked.

"Let's walk," said Fannie. "It will be easier to talk about last night."

"There's nothing to talk about," said Caleb.

"But Caleb—"

"I said, nothing."

So that's how it is going to be. I'll never know where he was. Walking the streets alone with his sorrow or being comforted by another woman?

★ ★ ★

The months after Miriam shared the news of her illness went by all too quickly. Fannie watched as her mother-in-law spent her remaining days as she had lived her life, thinking of her family before herself, treating each of them with love and affection. Whenever she felt up to it, she played with the children. Later she would say to Fannie, "I may be the tiniest bit prejudiced, but David and Avigail are so much smarter than other children their age. And beautiful—those blond curls and long eyelashes would make any woman jealous. Max looked just like that when he was a baby."

Fannie laughed. "I hope you don't let them wear you out," she said.

"No, Rachel makes sure they don't. But it would be worth it," said Miriam. "I'll be resting for good soon. And until I'm with God's angels I'll enjoy the two little angels I'm blessed with here."

She often took afternoon strolls with Fannie, even as her steps slowed, and she had to lean on Fannie's arm more frequently.

"How are you getting on Fannie? I've been worried about you since—"

"I'm fine, Miriam, really I am."

"You've been through the hardest thing a woman can face, Fannie. Next time I'm sure will be fine, and you'll have your Mama with you."

"I'll be happy when Mama is here, but no one could have taken better care of me than you did. I'll never forget how you got me through that time."

Occasionally, Mary joined them on their walks. They would chat and gossip as though they had all the time in the world.

One warm sunny day they stopped to rest on a bench. "I'm having a baby," said Mary, looking nervously at Fannie. "In March."

"I'm so happy for you," said Fannie. She squeezed Mary's hand, thinking back to when she told her she didn't want a baby. Had she finally decided it was time? Or perhaps the pessary wasn't foolproof? Either way, Fannie was genuinely happy for her. She knew her friend was worried about how she would take the news, but she was no longer bitter around women having babies. She knew the pain would never go away, but it didn't cause her the anguish it had at first.

"I never would have guessed," said Miriam. "I should have known no baby would dare ruin your beautiful figure. If only I were going to be here to see you and Simon when the baby is born."

"But—"

"No Mary, no pretending."

On Shabbos mornings Miriam often joined Max and Caleb on their walks. She told her sons it was fine if they wanted to talk about business; she was content just to be with them. At lunch she recalled pushing Max in the baby buggy, while Caleb, still in short pants, walked beside her. "He announced to everyone we passed he was the big brother."

"And he's never let me forget it!" said Max.

When Fannie looked over at Caleb she was glad to see him smiling. She worried about how withdrawn he was at home; afraid he would explode at any moment.

When the family wasn't gathering at the Fine's home for Shabbos dinner, they came to Caleb and Fannie's apartment. Miriam especially loved listening to Eve talk about the things she was learning in nursing school. "It's wonderful you'll be doing something so important," she said. "I'm happy I've lived to see the world changing for young women."

But not for me, Fannie wanted to say. She too was happy for Eve, but the choices she had been able to make weren't available to Fannie. Her marriage—her whole life—had been determined for her.

Gradually Miriam's good days grew fewer and further apart. More and more, the pain kept her in bed and the laudanum made her too sleepy to talk. When the family visited, they could only sit quietly at her bedside while she seemed to grow smaller under her satin quilt. When she woke, she could barely talk.

Finally, on the first Monday in September, Labor Day, while workers paraded and enjoyed a holiday, Charles summoned the family to say their goodbyes. They gathered in the parlor, taking turns to go into her room.

Before Max and Rachel went in, they sent David and Avigail to the kitchen with Bridget for milk and cookies. They wanted the children to remember their bubbe as a lively woman with a ready laugh, not the pale, shrunken old woman she had become. They came out after a few minutes, holding each other and weeping.

Caleb and Fannie went in after them. They sat silently on opposite sides of the bed, each holding one of Miriam's hands, waiting for her to open her eyes. When she did, she smiled and seemed to rally.

"I love you both," she said. "Be good to each other—and take care of Papa, Caleb."

"Yes, Mama," he said.

Fannie could barely speak. She wanted to throw herself on the bed and cry out in rage and despair. A whispered "I love you" was all she could manage.

They turned to leave, but before they reached the door Miriam called out to Fannie.

"Do you need something?" Fannie asked.

"I'd like to speak to you alone."

"But Mama," said Caleb.

"Please, give us a minute, son."

He left, shutting the door as forcefully as he dared.

"I know Caleb hasn't been easy to live with," said Miriam. "You're too good to have said anything, but I could see it. He has trouble showing his feelings, like his Papa. But deep down he's a good man. Promise me you'll take care of him."

Of course I'll promise. How can I deny you? But how can I take care of a man who pushes me away?

Miriam struggled for breath. "Please Fannie, I won't be able to die peacefully unless you promise me."

"I promise, Miriam. I'll always take care of him."

Miriam closed her eyes. When it was clear that she was sleeping again, Fannie opened the door to leave. Charles was waiting just outside. He looked as though he hadn't slept in days. I can see how Caleb and his father are alike, thought Fannie. Neither one of them asks for help and it makes their suffering worse.

As soon as she went back into the parlor, Caleb confronted her. "What did she want? What did she say to you that I couldn't hear?"

"She asked me to take care of you."

"I don't need taking care of."

"If that's what she thought, she wouldn't have asked." She sat down next to him and looked at him with compassion but made no move to touch him. "We all need to be taken care of sometimes."

The clock on the mantel ticked steadily. Max and Rachel brought the children upstairs and kept them close to them. The children sensed the somber mood of the adults around them and played quietly on the floor. Caleb sat at Fannie's side without a word.

It seemed like only minutes later that Charles returned from the room. Before he could speak, his knees buckled under him. Max and Caleb rushed to hold him up and lead him to a chair.

"She's gone," he sobbed. "My Miriam is gone."

★ ★ ★

The next morning Fannie looked up at the cloudless blue sky and thought how much Miriam would have enjoyed walking on such a beautiful day. Instead, they were burying her.

Overnight, Miriam had been taken to the funeral home, where members of the burial society had washed her body and wrapped it in a white shroud. They had watched and prayed over her until it was time for the service. It comforted Fannie to know Miriam had not been alone.

Before the service, the family gathered with the Rabbi, who approached each of them for the ritual *keriah*. One by one, he tore a piece of their clothing as a symbol of their grief. After he explained the funeral and the *shiva,* the mourning period they would observe for seven days, he opened the heavy wooden double doors to lead them into the chapel. Caleb and Max walked on either side of Charles, followed by Fannie and Rachel. The family and friends who had come to mourn with them rose as they entered.

It reminded Fannie of making her entrance into the sanctuary when she was about to be married. Then, she had to remind herself to smile at the room full of people waiting to celebrate. Now, she was numb with pain and saw sorrow reflected in every face she passed. There weren't many genuinely good people in this world. Today they were mourning one of them.

As they walked down the aisle behind the Rabbi, she saw Mary and Simon and Caleb's other friends, seated together amid dozens of neighbors, business associates and members of the shul, a sea of black dresses and suits. Every seat was taken. Fannie nodded to her brothers and Eve, seated in the second row next to Rachel's family.

"Miriam," Charles cried out when he saw the casket. Caleb and Max helped him to his seat in the first row. Fannie and Rachel slid in next to them. The chapel allowed men and women to sit together. If only sitting next to Caleb meant they would be consoling each other. Daniel reached over the back of the pew to put his hands on her shoulders. "We're here for you," he whispered. Her brother offered her a comforting touch. Caleb held himself apart.

Fannie looked around. The walls of the chapel were plain except for a Star of David in the front. Soft lights shone from brass sconces. There were no windows to let in the sun and a deep burgundy carpet muffled any noise. It was a place designed to contemplate death.

The service was short. The Rabbi understood her, thought Fannie during his eulogy. She saw people nod as he spoke about her kindness and generosity, her physical and spiritual beauty, and her devotion to her family. But how could he capture the smiles and gestures, the soothing calm of her glance, the solace of her embrace? How could he know what this woman had meant to Fannie? Miriam had taken a frightened young girl into her home and had been like a mother to her. She had nursed her through a terrible loss. *Did I do enough to tell her how much she meant to me? What did I give her in return? Not the grandchild she hoped for.*

"The Lord is my shepherd ..." the Rabbi recited. "Amen," said the mourners. Fannie envisioned Miriam sleeping peacefully, the lines etched by age and illness gone from her face.

Charles, Caleb, and Max rose to say the mourner's *Kaddish.* The ancient prayer didn't mention death but praised God's name. Why are we praising the God who took Miriam away thought Fannie, who took my baby away? It was getting harder and harder to believe in him. The family filed out, accompanied by prayers of comfort as they walked down the aisle.

At the gravesite, Fannie couldn't reconcile praying for Miriam to be "sheltered under God's wings" with the ugly hole in the ground and the pile of dirt next to it. Charles took a shovel of the dirt, emptied it onto the casket and handed the shovel to Caleb. He did the same and handed it to Max, followed by every man in attendance until the grave was filled. Each shovelful landed with a resounding thud, piercing Fannie's heart. She felt like part of her was being buried.

As the mourners turned to leave the cemetery, Fannie glanced back at the fresh mound of dirt. Miriam isn't there, she thought, she's on her way to the angels who have been waiting for her. She looked for Caleb, but he was already walking away with his father and Max. Rachel came over to take her hand and they walked out together.

At the front door of the Fine's home, they stooped to wash their hands in the pitcher of water that had been left there for them to wash away impurity from the cemetery. Inside, all the mirrors and family portraits were covered so the mourners would not be tempted by vanity. During the shiva they would sit on low, hard benches and refrain from shaving or wearing leather shoes or jewelry. A memorial candle would burn throughout the seven days.

As soon as they walked into the house the children ran to greet them. Charles bent down to take them both into his arms. "Your Bubbe has left us," he said, tears streaming down his face.

"Don't be sad, Zayde," said David. "Mama and Papa said bubbe is sleeping, and God is taking care of her. And we'll take care of you." He looked at his parents for reassurance. They nodded and went to take him and his sister from Charles.

"Let the boy stay with me," said Charles as they went into the dining room. He put his grandson on his lap as they sat down to eat the lunch Bridget and Clara brought out, which had been prepared by friends and neighbors. The meal began with hard-boiled eggs that symbolized new life, but none of them noticed what they were eating. They picked at the meal silently.

Almost as soon as they had finished the first guests arrived. They would come to comfort the family every afternoon and evening except for Shabbos, bringing food and sharing memories of Miriam. Every day the Rabbi and other men would come to form a *minyan*, the ten men required for Charles, Caleb, and Max to recite Kaddish. No work was permitted during shiva and Fannie wondered how Caleb would cope with being away from the factory so long. She expected that after the first few days he would sneak away for a few hours to check up on business.

Fannie was kept busy. It was she who made sure the guests were welcomed and told Bridget and Clara what was needed. She was grateful to have them, because although the guests were not supposed to burden the mourners, it was expected that coffee and tea would be offered, along with the cookies and cakes the visitors brought—sweets to take away the sadness. Rachel helped, of course, but she had to keep the children from getting underfoot and Max often asked her to sit with him.

At first, Fannie was offended when she heard the guests laughing in the parlor, but then she realized it was because of the joy Miriam had brought them. Why shouldn't they laugh as they remembered the good times they had together?

She wondered what would happen after shiva. Charles knew how to run a factory, but he had no idea what it took to run a house. Could Bridget and Clara handle the shopping, cooking, cleaning and laundry on their own? Would he simply give them the weekly household allowance he had given Miriam? Did he even know what they were paid? Fannie supposed she could help him decide and check on them frequently. After all, she had lived in the house for almost a year and knew how Miriam planned the week's work and what each girl did. She would speak to Rachel, since she was sure Caleb and Max hadn't thought about what came next.

She and Caleb rarely spoke. She sat with him as often as possible, but he had more to say to the guests than to her. He rarely initiated a conversation, even when they were alone in the bedroom. He didn't care that she too was suffering. One night, desperate to end the silence between them, she sat at the end of his bed.

"Talk to me, Caleb."

"About what? My mother is dead. What is there to say?"

"Can't I help?"

"We've been through this, Fannie. I don't need any help."

"I'm only trying to make things better for you."

"Well, you can't." He turned away from her and drew his covers up around him.

Fannie knew they were supposed to refrain from sexual relations during shiva, but she was still surprised that Caleb had made no attempt to come near her. Perhaps he was afraid the others would hear. As indifferent to her feelings as he usually was, at least it would be some form of connection, some indication that life went on. But the distance between them was too great. She went back to her own bed.

Finally, the seven days ended. The family got off their hard seats and walked around the block together to begin their re-entry into ordinary life. What would "ordinary" mean now, Fannie wondered.

PART V: TRANSITIONS, 1913-1915

Fannie stood on her toes, straining to see over the crowd. It was a hot, late summer day and there was barely any air moving in the great hall. She could feel the sweat dripping under her cotton blouse. She stared up at the giant American flag, realizing that three years ago she had known nothing about the stars and stripes. Now she knew what they symbolized, but all she cared about was seeing her family. When would Mama and Papa and the children come down the stairs? It seemed like hours since the last ferry had arrived at Ellis Island. Could anything have gone wrong? What if she never saw her Mama again? She bounced up and down, wishing she could do something besides wait. If only she could go to look for them.

"Calm down, Fannie," said Daniel. He spoke loudly to make himself heard over the hundreds of other anxious families. "You're making us all nervous."

"I can't," said Fannie, turning around toward him and throwing up her hands in frustration. "I don't know how you were able to wait for me and Papa. It seems like longer than three years since I've seen Mama and Freyda and Levi. I can't bear to wait another minute."

"You won't have to," said Daniel, spotting them over Fannie's head. "Look, there they are."

Fannie whirled around. "Mama, over here! Papa, Freyda, Levi," she yelled. "Pardon me, pardon me," she said as she began pushing her way toward them, "Mama—"

"Feige," Freyda threw herself into Fannie's open arms. "I've missed you so much!" Fannie looked at her sister, now nearly her own height. Her bright red curls had been tamed into two braids. She could see that at thirteen, she was on the verge of becoming a woman. Her small breasts were straining against the fabric of a dress Fannie recognized as one she had outgrown. Mama must have made it over for her.

Fannie looked down at her own clothes self-consciously. They were not new, because Caleb had stopped giving her money for clothes, but they were still more fashionable than anything from Kamenetz. Miriam had helped her fit in by buying her new clothes when she arrived, but how would she help Mama and Freyda? She had saved more money from her embroidery after Papa left, but it wouldn't be enough.

"And who's this?" she asked, bending down to look Levi in the eyes. "Who is this handsome man you brought with you, Freyda?"

"It's me, Levi. Don't you remember me?" Levi asked in alarm.

"But you've grown so much. Are you sure you're my baby brother?" He squirmed as she squeezed him tightly. Without his baby fat, he was starting to look more like Papa. Fannie noticed how clean the children and their clothes were. Mama must have worked very hard to keep them that way on the ship.

"My turn," said Daniel, lifting his brother high into the air. "Let's have a look at you." Levi squealed in delight. Daniel had left home before he was born and was a stranger to him, but he was won over easily.

"And I suppose you're too grown up to give me a kiss?" he asked Freyda.

Freyda looked up at him unsurely.

"Don't tease her, Daniel," said Fannie. "She's not used to you."

"I never would have recognized you Freyda," said Noah. "What a beauty you've become. And you, Levi, are you as naughty as Fannie says you are? Come say hello to Eve. You're just in time to dance at our wedding."

Eve bent down to kiss the children.

"Feigele." Mama said softly. She had been watching with pleasure as her children greeted each other.

Fannie turned to her mother's voice and fell into her open arms. "Oh Mama," she cried.

Her mother pushed her away to look at her. "I'm here now, my child. Papa and I are here."

Fannie saw that her mother had aged. There were more wrinkles lining her face and her hair had become grayer. *What does she see when she looks at me?*

"Miriam?" Papa asked.

Fannie shook her head, unable to say the words.

"When?"

"Two weeks ago."

"Two weeks? If only—" he began.

"No Papa. She wanted you to bring Mama and the children here, no matter when you'd get back. We were all there with her, holding her hands at the end. She was ready to leave us."

"Thank you, Feigele." He bowed his head and wept silently, only looking up as his sons approached.

Noah was first. "Papa, it's so good to have you back. Mama, this is Eve."

"I've heard a great deal about you, Eve. It will be good to get to know you," said Bluma with a warm smile. "Noah was barely a *Bar Mitzvah* when he left home, and here he is with a bride."

"I'm sorry, but we'd better go," said Daniel, embracing his parents quickly. He started to pick up suitcases and bundles. "We want to get you to Brooklyn before it gets dark. Make sure you have everything, children." He began to lead them out.

Fannie held onto Levi's hand. "Don't let go," she said. "Or you'll get lost, and we'll never see you again."

"I'm not a baby anymore," Levi complained, but held on tightly.

Asher and Bluma walked alongside them.

"Walk with us, Freyda, and tell us all about your journey," said Eve. She took one of Freyda's hands and Noah took the other. Fannie could see how pleased Freyda was at their attention.

As the ferry headed toward Manhattan, Fannie watched Freyda and Levi's faces as they saw the skyline for the first time. She still loved the view and began to tell the children about the skyscrapers and elevators to the top.

Levi was in awe of the elevated train. "How does it work?" he asked.

Daniel and Noah tried to explain, but for every one of their answers the curious six-year-old had another question.

Finally, Noah gave up. "You'll learn about it in school," he said. "Here in America all the children go to school."

"Girls too?" asked Freyda.

"Yes," said Eve. "Even me. I'm still in school, studying to be a nurse."

"A nurse?" asked Freyda. The two leaned their heads together as Eve began to tell her all about Florence Nightingale. Now she'll have another big sister, thought Fannie, feeling a little jealous. Eve was American, independent, and educated. And what did she offer? Staying at home to cook and clean? That was fine for a small town in Russia, but here Freyda would surely want more.

Mama was quiet, barely taking in her new surroundings. Fannie reached out for her hand. She was sure she was thinking about Miriam and worried about Papa. He hadn't said a word yet.

The lights were just coming on when they arrived at the Fine's home. Charles came to the door to greet them. "Cousin," he said, reaching for Asher. "She's left us." The two men hugged and wept together until Charles pulled away and collected himself enough to greet Bluma. It's been so long, Bluma. Thank God you're all here safe. We're so grateful that you gave us Fannie, but I'm sure you've missed her."

Bluma embraced him. "Oh, I have Charles, but I wish I had been here in time to thank Miriam. I can't imagine how my Feigele would have managed without her."

"She wanted to be here to welcome you," he said, beginning to cry again. Finally, he took out a handkerchief, blew his nose loudly and took a deep breath.

"Freyda, Levi, say hello to your cousin Charles," said Bluma when he was calmer. She took her children's hands and led them to him.

The children had never seen a man so overcome before and were unsure how to approach him. Charles bent down to them, kissing the tops of their heads and stroking their cheeks. "Forgive me, children, but I'm missing your cousin. She would have been so happy to have children living in this house again."

"How lovely you are," he said to Freyda. "Just like your mother and sister."

"Thank you, Cousin Charles."

He picked Levi up in his arms. "And you, young man," he said. "Are you ready for school? I hope you're a hard worker like your brothers."

"Yes sir," replied the little boy, bringing a rare smile to his cousin's face.

"Now, everyone, you must be hungry. Go get ready for din-ner," said Charles.

"I'll help you get settled," said Fannie. She took them upstairs to where Bridget was waiting to show them to their rooms.

"Clara has dinner prepared," said Bridget. "So just leave your things and wash up. I'll make sure everything is put away."

"You wrote to me," Mama said quietly. "But I had no idea how big this house really was—it's beautiful."

"Yes," said Fannie. "Bridget and Clara have been wonderful in the last few weeks, taking care of everything the way Miriam would have wanted it, but they need someone here to guide them. I'm glad you're here."

"Where's Caleb, Feigele?"

Fannie stiffened. There was so much she wished she could tell her. "I expect he'll be here soon. He's always worked late but it's worse now that he's running the factory on his own. Charles has only gone in a few times since shiva ended. He's just not ready."

"And how is Caleb?"

"He's heartbroken, mama, but he won't talk about it." Fannie busied herself with the children to avoid talking about it further.

She showed them the bathroom and how to use the toilet, letting them pull the chain to watch the water swirl and disap-pear as she had her first time and helping them use the tap to wash their hands before they went back downstairs.

Caleb was waiting for them in the dining room. "Welcome," he said to Bluma. "I hope your trip went well."

"We were hoping not to be too late," said Bluma, taking both his hands. "But God had other plans. I'm so sorry, Caleb."

"I'm just glad you're here now," he said. "It will be good for Fannie to have her own mama here."

"She was blessed to have Miriam," said Bluma. "I'll always be grateful to her."

Caleb turned abruptly toward the children. "Hello," he said. "You must be Freyda and Levi. I've heard so much about you."

He took Freyda's hand. "You're going to be as beautiful as your big sister, Freyda."

Freyda blushed.

"How do you like the big city so far?" he asked Levi. "Would you like to see my factory?"

Levi shook his hand solemnly. "I would like that very much, sir."

Caleb laughed. "Not 'sir,' Levi, just Caleb. We're brothers now. And I'll take you one day when you're not in school."

Fannie watched them. Caleb was warm and playful around children. It was a side of him she rarely saw. He would be a different person with children of his own. It would make them both happy.

"Let's eat," said Charles. "Asher, it's good to have you back to say the *brachas* for us."

Fannie's father said a short blessing. The meal started quietly, but soon the men started to talk about business and the children chattered about everything they had seen. Everyone talked at once. Like it was before, thought Fannie, when family dinners were noisy and happy.

Bluma had asked Eve to sit next to her. She was making her feel like part of the family, just like Miriam had made Fannie feel. "Fannie," she said, "Can you help me get Freyda and Levi to bed?" Levi had climbed onto her lap and was falling asleep.

"Of course, Mama. Say goodnight to everyone, children. Freyda, I know you don't need help anymore, but I'll just remind you where everything is. It took me quite a while to get used this big house."

"Goodnight," she said when they were both in bed. "I'll be back in the morning."

"Don't you live here?" asked Levi.

"No, Caleb and I have our own apartment nearby. You'll see it when you come for Shabbos dinner. But I'll be back tomorrow to help Mama."

"Papa and I will be right down the hall," said Bluma, tucking them in with a kiss. She and Fannie walked out together, leaving the door ajar.

"Clean sheets and peace and quiet." said Fannie's mama. "I never thought they'd mean so much."

"Yes, I'm sure you'll sleep well tonight. And Bridget and Clara will take care of everything until I arrive in the morning, so there's no need for you to do a thing. Just rest." She grasped her mother's hand as they began to walk side by side down the wide stairs. "I'm so glad you're finally here."

Caleb stood as soon as the two women returned to the dining room. "Let's go home," he said.

"Yes," said Fannie, suddenly realizing how exhausted she was.

Daniel, Noah, and Eve also got up to leave. There were goodbyes and some grateful tears. Bluma included Caleb and Eve in her embraces.

Their reunion was bittersweet without Miriam, but Fannie was grateful to be back in her mama's arms. Surely things would be better now.

★ ★ ★

A few days later Fannie arrived to find Mama and the children at the kitchen table.

"Feige," shouted Levi. "We thought you'd never get here!" He jumped up from the table to give her a hug. "We're going to school today. Daniel is taking us."

"Yes, I know," said Fannie. "But Levi, and you too Freyda, from now on you must call me Fannie. It's my American name. Do you think you can remember that?"

The children looked at her solemnly. "We'll try, won't we Levi," said Freyda. "Will we have new names too?"

"No," said Fannie, "Yours are perfectly fine. Where is Charles, Mama?"

"He's gone to work. Perhaps having Papa back was just what he needed to start getting back to his old self."

The children couldn't contain their excitement. "Where is Daniel? Will we be late for school?" asked Freyda.

"Breakfast first," Fannie told them. "You have plenty of time."

Clara had already set out cereal for them and now she was spooning sliced bananas and strawberries into their bowls.

"What is this breakfast?" Freyda asked Fannie. "Clara poured it out from a box."

"I'll tell you the words and you say them after me," said Fannie. "Corn flakes."

"Corn flakes," said the children.

"Straw-burr-ees."

"Straw-burr-ees," they repeated.

"Bah-nah-nahs."

"Bah-nah-nahs," the two of them echoed.

"Your first English lesson! Good for you!"

Clara poured cold milk over the fruit and cereal. They finished their bowls quickly.

"Can I have more, please," Levi asked timidly.

"Of course," said Fannie. "This isn't like the ship—you can have as much as you want. And Clara will show you the pantry and the icebox so you can get your own breakfast in the morning. But no sweets without asking!"

"Would you like to try some cereal and fruit, Mama?" Fannie asked. "Do you want your tea now?"

"Corn flakes. Straw-burr-ees. Bah-nah-nahs," said Bluma.

"Look children, Mama is learning English too," said Fannie.

"Yes, I would love to try some, but I'll wait to have tea when the children are gone," said Bluma.

Daniel arrived as the children were finishing.

"Are you ready to start becoming Americans?" he asked them. "Go wash your hands and faces and we'll be off." Fannie rose to walk them upstairs.

"Good morning, Mama," he said, leaning over to kiss his mother's cheek. "I see you're already enjoying an American breakfast."

"Yes, I am," she replied. "But are you sure I shouldn't go with you to the school?"

"We'll be fine. The school will listen to a man who looks and speaks like an American more than they would to you. Since the term has already started, they might give you a hard time."

"But I will need to go with them soon and how will I find my way? I can't read the signs on the street. How will I take care of my children, Daniel?"

"Mama, Mama, don't worry. We all felt that way when we came. Clara and Bridget will help you find your way around, and Fannie will too. And you can go to night school to learn English like she did. But today you stay here and rest and catch up with Fannie."

"I would like that. But I don't think I'll ever get used to calling her Fannie."

"Call her whatever you like, Mama. It was Caleb's idea and he's the only one who cares."

"Daniel, don't be unkind," said Fannie, who had returned to the kitchen just in time to hear him. "Fannie is my name now. But I'll always be Feigele to Mama and Papa."

"Off we go," said Daniel to the children.

Now that the time had come, they hung back, standing behind their mother's chair.

"Don't be afraid," said Fannie. "There will be children just like you at the school. They'll be learning English too. And Daniel will take good care of you. We'll see you later."

As soon as they were gone, Fannie asked Clara, who was standing near the stove stirring batter in a big yellow bowl, to come to the table.

"Clara, my mother doesn't speak any English yet, so I hope you'll help her like you helped me when I first arrived. And you'll soon see what a wonderful cook she is. Can we have our tea now, please?"

"Of course, Miss Fannie." Clara wiped her hands on her apron. "I'll bring it right over. And cookies? I baked some for when the children come home from school, but there's enough for the whole family."

"My mother doesn't like sweets the way I do, but perhaps I can convince her to try some."

Clara took away the empty breakfast bowls.

Fannie got up, opened one of the drawers under the counter and withdrew a packet. "Miriam bought this for you, Mama. She gave me one when I first arrived and said she had one for you too. I was afraid I wouldn't be able to find it, but here it is." She handed it to her mother.

Bluma untied the string and took off the brown paper. "What is this?"

"It's a book of recipes for American foods—all in Yiddish! Miriam said every woman she knew had one and ..." Tears came to Fannie's eyes. "She should have been here to give it to you herself. It wasn't supposed to be like this—"

"Sha, child. It's not for us to know what is supposed to be. We can only make the best of what is."

Clara brought over two steaming cups of tea, milk and sugar, and a plate of cookies. "I'll go help Bridget now," she said, leaving the two women alone.

"How was the trip, Mama? Was Papa sick again? Were you or Freyda and Levi? Was the food awful? How bad was the smell? Were there—"

"Slow down, mamaleh! You can imagine how the journey was, as terrible as yours, I'm sure. Papa was sick for a few days, but he said it wasn't nearly as bad as the first time. The children and I were fine. And now it's over and soon we'll hardly remember it. But I want to hear about you, Feigele. It's been so long since I was able to read a letter from you. Now here we are so you can tell me everything in person."

Fannie took a sip of tea and bit into a cookie. Then she began to speak, the words spilling out like a dam had burst.

"What can I say, Mama? I'm well. I'm still studying English, but I feel more and more like an American. I'll be able to teach you so much. I have friends. My sister-in-law, Rachel, is one of them. Mary is another. I sell my embroidery to the wealthy women she knows. And Eve of course. She's wonderful. You'll see how lovely our apartment is— nothing like this of course, but the building is new, and the neighbors are nice. Most of them are young like me. Caleb and I—"

"Feigele, Feigele," interrupted her mother. "I'm not going anywhere. You don't need to rush."

Fannie paused. "Of course, Mama. I just have so much to tell you about life in America."

"And I want to know all of it. But right now, I want to know about you. When we said goodbye, you were still a child. Now here you are, a married woman. And marriage must agree with you, because you're more beautiful than ever, and wearing such lovely clothes. I hardly recognize the girl who left Kamenetz."

"Thank you, Mama. Miriam and Mary took me shopping when I came. We'll have to go shopping soon, Mama, so you'll look your best for Rosh Hashanah and Yom Kippur and Freyda will have clothes that fit her properly for school."

"We certainly wouldn't want our clothes to embarrass you," said Bluma.

"Oh no, Mama, I didn't mean it that way. Everyone here buys new clothes for the holidays. And I could see Freyda is getting too big for my old dresses and I'm sure you didn't have enough room in the valises to bring enough dresses for her to grow into."

Fannie didn't want her mother to know that Caleb had stopped giving her money for new clothes until she had a baby. She didn't dare ask him for money for Mama and Freyda, but she had some money saved from her embroidery and she'd ask Daniel for help. Then she wondered why she was so worried about their clothes. Had she become like Caleb, worried about how her family's appearance would reflect on her? She was ashamed to have such thoughts.

"But you haven't answered my question. I know Papa told you about the babies I lost, although mine came sooner—I never got to see them or even know if they were boys or girls. But it doesn't matter when it happens, a mother never forgets. More than anyone, I understand this. So, tell me, how are you?"

"I'm sad Mama, but it's better now. Not as bad as it was at first."

"Yes, it gets easier with time. And Caleb, he comforts you?"

Fannie hesitated.

"Isn't he good to you, Feigele?"

"I have everything I need Mama, not just my nice clothes. But you saw a little of how he is last night. He has trouble letting people see how he feels—even me. He wants a baby very much and it's taking so long …"

"But surely you're trying again?"

"Oh yes, we're trying, but still nothing. It's all he—we—think about."

"Perhaps don't worry so much. Sometimes babies come when you're not trying so hard."

"I'll try, Mama, but I'm not sure I can convince Caleb of that," she sighed. "Have you finished your tea? Let me show you where everything is kept." What more could she say about Caleb before her mother guessed at her unhappiness? She longed to tell her, but for now she didn't want to burden her, especially when there was nothing she could do to help.

The two of them rose. Bluma put an arm around her daughter. Fannie leaned into her and the two of them stood silently for a moment. "Mama's here now, Feigele. We'll talk more."

★ ★ ★

Eve and Noah were married the following month, soon after the Jewish High Holy Days. It wasn't easy for her parents, Fannie knew, to see their son married in a Reform shul. Men and women sat together; no one covered their heads. Papa must have wondered if he was wrong to bless their marriage. But, as Noah had promised, they stood under the *chuppa*. The traditional blessings were recited and when he placed the ring on Eve's finger, Fannie saw both her parents crying. There was no mistaking the love their son and his new wife shared.

Mama looked beautiful in a pale blue satin dress. Her hair was pinned in an elaborate chignon. She had declined to wear feathers or sequined ribbons. "That's a fashion for you and the younger women," she told Fannie, "I'm too old."

"You're not too old Mama," Fannie chided her. "But you don't need any decoration to be beautiful." She kissed her cheek.

Fannie wore a dress in a darker shade of blue. Her hair was braided like her mother's but threaded with sparkling ribbons. Daniel had paid for the dresses for Bluma, Fannie, and Freyda. He had insisted Fannie take them shopping and buy herself a new dress too. He had done the same thing when Fannie had asked him to help her pay for their new clothes for the holidays and some new blouses and skirts for Freyda to wear to school.

"I have nothing better to spend my money on than making sure the women I love look beautiful," he'd said. "We'd rather see you with your own wife," said Fannie. "How can it be that you still haven't found a woman you care for?"

As usual, Daniel put her off. "Stop worrying about me, Fannie." Fannie did worry, but she was grateful for his help.

Papa had regained his color and some of the weight he had lost on the ship. With his hair and beard neatly trimmed, wearing formal clothes and a top hat, he looked handsome standing next to his wife. *Just like he looked at my wedding, only happier with his wife beside him.*

Caleb, who had been sullen and withdrawn since Miriam died, surprised her by being sociable throughout the evening. He danced often and was attentive to her parents. When he took Freyda onto the dance floor, spinning her around so that her dress twirled out behind her, the other dancers gave them room and smiled at the pure joy on the young girl's face. Fannie stood with them, clapping to the music.

Shortly after the wedding, when Fannie had gone to see Eve and Noah's new apartment, she had remarked that with only one bedroom, it would soon be crowded. "Oh no, not soon," said Eve. "We're not planning to have children for quite a while. We both want to find good jobs first."

Fannie was too embarrassed to ask her if she was using a pessary like Mary. Eve was a nurse and would know all about those things, but Fannie didn't want to pry. *How strange life is. Caleb and I are yearning for a baby, and other couples are making sure not to have one. And how will Mama and Papa feel when neither of their married children gives them a grandchild?*

Freyda and Levi thrived in school. Levi had quickly been moved up a grade. Freyda needed more time to adjust to English, but she had been making great strides since Daniel hired a private teacher to help her. Fannie had been worried about Mama, but she surprised them all with her determination to learn English. Many women her age never learned more than a few words. They never left their neighborhoods and were completely dependent on their husbands and children. Bluma, on the other hand, enrolled in night school and sat with Freyda and her teacher for extra help. After Fannie showed her around the neighborhood a few times, she shopped for everything the family needed on her own. With great trepidation, she even took a trolley to Fannie's apartment by herself.

Fannie was amazed at her mother's fortitude. She realized she had always just taken her for granted. She never thought about what it took to make a home for a husband and five children. And she never knew about the babies Mama lost. She would do her best to make sure Freyda and Levi understood what a remarkable woman their Mama was.

In the first week of the new year, Rachel gave birth to a girl. When Max named her Miriam before the congregation, they all wept, wishing she were there to see her granddaughter.

Fannie went to bring the baby a dress she had embroidered. When Rachel finished nursing, she handed her the sleeping infant. "I'll make some tea," she said. "You can enjoy her while she's well fed and content." Fannie kissed the baby's forehead and the fuzz on her head.

Would it be so terrible to settle for "Aunt Fannie?" She loved them and they loved her. She spoiled them as much as she wanted. But she wasn't quite ready to resign herself to "aunt" instead of "mama" and she knew Caleb was still counting on a son of his own to take over the business.

A few months later, Mary had a baby boy. Caleb, Fannie, and Charles went to the *bris* together. The circumcision was followed by a sumptuous lunch. As she looked around at the guests, Fannie saw several of her customers. They were wearing her shawls and an item she had just started embroidering, bolero jackets. These were more expensive than anything she had ever made before. Knowing these women were part of the same crowd, she made sure to never make two exactly alike – and charged more for "originals." Fannie had always loved to embroider, but now she surprised herself by being a good businesswoman.

She could see Caleb and Simon off in a corner, drinking. "L'chaim," they shouted, downing one glass after another. They were getting louder and redder in the face with each toast.

That night Caleb was even quieter than usual, and she made no attempt to talk to him. It seemed like everyone else had what they wanted, so what was there to say?

Just a few months later, Europe was at war. Papa had gotten Mama and the children out just in time. Fannie wasn't sure if President Wilson's promise to keep America out of the war was a good thing. She wanted Daniel, Noah, Caleb and Simon – all the young men she knew — to be spared from fighting. But what about the Jews in Europe? Papa's cousins, Eli and Gussie, who they had stayed with on their way to the train, had written to say they were making plans to come to America. What would happen to them? How would any of the Jews trying to escape the pogroms in Russia get across Europe? The one thing that was certain was that the longer the war went on the more the Jews would suffer. Still, she thought, it's better for America to stay out of it.

She saw from the kitchen clock that it was getting late and dragged herself up from the chair to finish making dinner. The heat made her drowsy and the fan she had turned on did little to help. The air coming through the window was hot and humid. She took the *kasha varnishkes* and vegetables she had made earlier out of the icebox. She would wait to take the lamb chops out until Caleb was home and fry them quickly.

She wasn't looking forward to his arrival or another tense dinner. She had started bleeding the night before, five days late. Foolishly, they'd allowed themselves to hope, only to be disappointed once again. When Fannie heard Caleb's key in the door she sighed. Would there only be silence, or would he berate her for another "failure?" There was no way to tell.

"I see you've read the news," said Caleb when he came into the kitchen. "I just hope we get into it soon."

"How can you say that? Why would you want us to fight?"

"Soldiers need supplies, Fannie, like mess kits and first aid packets. They'll need canned foods, and we're a big tin manufacturer. In fact, I'm thinking of expanding, maybe buying another factory. You'll see, there's no way we'll stay out of it for too long, and Fine and Sons will be first in line to sell to the government."

"You want war so you can make money?"

"I don't want war, but it's coming, and someone will get rich. Why shouldn't it be me?"

The thought of making money because young men were dying appalled Fannie, but she didn't argue. She wondered how he would feel if he had a son old enough to fight. Even the sons of rich men died in a war.

"I haven't discussed it with my father yet, but I'm sure he'll agree. This is the opportunity we've been waiting for."

There was nothing else to say. Only time would tell how the war would change their lives.

CHAPTER 17

Fannie sat in the living room, embroidering a jacket for a new client. Her head was bent over her work as she concentrated on the tiny French knots she was stitching. Her new eyeglasses were perched on her nose. Over the last several months she had found herself holding her work closer and having difficulty threading a needle. Finally, she went to see the eye doctor. "Make sure you have a good light and rest your eyes often," the doctor said. "Or your vision will get worse." Fannie's embroidery was too important to her to put her vision at risk, so she heeded his advice while she was embroidering or reading at home. But she was too vain to wear the glasses anywhere else.

Dinner had been ready an hour ago, but Caleb was even later than usual. She was keeping it warm in the oven. When she heard his footsteps in the hall, she barely had time to put her work away before he burst into the room and started shouting at her.

"You won't believe it. He has a bride. He says he loved my mother, and this is what he does. I—"

"Slow down, Caleb. What are you talking about?"

"My father, the old goat. As soon as we unveiled my mother's headstone, he went to the shadchen to find a new wife. He waited one year—not a minute longer—and then he went looking without telling us. And now he's found someone, and he plans to get married right away. Right away! He told us when we were ready to leave today. Max and I couldn't believe it." Caleb paced the room.

"Charles, married again so soon?"

"Isn't that what I just said? The wedding is next month."

"Sit down, Caleb, let's talk."

"Talk? It's my father who should have been talking, not keeping secrets." He dropped into his chair.

Fannie searched for the right words to calm him. And what would it mean for her family now that there would be a new wife to take over the Fine household?

"He loved Miriam very much, Caleb, but he's been lonely. I'm sure he didn't mean to hide anything from you."

"Oh yes he did, the devious bastard."

"Caleb, he's your father!"

"So? Doesn't my mother's memory mean anything to him?"

"I'm sure it does." Fannie proceeded carefully, not wanting to make him angrier. "But I think your mother would understand. She loved him too much to want him to be unhappy."

"Well, you haven't heard the worst. She's my age, a widow with a young son."

Fannie was taken aback. She had imagined a woman Miriam's age. Charles loved children, but did he really want another little boy in the house? Then she remembered how warmly he had welcomed Levi. But Levi was a cousin, not a son, a child to play with, not to discipline or worry about.

"You know how much your father loves children. The child will be a comfort to him. Have some pity, Caleb."

"He has three grandchildren already to comfort him." Caleb would not be placated. He stood up and started pacing again. "It's embarrassing for such an old man."

"Do you know when we'll meet her?"

"I have no idea and what difference does that make?"

"None, but think about what she must be feeling, marrying into a new family and having to face you and Max."

"I don't care what she's feeling and I'm not about to forgive my father."

"That's not what your mother would want, Caleb. Come, let's have dinner. Things will look different tomorrow."

That night, when Caleb came to her bed, Fannie prayed fervently for a baby. Caleb wouldn't care as much about what his father did if he had a son of his own.

The next morning Caleb was silent at breakfast. She could see from the way he held himself he was still angry.

"I'll go talk to my mother," said Fannie. "She'll know more about your father's plans."

"Fine, do what you want," he said. He stood up abruptly, "It won't make any difference."

When Fannie got to the Fine house later that morning Rachel was walking out the door. "I had some meat from my father's shop to drop off," she said. "My mother is watching the children, so I can't stay to talk."

"Only for a minute," said Fannie. "Tell me what Max said about Charles. Caleb was furious."

"Max was angry too," said Rachel, "but he calmed down."

"Caleb didn't. He was still fuming when he left this morning. And did Max tell you how young she is? And that she has a son not much older than your David?"

"Yes, that will be strange, won't it? But that happens in lots of families when a man marries again."

"I couldn't make Caleb understand."

"Well, Charles has decided, so it doesn't matter if Caleb understands or not."

"True, but it would be nicer if he was ready to get along. Do you have any idea when we're to meet her?"

"I think this week at Shabbos dinner."

"Then I don't have much time to convince him to be kind."

"I really have to run, Fannie."

"I'll let you go – give the children a kiss for me."

Fannie went inside to find her mother.

"Feigele, I'm glad you're here," said her mother when Fannie found her sitting in the kitchen. "Tea?"

"Thanks, Mama."

"So, I'm sure you've come to talk about Charles."

"Yes, Caleb told me yesterday. He was so angry I couldn't reason with him."

"It's hard now, but he'll get over it after a while."

"I'm afraid it will be a long while. When did you find out?"

Bluma got up to get cups and saucers and a plate of cookies she knew her daughter liked. Then she took the kettle off the stove.

"He told us about the shadchen right after the unveiling, but he asked us not to say anything," she said as she poured the steaming hot water. "He had no idea he would find someone so quickly. He only told us last night, after he told Caleb and Max, of course. He wanted his sons to be the first to know."

"How does Papa feel about it? He and Miriam were so close." Fannie took a cookie.

"Papa understands. He's seen how lonely Charles has been and was glad to see him smiling again. He couldn't hide his happiness when he told us about her." She paused to sip her tea. "Her name is Zipporah. She and her late husband came to America from Poland seven years ago. He died a year after their son, Gabriel, was born. She was left with no money, and her only family was an old aunt of her husband's, who took her in. She's been working six days a week for a milliner while the aunt watches the child. She sounds brave. I think we'll like her."

"Caleb won't. He's determined not to like her. And she's so young."

"What, he should only marry an old lady? What difference does her age make if she makes him happy and she'll keep a good home?

"But what about you and Papa and the children? Will you have to leave?"

"Charles said no. He promised us we have a home here as long as we want, but of course we won't stay. Don't tell Caleb, but Papa has been looking for a new job. It hasn't always been easy working for his cousin. But he got some good experience, and it gave him time to learn enough English to look for something else. They're impressed when he says he works for Fine and Sons. I hope he'll come home with good news today and then we'll tell the family."

"And a new place to live?" asked Fannie, reaching for another cookie.

"I'm not sure, but probably in Manhattan, Feigele."

"Oh no, so far?"

"I'm afraid so, *ziskeit*. One of the men Papa knows from the factory told him about an apartment in his building that sounds perfect for us, in a nice neighborhood. There are stores I can walk to easily and a shul only a few blocks away. It has three bedrooms, but we can afford it. The children will have to change schools, but I'm sure they'll make friends easily. And Freyda wants to go to the Stuyvesant Manual Trades high school next year, so it will be perfect for her."

"Papa approves of this for Freyda?"

Bluma put her hand over Fannie's. "Let it be between us for now," she said.

"So much change," said Fannie. "And so fast. Are you sure you won't stay in Brooklyn?"

"I can't say for sure, but I think Papa would like to start over."

"Just when I got used to having you close by."

"But we can still see each other often. This train you take all the time – it will be easy for you to visit, no? And I'm learning to make my way too."

"It won't be the same."

Bluma looked Fannie in the eyes. "Feigele, you're unhappy?"

"Oh, no—"

"Tell me, child."

Fannie burst into tears.

"Oh Mama, it's so hard. I don't think Caleb wanted a wife his father picked out, but I think it would have been fine if only we had a baby. He was angry when it took so long, but you should have seen him when I was expecting. It was just like I wrote - he was overjoyed. Then when I lost the baby, he got even angrier. He blames me."

She buried her head in her hands. "He can be so cruel," she said through her tears.

"My poor Feigele. I knew something was wrong."

"I didn't want you to know. I've tried to hide it. Daniel guessed, but I was hoping he was the only one."

"A mother knows," said Mama, taking both of Fannie's hands in hers.

"There's nothing I can do. I keep house, I spend time with my friends, I shop, I cook, and I embroider. It just doesn't seem fair."

"It may not be fair, but it's in God's hands. Come, will you take a walk with me?"

"Of course, Mama."

The two women rose. Bluma took Fannie in her arms and let her cry. "Go wash your face," she said. "I need to go to the grocer, and maybe we'll have time to stop in the candy store." She gave her daughter a squeeze. Fannie smiled wanly. If only her problems could be cured by candy, but she wasn't a little girl anymore.

When she got home, she opened the bag of chocolate kisses her mother had insisted on buying her, put one in her mouth, and started to think of what she'd say to Caleb. And somehow, life did feel a little easier.

CHAPTER 18

Fannie's family was gathered around the dinner table. Ever since Mama, Papa and the children had moved to Manhattan, they had rarely come to Brooklyn. Bluma would only take the subway if Asher was with her, and it was easier for Fannie to go to their new apartment and for Caleb to meet her there. It was closer for Noah, Eve and Daniel too.

She had taken extra care preparing for Shabbos. The immaculate white linen tablecloth she had embroidered with a blue border lay on the table without a crease. Crystal glasses sparkled and her treasured silver candlesticks from Mama gleamed. Dinner smelled delicious. The kugel was browned and crisp, just the way Caleb liked it. The aroma of the raisins and honey she had added to the roasted carrots filled the house.

Although the war news was on everyone's mind, most of the conversation was about the children's school. They spoke excitedly about their lessons, switching back and forth between Yiddish and English. She had helped them both get library cards and bought them a dictionary just like the one Noah had given her. Freyda had discovered "The Outdoor Girls" series and chattered on about her favorite character, Betty.

"When I'm a nurse I'll be brave, just like her." she said.

Freyda looked more grownup every time Fannie saw her. She hadn't had a chance to ask Mama about Freyda's plans for high school, but she was sure she'd go where she could prepare for nursing school.

Levi had brought some of the toy soldiers Daniel had given him to show Fannie and Caleb. "I'll be brave too," he said. "As soon as I'm old enough I'll fight in the war and kill all the Huns." He puffed up his chest and struck a pose.

"Sha, *tateleh*," said Bluma. "No talk of killing."

"But Mama, they're bad men."

"Yes, Levi, but killing is a terrible thing."

Caleb had promised he would be home in time for Shabbos, but he hadn't arrived yet. Darkness came early in the winter, and she couldn't wait any longer to light the candles. Just as she struck a match, he appeared in the dining room. They had all been so busy talking they hadn't heard him come into the apartment. She blew out the match to wait for him to sit down.

"Caleb!" Levi ran to show his brother-in-law his toy soldiers.

"Very nice," said Caleb, without looking at him.

Disappointed, Levi returned to his seat.

"Gut Shabbos, son," said Asher. "It's good to see you again."

"What's good about it," muttered Caleb. He remained standing in the doorway.

"Has something happened at the factory, Caleb?" asked Fannie. "Or is there news about the war? You're just in time for the candles. Come, sit down and we'll talk about whatever it is later."

Caleb looked around but made no move to sit.

"One big happy family," he sneered.

Fannie had been about to light the match, but she paused, taken aback by the hostility in his tone.

"You know what's missing from this happy family?" he said. "Babies. My brother has babies at his table, my friends have babies at their tables, but not me. Oh no, no baby at my table."

"Caleb, please," said Fannie. "Sit down and calm yourself. It's Shabbos."

Caleb paid no attention to her. "And you know who else is going to have a baby at his table? My father, that's who. Perhaps you haven't heard the good news? His new bride is expecting. My father will be a father — again — before me." His voice got louder.

"Caleb," Fannie tried again.

"What do you think about that, Fannie?" His voice rose. "Another man's wife is having a baby. But not mine." He glared at her. "The only baby my wife managed to give me didn't even live to take a breath."

Fannie jerked back as though he had slapped her.

"That's enough Caleb," said Daniel, getting out of his chair. "You and Fannie can talk about this later."

"Later? How much later? Another four years?"

"Caleb, please, it's time to light the candles," pleaded Fannie.

"Why bother? Why are you praying to a God who never listens?"

"Caleb." Asher started to stand. "How can—"

With two long steps, Caleb was beside Fannie. "Forget the candles, Fannie—there is no God." In a rage, he drew back his arm and swept the candlesticks off the table. They fell to the floor with a loud crash.

The family sat, stunned. For a moment, no one moved or spoke.

Fannie avoided looking at Caleb as she silently bent down to pick up the candlesticks. One of them had broken in half. She began to weep as she held the pieces out in front of her, staring at them in disbelief.

"Look what you've done," she cried. "My gift from Mama."

"I—" Caleb seemed as dazed as everyone else by what he had done.

Before he could finish, Daniel grabbed him by the shoulders.

"Get out. Go calm yourself somewhere."

"This is my home," said Caleb, trying to shake him off.

"And I'm telling you to leave it. Now," said Daniel, tightening his grip. "And if you ever hurt my sister—"

"Daniel, he wouldn't—" Fannie walked toward them.

Daniel ignored her, roughly shoving Caleb toward the living room. Noah took Fannie's arm to keep her from following them. "Stay," he said gently.

"*Got in himmel*," muttered Asher, dropping back into his seat. Bluma put her hand on his arm and reassured Freyda and Levi, who were white faced. "He didn't mean it," she told them. "He's just upset."

Eve got up, put her arms around Fannie, and helped her into her seat.

"Sit, Fannie. We'll start again." She put the candlesticks on the counter and picked the candles up from the floor. She took out a plate, lit a match and let the wax drip from the bottom of the candles so they would stay upright.

Fannie let Eve take over. She sat, numb, getting up only when the apartment door slammed, and Daniel returned. Then she stood up, struck a match, and covered her eyes.

Bluma stood beside her daughter and put her arm around her, holding her upright while she said the blessing.

"*Baruch atah* ..." Fannie whispered, tears streaming down her cheeks. She collapsed back into her seat when she finished.

Without being asked, Asher stood, raised his wine glass and led the Kiddush. Then he said the Motzi over the challah. Fannie started to get up to get the dinner, but Eve pushed her down firmly. "We'll take care of it," she said. "You sit."

"Fannie," started Daniel, "Has Caleb—"

"Daniel, not now," said Bluma, inclining her head toward the children.

The meal went on without the lively chatter that had preceded Caleb's arrival. Everyone complimented Fannie on the food, but she barely noticed and didn't utter a word.

As soon as Bluma, Eve and Freyda had cleared the table, Eve held out her hands to the children.

"Come let's sit in the living room," she said. "You can finish telling me about your English teacher."

"But we—"

Bluma silenced them with a glance. "Go with Eve," she said.

"Fannie, has he ever hurt you?" asked Daniel as soon as they were out of the room.

"No, Daniel, never. He may be harsh, but it's only words."

"Only? He uses words like weapons. He's making you miserable, isn't he?"

Fannie nodded mutely.

"This is true?" asked Asher.

Bluma answered. "He's been cruel, Asher. He's made her unhappy almost from the beginning, but it got worse after she lost the baby."

"And you've known this?"

"She tried to hide it, but I guessed." said Bluma. "She didn't want you to know."

Asher shook his head. "I thought I was doing the right thing," he said to Fannie. "I thought you'd have everything you wanted, married to a wealthy man in America."

"Don't blame yourself, Papa," said Fannie, "How could you have known?

"I'm sorry, Feigele, I wish there was something to do."

"There is something to do," said Daniel. "This is America. Fannie doesn't have to stay with him."

"What are you talking about?" said Asher.

"I'm talking about a divorce, Papa. And if Caleb won't give it to her, she can go to court. That's what they do in America."

"No," said Asher, "It would be a shanda—"

Noah couldn't hold back his anger. "You're more worried about being ashamed than about your daughter? Is some law from thousands of years ago more important than her happiness? Haven't you learned anything?" He turned to his mother. "Please do something," he said.

"I can't leave him," said Fannie.

"Can't?" said Daniel in exasperation. "Or won't?"

"I promised," said Fannie softly.

"You didn't have a choice," said Daniel. "You were a girl. No one will hold you to that promise."

"No," said Fannie. "I promised Miriam. She begged me when she was dying. She said Caleb was a good man underneath. I promised her I would take care of him. So, you see, I can't leave him."

"That's—"

"Let her be, Daniel," said Mama.

"Let her suffer?"

"Of course not, let her decide," she answered. "Let her make up her own mind."

"But—" began Asher.

"She's not a child anymore Asher. And Daniel is right. This is America. She must be allowed to decide for herself."

"Thank you, Mama." Fannie squeezed her mother's hand.

"You're exhausted, Feigele. Will you be all right here if we leave? Will Caleb—"

"I'll be fine, Mama. He's just mad about his father. He was hurt when Charles got married again so quickly after Miriam died, and now this. He doesn't know how to show his disappointment except in anger. He probably won't even come home."

"All the same, Fannie, I'll stay with you," said Daniel. "You can't be sure he won't turn violent again."

"No, Daniel. I know you mean well, but like Mama said, I'm not a child anymore. I'll work this out on my own."

The family began to bundle up against the cold and one by one kissed Fannie goodnight.

"We're here if you need us." Eve and Noah were the first to leave.

"I'll take care of you Fannie. I'm a big boy now, and Daniel is teaching me to fight," said Levi, putting up his fists.

Fannie looked accusingly at Daniel over Levi's head, but he only shrugged.

"I know you will, Levi." Fannie smiled through her tears.

Freyda hugged her sister tightly. Fannie saw in her eyes that her happily-ever-after illusions had been shattered.

"Feigele, I—"

"I know, Papa. I love you too."

She and her mother held on to each other wordlessly.

"Are you sure?" Daniel hesitated at the door.

"Yes, Daniel, goodnight." Fannie kissed him and closed the door firmly behind him.

Leaving dirty dishes in the sink for the first time in her life, she undressed and fell into bed. She was awake for what seemed like hours, listening for Caleb's key in the door and worrying about what she would do if he came home. Scenes from the last four years played again and again in her mind. Caleb disappearing after they lost the baby. Caleb pushing her away when Miriam died. She tossed and turned until exhaustion overcame her, and she fell asleep.

As she had expected, Caleb didn't come home until early the next morning. She was in the bedroom, sitting at her dressing table in her robe when he arrived, worrying about what would happen. He had gone too far, and she had to find the words to tell him.

"I'm sorry I broke your candlesticks," he said as he walked into the room. "I'll have them fixed. They'll be good as new, I promise." He went to the closet and began taking out fresh clothes.

"Oh, Caleb, it's not the candlesticks. Don't you understand?"

"I said I'm sorry, what more do you want?"

"Nothing," said Fannie. *At least nothing you can give me.* She walked out of the bedroom and sat in her chair in the living room, waiting to see if he would say more.

As soon as he had changed his clothes, Caleb prepared to leave. "I'm going to take a walk with Max. Maybe you'd like to go to a movie tonight? *Perils of Pauline*?"

"No, Caleb, I don't want to go to a movie."

"But I want to make it up to you."

"You can make it up to me by being a husband who cares."

"What the devil are you talking about?"

"I'm talking about how you treated me last night—and how you've been treating me for four years."

"I haven't got time for this now, Fannie."

"Yes, I know," said Fannie softly.

"Well, I'll see you later," he said curtly as he left.

She stared at the closed door as though she could see through it and watch him walking away, still oblivious to the depth of her feelings.

The future of our marriage isn't up to him anymore. It's up to me.

CHAPTER 19

Fannie made quick work of the kitchen and got dressed to go out. It was cold, but sunny, so she decided to go for a walk in Prospect Park, where she and Caleb had walked when they first met. She had gone back often and thought of it as a refuge. It wouldn't be crowded, and she wasn't likely to meet anyone she knew as she thought about what to do. As she entered the park, she tightened her scarf around her neck and pulled her hat down over her ears. The trees that had shaded them on their picnic that summer day were bare now. The sun shone brightly in the pale gray winter sky, but the air was cold.

As she suspected, there were hardly any people on the path. Two women, also bundled up against the cold, were pushing prams ahead of her. If she left Caleb, would she be giving up any chance to walk here with a baby of her own?

Her brothers told her she could go to the American court. But was that a good thing, to end a marriage? She argued with herself as she walked. They had been married under the chuppah, made promises to each other before God. Even in America, didn't that still mean something?

Caleb put a roof over her head. He didn't beat her. So she was unhappy. There were unhappy wives in Kamenetz, she'd heard Mama talk about them. But none of them got divorced. She thought about Gittel and Raisel. What would they tell her? When they were young, she and her friends knew they would be expected to be good wives and mothers, no matter what their husbands were like. But what did they understand then of unhappiness, of loneliness?

She started to think about what her family would say. Her brothers were urging her to leave. They meant well, but did they really understand what life would be like for her if she left Caleb?

And Papa? It had been so hard for him to give his blessing to Noah and Eve. Could he accept a daughter who got a divorce? He was sorry her marriage didn't work out the way he'd hoped, but she doubted he'd think her feelings were reason enough to leave. He had said it last night—it would be a disgrace. She couldn't bear it if Papa turned his back on her.

But Mama would convince him, wouldn't she? Fannie had seen how she let Papa think he was in charge while getting him to do what she thought was right. Mama had brought her up to be a good wife, and until now Fannie thought that meant obeying her husband and suffering in silence. But in America, Fannie saw another side of Mama. She said giving women the freedom to choose for themselves was a better way. If Mama hadn't said it was up to Fannie to decide, would she even be thinking about leaving Caleb?

A man coming from the opposite direction stared at her. She must have looked strange, talking to herself. She began to walk faster. The sun was already disappearing and with it any warmth. Her fingers were starting to get cold, even under her thick wool mittens. She slapped her hands together, trying to warm them. If only the choice was clear to her.

And how could she break her promise to Miriam? It hadn't been fair of her to ask when she was dying, when she knew Fannie couldn't refuse. But she did ask, and Fannie said yes. It was easier to think about breaking her wedding vows than breaking her promise to Miriam. She had welcomed Fannie into her home and family. She had taken care of her when the baby died. *What should I do, Miriam? If only you were here now so I could explain.*

Miriam had asked Fannie to take care of Caleb, but he wouldn't let her. Perhaps he was feeling as trapped and unhappy as she was. Miriam wouldn't want him to be unhappy, would she? Maybe leaving would be a relief to him and he would find a wife he wanted. *Will you forgive me, Miriam?*

And, finally, she tried to envision what Caleb would say. What did he think now, four years after he introduced the "greenie" bride his father had picked out to his friends in this very place? *We talked about children that afternoon. You wanted sons, and I said I wanted a daughter too.* Now they had neither. Was that why he treated her so badly? She conceived once, but it might never happen again. What if another baby died? She picked up her pace, the end of the path in sight. *Is there someone else, Caleb? Where do you go when you don't come home? Have you broken God's commandment? Are you thinking of leaving me?*

Husbands left all the time, she knew, so many they filled a page every day in the *Forverts,* "The Gallery of Missing Husbands." Of course there was no gallery of wives who ran away. Where could they go? How could they earn enough money for food and a place to live? Fannie was luckier than most. Caleb was obligated to give her money, and she had a family who would take care of her. She had no children to feed. But was she a child that she should go running home to Mama and Papa? They'd settled into their new apartment. Would Mary's wealthy friends still buy embroidery from her so she could give Papa money for the expenses she added?

Fannie came to the park exit. She was back where she started, not knowing what to do. She stopped walking for a moment. No, she wasn't back where she started. She was no longer the girl who got off the boat, innocent and scared, and let her future husband change her name. She'd gone to school, made friends, and earned good money. *If life with Caleb is too painful to bear, I can start again. This is America; I can leave him.* She paused again. *I will leave him.* She stood up tall and strode out of the park.

★ ★ ★

Fannie was afraid her resolve would weaken by the time Caleb came home. She sat in her chair, holding her embroidery in her lap without making a stitch. Finally, she heard his steps in the hall.

"I'm sorry I'm late, but we can still make the movie if we hurry," Caleb said as soon as he opened the door. "Come, put on your coat."

"Didn't you hear me this morning? I don't want to go to the movies," said Fannie. "Sit down, Caleb. I'd like to talk."

"But it's one of your favorites."

"No," said Fannie firmly. "Not tonight."

"Fine, I was just trying to do something nice for you." He hung up his hat and coat.

"Caleb, I'm leaving."

"You're what?"

"I'm leaving you. I'm going home to my family until I decide what to do with my life."

"You can't." He sat down in his chair with a thud. "I said I was sorry. I said I'll fix the candlesticks. What more do you want?"

"What more? I'll tell you what more. I want someone who cares about me. I want someone who doesn't blame me for not having a baby — someone who knows he's not the only one suffering."

Caleb remained silent.

"Please, Caleb, think about it. You didn't want to marry me in the first place, did you? You wanted to choose your own wife."

"What difference does that make. We're married now."

"Yes, we are, but can you honestly say you'd be unhappy without me? Where are you when you stay out all night? With other women? With the same woman? Should I just wait for you to abandon me?"

"Don't be ridiculous. Lots of men stay out—their wives get used to it." Caleb got up. He stood with his arms folded in front of him.

"I won't."

"It's your brothers. They've put these crazy ideas in your head."

"No, they've only opened my eyes to what a woman can do in America."

"So, you think because this is America you can just pick up and leave?"

"I know it won't be easy." Fannie sighed.

"You can't do this to me. People will say I was a bad husband."

"Is that all you care about? What people will say?"

"Of course I care. I'm an important man. You should care too."

"Did you care what people thought when you punished me by not allowing me to buy new clothes?"

"New clothes. I should have known. Is that what this is about?"

"Just listen, Caleb, listen to me for once." Fannie rose to stand opposite him. "I don't care about new clothes," she said slowly. "I didn't have them before we were married, and I can do without them again. I'm an American now, just like you, and I'm going to decide for myself."

"And a baby, Fannie? I thought that was important to both of us."

"And what if that never happens? I never thought I'd be saying this, but some things are more important." She glared at him. "I will never—ever—forgive you for what you said last night."

"Stop being hysterical. You know I was just angry about my father." He began to pace.

"Stand still and look at me when I talk to you," Fannie shouted at him. "It wasn't just last night. You have always blamed me. Where were you when our baby died, and I needed you to comfort me? You take your anger out on my body, without pleasure for either of us, I think. Have you even once thought about how I was feeling? Or were you too busy taking your pleasure somewhere else to care?"

"Fannie—"

"It's too late now. I'm leaving."

"And what about your promise to my mother? Doesn't that count for anything?"

"How dare you! I tried—you know I tried. You pushed me away."

"You promised her."

"Leave your mother out of this, Caleb. I loved her more than you'll ever understand. You wouldn't even let me mourn her with you. She, more than anyone, would know that this is best for both of us. I'm leaving and I want a *get*."

"Fine. We'll go to the *Beis Din* and I'll tell the Rabbis you couldn't give me a child. They'll take my side and approve the divorce. But I'm not giving you any money. See how many new clothes you'll have then," he said with a scornful smile.

"But the ketubah says—" Fannie sat down, gripping the arms of her chair. His threat took her by surprise. How would she manage without his money? But she would find a way. There was no turning back now.

"I don't care what the ketubah says, and the Rabbis won't either. Not when I tell them this was all your idea." Caleb stood, looking down at her. "See how you'll feel then."

Fannie stood to face him. "I'm sorry, Caleb. I was hoping you'd understand this will be better for both of us. I'd like a few days to pack my things and then I'm going to stay with my family."

"Fine."

They looked at each other, uncertain what to do next. Caleb put his hat and coat back on and opened the door. "I'm going to tell my family," he yelled as he left.

Fannie locked the door behind him and sat down. *Now what?*

★ ★ ★

Once Caleb had agreed to grant her a get, she saw him only once. It was the day she went to take her things from the apartment.

Daniel and his friend, Tony, loaded everything onto Tony's truck. When they had a moment alone she asked Daniel, "How do you know a man with a truck?"

"I have many friends," he answered. "None of them are scholars like my brother, so they actually have useful skills in life."

"So many mysteries. And why aren't you working now? It's the middle of the day."

"Fannie, I've told you before, stop asking so many questions." He picked up the last box, gave her a quick kiss and headed out the door. "We're off. I'll see you at Mama and Papa's.

She had expected to have very little to pack, but her clothes alone filled quite a few valises and boxes. How different from when she left Kamenetz. She took nothing from the kitchen except the tablecloths she had embroidered, although she couldn't imagine Caleb using any of the pots and pans. Would another wife use them or want new ones? She left the sheets and pillowcases she had embroidered before she knew anything about the man who would be sleeping on them, although she was sure Caleb would get rid of them before another woman shared his bedroom. He wouldn't want to explain about her.

She took special care wrapping the candlesticks. Papa said he would take them to be fixed at the place where he'd bought them. She wondered if she'd ever use them again in a home of her own. It was Daniel who had suggested she take her chair and footstool, so she had telephoned Caleb at his father's house to ask if she could take them. He wasn't there, but Bridget took a message and called her the next day to say he had agreed. Fannie was surprised he said yes, but perhaps he wanted as few reminders of her as possible.

"I don't mean to overstep, Miss Fannie," said Bridget. "But Clara and I will miss you. We wish you good luck."

"I'll miss both of you too, Bridget." The reality of how many people she was leaving behind was starting to sink in.

Rachel had been the hardest goodbye. "I'm sorry I couldn't bring the children, Fannie, but Max has forbidden me to see you again. He would be furious if he knew I was here and they're too little to keep a secret. I can't even sit, just say a quick goodbye."

"I understand, Rachel. I'm so grateful you came."

She grasped her sister-in-law's hand. "You've been like a big sister to me. Do you remember how frightened of marriage I was the first time we met? And we've been through so much together. Who would have thought we'd lose Miriam?"

"And now I'm losing you," said Rachel. "What will you do, Fannie?"

"I honestly don't know yet. But I'll be moving in with my family and looking for work soon. You'll let your friends know if they want embroidery, won't you?"

"I'm not sure I can, Fannie, and I don't want to make a promise I can't keep."

"I see," said Fannie, although she didn't see at all. Caleb refused to give her money. Was he also going to prevent her from earning it on her own?

"But will you take my parents' number, just in case?" She handed Rachel a folded-up piece of paper from her pocket. Rachel took it and buried it deep in her purse.

"Oh Fannie, if only it didn't have to be like this. Surely you could have tried harder."

Fannie dropped Rachel's hand. "I tried and tried, Rachel. It was Caleb who wouldn't try.

Rachel shook her head sadly. "*Shalom Bayit* takes time, Fannie. It's hard work to make peace in the home."

"I wish I could make you understand."

"I'm afraid I don't, but I'll keep the good memories of our time together." said Rachel. "And I know the children will miss their Aunt Fannie."

"You'll give them a kiss goodbye from me?"

"I will, I promise, but now I really must go. God bless you, Fannie."

"And you too," said Fannie.

The two held on to each other briefly before Rachel turned to leave. Now she was neither "mama" nor "Aunt Fannie." *Who am I going to be now?* She tried not to feel sorry for herself, but a few tears rolled down her cheeks.

She had tried calling Mary several times, but none of her calls were returned. How could she be so cold? Even though she was Caleb's friend first, they had spent four years shopping, dining out and sharing confidences between women. And not even a goodbye? It was probably Caleb's doing.

Fannie walked around the apartment, remembering the day she had looked at her new things and wondered about her married life. Only a single toothbrush and towel remained in the bathroom. She had moved Caleb's chair and rearranged the lamp to cover up the marks in the carpet where her chair and footstool had been. It was as though she had never been there.

Her dressing table was bare. Samuel's button was in her purse. If ever she needed a good luck charm, it was now. She was still wearing the rings Caleb had given her. If she didn't find a job, she would ask Papa to sell the diamond. She checked one more time, although she had thoroughly cleaned and dusted that morning, before laying her key on the kitchen table.

"Fannie."

She jumped at Caleb's voice behind her.

"I'm sorry, I didn't mean to startle you. I thought you'd be gone."

"I was just leaving. Here."

She picked up the key and handed it to him.

They looked at each other, neither of them sure what to say.

"It wasn't all bad, was it?" Caleb asked.

"No," she said quietly as she walked out the door.

CHAPTER 20

The door to Mama and Papa's apartment opened before Fannie had a chance to knock.

"Feigele, I saw you from the window!" Fannie's mother reached out to her, and in spite of telling herself all the way from Brooklyn she wouldn't cry, Fannie burst into tears.

"Sha, mamaleh, everything will be fine. Put your things down and come sit. We have plenty of time before dinner and you're the first one here. Sit, and I'll bring some tea."

"I'm not a guest for you to serve, Mama."

"Of course not. But just for now, listen to your mama and sit. I can see how tired you are."

Fannie sank into her chair gratefully, closing her eyes and thinking about everything that had happened since she told Caleb she was leaving. She could still hardly believe she had done it.

"Fannie." Her mother's voice startled her.

"I'm sorry, Mama, I must have dozed off. I was thinking about my things. Do you remember the day you and I packed my embroidery in Kamenetz?"

"Yes, and I said you shouldn't worry about them being fine enough for Caleb's family and friends. And look how successful your needlework business has been here."

"You were right, as usual." Fannie thought her mother looked especially lovely this evening. The circles under her eyes were gone now and there was color in her cheeks. Having the family together again and the move to a place of her own agreed with her. Even Fannie's divorce didn't appear to have spoiled her peace of mind. And even though Mama said she looked tired, it hadn't spoiled hers.

She took the cup of tea her mother held out to her and had just taken a sip when Freyda and Levi came running in, tossing off their coats, hats, scarves and gloves in their haste to get to Fannie.

"You're here, you're here!" they shouted.

"We're not supposed to talk about it, Fannie, but are you very sad?" asked Levi. "Are you going to cry?"

"How could I be sad when I'm with you? Let me kiss that cold nose of yours. And then you'd better pick up your clothes before Mama gets angry and makes me leave."

Freyda hugged her sister. "I'm glad you're here." she said. "Since you're going to be here all the time now will you teach me to embroider?"

"Of course. We can start with this daisy stitch. She took a piece she was working on from the bag she had placed next to her chair to show Freyda. "It would look pretty on the belt you're wearing. But for now, let's see what we can do to help Mama. Daniel will be here soon with my things and Noah and Eve are coming from school."

Dinner was lively. If anyone was thinking of the last time they had eaten together, it was never mentioned. Only after the children had gone to bed did Daniel talk to Fannie about her future. "That *mamzer*," he said. "You need to make the bastard pay."

Bluma shook her finger at her son. "Daniel, such language in my house."

"I'm sorry, Mama," said Daniel. "But Fannie, listen to me. You can take him to court for what is rightfully yours. It's called alimony – money he will have to give you, at least until you marry again."

"And if I never marry?"

"Don't be silly, you're too beautiful to stay unmarried long. But let's not worry about that now."

"And what exactly happens in court?"

"You go with a lawyer in front of a judge to tell him your story, and he decides how much to give you."

"And does Caleb tell his story? He'll be there too?"

"Yes, but you don't talk to each other, only to the judge. And the lawyer will help you. I have a friend, Michael, who's a lawyer. I told him about you, and he'll take your case."

"Truck drivers and now lawyers, what interesting friends you have, Daniel."

"Well, will you?"

Fannie looked at her parents. "You know the Beis Din will side with Caleb," she said. "I'll have my get, but nothing to contribute to the family."

"We'll manage, Fannie. People do on far less," said her father. "But I know nothing of how this is done in America, so perhaps it's wise to listen to Daniel."

"Listen to him, Fannie," said Noah. "Get what you deserve." Eve nodded along with him.

"I'll let Michael know right away. It takes time to get a court date."

"Fannie hasn't said yes yet," said Bluma. She reached out to hold Fannie's hand. "It's up to you."

Fannie bowed her head and took a deep breath. From now on, she vowed, every decision she made would be her own. "Yes," she said. "I'll go to the American court."

★ ★ ★

Fannie was desperate. She had been looking for work for three months. There was still no word from the court about her alimony, her savings were rapidly disappearing, and she still didn't have a job. She had lost count of all the shops she had tried, hoping to avoid working in a factory. Things had gotten better since the Triangle Shirtwaist fire, and of course she would do whatever was necessary to help the family, but she wanted to try her luck in a shop first. Today she'd gone out again, dressed in one of her newest black skirts and a pristine white pintucked blouse she had made for herself. She added a belt she had embroidered in bright colors and wore the still elegant pearl-gray boots she had bought when she'd first arrived. She carried some of her shawls and jackets in a small carpet bag, hoping that even if they didn't offer her a job, one of the shops might sell them.

She'd had no luck. Not sure where to try next, she had stopped for a cup of tea and a roll and butter and was walking aimlessly near Central Park, when she happened to glance up at the window of a brownstone and saw a sign, "Wanted – experienced seamstress for a dressmaking establishment; references required." She had no references, but she had her samples, and she'd made what she was wearing. Maybe she could convince them to give her a chance. She went up the three stone steps and rang the bell.

The woman who answered the bell was wearing a pink smock with a dark red "S" embroidered on the breast pocket. She had a tape measure around her neck and was carrying a pin cushion. "Yes?' she asked brusquely after removing some pins from her mouth.

Fannie gave the woman her best smile. "I'm here about the job," she said with more confidence than she felt.

"Where have you worked?"

"I've been working on my own —"

"Not interested," said the woman, starting to shut the door.

"Please," said Fannie. "Let me show you." She put her foot in the door and quickly reached into her bag to pull out a shawl and one of her new boleros. "I designed these myself. They're one of a kind. You can offer them to your clients as custom accessories, or I can add embroidered designs to your clothes. You'll have something other dressmakers don't. And I can do basic draping and finishing too. Look — I made this myself." She started to unroll her sleeve to demonstrate the quality of her stitching.

"Come in," said the woman, her interest piqued. She took Fannie through a door on the right of the hallway.

Fannie entered a room carpeted in a soft pink with a platform in front of a three-way mirror, some velvet chairs and small tables, and a painted screen in the corner. She could hear voices from the other side of a door near the screen.

"What is your name?"

"Fannie, Fannie Dorfman." Fannie was still married, but she didn't want anyone to connect her to the Fine family. They were too well known in New York. The dressmaker had a slight accent. Maybe she too was an immigrant and would take pity on Fannie.

"I'm Sylvia. "Designs by Madame S" is my business. You can go behind the screen there and take off your blouse." She turned the blouse Fannie gave her inside out and handed it back over the screen.

"Good work. Now tell me more about your embroidery," she said when Fannie was dressed again. "Is the belt you're wearing your work too?"

"Yes, it is. Don't you think it adds something to my ensemble?"

Fannie's desperation made her bold. She was determined to make this woman hire her. She remembered Miriam saying someday her things would be in a lady's magazine. This could be her start. She took off her belt to let Sylvia look more closely.

"My grandmother taught me to embroider when I was a child. When I came to America, women saw the things I made for a friend and asked me to embroider for them. At the beginning, they brought me a plain shawl and told me the colors they wanted. My fee depended on how complicated the design was."

Fannie held out a shawl covered in red roses and dark green leaves, similar to one of the designs she had created for Mary. "This is one of my more elaborate pieces. And you can see when you turn it over that you can't tell the front from the back. Not everyone can embroider like that."

While Sylvia examined Fannie's craftmanship, Fannie pulled out a jacket. "Last year I started making boleros like this one. They've been very successful. My clients are wealthy, fashionable women — like yours, I'm sure. They've paid whatever I've asked."

"I'll tell you what, Fannie. I'll hire you to sew at seven dollars a week to start. If it works out, after six months you'll get a raise to seven dollars and fifty cents. And I'll put a shawl and jacket in the window and on display inside near my clothes. If they sell, I'll split the profit with you fifty-fifty."

Fannie thought quickly. Fifty percent when the work was all hers? But it was a chance to build up a new clientele. And she had nothing else. "I'll do it for seventy-five," she said.

"Oh my, a businesswoman as well as a seamstress. I like that. Take sixty and we have a deal. You can start tomorrow."

Sylvia held out her hand. Fannie shook it.

"We start at 8 o'clock sharp. There's tea in the workroom and you can bring your lunch and eat with the other girls. We finish at six unless there's a big order to finish. I assume your husband will approve?"

Fannie had left her wedding ring on to avoid unwanted attention when she was out alone. "My husband died last year," she said, hating the lie but knowing that a widow was more acceptable than a divorced woman. I live with my family."

"Children?"

"No."

"So, you're on your own, like me. We'll get along well, you and I."

Fannie started to put her things away.

"Would you like to leave the shawl to display?"

"Yes, please," said Fannie. "And you won't be sorry, I promise you."

Sylvia showed her to the door. "I'll see you tomorrow morning," she said.

Fannie skipped down the stone steps. When she looked back, Sylvia was draping her shawl around a dress form in the window.

"I did it!" Fannie congratulated herself as she started toward the subway. She couldn't wait to tell the family.

* * *

"Fannie, wait!"

Fannie turned to see Molly, one of her new co-workers, running up the street behind her and stopped to wait. It was a beautiful spring morning, three months after she had started her job, and she was happy to spend a few more minutes in the sun before working inside all day. She tilted her face up and closed her eyes to feel the warmth, unaware of the admiring smile of an elderly gentleman walking by with his cane. She often met Molly or one of the other girls when they got off a subway or trolley nearby. Fannie had come south from 119th Street; Molly came north from Greenwich Village.

Molly caught up with Fannie and stopped to catch her breath. Her black curls had come loose from the wide blue ribbon that matched the skirt and jacket she wore; she took a moment to retie it.

"How pretty you look this morning," said Fannie. "Your clothes bring out the color of your eyes."

"You're the beauty," said Molly. "And what a lovely green dress. To be sure you look like spring itself."

"I'm just so glad to leave the cold winter behind."

"And isn't it a grand day," said Molly, smiling and linking her arm with Fannie's. "It's bound to put the new client Sylvia's been talking about in a pleasant mood. She wants a whole new wardrobe for her honeymoon. Can you imagine?"

Fannie could imagine, but she had never talked about that part of her past with her new friends, so they knew nothing of the wealth she had left behind.

Molly and Rose had started at "Designs by Madame S" when the shop had moved to the brownstone, Emma the year before. Fannie had been surprised at how young they were, but they each had experience doing piecework or sewing in factories. Molly had worked in the dressmaking department at Macy's. Fannie realized soon after she started that Sylvia had hired the girls carefully. She knew the kind of clothes she wanted to make and wanted them to do justice to her designs. She was hoping to attract the kind of clientele that would make her business a success. It made Fannie even more grateful that Sylvia had given her a chance.

She was as excited as the rest of them about the prospect of a big, important client who could spread the word about them. She knew one person could make a difference, as Mary had for her. Their work had been steady, but today's client would be a coup for the small shop.

"Just in time," said Sylvia as she opened the door for them, looking quite different from the day she had tried to chase Fannie away. Her light brown hair was carefully arranged in Marcel waves, framing her pretty oval face. Instead of her usual smock, she wore a stylish navy blue and white striped dress with long sleeves, a square neck and a row of buttons down the front. A narrow belt showed off her small waist. They had just finished making the dress a few days ago.

"She has to see what we're capable of making," Sylvia had said when she showed them her design. "And believe we're as stylish as any of the more established dressmakers she could go to."

Fannie noticed vases of fresh cut flowers and new editions of fashion magazines on the tables. She would look at the magazines for ideas for own creations later, but for now she and Molly hurried to join the others in the workroom to have tea, don their smocks, and start working. There was plenty to do before they could start a new order.

They each had specialties, like cutting and pattern making, but Sylvia made it clear everyone was expected to help with every aspect of making the clothes. When Fannie started, the girls had "oohed and aahed" over her embroidery, but that meant nothing until she proved she was able to work alongside them.

Now she considered them friends. At eighteen, Molly and Rose were the youngest. Molly was never without a smile. She had a beau, James, who often came to pick her up after work. They anticipated making her wedding dress soon.

Rose had just gotten married. She was petite like Molly, with brown eyes and auburn ringlets she was never able to tame.

She and her husband Leib, a printer, were saving for their own haberdashery shop.

Emma was tall and slender like Fannie, with hair as light as Fannie's was dark. She was plain, but her dark brown eyes were warm and drew people to her. She was the quietest among them, except when she talked about her two-year-old son, Jesse.

After reading so many terrible stories in the *Forverts* about how poorly workers in America were treated, Fannie had been relieved to find a different atmosphere at "Designs by Madame S." Sylvia had immigrated from Germany as a twelve-year-old girl. She lived and worked with her aunt, who hired girls to work in her apartment on the sewing machines she owned. Although her aunt was kind, Sylvia left to work for a dressmaker when she was seventeen, saving for the day she could start her own business. It had been eight years since she opened her shop, and three since moving to the brownstone. To her clients, she was Sylvia Lamond, a European-trained dressmaker whose faint accent might well be French.

Sylvia was a demanding, but fair, even generous employer. She allowed the girls to use her machines to work on their own clothes and she let them have leftover fabric ends she could no longer use. In return, they were hard-working and loyal.

Fannie had told them about herself without discussing the details of her marriage. She shared stories about her trip with her father and the arrival of the rest of her family just before the war started, but she never mentioned Caleb's name or talked about the Fine family. They assumed her sadness was due to her husband's death and knew nothing of the real reason. In their eyes, she was a beautiful young widow, ripe for matchmaking. Emma had three older brothers and never lost an opportunity to tell Fannie how well situated they were.

"Ethan, the oldest, he's the one for you. He has a good job in an office," she said. "Now all he needs is a beautiful wife."

Fannie held them off, asking for more time to get over her grief. And she wasn't lying. She was nowhere near ready to try again—and maybe never would be. She loved her work, earned enough to give Papa money for the rent and still have some left for an occasional movie or night out with her new friends. That was enough for now.

The girls finished their tea at a table at the far end of the workroom and got to work. Molly was deftly wielding a pair of shears around a pattern that was pinned to a piece of silk. Rose and Emma were sewing at the machines, moving the hand cranks slowly to control the stitching. Fannie was bent over the sleeve of a dress, finishing the cuff by hand. They worked silently, concentrating on their tasks. Mistakes were time-consuming and, if the fabric was cut incorrectly, costly.

At around half past ten they heard women's voices in the fitting room. Sylvia knocked on the door and asked Molly to bring them tea and cookies. Molly put the good china teapot and cups on the silver tray they kept for customers. Fannie held the door open for her.

"Fannie, can you come in for a moment?" asked Sylvia.

Fannie smoothed her hair, brushed some loose threads off her smock and walked into the showroom.

"Miss Abbott was admiring the shawl in the window and was wondering if you could embroider a full-length cape for her to wear to the opera. She'll wear it over this dress, which we'll make in white." Sylvia showed Fannie a picture in one of the magazines.

"Of course, Miss Sylvia," said Fannie. "Perhaps in silver and gold?" she asked the pretty young girl. "Or would you prefer pastel colors? Either would set off your fair complexion and blond hair."

"Silver and gold," the girl's mother answered for her. "She'll look like a princess."

"Yes," said the girl. "And no one else will have anything like it."

"Thank you, Fannie." Sylvia smiled with approval. "And Mrs. Abbott would also like to buy the shawl in the window."

Fannie nodded to the girl's mother. "Thank you, Madam. I hope you'll enjoy it."

Emma, Rose, and Molly were waiting eagerly on the other side of the door.

"What did she want? Are things going well?"

"She wants me to make her a cape and her mother is buying one of my shawls!" Fannie couldn't contain her happiness. "And from the pile of sketches I think it's going very well. Lots of work ahead of us, girls."

The girls were giving Fannie a hug when Sylvia poked her head into the room.

"You did well, Fannie. Molly, can you bring out some of the white silk?

Molly rushed to find the right bolts of fabric. The other girls got back to work, but Fannie could barely concentrate. She wondered what Sylvia would charge for the cape. It would certainly be a tidy sum to add to her savings.

They ended the day in a celebratory mood. Sylvia showed them sketches of a dozen dresses and suits Miss Abbot had ordered. "She came prepared with pages from *Vogue* and *Pictorial Review*," she said. As they had hoped, it was a very large order. "We're on the way, girls, said Sylvia as they were leaving. "This is the success I've always dreamed of."

Fannie thought about her own dreams. Perhaps she'd be a wife and mother one day, but for now she wanted her embroidery to be a success. Maybe she'd even have her own shop one day, with girls working for her. Miss Abbot's cape was only the start.

Fannie arrived home bursting with her good news, but before she had a chance to say anything, her mother handed her an envelope. It was from the court. Fannie opened it and read quickly. She looked up at her mother. "The judge has denied my request for alimony," she said. "It doesn't give a reason, but the lawyer warned me that the judge wouldn't want to anger the Fine family." Fannie held her arm out straight in front of her and crumpled the letter in her fist.. "It's not fair, Mama, but my old life is over. Now let me tell you about today."

PART VI: ROMANCE, 1915

CHAPTER 21

Fannie was adjusting Miss Abbot's beaded blue chiffon gown on a mannequin. She was kneeling on the carpet with her back to the door when she heard the bell jingle and the door open.

"Excuse me, miss," said a man's voice. "I'd like to inquire about the shawl in the window."

"I'll be right with you," said Fannie, placing a final pin. As she started to stand, her heel caught on the hem of her skirt, and she stumbled.

"Let me help you." The man came across the room quickly to grab her elbow and help her regain her balance.

"Thank you," said Fannie, turning toward him.

"Feige?"

Fannie stared at him. "Samuel?" she said when she found her voice.

"Feige, I don't believe it. I remembered what you told me about your embroidery when I saw the shawl, but I never thought ..."

"It's Fannie now. I mean my American name. It's Fannie," she stammered.

"You're as beautiful now as you were when we met."

Fannie blushed, still barely able to speak. In the early days she thought of him every time she glimpsed a man with red hair on a street corner or a passing trolley. And as Caleb grew colder, she often thought of what might have been if she hadn't been betrothed when they met. Gradually the memories faded, but now here he was, holding her arm. And he hadn't changed. He was as handsome as she remembered, wearing dark blue pants with a crisp white shirt and blue suspenders. He held a tweed cap in his hands.

"When do you finish?" he asked. "We have so much to talk about."

"Not until six."

"I'll wait for you outside. We'll have dinner."

"I don't think ..."

"Fannie?" Rose came in from the workroom and saw Samuel holding Fannie's arm. "Is everything all right?"

"Yes, it's fine," Fannie said, taking a step back. "This is Samuel, Rose. Our families met on the ship. He just saved me from falling when I tripped."

"Pleased to meet you," said Samuel.

"Likewise," said Rose.

"I came in to buy a shawl for my mother's birthday," explained Samuel.

"It's three dollars, Samuel. Should I wrap it now?"

"I don't have that much money with me today, but can I come for it next week? It will be just in time. And we'll have dinner?"

Rose was still standing near them. She looked at Fannie with raised eyebrows.

"I don't know about next week," said Fannie, trying to appear nonchalant. "But we'll make a plan. I want to hear about the boys. They must be so grown up by now."

"Goodbye until next week then."

"Goodbye, and be sure to give my love to Hannah. I can't wait to see her."

"A beau?" asked Rose as soon as Samuel left.

"Don't be silly," said Fannie. "Just an old friend."

"Old friends don't look at each other like that," said Rose, smiling. "And he wasn't wearing a wedding ring, so why not?"

"I hadn't noticed," said Fannie, thinking, why not?

Rose laughed. "Of course you didn't," she teased. "But come back to the workroom, we need your help on the red suit jacket. You know, the one that matches the color your face is right now."

Fannie followed Rose into the other room, not sure how helpful she would be. Thoughts of Samuel pushed everything else from her mind. At the end of the day, Sylvia asked her to stay after the other girls left to talk about her latest sale and what would go in the window next.

"Congratulations," said Sylvia. "And how nice it's a gift for someone you know. Now run along. I have some work to finish so I'll be here for a while longer." Sylvia almost always stayed another hour or two after the girls left.

Fannie walked down the stairs from the brownstone. It wasn't quite dark as she turned to walk up the street toward the subway.

"Fannie." Samuel stepped out of the shadows.

"I was hoping you'd wait," she admitted.

"There's a café just a few blocks from here. Come with me."

Fannie hesitated. This was America, she reminded herself. A woman could have a cup of coffee alone with a man. She looked at Samuel, remembering how it felt to hold his hand. She might not get another chance.

"I'd love to," she said.

They walked, making small talk and comparing the adventures of their younger siblings, until they were seated at the cafe.

"I see—"

"Did you—"

They both started to speak at once.

"You first," said Samuel.

"I don't know where to begin," said Fannie. "I married the man I was betrothed to when we met. He was very wealthy, and I had a life unlike anything I had ever imagined."

"And now?" he asked.

"It ended," said Fannie. "I have my get, I'm only waiting for the divorce papers from the State of New York. Please don't ask me to say more."

"And you never had children?"

"I had a stillborn son."

"I'm so sorry, Fannie. I know how much you wanted children." He took her hands in his and waited for her to go on.

"I live with my family now—Papa went back to get Mama and the children just before the war started. She paused. "And you?"

"Not married. I went to school as soon as I got here and I'm a doctor, just like I told you I would be. I specialize in problems of the eyes."

"I never doubted you would do it. My brother Noah's wife is a nurse at Bellevue Hospital. I often wondered if your paths would cross. Perhaps you know Eve Dorfman?"

"No, but I work at The Mount Sinai Hospital, so it's unlikely we'd meet."

"Now my younger sister, Freyda, wants to be a nurse. Life for girls is so different here."

"Yes," said Samuel. "More than we expected when we left home. When Freyda is ready, tell her we have a fine nursing school."

"I will."

"And your job at the dressmaker's, Fannie, how did that happen?"

"I started selling embroidered clothes before I was married. A very stylish friend of my husband's wore one of my shawls and told anyone who admired it that I had made it. Before I knew it, they all wanted one. It was something I loved to do, and I charged them a lot of money. If you'll permit me to boast a little, I was able to help Papa pay for his trip back to Russia."

"You should be proud."

"I was having no luck finding work after my marriage ended. I was just about to give up when I saw a sign for a seamstress at the shop where you found me. The owner tried to turn me away because I'd only ever worked for myself, but I wouldn't leave until she saw my work. I convinced her to put my things in the window and split the profits on anything that sold. I also do custom work on the dresses she designs and plain sewing just like the other girls."

"So it was your bravery that brought us together again. I just happened to be walking by when I noticed the shawl in the window. It would be perfect for my mother, I thought, never suspecting it would bring me to you."

"You told me I was brave, but I didn't believe it then."

"Are you happy, Fannie?"

Fannie was quiet. No one had asked her that in a long time. "I am, Samuel."

"And you haven't been in love again?"

"There has been no one since my husband."

"That's not what I meant."

It took Fannie a minute to understand. "No, not since you and I said goodbye."

"Neither have I."

"Look," said Fannie. She reached into her purse for Samuel's button.

"You kept it."

"And now it's brought you back to me."

They sat, holding hands, letting their coffee get cold. When the waiter came over to see if they wanted anything else, Samuel threw some coins on the table and waved him away.

"I can't lose you again, Fannie. I'm working late for the rest of the week to handle emergency patients—but next Tuesday I'll wait for you again and we'll have dinner?"

Was this a new beginning for them? Could they pick up where they left off when they let go of each other on the ship? Was it *bashert?* Was it meant to be? She leaned toward him, ready for whatever might come.

"Yes, let's."

★ ★ ★

The following Tuesday, Fannie smiled to herself as she dressed. She told her mother that she was going out to dinner and a movie with the girls, so it wouldn't be unusual for her to take extra time with her clothes and hair, but she was afraid her nervousness would give her away.

"Goodbye, Mama," Fannie said as she took her jacket off the hook by the door. "Remember, I'll be late."

"Is everything all right, mamaleh?" asked her mother. "You seem far away this morning."

"I'm fine," said Fannie. "Just thinking about what I have to do to finish the cape." It was too soon to tell her about Samuel.

At work, the girls had been teasing her mercilessly ever since Rose told them about Samuel. "Tell us everything," they demanded.

"There isn't much to tell," said Fannie. "I slept on the bed near his mother and younger brothers, and we met the day the ship sailed. Neither of us got sick, so we saw each other up on the deck almost every day. We talked and talked. Perhaps, if things had been different ... But I was betrothed, so we said goodbye. I never expected to see him again."

"He's so handsome," Rose told the girls. "And you should see the way he looked at her."

"We'll meet him tonight," said Molly. "And make sure he's good enough for our Fannie."

Fannie did her best to concentrate on her sewing. The hours until six o'clock dragged on. True to their word, the girls all walked out with her. She introduced each of them and was happy to see their smiles. "Have a nice evening," said Molly with a wink.

Fannie and Samuel strolled away arm in arm. Samuel told her about a difficult case he had and the satisfaction he felt when he cured someone. He said it was only a matter of time until America entered the war, and he would serve as a doctor. "I've only just found you again," said Fannie. "Don't talk about leaving."

They had walked about a half mile when Samuel paused. "Fannie, we're almost at the restaurant, but my apartment is also nearby. It's really only a room, but it's clean. And I have some food I saved, since I'm sure you're hungry – will you come with me?"

"I don't—"

"No one will be home tonight. Your reputation will be safe, I promise."

"But still—"

"Do you trust me, Fannie?"

"Of course, Samuel."

"Then you'll come?"

Fannie nodded.

They walked another few blocks until Samuel led her into a six-story brick building.

"It's one flight up," he said.

Fannie hung back. She was no longer the shy girl from the ship, but she was frightened by what lay ahead. Was this what she wanted?

Samuel held out his hand and, after a moment's hesitation, she took it. When they got to his door, Samuel fumbled with the key. He was nervous too.

He had been telling the truth. It was a just a small room, barely big enough for the desk that was covered with books and papers, a table with a hot plate and a few dishes, and his bed, which she struggled not to stare at. The walls were a dingy gray, and she could tell from the brick wall outside the single window that the room got hardly any light.

"Fannie." Samuel kicked the door closed, took her in his arms and looked at her.

"Yes," she said. "Yes." The years slipped away. She and Samuel were back on the ship, alone on the deck. She was ready to be his.

His first kisses were slow. He held her away from him, never letting his eyes leave hers as he unbuttoned her blouse, then bent to kiss her throat and the top of her breasts. He waited after every touch, looking at her for permission to go on. She looked back at him steadfastly and grasped the back of his head to pull him down for more.

"Your skin is so soft," he said.

"Don't stop," said Fannie.

He reached around the back to open her skirt, which dropped to the floor. Then he slowly unlaced her corset, stopping often to kiss her, his tongue deep in her mouth.

Emboldened by her own desire, she lifted her arms to take off her chemise and then stepped out of her drawers, standing naked before him, enjoying the yearning in his eyes. She had never felt like this before, not during all her years of marriage.

He brought her to the bed and sat her down, kneeling in front of her to take off her boots. He laid her down gently, kissing the soles of her feet, the inside of her thighs, her belly, and her breasts.

Fannie trembled, losing awareness of everything but the sensations in her body. Her nipples were hard, she could feel the throbbing between her legs. She wanted more.

"I've dreamed of making love to you," he said, unbuttoning his own shirt and pants and pulling off his shoes.

"I didn't know it could be like this," she murmured.

He eased his own body on top of hers and began kissing her again, letting his tongue linger on every part of her body. She gasped when he put his head between her legs and kissed her there too. She moaned, but then stopped herself and pushed him away.

"Someone will hear us."

"There's no one home at this hour," said Samuel. "Let me make love to you the way I've always imagined."

"Yes," she said.

He started over. She felt herself getting wet and arched her body until spasms overtook her and she felt herself rise off the bed. Only then did he slide into her and begin to thrust, at first slowly and then more urgently. They moved together until his final thrust, until he collapsed on top of her. They were both breathing heavily, their bodies slick with sweat.

"Fannie, was it—"

"Shh," said Fannie, putting her finger over his lips. "Don't say a thing."

They remained locked together, breathing deeply, exploring each other's bodies with touches and kisses until she felt him growing hard and they began again.

"I promised you food," said Samuel after a while. He brought over a basin of water and a cloth and began to wash her slowly. Fannie could feel herself becoming aroused again.

"Give me that," she said playfully. "There isn't time for more."

"There's always time," he said. He didn't stop until he had satisfied her again.

After they dressed, he produced some soup and cold chicken, and Fannie discovered she was ravenous.

"I have to leave, Samuel. It's very late and Mama will worry."

"Of course, I'll take you home. It was—"

"Perfect," Fannie finished for him.

"And we'll see each other again soon?"

"Yes," said Fannie, wondering how she could do without his touch until the next time.

Samuel went to the door and looked out to make sure no one would see them.

"It's fine," he said, but before Fannie could walk out, he shut the door and kissed her again.

"Let me go," said Fannie. "Or I'll never leave."

"Just what I had in mind," said Samuel. "We'll be together forever."

"We will," said Fannie. Now nothing would come between them. Their feelings for each other were stronger than when they parted years ago, and they were both free.

"Next week then?"

This time it was she who kissed him. "I'll be counting the hours," she said.

CHAPTER 22

Miss Abbott was trying on her new cape. "I love it!" she said as she twirled around in front of the mirror, admiring herself from every angle. Her mother looked on with approval.

Fannie had been pleased with the work as it progressed, but until this moment she hadn't realized how truly beautiful it was. She could only imagine how it would look at the opera, the intricate silver and gold embroidery glowing in the light of the chandeliers.

"I'll be the envy of everyone who sees me," said the young woman. "You have truly outdone yourself."

"Yes, she has," said Sylvia. "We're so glad you like it."

Fannie enjoyed the praise, but what mattered even more to her was the additional money she would earn. She had already decided she was going to ask Sylvia for a greater share of the profits. She couldn't wait to discuss it later with Samuel. It was Tuesday, which had become their night together for the last few months.

Just a few more hours until he would hold her again. She felt her body grow warm. He had unlocked feelings in her she never knew were possible. This was the love she had been denied. Now that they were together again, she had given herself to it completely. Every cliché in the lady's magazines and novels was true. She floated through her days.

She still hadn't told her mother, although she was sure she suspected something. How could she not notice the happiness that Fannie saw every time she looked in the mirror? But could she tell her without revealing the intimate nature of their love? Her mother had become much more broad-minded in America, but Fannie didn't think that would extend to the physical passion she shared with Samuel. For now, that was her delicious secret.

She went back into the workroom, told the girls about her triumph and got to work. They were too busy with the rest of the Abbot order to stop and celebrate. A short while later, Sylvia came in to tell her there was a woman who wanted to talk to her about a shawl. "She insists on talking to you directly," said Sylvia. "She said she knows you from before."

Fannie wondered who it could be. No one from before she left Caleb knew she was here. "I'll go right out," she said.

The woman in the showroom was fingering the shawl in the window. She turned around when Fannie walked in.

"Hannah, what a happy surprise!" cried Fannie as soon as she realized who it was. She threw her arms around Samuel's mother. She had asked him a few times to arrange for her to see Hannah and the family, but there never seemed to be a time when he wasn't working late, or the family didn't have other plans. And once she fell into his arms, she forgot everything else.

"Feige, it's so good to see you again," she said.

Fannie looked at Hannah. The last time she saw her was when the ship docked, and she was drawn and pale from seasickness. She looked healthy now. Her face had filled out and she had more color. Her hair was a little grayer and she had a few more wrinkles, but she was still a handsome woman.

"I hope I don't bring shame on you by coming here in my old clothes."

"Hannah, please. You look beautiful."

"Feige, I mean Fannie—Samuel told me about your new name, forgive me for not remembering. And he told me you looked well, but he didn't do you justice. Life must be good for you."

"Yes, it is." *If only I could tell you how your son makes me feel every night we're together.*

"And your Papa?"

"Good, thank you for asking. He brought Mama and the children here last fall. He has a good job and the whole family is well."

"I'm glad. America has turned out well for all of us."

"But Sylvia said you came about a shawl? I hope nothing is wrong with the one Samuel gave you?"

"Oh no, it's perfect. It was such a nice surprise on my birthday, especially since you made it. No, I've come to buy one for Judith."

"Judith?"

"Samuel's betrothed. I'm sure he's told you all about her."

Samuel, betrothed? How could that be? Fannie tried to remember everything he had said that first night at the coffee shop. He said he wasn't married and never said anything about a betrothed. She was sure of it. She wanted to scream but forced herself to keep smiling.

"Of course, I forgot. Is there an occasion?"

"Yes, her birthday is in August."

"I'd be happy to make it for you," said Fannie.

What else could she say to his mother? Your son lied to me? I hate him and I never want to see him again?

"Thank you so much, Fannie. Now I'll let you get back to work. Should I come at the end of July?"

Fannie was finding it difficult to breathe. "Yes," was all she could manage. She walked Hannah to the door, praying she would leave before she realized something was wrong.

"Goodbye, dear. I'm so glad you and Samuel are friends again."

As soon as the door closed Fannie collapsed onto the floor, sobbing.

"Fannie, what's wrong?" asked Rose, who came out when she heard the noise and knelt beside her. "Did that woman have bad news?"

Fannie gulped for air. "Yes, she did."

"Has someone died? Someone from the old country?"

Fannie couldn't speak.

Rose helped her up into a chair. "I'll get you some water."

Fannie drank eagerly from the glass Rose handed her.

"That was Samuel's mother."

"What happened? Is he ill? Was there an accident?"

"He's betrothed."

"Betrothed?"

"He lied to me. All this time, he's been lying."

Rose sat down next to Fannie. "I'm so sorry, Fannie. I wish there was something I could do."

"I thought he loved me. I've been a fool, a stupid fool."

"No Fannie, you haven't. I've seen how he looks at you. I'm as shocked as you are."

Rose didn't know. She thought they went to dinner, maybe stole a kiss. She didn't know how Samuel made love to her. Desire had made her weak—she had been a fool to trust him.

"What will I do, Rose? He's coming tonight. How will I say goodbye?"

"Are you sure it has to be goodbye? You can't find a way to forgive him?"

"Never. How could I ever trust him again?"

"Lots of women have learned to forgive, Fannie. At least wait until you've spoken to him to make up your mind."

"What could he possibly say?"

"Then you'll just have to be brave."

"Brave? I'm tired of being brave. I just want to be happy. Don't I deserve that?"

Rose took Fannie's hand in hers. "I need to go back to work," she said. "Why don't you rest here a little. I'll tell the others you've had a shock."

Fannie nodded. "But please tell them I'd like to be alone for a while. I need some time to think."

"Take your time," said Rose.

Fannie didn't sit for long. She went back to work, hoping to take her mind off what was coming. But it didn't help. *If only I'd known which kiss was going to be my last. How will I bear it without him?*

At six o'clock, as they readied to leave, the girls each gave Fannie a hug or squeezed her hand, without saying a word. They walked out with her, but when they saw Samuel waiting, they quickly walked away to leave them alone.

"Where is everyone off to in such a hurry?" asked Samuel, taking Fannie's arm.

Fannie pushed him away.

"What's wrong, Fannie?"

"Your mother came today."

"She's been talking about stopping by to thank you for the shawl, but I told her to wait until we could all get together. I didn't know she'd come without telling me."

"She came to buy a shawl for Judith."

Samuel turned pale and stood still.

"Judith, the woman you're betrothed to. The one you never told me about."

"Please Fannie, I can explain." He held out his hands, pleading. "Please, just give me a chance to explain."

"What is there to explain? You lied. You said you loved me and took me to your bed. And I loved you in return. I've never been happier—but all this time there was someone else."

"I do love you, Fannie. I have since the moment we met on the ship's deck. I never stopped loving you, even when I met Judith. She's my best friend's sister. We were thrown together at dinners and went to the movies a few times and people started to assume we'd marry. My family liked her and pushed me to ask her. So, I finally did, but I kept putting off the wedding. And then I found you again."

Samuel moved toward her, but she held up her hands.

"Don't touch me," she said.

"I thought I'd never see you again, Fannie. What was I supposed to do? I wanted a wife and family, even if I had to settle for someone I knew I couldn't love like I loved you."

"But you did see me."

"And I've never been so happy. I wanted to tell you, but I was afraid I'd lose you. I was going to break it off. I just needed a way to tell her and my family. I was wrong, Fannie. Please forgive me." He put his hands together as if in prayer.

"Happy? With a betrothed his family likes and a lover to enjoy besides, what man wouldn't be happy? I thought you were different from other men, but I was wrong. I never want to see you again." She stepped further away from him.

"No, Fannie. I'll break it off. I'll leave her and you and I will be married. Isn't that what you want, for us to be together forever?"

"I do—I did. You shouldn't have waited for me to find out like this. I didn't believe you when you told me I was brave, now it turns out you're the coward."

"You're right. But do you really want it to end?" His eyes held hers.

Fannie couldn't answer.

"If there's one thing I'm sure of, Fannie, it's that happiness like ours only comes once." He stepped toward her and reached out to caress her cheek. "Don't end it Fannie. Please, find it in your heart to forgive me, and we'll find a way."

Fannie brushed his hand away. She wanted to say yes. *Yes, leave her Samuel, let's be together as we were meant to be.* She wanted to be in his arms, tonight and every night. She could barely see him through the tears that began to fall.

"You betrayed me. And even if I could forgive you, how could I be happy knowing it was because you hurt someone else? How will your best friend feel, and your family? Even if I forgive you, will they? To them, I'll always be the other woman. What if they won't accept me? I can't do it, Samuel. You need to go."

"You can't mean that, Fannie. Please don't make me go. I can't lose you again."

"Oh, Samuel, I want you so much, but not like this. Please, just go and leave me in peace."

"No, I won't let you do this." He took her in his arms.

Fannie struggled briefly but gave in when he kissed her.

She kissed him back fiercely. *Maybe he's right. I would be a fool to give this up.* She had done the right thing once before and it had brought her nothing but pain. Why sacrifice herself again?

"No, I can't," she cried, wrenching herself away and turning her back on him.

"Fannie—"

She ached to turn around but didn't move until she heard his footsteps recede.

She turned. He was still close enough to call. One word, one word and she'd have the happiness she thought was going to be hers.

"Samuel," she whispered. She took his button from her purse and tossed it into the street.

In a daze, she went back to the shop and dragged herself up the stairs. "Sylvia," she cried out as she pounded on the door. "What have I done?"

PART VII: MOVING ON, 1915 - 1916

CHAPTER 23

Fannie got through the days one at a time. She worked, went home, cried herself to sleep, and started over the next morning. The girls at work tried to cheer her up. They tried to coax her into joining them when they went out after work, but she turned them down. She didn't want to ruin their good times.

The night she turned Samuel away, her mother knew right away something was wrong. She listened as Fannie wept and told her what had happened, leaving out the details of their nights together.

"What's wrong with me, Mama? Have I given up the only happiness I'll ever know?"

Her mother took her in her arms to comfort her. "We can't know the future," she said. "You're young, child, and beautiful. Give it time."

Fannie heard her, but what else would a mother say? The moment she let Samuel leave haunted her. Had it been foolish pride that made her let him go? What made her think she was better than other women who had forgiven men for worse things? What good was it to be young and beautiful if she was so unwise?

Hannah didn't come for the shawl. Fannie wondered if Samuel was already married. What did he tell Hannah to prevent her from coming back?

The only bright spot in Fannie's life was the increasing popularity of her embroidery. She had negotiated a raise from Sylvia, letting her know that as much as she loved "Designs by S," she would leave if she had a better offer. Sylvia readily agreed.

Summer turned to fall. When the August heat broke, people began to move about the city with new energy. Even Fannie felt invigorated and started to join her friends for an occasional evening out.

One sunny afternoon in late October, after buying thread for some new commissions, Fannie decided to treat herself to cherry pie at the Horn and Hardart. She had just put her coins in the slot and was reaching for the dish when she heard someone call her name.

"Fannie, over here!"

It was Anna, her friend from night school, sitting with a young man.

"Come, join us," Anna called out.

Fannie took her pie over and sat down.

"It's so wonderful to see you again. This is my husband, Nathan," said Anna.

"It's good to meet you," said Fannie. "Anna told me all about you before she left Brooklyn. Do I remember correctly that you are in the fur business?"

"Yes, I am. And—"

"And he just got another promotion," Anna interrupted. "I came downtown to celebrate with him."

"Please, Anna," Nathan blushed.

"No, she should share such good news. Mazel Tov."

She turned to her friend. "I was so sorry not to hear from you after you moved, Anna."

"But I left so many messages," said Anna. "I gave up when you never called."

"Messages?"

"Yes, with Caleb."

"I never got them, or I would have called right away."

"I should have known there was a reason," said Anna.

Could he have put them away somewhere and forgotten? No, it was more likely he didn't want her to have a friend of her own. "Maybe you won't be surprised that we're no longer married," she told Anna.

She turned to Nathan. "I had planned to dance at your wedding."

"And you could have come to the bris," said Anna. "Our son was born last winter. But maybe there'll be another bris in the spring." She pointed to her slightly rounded belly.

"Mazel Tov again," said Fannie. "You're one of those women who glows when she's expecting, Anna, but I'll always think of you as a schoolgirl." Anna's plain black skirt and white blouse reminded Fannie of the night they met, although her hair was bobbed and there was no red bow.

"And you?" asked Anna. "Do you have children?"

"No, my baby was stillborn," said Fannie.

"I'm so sorry," said Anna, reaching for Fannie's hand.

They continued talking about their lives since night school until Fannie noticed the time. "I hate to leave, but I'm expected back at work," she said.

"Well, now that we're together again, you'll come for Shabbos dinner," said Anna as Fannie stood to leave. "Can you come next week? Both our families will be there."

Fannie was about to refuse, not quite ready to be among strangers, but she couldn't bring herself to disappoint her friend. She would put on a happy face and go. "Yes, I'd love to," she said, and realized that she meant it.

"Here's my address," said Anna, scribbling on a napkin. "And the number for the telephone We're on E. 115th Street."

"We're practically neighbors," exclaimed Fannie. "I live with my family on 119th Street."

"Wonderful. We'll see you at seven?"

"Seven is fine. I work until six."

The two friends hugged, and Fannie shook Nathan's hand.

"You've made my wife very happy," he said. "I'm sure we'll all be friends."

"Oh, I almost forgot, Fannie," said Anna. "I'm almost certain I saw your brother Daniel here a few weeks ago, with a pretty blond girl. I thought he recognized me when I called out to him, but he rushed off. I must have been mistaken."

"I'll ask him the next time I see him," said Fannie.

Fannie told her mother about Anna as soon as she got home. "I'm sure Caleb threw her messages away, Mama."

"Perhaps, but there's nothing to be done about it now. The important thing is that you found each other again—and that you're smiling." She gave her daughter a hug.

"I've already had my dessert, but I could eat some dinner now."

"Come, Papa and the children have already eaten. He's in our room reading and the children are outside playing until it gets too dark. I saved you some and you'll tell me more about your friend while you eat."

★ ★ ★

Fannie hurried toward the address Anna had given her. She had been late leaving the shop and had no time to spare before Shabbos started.

"Welcome," said Nathan as he ushered her into their apartment. "Can I take your jacket?"

"Thank you," said Fannie. "And this is for you." She handed him a tin of Almond Kisses she had tied with a ribbon.

"Oh, excellent," he said. "Anna has always loved these, but even more now that she's expecting again. There never seems to be any left for me."

Fannie laughed. "Then I'm glad I brought you a new supply."

"Come meet the family."

Anna and Nathan's families were gathered in a small, somewhat crowded living room. The sofa and two armchairs had been pushed back to make room for a long table and chairs. The table was set for Shabbos with a white cloth, white china with a gold rim, and sparkling glassware. Candles in tall brass candlesticks, two challahs covered with a patterned cloth, and the Kiddush cup and wine were at the head of the table.

"These are Anna's parents, Mr. and Mrs. Vogel," said Nathan. "And these are my parents, Mr. and Mrs. Schwartzman. And did you meet Anna's brother, Jacob, when you were together in school?"

Jacob, who was seated in one of the chairs with his nephew on his lap, handed the baby to his mother and rose to greet her.

"No, we never met," said Fannie. "But Anna told me so many wonderful things about you."

"I'm sure she exaggerated, but she certainly didn't exaggerate about her beautiful friend."

Fannie felt her face turning red. Anna had told her how smart her brother was and that he took good care of his family. She hadn't expected him to be such a smooth talker—or, for that matter, so good looking. He had brows that met in the middle of his forehead, a narrow nose and a pencil mustache over full lips. His thick, straight brown hair was parted on the side. He wore a distinguished looking blue three-piece suit with a blue striped tie. He was slightly shorter than Fannie but held himself confidently. Ordinarily, Fannie would try to make herself appear shorter, but somehow she sensed it didn't matter to him. He seemed at ease with himself. His dark eyes were openly examining her.

Anna saved her from more embarrassment by coming in from the kitchen and asking everyone to be seated. "You've met everyone, Fannie? Come sit next to me," she said.

Fannie was relieved not to be seated next to Jacob, only to discover he was directly across from her. He had managed to disconcert her with only a few words. What would the rest of the evening be like?

Anna said the blessing and lit the candles. Nathan said the prayers over the wine and challah and then gazed lovingly at his son and his wife as he gave them his blessing.

"Let me help you," said Fannie as Anna rose to start serving the meal.

"No, sit. Talk to Jacob."

Fannie couldn't think of anything to say.

"Anna tells me that you work for a dressmaker," said Jacob. "Do you like your work?"

"Yes, I do," said Fannie. "My specialty is custom embroidery. Sometimes I work on the dresses the owner designs, but often I make shawls and jackets, and even an opera cape, to order. That's how I met Anna again. I had just finished buying some silk thread and decided to treat myself to some cherry pie."

"A sweet tooth?"

"I'm afraid so. And you?"

"Only sugar in my tea, but I'm happy to indulge my friends—and Anna's friends too, of course."

"What about Anna's friends?" asked Anna as she carried in a tray of steaming bowls of matzo ball soup.

"All you sweet women enjoy sweets."

"Has Jacob told you about his university?" said Anna. "He's studying to be an engineer at the Cooper Union for the Advancement of Science and Art. He's brilliant."

"Anna, please, everyone here is tired of hearing about it."

"No, tell me," said Fannie. "I'm not sure I know exactly what engineers do. Do they build bridges like the Manhattan Bridge?"

"Some do, and that's the kind of engineer I'd like to be some day."

"Then I'm sure Anna's right. You must be very smart. Tell me about the classes you take."

Jacob was happy to tell Fannie about his studies, and patient with her questions. He told her that when America went to war, he wanted to be an engineer in the army.

"When, not if?" she asked.

"I think so," he said. "It's only a matter of time."

"Every man I know says that. Why are you all in such a hurry to fight? Didn't we leave home to get away from violence?"

"I don't want to fight," said Jacob. "And I probably can't because I'm deaf in this ear from scarlet fever when I was a child." He pointed to his right ear. "But I do want to serve my country."

Jacob was surprisingly easy to talk to. He was obviously a learned man, but he seemed genuinely interested in what she had to say and laughed at the stories she told about the girls at work. They had even read some of the same novels. Both of them liked Willa Cather.

Before she knew it, the meal had ended, and it was time to leave.

"Thank you so much, Anna. I've had a lovely evening."

"Then you'll come again soon."

"I'd love to, and you'll come to my house too."

The two friends embraced, and Fannie said goodbye to Nathan and the rest of the family.

"Jacob will walk you home," said Anna.

"Oh no, I'm fine on my own. It's quite safe."

"I insist," said Jacob, helping her into her jacket. "The night air and the walk will do me good." He took her arm.

They walked slowly up Second Avenue, continuing their conversation from dinner until they turned onto 119th street and reached Fannie's building.

"I hope you won't think this too forward of me," said Jacob when they got to her door. "But would you go to the Yiddish theater with me next Sunday?"

Fannie hesitated. She had enjoyed his company but didn't want to give him the wrong idea. The last thing she was interested in right now was another man in her life. Two bad endings were enough.

"I don't know, Jacob."

"Anna and Nathan are going too. I know you'll enjoy it."

"Then yes, I will," she said.

"I'll pick you up at noon. We'll have lunch first."

"That sounds wonderful."

"Good night, Fannie." He leaned in and for one terrible moment she thought he was going to try to kiss her, but he was only opening the door.

"Good night, Jacob."

★ ★ ★

Lunch on Sunday was more pleasant than she expected. She had been nervous when Anna and Nathan had to cancel at the last minute, but Jacob was once again easy to talk to. At first, they only talked about the news of the day. The *Forverts* didn't approve of "The Boy Mayor" of New York's plans for education reform.

"I wonder what his plans will mean for my sister Freyda, who wants to be a nurse," said Fannie."

"And your father approves?"

Fannie was taken aback. She remembered Anna telling her Jacob favored giving women the vote. And now he expected Freyda to get her father's approval to continue her schooling?

"It's Freyda's decision," she said. "And after all, his daughter-in-law is a nurse."

"Of course," said Jacob. "I was only wondering how he felt about it. Sometimes it's hard for men of our parents' generation to change."

Fannie nodded, reassured.

"Tell me more about your family," he asked. "Are you the oldest child?"

"No, I have two older brothers who came here a few years before me. Daniel is the oldest. I'm not exactly sure what he does, and I worry he may have fallen in with the wrong kind of men, but he's been kind and generous to me from the time I was a little girl."

"Well, that's the most important thing, isn't it?" said Jacob.

"The next oldest is Noah. He's studying business at the College of the City of New York. His wife, Eve, the nurse, works at Bellevue." Fannie found herself telling him about Papa's anger when Noah and Eve pledged to marry without consulting him.

"It took a long time for him to give in," said Fannie. "My mother was still in Russia and I didn't know how to help."

"That's exactly what I meant before," he said. "Difficulty changing. I'm glad it had a happy ending."

Fannie told him how hard it had been to leave Mama and her friends. "I came to be married," she said. "They are a very wealthy family. They paid for our passage and gave my Papa a job so he could earn enough to bring my Mama and the two younger children here."

Jacob didn't press her for any more information. After she told him about Freyda and Levi, he talked a little about his own family, and how he had worked to bring his parents, Anna and several cousins from Poland. "I saved all my money to send for them. Now it's up to them to bring their families, but with this war, who knows when that will be?"

"We were lucky," said Fannie. They were both quiet, thinking about friends and family trapped in Europe.

"What work do you do now? I don't think Anna ever told me."

"I work for a diamond dealer," said Jacob. "Zalman, a friend of the family from the old country. He has a very successful business and hired me as soon as I arrived. Until the war started, I traveled frequently to Antwerp to buy diamonds."

"The city where Papa and I boarded the ship?"

"Yes, it's occupied by the Germans now, so I can't go back. I miss it."

Fannie sighed. The war had already changed their lives. But war was far from her mind as they entered Thomashefsky's National Theater, the newest Yiddish theater on the Lower East Side of Manhattan. It had been built to rival the theaters on Broadway. She and Caleb had gone to Broadway shows often, but in his determination to be a "real American," he would never have come to a Yiddish theater. Fannie was looking forward to it.

Most of the audience, she saw, was dressed simply, even those in the orchestra seats below them. She and Caleb had always dressed up for the theater, but tonight she wore a plain, dark green skirt and white blouse with a wide belt she had embroidered. Jacob noticed it and complemented her. She had purchased the new black boots she was wearing with money from one of her commissions from Sylvia. Jacob looked relaxed in his black pants, white shirt, and gray knitted vest.

Fannie laughed so hard at the performance she had tears in her eyes. She stole a glance at Jacob, who seemed to be enjoying himself as much as she was. Even though it was only their first time together, she wondered if he would reach over and take her hand. She wasn't sure if she was relieved or disappointed when he didn't.

I wonder what his experience with women is? Has he ever known the kind of love I had with Samuel? She chided herself for thinking about it. Hadn't she sworn she wasn't interested in having another man in her life? Yet she was keenly aware of Jacob's presence and his dark good looks.

The audience roared at the antics on the stage. When the actors took their final bows, they were called back again and again. As soon as the curtain fell for the final time, Jacob led Fannie down from the balcony, with Anna and Nathan following close behind. "I think it's still early enough for a piece of cheesecake at Ratner's. Can I tempt you?" he asked.

"You're taking advantage of my weakness," said Fannie. "I'd love to."

"And will you join us?" he asked Anna and Nathan. "You can make up for missing lunch."

"For sure this baby will be born with a sweet tooth," laughed Anna, patting her belly. "But I think we have time?" She looked at Nathan to be sure.

"Yes, let's," he said.

The foursome walked to the restaurant where each of them selected their favorite cheesecake. They talked and laughed until it was time to leave.

"We need to be off," said Nathan. "Or we won't be able to ask my parents to watch the baby again."

Jacob and Nathan paid the bill and the four of them began walking to the subway. Fannie and Jacob stayed on the train after Anna and Nathan got off, but it was only a short ride to Fannie's stop and a two-block walk to her building.

"I had a lovely day, Jacob."

"Thank you for the company," he said. "I've enjoyed it. Perhaps next week you'd like to go with me to the Metropolitan Museum of Art? I've never been, but perhaps we can explore the paintings together?"

"I lived near the Brooklyn Museum," said Fannie, "But I never went. It sounds wonderful. But please save the Sunday after that to celebrate Hanukkah with my family. I'll be asking Anna and Nathan and your parents, too, of course. We'll light the candles and have *latkes* and the children can play *dreidel*."

"Then I'll bring shiny new pennies for them," said Jacob. He squeezed her hand and said goodnight.

"Goodnight, and thank you again," she said as he turned to go.

Once she got inside her apartment door and took off her coat, Fannie leaned against the door and smiled to herself.

"I heard you come in," said her mother as she came out of her room. "You're smiling again."

"He treats me like I'm special, Mama."

"You are special, ziskeit. Come, tell me all about it."

CHAPTER 24

"What's wrong, Daniel? I can tell something's wrong."

She and Daniel were sitting at a table in the tea gardens at the Biltmore Hotel, next to the ice rink where she and Jacob had spent the afternoon skating. Every Sunday for the last several months he had he found something new for them to do together, often including their siblings as well. Her cheeks were still red from the cold, and she hadn't removed her scarf and gloves yet. She couldn't wait to put her hands around a cup of steaming hot cocoa.

Daniel hadn't told her why he wanted to talk to her. She was sure this meant it was bad news and had tried not to let her anxiety ruin her time with Jacob. Now she braced herself for whatever he was going to say.

"So, you like this fellow, Jacob?"

"Yes, I do, but that's not why you asked me here, is it?"

"No, it's not, but before I tell you why, I want you to know I think he's a good man and I think he'll be good for you. Don't turn him away, Fannie, don't think you need to be alone because Caleb was such a *mamzer.*"

"We're just getting to know each other. It's too soon to talk about being serious."

"No, it's not. I've seen how he looks at you. He's already serious. Don't wait too long to be happy."

"Daniel, you're speaking like someone who won't be here much longer. Are you ill? Is that what you need to tell me?"

"No, I'm fine."

Fannie looked at him. "Then what's wrong?"

"Do you remember when your friend Anna told you she had seen me at the Horn and Hardart with a woman and I told you she must have been mistaken?"

She nodded.

"I'm ashamed to say it, but I lied to you, Fannie. I was there, and I was with a woman. Her name is Susan and we're getting married in a few weeks."

"I'm happy for you—I'd thought you'd never settle down—but a few weeks? Why haven't we met the woman who finally captured your heart?"

She searched his face for an answer, but his expression gave nothing away.

"What aren't you telling me?"

"She's not Jewish. We're going to be married by a judge."

Fannie sat back, stunned.

"I love her. The way Noah loved Eve and was willing to go against Papa to marry her. You understand, don't you?"

"But this is different," she said, finally finding her voice. "He'll never approve."

"I know. I was just there. I'm dead to him, Fannie. Papa turned his back on me, ripped his shirt and announced he would sit shiva."

"And Mama?"

"She won't go against him on this, so I'm dead to her too."

"I don't think there's anything I can do to change their minds," said Fannie, attempting not to cry.

"I wouldn't even ask you to try."

"You know I'm not like them, don't you? I'd like to meet your bride. And if you love her, I'm sure I will too."

"She's lovely, and I'm sure you would, but there's more to tell you." He paused, struggling to go on. "We're leaving right after the wedding, and we don't plan to come back."

"I don't understand. Why? Where will you go?"

"Somewhere we can start over."

"Are you in trouble? Tell me the truth, Daniel. Enough with the lies."

"You're right. I'm not in trouble, but I'm a gambler. I can't talk about it openly, but I make a lot of money playing cards. There were times I thought you'd guessed, but I see I was wrong."

"So that's why you always avoided my questions. I knew there was something, but a gambler? Does Noah know?"

"Yes, he realized it when we were living together. I told him and Eve about Susan a while ago and swore them to secrecy."

"Are you in danger?"

"Not if I'm careful. It's illegal, of course, but I only play with men I know or who someone can vouch for."

"And Susan is willing to leave her family and go who knows where with you?"

"Her family is no happier than ours. Once she marries a Jew, she won't be welcome in their home. So, with both of our families unwilling to accept us, we've decided to start over somewhere else."

"I'm so sorry for you both. But how will I reach you?"

"I'll send you a postcard. But one more thing, Fannie. It won't come from Daniel Dorfman, but from Danny Diamond. It's the name I go by and I'm legally changing it before the wedding."

Fannie looked at him, unbelieving.

"You're giving up the family name. Then you might as well be dead to us," she said.

"Please don't say that. And promise you'll write. I want to hear about you and the family—and most of all about your happiness."

"My big brother, the one I've always adored, will be gone. And you talk about my happiness?" Fannie stood up and took her things. She turned to leave but couldn't make herself take the first step. When she turned back, Daniel stood, took her in his arms and let her sob.

"I'll write soon," he said into her ear.

She looked up at him. "I'll always love you, Daniel. Please take care." This time she walked away.

When Fannie arrived home, Papa was sitting stiffly at one end of the sofa and Mama at the other end, clutching her tear-soaked handkerchief.

"My son has died," Papa said.

Fannie stood with her hands balled into fists at her side.

"No, Papa, he has not. I had a son who never drew his first breath. Yours is very much alive. And maybe soon he'll have a son of his own, but you'll never know."

"My son is dead. He is no longer a Jew."

"Fannie, please," her mother began.

"How could you, Mama?"

"Leave her be," said Papa. "He made his choice."

She held her breath for a moment, afraid her anger would make her say something she couldn't take back.

"And I've made mine. I will go on loving him. And now I'm going to talk to Freyda and Levi. They must be confused about what is happening."

"I make the decisions in this family."

"Yes, you do, Papa, but surely you didn't tell them Daniel died?"

He wouldn't look at her.

"I'm going to talk to them, and since I won't sit shiva for a brother who is still alive, I'll go stay with Noah and Eve for the rest of the week."

"Please take Freyda and Levi with you," Mama said softly.

Fannie longed to embrace her but didn't want to come between her parents. Mama was in enough pain. She walked out of the room to find her brother and sister.

★ ★ ★

Fannie kept her anger and grief to herself at work. A few days after Daniels' devastating news, she, Molly, Rose, and Emma were leaving the shop after a long day cutting and sewing clothes for the next season.

"Fannie." Jacob was waiting at the bottom of the stairs.

"Jacob, what are you doing here? Is everything all right?"

"That's what I came to ask you. Can we talk?"

"I don't understand. Of course we'll talk, but first let me introduce you to my friends. Molly, Rose, Emma, this is Jacob."

Jacob nodded to each of them. "Fannie has told me so much about you. Not everyone is lucky enough to have such good friends at work. I'm happy for her."

"And we've heard about your wonderful adventures on Sunday afternoons," said Rose.

"But she didn't tell us how handsome her new beau was," said Molly, playfully poking Fannie with her elbow.

Fannie blushed but said nothing. What would Jacob think? She had only ever referred to him as a friend, but she had to admit he had become more than that. She just wasn't sure how much more she wanted him to be.

"And who would notice what I look like when I'm next to her? She's the beauty."

"Ooh," said Molly. "Gallant too."

"Now, do you mind if I steal her from you for a few minutes?" asked Jacob.

"We're all off for home," said Molly, taking the other girls' hands and leading them away. "She's yours for as long as you like," she added with a grin.

"Can we stop for a cup of tea?" Jacob asked as soon as they had walked away.

"Yes," said Fannie. "We certainly can't stand here in the cold."

Jacob took her arm and guided her briskly to a restaurant up the block.

"Now, please explain," said Fannie as soon as they were seated and hot tea was in front of them.

"I called to make plans for Sunday," said Jacob. "Your mother said you had gone to stay with your brother and sister-in-law for the week. When I asked her if anything was wrong, she didn't answer. She only said I should call there. I decided to come talk to you instead. I hope it wasn't inappropriate, but I was concerned."

"I'm glad you came," said Fannie. "And yes, something is very wrong."

"I knew it from your mother's voice. Is someone ill? Is there anything I can do to help?"

Fannie took a sip of her tea and thought about how to tell him the news. "It's Daniel. He's getting married."

"But isn't that good news? You've been hoping he would settle down."

"I wish it were, but she's not Jewish. My parents are sitting shiva. I refused and decided to leave. I couldn't bear to stay while they pretended Daniel had died. Mama asked me to take Freyda and Levi with me. She will do what Papa says, but she wanted me to take the children out of the house."

"What do you mean, you refused?'

"My brother is not dead. He's alive and marrying a woman he loves, and I'll miss him. Sitting shiva for him is unthinkable." By the time she finished telling him she was crying.

"But Fannie," said Jacob. "He's marrying outside the faith. He's lost to us—to your family and to the Jewish people. That's the same as a death and shiva is our way to mourn."

"Our way? No. Maybe yours and Papa's, but not mine. I will miss him every day, but I hope he'll be happy."

"Does he deserve happiness when he's abandoned his people? Think of the pogroms, Fannie. They want to see all of us gone, and he's helping them. We can't afford to lose even a single Jew from this world. Daniel has betrayed us. Your Papa is right."

Fannie banged her cup down so hard the tea splashed onto the table. "No."

"It has to be this way."

"How can you say that? I thought you said the older generation has trouble changing, but now I see you can't change either."

"I can change, Fannie, but about this, I choose not to."

"I'm disappointed. I've always known you and I were different, but not this much."

"And I'm disappointed that you don't understand what this means to me. I respect your decision, but please don't ask me to agree with you."

"Thank you for worrying about me and coming by. I should be going now." Fannie stood up to put on her coat and scarf.

"I'll take you back to Noah and Eve's."

'No," she said, tugging on her gloves. "I'll be fine."

"Please don't go away angry."

Fannie shook her head. "Not angry, sad. I need some time to think."

"Of course. I'll see you Sunday?"

"Not this week, Jacob. I need to take the children home, and I think I'd like to spend some time with the family."

"May I call after that?"

Fannie could see how distressed he was, but so was she. She really did need time to think.

"You can call," was all she said before turning to leave.

When she arrived at Noah and Eve's, Freyda, Levi, and Noah were doing homework at the dining room table. Eve was in the living room, reading. "You're later than we expected," she said. "But I saved you a plate. Can you eat it in here or should I ask Noah to move?"

"Don't bother him. And don't get up, I'll help myself."

"What are you reading?" she asked when she came back from the kitchen.

"A short story, *The Yellow Wallpaper*. It's quite sad. A young mother is sick, and her husband and doctor treat her as though she has no mind of her own. Would you like to read it when I'm done?"

"Yes, I would, thank you."

Eve looked back down at her book and Fannie began to eat. But she had no appetite and put her plate down.

"It's still true, isn't it?" said Fannie.

"What is?" asked Eve.

"That women are treated like they're ignorant."

"Well, some are, but it's different for many of us. Is there something on your mind?

"It's Jacob."

Eve closed her book and waited for Fannie to explain.

"He came to see me after work today. That's why I was late. Mama told him I was here, and he was worried something might be wrong."

"But that was so thoughtful. Or didn't you think so?"

"I did. But when I told him about Daniel, he agreed with Papa that it was right to sit shiva. I couldn't believe it. And I didn't even tell him about the gambling and that he was going to change his name."

"And he said you were wrong?"

"Well, not exactly. He said he didn't agree, but that he would respect my decision."

"But then he's not treating you like the woman in the story at all."

"I suppose you're right. Daniel told me he was a good man and not to turn him away, but what if this is just one example of how different we are? What if he's more like Papa than like Noah?"

"I don't think he is. Are you going to marry him?"

Fannie laughed. "He hasn't asked me yet, but I think he will. The thing is, I'm not sure I want to marry him or any man, at least not for a while. I'm not ready to give up making my own decisions."

"Then don't. If he asks and you're not ready, ask him to wait. If it's *bashert*, he will. But I agree with Daniel. I think he's a good man and he'll make you happy. And don't only think about what you might lose – but what you'll gain. A companion, a lover, a father for your children. Isn't that what you've always wanted?"

"You're very wise, Eve." She got up to return her plate to the kitchen. "Can I get you some dessert?"

"No thank you, I had mine earlier," said Eve.

Fannie returned with a slice of cake and picked up a lady's magazine she had brought home from the shop.

After a few minutes of eating her cake and flipping through the pages, she looked up at Eve.

"I have a lot to think about, unless I've already scared him away."

"I don't think he'll scare that easily. I think you've enchanted him."

"We'll see," said Fannie. "We'll see."

★ ★ ★

Fannie and Jacob resumed their times together. She had decided to accept his word about respecting her decisions. A few weeks later he took her, Eve, and Freyda to the Cooper Union to hear Henrietta Szold speak. Szold's organization, Hadassah, was sending nurses to Palestine. Szold told the audience she had refused an offer by a male friend to say Kaddish for her mother. She would do it herself. "Women were just as capable of fulfilling the obligations of their faith as men," she said.

Fannie was shocked. Women saying Kaddish? She tried to imagine standing with the men after Miriam died. But why not? Wasn't her grief as great as theirs? She was sure Jacob had no idea Szold was going to mention such a radical idea. His attitudes about secular matters were liberal, but, as she had learned from their disagreement about Daniel, not his religious beliefs.

Fortunately, the rest of Szold's talk was about health care in the Holy Land. Eve and Freyda were thrilled to hear about the nurses' training program and that was all they talked about on the way home.

The evening reminded Fannie of everything she loved about Jacob. He planned things for them that opened up new worlds for her. But was that enough to overcome their differences?

★ ★ ★

Fannie covered her eyes as the *mohel* prepared to circumcise Anna and Nathan's eight-day old son, Jonathan. He had given the baby some gauze soaked in wine to dull his senses, but that didn't stop from letting out a lusty cry. The mohel rewrapped him in the white blanket Fannie had knitted and lifted him from the silk pillow on Jacob's lap. As the baby's godfather, Jacob had been given the honor of holding him during the ritual. It didn't seem like an honor to Fannie, but fortunately Jacob didn't mind the sight of blood.

"Mazel Tov!" shouted the crowd.

Fannie took the baby to bring him to Anna, who had remained in the bedroom during the ceremony. The other guests headed toward the tables of food to have a quick bite and a glass of schnapps before heading off to work.

"Oh, my poor baby," said Anna, offering him her breast. "How could they hurt you like that?"

"Luckily, he won't remember," said Fannie. She noticed a red ribbon tied to the baby's cradle. What's this?" she asked.

"A *kine hara*," said Anna. "To ward off the evil eye. My mother put it there. Nathan and I don't believe in such a silly superstition, but it makes her happy."

"Maybe it's a bubbe's love that keeps danger away."

Anna laughed. "Go mingle with the guests, Fannie. I'm fine."

"I can't. It's already late and I have to get to the shop. You have Nathan and your mother to help, but I'll stop by on my way home if you'd like."

"Jacob will be here too," said Anna. He has the rest of the day off and he's going to take Elijah to walk in the park. He'll be such a good father someday."

"I'm sure he will," said Fannie, avoiding Anna's eyes. She knew Anna was eager for them to marry. And she wasn't the only one. Both their families were expecting a proposal soon.

"I'm off," she said.

Later that evening she stopped by Anna's to say good night.

"I'll walk you home," said Jacob. "It will be nice to talk to a grown-up after playing with Elijah all day."

The two of them strolled at a leisurely pace, enjoying the perfect spring evening. Suddenly, just as they were about to cross 117th Street, Jacob stopped, turned to face Fannie, and took both her hands in his.

"I had planned to do this at a fancy dinner, with flowers and candles, like in the movies," he said. "But I can't wait. I'm sure you know how I feel about you. And all I could think about today was starting our own family. Fannie, will you marry me?"

"Oh no," she said. "I wasn't expecting this."

"But surely you knew I would be asking, and I thought you had feelings for me."

"No. I mean yes. I mean yes, I knew, and yes, I do. But so soon? I don't know what to say."

"Say yes."

"I don't care about flowers and candles," said Fannie. "But there are other things. Let's go sit in the park and talk."

They walked silently. Fannie thought about how to explain her hesitancy without hurting Jacob's feelings.

"You surprised me," said Fannie, adjusting her dress around her on the bench. "I don't want to ruin today's happiness, but I need to tell you how I'm feeling. You said you imagined the family we'll have together. You know I was married before, yes, and that my baby didn't live? What if I can't give you a child? I saw the way you looked at Jonathan today. You should be a father."

"I do want a child, but being with you is enough. I'm not him Fannie, the man you're remembering. I'll be good to you, no matter what."

"I believe you. But what about our differences? I'll keep a kosher home and light the Shabbos candles. But you know I don't agree with you about marrying out of the religion and there may be other things. Can we be happy together?"

"I'm sure we can. We don't need to agree about everything. The important thing is that I love you." He took her hand.

"I care about you, Jacob, I do. I'm happy when we're together. But I'm not ready to marry again. Can you wait? Can I have more time to get used to the idea?"

"I won't pretend to be happy, but I'll wait if you tell me there's hope."

"I just need some time. Perhaps after the holidays?"

"Or before? Wouldn't it be wonderful to go to shul together on Rosh Hashanah and announce our engagement? And by then I'll have a new job, and I can take care of you the way you deserve. Please say that's not too much to ask."

"No, it's not too much. Ask me again at the end of the summer."

"I guess I'll have to be satisfied with that for now."

When they arrived at Fannie's door, Jacob surprised her by taking her in his arms and kissing her gently on the lips. His lips were soft and warm, and she kissed him back. The kiss deepened until he stepped away.

What would it be like to be made love to by this man? She had known passion, and she wanted it again. She couldn't imagine him being selfish like Caleb, but would he excite her the way Samuel had? Could she settle for anything less? On the other hand, what else besides passion did she have with Samuel? Looking back, she realized lust had dominated their time together. Jacob was a good man. He took her interesting places and listened to her as though she was his equal, even though she knew she wasn't. There was so much to think about.

"Goodnight, Fannie."

"Goodnight, Jacob." She wanted him to kiss her again, but he walked away.

"How was the rest of your day?" Fannie's mother asked when she got inside the apartment.

"It was an ordinary day at work, but I had a big surprise just now. Jacob proposed."

"But surely you knew this was coming? We were all expecting it. I'm so happy for you—and for us. He'll be a wonderful son-in-law — and brother-in-law too. Eve and Noah have so much respect for him and Da—" She caught herself before mentioning Daniel. "Levi looks up to him," she went on. "And Freyda will be beside herself at the prospect of a wedding. And I am too, Fannie. This time I'll be standing next to you when you get married. Look, I'm already teary-eyed." She took out her handkerchief to wipe her eyes.

"Not so fast, Mama. I didn't accept."

"But why not? I thought he made you happy. Come, tell me." She patted the sofa cushion next to her.

Fannie sat down and leaned her head on her mother's shoulder.

"I can't explain it, Mama. But I'm happy the way things are now. I like my job; I like not worrying about what a husband wants."

"But what about children?"

Fannie sat up straight. "That frightens me, Mama. He says he doesn't care if I can't have children, but he doesn't know what it's like to lose a baby. What if he blames me like Caleb did?"

"There's no reason you can't have a healthy baby, Fannie. And Jacob is a different man. He's a *mensch*, the kind of man who'll stand by you. I'm sure of it."

"He said he'd wait until the holidays. That's almost three months for me to decide."

"Don't be alone, Fannie. It may be a good life when you're young but think about the future. Jacob is a man you can grow old with."

"I think so too. We're friends."

"And you couldn't ask for a better way to start a life together. Now get some sleep and I'm sure you'll see things more clearly in the morning."

"Thank you, Mama. I'm sure you're right, as always." She hugged her mother tightly and kissed her cheek. "Good night."

"Good night ziskeit. Sweet dreams."

★ ★ ★

The workroom was quiet. Fannie and the other girls were bent over their work, concentrating on the details they were finishing by hand. No one spoke; the only sounds were the electric fans whirring steadily and an occasional snip of a pair of shears.

"Ouch!" Fannie quickly stuck the finger she had just pricked into her mouth. A speck of blood would ruin the fine linen she was embroidering. She'd have to start over, not to mention pay for what she had spoiled.

"What's wrong with you?" asked Emma. "That's the second time today."

"She has her head in the clouds," said Molly. "Dreaming about that good-looking man of hers, I'll wager."

"He asked me to marry him yesterday," said Fannie softly, her head still bowed.

"What? Did you hear that, girls?"

Emma, Rose and Molly put down their work and rushed to embrace their friend.

"It's about time," shrieked Molly. "When's the wedding?"

"Mazel Tov," said Emma. "I'm so happy for you."

"Me too," said Rose. "You deserve to be happy, Fannie."

"We'll start planning your dress." Molly couldn't contain her enthusiasm. "I'm thinking silk."

"Wait," said Fannie.

"Nonsense," said Molly. "Pale blue, I think. With a matching hat and a short veil."

Just then, Sylvia walked in. "What's all the fuss?" she asked. "What will be blue?"

"Fannie's dress," said Rose. "She and Jacob are getting married."

"That's wonderful, Fannie. I'm so glad you found someone."

"No, no, no," said Fannie. "Please listen to me. I haven't accepted him yet. I asked him to wait."

The girls were shocked. Sylvia took a seat and waited for Fannie to explain.

"But why on earth not?" Rose finally asked. "You seem so happy whenever you talk about him."

Fannie struggled for the right words. "I'm just not ready," she said. "It feels too soon after—"

She looked down at her hands, folded in her lap. "I like my life now. And you know I have terrible luck with men." She had never told them the truth about Caleb, but they had seen her suffer after Samuel's betrayal.

"If you're thinking about Samuel, you can't judge all men by him," said Molly. "It's time to move on." She picked up Fannie's hands and looked her in the eye. "Look at the three of us. We've all found good men. I was never as happy as I am now, married to James. You can have that with Jacob."

"What if I want to be like Sylvia, the owner of a successful business, not answering to a man." She looked at Sylvia. "Maybe yours is the right life for me."

"Oh no, Fannie," said Sylvia. "I'm flattered you want to be like me, but don't make the same mistake I did. I'm very proud of what I've done, but it's a lonely life." She sighed. "When you all go home at night, I have no one. I had a suitor once when I was young. I was afraid he'd make me give up my ambitions, so I turned him down. There were never any others. I'm glad I have this," she said, pointing to the work spread out across the room, "But I'm too old to find anyone else."

"It's not too late," said Fannie.

"Don't fool yourself," said Sylvia. "You don't have much time left before you'll be a spinster too."

Fannie shook her head, but she knew Sylvia was right.

"And I missed my chance for children. I would have liked a family of my own. Isn't that what you want?"

"I didn't know."

"It's not something I like to talk about." She stood up. "Come, girls, let's get back to work. Fannie can tell us more about Jacob while we finish up this order. Our client is expecting it at the end of the week."

The girls went back to their tables as Sylvia walked around inspecting the work. Fannie returned to the trim she was embroidering on a pair of sleeves and remained silent.

"Out with it, girl," said Molly. "We know he's handsome, but what else? If you didn't say no outright, there must be things you like about him."

Fannie thought for a minute and then put down her work. "I'm not very smart," she said. The girls started to protest, but she held up a hand. "No, it's true. I only started to like school here in America. I started to like books when I was learning English. Jacob, he's so smart he's going to the university without paying. But he doesn't look down on me or mind when I ask questions. We talk about the news all the time. Did I tell you he thinks women should vote? And we learn about things together, like the paintings in the museum. I guess what I'm trying to say is he treats me like I'm smart too."

"You're smiling," said Rose.

"That's what my Mama says. She says I smile whenever I've been with him."

"Tell us more," said Rose.

"Sylvia asked me about children. I've never told you all that I had a baby. He was born too soon and never took a breath." She paused to collect herself. "I never conceived again."

"Does Jacob know?" asked Rose.

"Yes, I told him. And you know what he said?" She looked at her friends.

"He said it's me he wants. That makes me glad, but how can he know for sure? I've seen how he lights up with his nephew. I'm afraid of what will happen if I can't have children."

"Oh, you poor thing," said Emma. She was the only one among them who had a child. "But lots of women lose babies and go on to have healthy children. You shouldn't worry."

"But I do. That's why I had to tell him."

"And he said being with you is more important than a child. I think you should trust him."

"I'm trying. We do have our differences, you know. He's more traditional than I am, but he says he'll respect my decisions. So I guess I'll have to trust him about that too."

"You know more about Jacob than most women know about their husbands before they're married. It sounds to me like he's a good and kind man. What more can you ask for?"

"Well, he did kiss me." She grinned and started to blush. "And it was nice. I can ask for that."

"Fannie," said Rose. "You may never be one hundred percent sure, no matter how long you wait. I certainly wasn't."

"Everything you've said and the expression on your face says go ahead and marry this man." said Sylvia. "And something tells me you'll stay with us and keep up your embroidery too—if you want to, that is. With Jacob, you'll have the best of both worlds—a loving husband and work you enjoy."

Fannie couldn't think of anything else to say. Where would she be without her friends?

"Let's start planning the dress, girls!" said Molly.

CHAPTER 25

Fannie had been mulling over her decision for months. Everyone who cared about her told her to marry Jacob. Mama, Eve, the girls at work. She knew they were right, but still she hesitated. Papa's choice had led to disaster. But now, with the freedom to decide for herself, she worried about being wrong. Wasn't Samuel proof of her poor judgement? She couldn't find fault with Jacob. No, more than that, everything about him said he was a decent, generous man who would take care of her. They would, as Mama said, grow old together. And marital relations? Well, she was no longer a girl who didn't know how to ask for what she wanted. And from the look in his eyes, not to mention the kisses neither of them could resist when they were alone, she suspected he would be a good lover. Didn't that all add up to love? It was time to tell him.

That Sunday, a sultry August afternoon, Jacob took her to Central Park. They sat facing the lake, watching the swans glide by. It was such a romantic setting, surely he would ask her now.

"Fannie," said Jacob, turning toward her. "Will—"

"Yes," said Fannie before he could finish.

"Yes?"

"Yes," said Fannie. "I love you."

Jacob's eyes held hers. Then he leaned over to kiss her lips. "I was hoping that's what you'd say." He reached into his pocket for a small black velvet box and handed it to her. "I've been saving this, praying I'd be able to give it you."

Fannie opened the box to find a diamond heart on a delicate silver chain.

"I've collected these diamonds over the years," he said. "Waiting for the right woman to have them made into something special. I knew that was you the first time we met. May I put it on you?"

Fannie turned around to let Jacob fasten the chain around her neck. "There," he said. When his lips grazed the back of her neck she trembled. She took out her compact to see how it looked; the way the stones sparkled in the light took her breath away.

"I've never had anything so lovely. Thank you."

"It barely does you justice."

"And I was also hoping today would be the day," said Fannie. "I have something for you too, although it's not nearly as grand as what you've given me." She withdrew a small package from her purse.

Jacob opened it to find an intricately embroidered yarmulke. At the center of a pattern of flowers and vines, a dove held an olive branch with the word *shalom* underneath. He immediately replaced the one he was wearing. "It's beautiful, and one-of-a-kind. I'll treasure it. When should we get married?"

"After the holidays, at the end of October? It's so pretty when the leaves turn color."

"And you can plan everything by then? I remember how much Anna and our mother did to get ready for the wedding."

"I'd like a small, simple wedding. And believe it or not, the girls at work have already designed my dress! They knew before I did that the answer would be yes."

Jacob laughed. "I knew I liked those girls." He took Fannie in his arms and kissed her again until Fannie pulled away.

"Jacob, you know I'm not a girl anymore. I've been married before. I am—that is—what I'm trying to say is that we don't have to wait to be together."

Jacob was silent.

"I've offended you, haven't I?" She looked at him anxiously.

"No, of course not. I'd lay you down and make love to you right now if I could. You're the most desirable woman I've ever met. But I'd like to wait for our wedding night. I want to start our marriage with a night so special it drives away all memories of your first husband."

"Then we'll wait."

"Now, we'd better leave. I know it's early, but if we don't stop to see Anna before I take you home, she'll never forgive me." He helped Fannie up and kissed her again. "Waiting may be harder than I thought," he murmured in her ear.

Jacob insisted they take a cab. They leaned against each other, holding hands. Neither felt a need to speak, only to occasionally look at each other and smile.

"Finally," Anna shouted as she flung herself into Fannie's arms. "Now we'll be sisters."

She reached out to her brother. "And just remember, big brother, you have me to thank."

"I do," said Jacob. "From the bottom of my heart."

"My turn," said Nathan, hugging them both.

"And don't forget your Mama and Papa." Jacob's mother took Fannie in her arms. "We couldn't be happier, Fannie dear. Welcome to the family."

She motioned for her husband. "What are you waiting for, Sid, come welcome Jacob's beautiful kallah."

"Look what she made me, Papa." Jacob showed his father the yarmulke.

"Beautiful and talented. My son's a lucky man," said his father.

"The wedding will be in October," Jacob announced to the family.

"Now we must go tell my family," said Fannie. "They're waiting for the good news."

They left after another round of hugs and tearful goodbyes.

Freyda ran to them as soon as they came through the door. "Are you getting married?"

"Yes," Fannie and Jacob answered together.

"I knew it," said Freyda, dancing around them.

'God bless you both," said her father, wiping his tears with his fingertips.

"And may you have a lifetime of happiness," added her mother, embracing them both.

"Thank you," said Jacob. "I promise I'll take good care of her."

"Bluma, get some glasses," said Asher. "It's time to celebrate." He went to get the schnapps from the cabinet.

"Levi, look what's happened in America. First a sister-in-law-and now a brother-in-law." Fannie bent to give her little brother a kiss.

"I'm happy for you," he said solemnly. Fannie and Jacob took him in their arms and laughed.

"Mazel Tov. And what a beautiful necklace, Fannie," said Eve. She picked up the heart to look at it more closely.

Fannie showed it off to the rest of the family.

"You've chosen well, Fannie," said Noah, hugging his sister tightly. "Daniel would be proud of you," he whispered.

Fannie began to cry. Jacob handed her his handkerchief.

"It's because I'm so happy," she said.

"L'chaim," said Papa. "You've made Mama and me very happy."

"L'chaim," echoed the rest of the family. "To a long and happy life."

★ ★ ★

Something was wrong with Jacob. It was a beautiful fall Sunday, the day after Yom Kippur. He had come to her parents' apartment so they could bring a few of their things to the apartment they would be living in after the wedding, now only three weeks away. But Fannie could see right away he wasn't himself. He had been unusually quiet when they had broken the fast the night before, but she had assumed that was from the long day without any food or drink. They had all been tired.

But today he hardly said a word when he greeted her and her parents, only asked where the bundles were and said the cab was waiting. He barely acknowledged the map of Europe Levi had cut out of the paper and marked with battle sites.

Fannie was upset. "Jacob, he's been waiting all day to show you that," she said when Levi left to put the map away. "You know how much he looks up to you."

"Of course, I'll apologize."

He put his hand on the boy's shoulder as soon as he came back into the room.

"I'm sorry, Levi," he said. "We'll sit at the table and look at it together the next time I'm here."

She waited for him to explain, but he said nothing while they were in the cab. Normally talkative, he only nodded or said one or two words as she talked about the congratulations they had received at shul. He revealed nothing about what was troubling him.

Unable to contain her worry, she confronted him as soon as they were inside the apartment. "What's wrong, Jacob? You haven't been yourself since before the holiday."

"I didn't know how to tell you. I still don't. Please, sit down."

Fannie sat. "You've changed your mind. You don't want to go through with the wedding." She couldn't look at him, even when he sat next to her and took her hands.

"How could you think that? I can't wait to be married to you. But maybe you're the one who will feel differently when I tell you. Maybe you'll want to call it off."

She looked up at him, bewildered. "Are you ill?"

"No, thank God. I'm not sick. I'm angry. And ashamed."

"But why? What are you talking about?"

"I didn't get the job, Fannie."

"I'm so sorry. I know you had such high hopes. But I'm sure there will be others. You told me yourself that companies want to hire graduates from Cooper Union. I've already picked out the place to hang your diploma." She pointed to the wall over one of the bookcases they had bought.

"You can forget about that now," he said, his voice harsh.

"I don't understand."

"I ran into one of my professors at lunch time the day before the holiday. We had both stopped to look in the same bookstore window."

Fannie had to smile in spite of Jacob's distress. It was so like him to spend what little free time he had looking at books.

"He didn't seem surprised when I told him I had been rejected again, so I pushed him to tell my why."

Jacob stood up abruptly and began pacing. "It's because none of those firms will hire a Jew."

"What? No!"

"Yes. I only wish someone had told me years ago. Why did they let me waste my time studying if they knew I'd never get a job? And you thought I was so smart? I'm an idiot."

"Don't say that, Jacob. You'll keep looking. They can't all be prejudiced like that. This isn't Russia."

He sat down again. "It's worse. At least there they don't pretend."

Fannie took his hand, unsure what to say.

"The professor said it was impossible. Oh Fannie, I wanted you to be proud of me. 'My husband the engineer' you would boast. Now that will never happen."

He put his head in his hands and wept.

Fannie put her arms around him and let him cry.

As his sobs subsided, she drew back to look in his eyes. "You're a smart man, Jacob, a very smart man," she said fiercely, tears in her own eyes. "And what's more important, you're a good man. I'll always be proud of you."

She paused, thinking of what to say next.

"Listen to me. I'm sorry it's not what you dreamed of, but maybe that will come someday. Meanwhile, you have a good job. And perhaps when this terrible war is over, and you can go to Antwerp again, you'll take me with you. I'll see it as the wife of a successful diamond merchant, not the frightened refugee I was the first time."

"Yes, I'll take you." Jacob blew his nose and sat up straight. "I'll show you off and everyone will wonder how I managed to persuade such a beautiful woman to marry me."

He wrapped his arms around her and kissed her. "You're the smart one, Fannie. I love you."

"And I love you," she murmured as she kissed him back.

"Fannie?"

She saw the hunger in his eyes.

"I know what I said about waiting, but—"

"Yes," she said, as their kisses deepened.

He unbuttoned her blouse and slid it off her arms. He kissed her neck, then lowered the straps of her chemise and cupped her breasts. "How beautiful you are. I've dreamed about this."

She could see the bulge in his trousers and started to unbutton them. "So have I."

"No, wait." Jacob sat up abruptly and caught his breath.

"Why? What's wrong? Don't stop."

"I want you, but not like this."

Fannie tugged her chemise over her breasts.

"I want our first time to be a celebration, not a consolation, not from pity. Can you understand?"

"Of course, but I'm glad it's only three weeks. I'll have a hard time looking at you and not thinking about this."

"I know what you mean," said Jacob ruefully.

PART VIII: A NEW LIFE, 1916-1917

As Fannie and Jacob stood under the chuppah with their fingers entwined, Fannie let the Rabbi's blessings wash over her. She thought about her first wedding, which seemed like a lifetime ago. She remembered guests dressed in elegant evening clothes, extravagant flowers, music, and a five-course dinner, but most of all she recalled her fear and the feeling that except for Papa, she was alone. Mama, who wept quietly beside her now, hadn't been there. Today, they had each taken one of her arms to bring her to Jacob.

"Be happy," whispered Mama as she let her go.

"He's the right one," Papa said into her other ear.

She had spent her first wedding dreading what was to come. Now, as she stole a glance at Jacob, handsome in his dark suit and the yarmulke she had embroidered for him, she couldn't help but think about the afternoon in their new apartment. She was looking forward to their wedding night and wondered if he was smiling for the same reason. *Sha!* she scolded herself. This was not the time for such thoughts. She made herself turn her attention back to the Rabbi.

Jacob placed the ring on her finger and repeated after the Rabbi, "With this ring ..."

After they each sipped from the same cup of wine, the Rabbi handed Fannie the ketubah, the contract that was written to protect the bride. When Caleb refused to honor the one he had signed she had thrown it in the trash. Today, she trusted the man making promises.

Finally, Jacob stepped on the glass and their guests shouted *Mazel Tov!* as they turned to walk back down the aisle toward the room where they'd be alone for eighteen minutes.

Noah took her hand briefly as she walked by. Molly, Emma, Rose and Sylvia blew kisses and joined the others in clapping their hands in a lively rhythm. Eve and Nathan's families were all smiles. If only Daniel had been there. She wondered what his wedding had been like. There was no chuppah, and no Rabbi, but what did that matter? Surely a merciful God was watching over him.

As soon as they were alone, Jacob took her in his arms and all unhappy thoughts vanished. "I can't believe we're finally married," he said.

Fannie held up her hand to look at her ring. "I love you," she said. "I'm only sorry it took so long to realize it."

"It doesn't matter now. We have the rest of our lives." He slipped off the ring to read the inscription: *"Ani l'dodi v'dodi li, I am my beloved's, and my beloved is mine."*

Fannie wept. Jacob wiped her tears away with gentle kisses. She melted against him. "I'm looking forward to tonight," he said.

"Me too," she said. They stayed in each other's arms until the eighteen minutes ended, then rejoined their guests and posed for their wedding portrait and family pictures. Bluma, Freyda, Eve and Anna stood on either side of Fannie as they posed for one last picture. "If only photographs had color," said Fannie, admiring the rich autumn shades of their lace dresses and matching jackets.

Eve's golden blond hair shone against her dark red dress. Anna, who had the same coloring, looked equally pretty in pale green. Freyda's burnt orange dress set off her dark red curls, which she had just begun pinning up. She had her mother's hazel eyes and was as tall as Fannie. At sixteen, she had blossomed into a beautiful young woman, already leading a different life from the one that had been chosen for Fannie when she was that age. Fannie was proud of her, and of Mama for enabling her to pursue her nursing studies.

"Stand up straight," said Bluma. "Yes, Mama," both Freyda and Fannie replied. Some things never changed. Bluma had refused anything brighter than the ecru dress she was wearing, but even the subdued color couldn't hide her beauty. It was easy to see who Fannie and Freyda took after.

After a great deal of discussion, with Molly still arguing for pale blue, Fannie had decided on deep gold for her dress. "You win, it will be perfect for your chestnut hair and dark brown eyes," said Molly. "But then again, you'd look good in a potato sack!"

"You're the bride," Sylvia had insisted. "Tell us what you want, and we'll do the rest—my gift to you."

Today, the silk dress shimmered, its glow matched only by her complexion and the happiness she radiated. They had designed it with a deep v-neck to show off her diamond heart. She wore one of her own embroidered bolero jackets.

During lunch, Fannie and Jacob walked around to each table to thank their guests. "You made my bride look even more beautiful." Jacob told Sylvia and the girls from the shop. When they got to Zalman, he complimented Fannie on her diamond heart. "Jacob knew what he was doing," he said. "He picked the right stones—and, if I may be permitted to say so, the right bride."

"Fannie wants to see Antwerp," said Jacob. "I'm going to take her as soon as the war ends."

When it was time for goodbyes, Fannie and Jacob stood by the door. There were embraces and tears of joy until the last guest left and they were ready to go home. Just before they stepped into the cab, the caterer came running up to them with a big brown bag.

"Some leftover food," he said. "And a big slice of wedding cake."

"Thank you," said Fannie. "Are you hungry?" she asked Jacob. "Neither of us has had a bite to eat all day."

"I'm starving," said Jacob. "But it's you I want," he whispered in her ear.

When they arrived home, they dropped the package on the kitchen table and clung to each other all the way to the bedroom. Jacob took the pins from her hair. Suddenly awkward, they stood next to the bed until Jacob started to unbutton the row of tiny silk buttons down the back of her dress and let it fall to the ground. Fannie raised her arms to help him lift off her chemise and remained still as he lowered her slip and panties. He made no move to touch her, only gazing steadily into her eyes. She stood still, naked, waiting for what he would do next. He lay her down on the bed gently, never taking his eyes off her as he took off his own clothes.

She looked up at him. His body was pale, his chest lightly covered with dark, curly hair that came to a vee at his navel. She stared at his erection, shivering with anticipation.

"You're so beautiful," he whispered, and began to kiss her lightly, first on her lips, then her neck, her shoulders, her breasts. He lingered on each breast until her nipples hardened. She moaned softly. He moved his hand down her body, his fingers caressing her gently between her legs until she was wet. She started to breathe heavily and began to move under him, eager to feel him inside her.

"Now," she begged.

Her hips rose to meet his as he began to move. She was aware of nothing but the sensation of him inside her until she came in waves. She held him deep inside her as he began to thrust more quickly, until he too stiffened and exploded inside her. "Fannie," he cried out. He shuddered and collapsed on top of her.

They were both still for a while.

Jacob lifted himself on his elbows to look at her. He brushed his lips across hers and slowly worked his way down her body. She began to respond and felt him getting hard. He came into her and then took her by surprise when he turned them over so that she was sitting on top of him. While he stroked her nipples with his thumbs, he began to push upward into her. She had never felt anything like it before. He let her take control, riding him, setting their pace, faster and faster until neither of them could hold back.

"Yes," cried Fannie. This time she collapsed onto him. And to think she had once been afraid he wouldn't be a good lover she thought as her breathing started to return to normal. They fell asleep in each other's arms.

In the morning, she awoke to find him staring at her. She held out her arms for him. Their lovemaking was slow as they explored each other's bodies.

"Let me wash up and get breakfast," she said.

"Stay," he said, "I'll run a bath for you."

No sooner had Fannie lowered herself into the steamy water than Jacob got in with her. He ran a soapy cloth over her breasts and drew her to him so that she was sitting on him. They hardly noticed the water getting cold.

"It's a good thing I have the day off. I'd never be able to go to work with you tempting me like this," he said when he was able to speak again. He got up, wrapped a towel around his waist and turned the faucet to add hot water to the bath.

"I'll be right back."

He came back shortly with a plate of wedding cake and a fork. "Are you ready for dessert?" he asked playfully. He balanced himself on the rim of the tub and began to feed her.

* * *

The next few months passed in a blur as Fannie and Jacob got used to their life together. They had tea together in the morning before they left for work. Fannie arrived home first to prepare dinner. She had quickly gotten to know the best places in the neighborhood to buy meat, groceries and fresh baked cookies and cakes. She smiled every time a shopkeeper addressed her as "Mrs. Vogel."

Jacob came home soon after she did, often with fresh flowers or a bag of candy. After dinner they sat together, reading, or Fannie worked on a piece of embroidery while Jacob read. If he found something he thought she'd like, he read it aloud to her. Often, they would look up at each other, put down what they were doing and spend the rest of the night in their bedroom, learning new ways to please each other. Jacob never brought up having a baby. Fannie knew he was being sensitive, but she wouldn't have minded. She was sure it wouldn't be long before she conceived. But as much as she wanted a child—his child— she couldn't push her fear away completely. Was love enough for a baby to survive?

As soon as they had moved in, Jacob had unpacked all his books and arranged them in the mahogany bookcases with glass doors that were the first pieces of furniture they purchased. She had sat on the floor with him as he took the books out of the cartons, dusting each one before he put it away. First there were the physics and philosophy books in Russian, German, and French. "I should probably give these away," he said. "Or maybe I can sell them. They're of no use to me now." He couldn't keep the bitterness out of his voice.

"No, not yet," said Fannie. "You never know ..." But she agreed to give the five volume *Everybody's Encyclopedia* to Levi to help him with his schoolwork.

The second bookcase was filled with novels, plays and biographies, most of them in English. These he had organized by author. Fannie loved having Jacob's books in the living room. They were an example of what she loved about the man she had married. "But we're going to run out of room soon," she had teased him. "Do you think you can resist going to Fourth Avenue for more books for a while?"

The kitchen was her domain, with its new gas stove opposite the sink and icebox. She had made white curtains for the large window on the third wall. The view wasn't as good as the one they had of Crotona Park in the living room, but it let in fresh air. There were ample cabinets for pots and pans and everyday dishes. The good dishes were stored in the breakfront in the dining area, where she also kept her prized silver candlesticks. Mama had brought them over as soon as they had moved in, welded and with a new inscription, "God Bless My Daughter in Her New Home. Your Loving Mama, October 1916." Each time she lit the candles she was grateful for everything she had.

★ ★ ★

"We're ready. So no matter what happens tonight, the Seder will go on, as it always has," Mama sighed. "But I don't think there's much doubt, Fannie, do you? America will go to war."

They had spent the afternoon cooking together and preparing special foods for the Passover Seder plate, chopping the nuts and apples for the *haroset*, grating horseradish for the *maror* and soaking a hard-boiled egg in tea to make it look roasted. The shank bone Mama had gotten from the butcher was in the ice box. Tomorrow, Freyda would be home from nursing school. She would help cut up the greens, put salt water in small dishes, open the boxes of matzo, and set the table.

"I'm sure of it," said Fannie. "Jacob can't fight because he's deaf in one ear. But Noah?"

"I'm trying not to think about it. We'll know soon enough. Thank God Levi is too young. All he talks about is being a soldier and fighting the Huns."

"Jacob told me he wanted to serve when we first met. It didn't mean a lot to me then, but now I couldn't bear to lose him."

"Try not to let the news upset you. It's not good for the baby."

"Mama!" Fannie's hands flew to her belly.

"Did you think I couldn't tell?"

"But even Jacob doesn't know for sure yet. I was going to tell him before the Seder so we could share the news with everyone then."

"Don't worry, I won't spoil your surprise. How are you feeling?"

"I'm fine. I haven't had the sickness I had last time. But there were never any signs that anything was wrong until I lost the baby, so what difference does it make how I'm feeling now? I'm scared, Mama."

"God willing, this baby is coming when he's big and healthy. And I'll be holding your hand the whole time. Now, go tell your husband, because I can't keep this news to myself much longer."

Fannie went home and, as she got their dinner ready, planned how she would tell Jacob. She'd wait until he was ready for his tea and give it to him along with the kiss she gave him every night as she handed him his glass. He called it his sugar. But the minute she heard his key in the door she ran to greet him.

"I have news," she blurted.

"Me too," said Jacob. "I enlisted. Of course I can't fight, but I'll have a desk job on Governor's Island, here in the city."

Fannie burst into sobs.

"What's wrong? I won't be in any danger, I promise. It's my duty, Fannie. I told you that when we met."

"But I'm having a baby," she cried. "I need you."

Jacob took her hands in his and looked up into her eyes. "A baby?"

Fannie nodded.

"I thought—I hoped. I'm going to be a father? Are you all right? When?"

"I'm fine, and around the new year."

"I love you," he said. "And I promise I'll be with you. Let's just pray the war will be over before our child is born."

"Come," said Fannie. "Let's eat. I was so busy cooking with Mama all afternoon I haven't heard the latest news. You can tell me what's happening in the Congress."

They walked into the kitchen. "You weren't working too hard this afternoon, were you? Freyda should help."

Fannie laughed. "She will. She was at school today. It was easy for me to help since Sylvia closed the shop a day early for a long weekend. Luckily, our holiday and Easter are at the same time so we could all be home for *Pesach.*

"Can we tell everyone at the Seder tomorrow?"

"Of course, I can't wait."

That night, Jacob lay beside Fannie, picked up her nightgown, and stroked her bare, still flat belly. "My child," he said. "I hope you look like your mother."

"And I hope you're smart like your father," said Fannie.

He made love to her, slowly and gently, before they both fell into an untroubled sleep.

In the morning, when they both had the rare luxury of a day off, Jacob got dressed and ran to the nearest newsstand to grab a handful of morning papers. "It's official," he told Fannie. "The House voted at three o'clock this morning. President Wilson will sign the declaration of war this afternoon."

Fannie reached over for the *Forverts*. "Listen to this." She started to read from 'Milkhome Brief,' letters from German and Russian soldiers at war, searching for their families in New York.

> *Beloved, dear father,*
>
> *I'm writing after a long time to tell you that I'm well and am now eight versts [5.5 miles] away from where the war still rages. I'm now among soldiers prepping guns and bullets for those at the front lines. Though I'm several miles from the battles, the bullets reach us. One witnesses such dreadful things my entire body trembles.*
>
> *Blood flows like water and people fall like flies—*

She couldn't go on. "This could be Noah, or Daniel."

"We have to stop them from taking over Europe, Fannie."

"I know, but I'm afraid. If not for you then for all the other men."

"Please, let's not talk about it anymore. It can't be good for you or the baby. Let's take a walk in the park and see the dogwoods blooming before we go to your parents."

"I'd like that," said Fannie.

"Wear your jacket—it's still a little cool." He helped Fannie into her jacket, and they went out, hoping to put the news out of their minds for a while.

Later that evening, as soon as they were all seated, Fannie and Jacob shared their news. "Mazel Tov," said Asher. "There couldn't be better news, especially today, when we tell our children the story of the exodus. Now we have another child to look forward to. Soon you won't be the youngest, Levi. Fannie and Jacob's son will ask the four questions at the beginning of the Seder."

"It will take a while, Papa. And it could be a girl, you know," said Fannie. She wondered if her father would allow a girl to read the questions. It was years away. Perhaps he would change by then.

"Yes," said Jacob, "A little girl as beautiful as her mother—and her grandmother."

Bluma smiled. "Boy or girl, we're more than ready to be bubbe and zayde," she said.

"Let's begin," said Asher. "Bluma, will you light the candles?"

After the blessings, the ritual foods, the retelling of the story of the journey out of slavery, and the obligatory four cups of wine, Fannie felt herself getting drowsy, but she was too happy to think about leaving.

"I have some news, too," said Noah. "I've enlisted. I'll be leaving as soon as the army is ready to send troops overseas."

Everyone was quiet.

"What can I say, son?" said Asher. "We'll pray for your safety."

Bluma began to cry. "Mothers everywhere are probably hearing the same thing tonight. And wives. It will be hard, Eve, but you know you can always come to us. We're your family too."

"I'm going with him," said Eve.

"What?" Fannie was the first to speak. "What do you mean you're going?"

"The army needs nurses to care for the soldiers. And shouldn't every wife and mother know their husbands and sons are being cared for by someone trained to save their lives?"

"But it's too dangerous, child," said Bluma. "Women aren't meant to go to war."

"That's how nursing started, Mama, in the wars. How can I let Noah put himself in danger and do nothing?"

"We've talked about it," said Noah. "I'm proud of her."

"You're so brave, Eve," said Freyda. "I wish I were old enough to go."

"Thank God you're not," said Bluma.

"You may have a chance to do your part when you've finished your studies," said Eve. "Although you'll still be too young to go overseas, they'll need nurses here in America to care for the wounded soldiers when they come home."

"Let's pray there aren't too many of them," said Bluma, looking at her son.

Fannie said nothing. She had counted on Eve to be with her when the baby came, but how could she put her needs ahead of the soldiers?

"This war will touch all of us in some way," said Jacob. "But let's hope H.G. Wells was right and it really is 'the war that will end war.'"

There was nothing left to say. Their goodbyes were subdued as Fannie, Jacob, Noah, and Eve got up to leave.

CHAPTER 27

annie had her feet in Jacob's lap. He was massaging them as he did every evening. She smiled as he chatted with their unborn child. He told the baby about the weather, a funny article in the paper, or a particularly delicious meal Fannie had made. Anything except the war news.

Sometimes he made an exception for one of Noah or Eve's letters. "This is from your aunt," he'd say. "You'll meet her one day after you're born. She said the soldiers are flirts. And Uncle Noah says the food is terrible and he's getting skinny." In truth, neither of their letters said very much. They were either censored or they were withholding the worst.

Eve had written that she was closer to the front than she had expected, and she didn't know where Noah was. The newspapers filled in the rest—about the trenches, the gas, and the shell shock. Badly wounded soldiers started to appear on the streets of New York. It was early September; Noah had been gone since May, Eve since July.

Fannie didn't tell Jacob, but she had also gotten a letter from Daniel's wife, Susan. Daniel had enlisted and, like Noah, had left in May. She promised to keep in touch. Fannie wished she could hear from Daniel himself, but at least she had something to hold onto. She shared the news with Mama.

Fannie had already started wearing maternity clothes. The midwife had been to see her the day before and assured her everything was going well, but she was still fearful. She tried not to burden Jacob with her fears, but tonight she needed him to comfort her.

"How will I ever get through these next few months, Jacob? I'm so afraid."

"It will be fine, Fannie, you'll see."

"You can't know that. No one can."

"You're right, but please try to have faith."

The baby began to kick, which delighted Jacob. "Be nice to your Mama," he laughed, but Fannie was silent.

"Come," said Jacob, "rest on me."

She curled up in his arms and closed her eyes. Nothing made her feel safer than being held by Jacob and soon she dozed off.

A sudden loud knocking woke her up.

"Someone's at the door," said Jacob. "I'll get it."

Fannie was seized with dread. No one would come this late without calling.

When Jacob returned, holding a yellow envelope, she began to keen. "No, no, no, not Noah."

Jacob held it out to her.

"I can't," she said.

He read silently to himself before looking up at Fannie.

"Tell me," she pleaded.

He read aloud:

Noah wounded. At hospital with him.

Tell parents. More news soon.

Pray for us.

Eve

"He's alive Fannie. He's alive. And Eve is with him."

Fannie sobbed with relief. "He's alive," she repeated. "But what else do we know? I hate this war!"

"Don't get yourself too worked up, Fannie. I'm sure we'll hear more from Eve soon. Tomorrow I'll go with you to your parents to tell them in person."

"They'll guess as soon as they see us."

"Probably, but we'll stay to make sure they're all right. Come, let's go to bed."

"I won't be able to sleep."

"I'll hold you until you do."

They didn't hear anything else for three weeks. The wait was agonizing. She was afraid to get the mail. What if another telegram came, this one from the army? What if it came when Jacob wasn't there?

Finally, a letter came from Eve.

Noah is well enough to be moved, but his wounds are still very serious. They are sending him to a hospital in ▆▆▆▆ *and I'll go with him. From there we'll both come home. I will try to let you know when.*

Fannie read the letter again and again. It didn't sound good and because of the censors they had no idea where he was. The news reports were terrifying. They had to be prepared for the worst. Every week, she and her mother went to shul with Jacob and her father to say the *Mi Shebeirach*, the prayer for healing, for Noah and all the other soldiers.

Another letter came, this time from England:

The crossing was difficult. Noah still has a fever, but he seems to be getting better.

There was no word about coming home. What was she not telling them?

Fannie decided to make Noah a blanket. If he still needed to recuperate when he came home, at least he'd have something cheerful to keep him warm, and it gave her something to do.

She had stopped working in the shop. Sylvia brought her work to do at home, but she had ample time for an additional project, especially since she refused to make anything for the baby. Whatever they needed they would buy, or her mother would make. The closer she got to when she lost the first baby, the more anxious she became. Jacob held her each night, trying to reassure her.

He loved taking off her clothes and staring at her naked body. She was worried that she looked fat and unattractive, but he seemed to desire her even more. "You're more beautiful than ever," he would say, kissing her swollen breasts and her belly, arousing her with his fingertips and making love to her gently. She would fall asleep in his arms.

In November, as she entered her eighth month, she finally began to believe she would deliver safely. When she complained about how big she was, the midwife and Mama laughed. You'll grow even more from now on, they told her. Jacob continued to dote on her. He massaged her feet, rubbed vitamin cream on her belly, helped her get into the tub and washed her back and her hair. The bigger she got the more erotic he found her body, and the more he wanted her the more aroused she became. No one had told her about that part of expecting a baby.

Only her fear for Noah kept her from being truly happy. Eve had written to say she thought they'd be home soon. It depended on when there was a ship that could take them. Another letter had also come from Susan. She thought Daniel was in Germany, but there was no real news.

Waiting and more waiting. For the baby. For Noah. If only they could know how the wait would end.

★ ★ ★

Fannie was napping on the sofa when Jacob burst through the door. "They're home, Fannie. Thank God, they're home."

Fannie eased herself up into sitting, still half asleep. "What time is it? Who's home?" she asked groggily.

"It's four o'clock. Noah and Eve. Your Papa got in touch with me at the base. They let me go as soon as I explained."

"But when?"

"The ship arrived a few days ago, but they needed to get Noah settled. They didn't let anyone know until today."

"But why didn't Papa call me?"

Jacob threw his hat and coat onto a chair and sat down next to her.

"What's wrong?" she asked. "Why did you have to come home to tell me?"

"We can go see them soon, when Noah has had a chance to rest from being on the ship."

"Tell me, Jacob." Fannie insisted.

Jacob hesitated. "It could have been worse, Fannie. He's alive and he'll heal. He'll be able to work. It will just take time."

"Tell me."

He took her hand. "They had to cut off his right leg, Fannie."

Fannie was quiet.

"He'll be all right."

"All right?" she spat out. "What does that mean, Jacob? He went to war. He almost died. He lost his leg. What does 'all right' mean?"

"Fannie, please don't excite yourself. Think of the baby. And Noah is going to need all of us to help him rebuild his life."

Fannie began to cry. Jacob took her in his arms. "Do you think you can you be strong for him, Fannie? He'll need all of us to be strong."

"I have to be, don't I?"

"He's at the Hospital for the Ruptured and Crippled. It's the finest hospital in New York for amputees. He'll get excellent care there."

"And Eve?"

"She's staying overnight with him, at least for now. That's all I know except that your parents will see him tomorrow afternoon. They'll come here after they've seen him, so we'll learn more."

"Poor girl. She wanted to be there for the soldiers, and it turned out it was Noah she had to nurse." Fannie was calmer.

"Can I get you some tea? A glass of water?" Jacob offered.

"Don't fuss, I'll be all right and we'll have dinner. There's chicken in the ice box. Should I heat it up or will you eat it cold?"

"Cold is fine, but no rush. Let me hold you a while longer." He rested his hand on her belly. "How are you feeling today? Has the baby been kicking?"

"Like a football player. I think he's getting ready for his big entrance. Oh, Jacob, what a terrible world we're bringing this child into."

★ ★ ★

Fannie's parents arrived the following day just as it was getting dark.

"Mama, Papa." They stood by the door holding each other, unable to speak. When they broke apart, Jacob took their coats, and they sat.

"I hardly recognized my own son," said Bluma, getting out her handkerchief. "You must prepare yourself, Fannie."

"Perhaps she should wait," said Jacob. "This close to having the baby."

"No," said Fannie. "I want to go. Is he in much pain Mama?"

"Yes. But it's not just his body, it's his soul. I'm afraid his spirit will be harder to fix than his leg." She began to weep.

"Perhaps a little schnapps, son?" Asher asked. "It's been a long afternoon."

Jacob went to get his father-in-law a drink.

Asher threw back his head and downed the shot of whiskey. "I didn't know what to expect. And Eve said this is already better. God only knows what my boy has suffered." Jacob poured him another drink and took one for himself.

The four of them sat quietly for a while.

"How long will he be there?" asked Fannie.

"Eve doesn't know," said her Mama. "The stump has to heal before he can get a new leg and then he needs to learn how to walk with it. It could be months."

Fannie cringed at the word stump.

"Oh Fannie, there were so many boys. Without arms, without legs."

"But he's come home, Mama. We'll take care of him and make him better."

Her Mama sat up straighter. "And you, Fannie? Wasn't the midwife here today? What did she say?"

"Soon, Mama, soon. Only a few weeks."

★ ★ ★

The next day, Fannie stopped just before the doors to Noah's ward, steeling herself for her first glimpse of her brother. *I must be strong for him.*

"Are you ready?" asked Jacob.

"No," said Fannie, clutching the brown paper package with the blanket she had made. "But let's go."

She saw Eve first and tried not to let her see how shocked she was. With all the talk of Noah, no one had mentioned how pale and thin Eve had become. She looked years older than when she had left. But she smiled as soon as she saw Fannie.

"Fannie, look at you! If they had a maternity ward at this hospital they would have rushed you straight there. You look wonderful." She embraced Fannie and held on as tightly as she could with Fannie's big belly in between them. "Try not to cry," she whispered. "He's getting better, I promise."

"And how is the Papa to be?" She reached out to hug Jacob.

Fannie broke away and approached her brother's bed. The man she saw there was a stranger. She could see Eve had made an effort by combing his hair and trimming his beard, but his face was gaunt and as gray as the blanket that was tucked up under his chin. She couldn't help glancing toward his legs, but looked away quickly before she could detect the empty space. His eyes were sunken and staring into space.

She forced herself to smile.

"Noah," she said, bending over to kiss his forehead. "It's good to have you home."

"Fannie, you're so big." He gave her a weak smile, hardly more than a grimace. His voice was so soft she could barely hear him.

"Yes, I am. I'm quite ready for your niece or nephew to be born so I can see my toes again."

Jacob came to her side. "Welcome home, Noah."

"Are you taking good care of my sister?"

"Doesn't it look like it?"

Noah managed another wan smile.

"You'll be an uncle soon. Your mother is sure it's a boy."

"I'm afraid I won't be at the bris."

"Just take your time and get well," said Fannie. "I've brought you something to cheer you up."

Eve took the package and sat down next to Noah to unwrap it for him. "Look," she said. "It's the rainbow God gave to Noah as a sign." She spread the patchwork blanket over him, the bright colors standing out in the drab ward.

Fannie had worked on the blanket steadily since hearing he'd been wounded, but she had imagined him at home, sitting up in bed, chatting. Now, given what he was facing, it felt like a pitiful gesture.

"Thank you, Fannie. It's beautiful." This time his smile reached his face. "I know I'll get better now."

Fannie put a hand on his shoulder. "I love you, Noah. I know you will."

"Just look at these colors," said Eve, fingering the soft yarn. "It's like being outside in the park on a sunny day."

"And soon he will be," said Fannie.

A tear fell slowly down his cheek, which she wiped off with her handkerchief. His eyes began to close.

"We'll let you rest," said Fannie, kissing him goodbye. "We'll be back soon."

Eve walked out with them. When they were out of Noah's hearing, she broke down, sobbing. Fannie and Jacob held her close and let her cry.

"Thank you both," she said when she was able to speak. "I know how hard that was. But you have no idea what this meant to him—and to me. It's the first time I've seen a real smile on his face."

"You're not alone anymore, Eve. Go outside while Noah is sleeping and put some color back in your cheeks. It will do you both good."

"I will, I promise." She reached out to touch Fannie's belly. "I don't think you'll be back to visit for a while, but the news will make Noah happy."

"We'll let you know." She and Jacob turned to leave.

"And I think Mama's right, Fannie. I think it's a boy."

CHAPTER 28

"Jacob, wake up!"

Fannie stood near the bathroom door and stared at the puddle at her feet. She had been on her way back to bed when her water broke. If she bent down to clean it up, she wasn't sure she'd be able to get up again. She held onto the door frame as the first pain came and called him again.

"Jacob, it's time!"

She stepped over the puddle and went to shake him awake.

"Get up," she said. "Get up now."

Jacob sat up. "What? What's wrong? Is it the baby?"

"Yes. You've been sleeping on your good ear. I couldn't wake you," she said frantically. "You need to call the midwife and Mama now. My water broke and the pains have started."

Jacob moved toward her, but she held up her hand.

"Be careful over here. The floor is wet. Don't worry about me, just go make those calls."

Fannie lowered herself back into bed, waiting anxiously for the next pain. She couldn't remember what it had been like the first time. Was this the same?

Jacob was back in minutes. "They're on their way. I'll put some clothes on before they get here."

Fannie started to cry, and Jacob rushed to her side.

"Is the pain very bad?"

"No, it's not the pain. I'm frightened. What if—"

"Everything will be fine." Jacob sat down and squeezed her hand. "I won't leave you."

"No, you were right. It won't do for you to be in your pajamas when they get here. Get dressed and mop up the water if you can."

"Of course." He stood up and went to get his clothes. "I love you, Fannie."

"I—" The pain came in a wave. It gripped her belly like a vise but subsided quickly. She squeezed the blanket and tried not to cry out.

Jacob got dressed and mopped up the puddle as best he could with some dirty towels from the hamper. "Are you having more pains?" he asked as soon as he sat down with her again.

"No. The midwife said they would come slowly at first, so I think that's a good thing."

"What else can I do?"

"Just stay with me. Tell me again you love me, and our baby will be healthy."

Jacob leaned over to kiss her. "I love you very much and we're going to have a healthy baby, and I'll love him too."

"Or her." Fannie smiled.

"I'll love you both, no matter what."

Another pain came. Fannie clenched her teeth and groaned. "Where are they? Where's Mama?"

"They'll be here soon, Fannie. It may have been hard to get a cab this time of night."

Fannie closed her eyes and dozed in between the pains while Jacob paced the floor until the midwife arrived.

"Deborah," cried Fannie. "Is my baby all right?"

"I'll check in a moment, Fannie, just let me wash my hands. Jacob, you can get some clean sheets and a basin of warm water."

"Everything looks good," she said when he returned. "The baby is in perfect position and Fannie is just about ready. It's time for you to give her a kiss and go wait in the other room. It may still be a while and Fannie may scream, but that's perfectly natural."

"Are you sure I can't stay and hold her hand a little longer?"

Deborah laughed. "Time to go!"

Fannie clutched Jacob as he bent over to kiss her. He loosened her hands from around his neck and kissed each palm. "Don't be afraid. I love you," he said.

"How lucky you are, Fannie. Most men can't wait to run away," said Deborah.

Mama arrived as he was walking out of the room. "She'll be fine," she said when she saw his look of dread. "They both will."

The pains started to come quickly, one running into the other. Fannie yelled as she bore down.

"Well, someone's going to be a redhead," said Deborah. "The baby's head is almost out. When the next pain comes, push as hard as you can."

Fannie gripped her mother's hand.

"Now push, Fannie, push."

Fannie pushed with every bit of strength she had and fell back onto the pillows. The baby's cry was faint at first, and then louder.

"It's a boy, Fannie. You have a son."

Fannie looked at her mother, who was too overcome to do anything but nod.

"A boy? And he's healthy?"

"See for yourself." Deborah cut the cord and laid him on Fannie's chest.

With tears streaming down her face, Fannie examined her son. Dark red hair, a rosebud mouth, a wide nose. She counted ten perfect fingers and tiny toes.

Bluma went to get Jacob. "Come meet your son," she said.

Jacob stood beside Fannie and the baby. "God has been good to us," he said quietly, taking her hand.

Fannie looked up at him. "Yes," she said, looking down at her son.

This was it, the perfect love she had been waiting for.

The love she had hoped for as a young girl leaving home to marry a stranger.

The love that had eluded her for so long and that she had resisted when it came.

As she picked up one of the baby's hands to kiss it, he grasped her finger.

Photo Credit: Mark Holmes

ABOUT THE AUTHOR

Two events inspired me to write this novel. First, I heard an author describe how her grandmother carried her candlesticks from Romania wrapped in her skirt. I have my grandmother's silver candlesticks; I think of her whenever I light the Sabbath candles. But I realized then I had no idea how old they were or where they came from. Shortly afterward, a cousin sent me a picture of our grandparents. He is seated on a park bench. She is kneeling beside him with her head on his knee. When I told my cousin I didn't remember our grandparents being that affectionate, she laughed. That man wasn't our grandfather, she informed me.

Who was this woman I knew until she died when I was in my 30's? I had to know.

I don't remember the exact moment when my occasional blog posts about her turned into a novel. I only know I had to tell her story. I have no idea if my version resembles her real life, but I hope she would be proud.

Although my grandmother did immigrate to America in 1910 and marry shortly after she arrived, other than the basic facts of her birthplace, the year she left Russia, the ship she sailed on, and her wedding date, this is a work of fiction. All the thoughts and actions attributed to the characters are derived from my imagination. I have made every effort to describe the time period accurately, but I have changed the dates and details of some recognizable events to suit the narrative.

ACKNOWLEDGMENTS

I began writing about my grandmother as part of a writing group that emerged from "Writing Your COVID Memoir," a class I took in 2020. Wayne Bizer, Michael Goodman, Greta Phinney, Steve Rubin and Betsy Smith have been there from the beginning.

My cousin, Debbie Viniar, sent me a picture of my grandmother with a man who wasn't my grandfather, which is how this all started. As I started to wonder about Fannie's "true" story, I worked with genealogist Keren Weiner. Her research became the springboard for my imagination.

When I realized I wanted to write a novel, I reached out to Sonia Pilcer, author of *The Holocaust Kid*. She became a teacher, editor and friend. At the 2023 Under the Volcano writing residency, I worked with Reyna Grande, author of *A Ballad of Love and Glory,* who helped me get the manuscript to the next level. Former Random House editor Diane O'Connell then got me to the finish line.

Many thanks to my beta readers, Elaine Padilla, Carole Siegel and Betsy Smith. Their comments and edits (especially Betsy's removal of all the "that's") were invaluable. The last time I acknowledged Elaine's support was in my doctoral dissertation in 1984. We're still hanging in together.

Thanks to Charlie Sullivan for his legal advice, and to other friends and family too numerous to mention for their ongoing encouragement.

Thanks to the team at Sibylline Press for believing in me and for their ongoing support, with a special thanks to Alicia Feltman for her gorgeous cover.

My daughters, Gwen Shusterman and Robin Hoffberger, are my pride and joy. I can never thank them enough.

STUDY GUIDE QUESTIONS

1. Was Fannie's father right to arrange her marriage to Caleb? What might he have done instead?

2. How is Caleb a product of his upbringing? What are the positive aspects to his character?

3. Who are the women in Fannie's life who support her journey to independence?

4. What is the role of work for the women in this story?

5. What are the religious and cultural clashes between Asher and his children? How do these reflect what you know about immigrants?

6. How is Fannie a different woman in each relationship she has with a man?

Sibylline Press is proud to publish the brilliant work of women authors over 50. We are a woman-owned publishing company and, like our authors, represent women of a certain age.